Praise for Libby Fischer Hellmann's
Set the Night on Fire

"A top-rate standalone thriller that taps into the antiwar protests of the 1960s and 70s...A jazzy fusion of past and present, Hellman's insightful, politically charged whodunit explores a fascinating period in American history."
Publishers Weekly

"Superior standalone novel...Hellmann creates a fully-realized world...complete with everyday details, passions and enthusiasms on how they yearned for connection, debated about ideology and came to belief in taking risks to stand up for what they believed."
Chicago Tribune

"Haunting...Rarely have history, mystery, and political philosophy blended so beautifully...could easily end up on the required reading list in college-level American History classes."
Mystery Scene

"Politics, suspense, and action all blend seamlessly together to create a fine thriller."
Deadly Pleasures

"[H]er best novel yet...This wonderfully written roller-coaster ride will make a fan out of anyone who hasn't read this author before...A beautiful, suspenseful, and altogether amazing novel, this is one that shouldn't be missed."
New Mystery Reader

"Libby Fischer Hellmann masterfully combines contemporary suspense and historical elements in equal parts...A terrific read."
Midwest Book Review

"The author creates the atmosphere of the sixties perfectly...This is a terrific book for those who want to relive those times when we thought we could do anything."
Murder by Type

"The 1960s-set backstory is compelling...this is an exciting book for readers who enjoy an action-packed thriller mixed with their historical facts."
Nanette Donohue, *Historical Novels Review*

"Hellmann has done a superlative job with the 60s Chicago setting. I felt as though I had entered a time machine and been transported back. She makes the entire time come alive, recreating a historical time in perfect detail."
Reviewing the Evidence

Also by Libby Fischer Hellmann

Set the Night on Fire

♦

THE GEORGIA DAVIS SERIES

ToxiCity

Doubleback

Easy Innocence

♦

THE ELLIE FOREMAN SERIES

A Shot to Die For

An Image of Death

A Picture of Guilt

An Eye for Murder

♦

Nice Girl Does Noir (short stories)

♦

Chicago Blues (editor)

A
Bitter
Veil

LIBBY FISCHER HELLMANN

 ALLIUM PRESS OF CHICAGO

Allium Press of Chicago
Forest Park, Illinois
www.alliumpress.com

This is a work of fiction. Descriptions and portrayals of real people, events, organizations, or establishments are intended to provide background for the story and are used fictitiously. Other characters and situations are drawn from the author's imagination and are not intended to be real.

Book and cover design by E. C. Victorson
Front cover images:
Woman by Daniel M. Nagy/Shutterstock.com
Backgrounds by ilolab and pavila, both Shutterstock.com
Tile border by kasia_ka/iStockphoto.com

Publisher's Cataloging-In-Publication Data
(Prepared by The Donohue Group, Inc.)

Hellmann, Libby Fischer.
  A bitter veil / Libby Fischer Hellmann.

  p. ; cm.

  ISBN: 978-0-9831938-1-4

  1. Iran--History--Revolution, 1979--Fiction. 2. Political prisoners--Iran--Tehran--Fiction.
3. Americans--Iran--Tehran--Fiction. 4. Iranians--Illinois--Chicago--Fiction. 5. Intercountry
marriage--Fiction. 6. Historical fiction. 7. Love stories. I. Title.

PS3608.E46 B58 2012
813/.6   2012932763

*For all those who've been brave enough to take
a stand against tyranny…whatever its guise*

*Out beyond ideas of wrongdoing
and rightdoing there is a field.
I'll meet you there.*

—Rumi

A BITTER VEIL

PART ONE

One

Summer, 1980

Anna was deeply asleep, which was unusual for her. She generally tossed and turned until the desperate hours of the night passed. But tonight she'd succumbed almost immediately.

The first knock seemed like part of a dream, and her brain started constructing a story around it. As she swam up to consciousness there was another knock. The sound left a residual imprint in her ears, and for an instant she tried to figure out its intent. Was it an angry thump? A frightened plea? A perfunctory tap? She checked the clock and grew immediately wary.

She threw the covers aside, grabbed her chador, and draped it over her baby doll pajamas. Nouri was not home. After what had happened earlier she wasn't surprised, but it meant she had to answer the door. Still, she hesitated. Whoever was there would see her sharp features, pale green eyes, and blonde eyebrows. They would know she wasn't Iranian. They might even suspect she was from the decadent West, perhaps the Great Satan itself. And if that happened, whatever mission brought them would be tainted with that knowledge.

She carefully pushed the curtain aside and looked out. It was summer in Tehran, a hot, arid time that reminded her of the dog days of August in Chicago. She and Nouri lived on an upscale street in Shemiran with walled-off houses set back from the road. At this hour the street was quiet and dark, save for a black Mercedes parked by the gate. The engine was off, but its headlamps were still on, and two precise beams of light illuminated tree trunks and overgrown bushes.

Three uniformed men, all bearded, crowded the door. One had his hands planted on his hips. The other two stood hunched over, arms folded around machine guns. Somehow they'd been able to break through the gate. Fear pumped through her veins. Revolutionary Guards. She had no choice. She had to open the door. If she didn't, they would break in, claiming knowledge of crimes she'd committed against Islam and the Republic. They might confiscate her books, her makeup, and Nouri's stereo, for starters. She didn't need that. Not now. Not with all the other troubles.

She padded out of the bedroom in her bare feet. Clasping the folds of the chador under her chin, she took the steps down, cursing inwardly at the garment's awkwardness. How could any woman manipulate the yards of heavy black material without feeling clumsy? When she reached the first floor, she slipped into a pair of black ballet slippers she kept by the door. If the Guards saw her toenail polish, they could report her.

She held the chador with one hand and opened the door with the other. One of the men's hands was high in the air, as if he was just about to knock again. He stepped back, looking startled.

"*As-Salâmo 'Alaikom*, Sister," he said stiffly, lowering his arm.

She gave him a curt nod.

"You are the wife of Nouri Samedi?" he asked in Farsi.

Her heart caromed around her chest. She and Nouri had argued viciously, and he'd threatened to have her arrested. Is that why they'd come? She nodded again, more uncertainly this time.

The men appraised her. Women were supposed to keep their eyes down in the presence of men, to be submissive and quiet. But men had no such limitations, especially Guards. They were free to ogle. Make demands. And if those demands were not met…she shivered, recalling the stories she had heard.

One of the other men stepped up to the door. His lips curved in a predatory smile. She tightened her grip on the chador, for once thankful it covered her body. If she was back home, she would call the police, report them as intruders. But here these intruders *were* the police. Or what passed as security.

"Your husband..." he said, his voice dripping with scorn. "Do you know where he is?"

She shook her head and looked at the floor. Oh god, were they going to beat her up? She knew people who claimed they were beaten during nighttime visits by the Guards.

"You are certain you do not know his whereabouts, Sister?"

She stole a look at him. His smile had disappeared, replaced now with a scowl. "You have been home all night?"

She nodded. She never went out much, certainly not alone.

His eyes narrowed in disbelief.

"What is it? Has something happened?"

"You already know."

Always the charades. The brinkmanship. Anger roiled her gut, but she could not show it. "No."

"Your husband is dead. His body was found in an alley nearby. He was stabbed."

She gasped. A steel gate plunged down the center of her brain, separating her emotions from her thoughts. She wished she was wearing a burqa to hide her face as well her body. Her jaw dropped open. Through her fingers she heard herself cry out, "No!"

Despite the Supreme Leader's admonition to limit eye contact between the sexes, the men stared hard at her. If she were Iranian, she would cry out, collapse, even faint. But she was an American, and Americans were not demonstrative. Odd to be thinking of cultural differences at such a moment.

She drew a ragged breath. "That cannot be," she lied. "He was with his friend Hassan tonight. Hassan is a Guard," she added, as if that gave her legitimacy. "He said he would be home late, because—"

"We have notified his family. They are coming to identify the body."

What game were they playing? *She* was Nouri's family. But she said nothing. At least they do not call her on her lie.

3

The man who'd been talking suddenly shoved the door open wider and barged in.

Panic tickled Anna's spine. "What are—where are you going?"

He and another Guard pushed past her and went into the kitchen. She started to follow them, but the third man aimed his machine gun at her. "Stop," he barked. "Don't move."

She froze.

She heard murmurs from the kitchen. Then a cry of triumph.

The first man returned from the kitchen, brandishing a steak knife. She and Nouri didn't eat much red meat, except lamb—in kababs and meatballs, but she'd brought the wooden block of knives from the States with her when she came. It reminded her of home.

"There are only five knives," he said. "Where is the sixth?"

She stiffened. "I don't know what you're talking about."

He nodded and the man with the machine gun shoved her into the kitchen.

"Six slots. Five knives. You see?"

He was right. She turned to him. "It's been missing for a while. I don't know where it is." She bit her lip. A weak excuse. They could tell.

A victorious smile curled his lips, as if he knew he'd won. "Ah, but *we* do. We have it. It was the murder weapon. You murdered your husband. Killed him so you could escape Iran and return to America. Now you will never leave. You will die in Iran, just like your husband."

Two

January 1977

The dusty smell of books, both new and used, was reassuring. Anna wound through the store's narrow aisles, thinking of the hours she'd spent in the library when she was a little girl. She had never been popular; her schoolmates kept their distance. So she'd spent a lot of time by herself. But her governess—or nanny, as they called them here—permitted her to ride her bike to the library after school, and it became her refuge, a place to lose herself in the stacks. The children's librarian would suggest novels, which she wolfed down like a starved animal, sometimes two or three in as many days. It wasn't long before she'd tackled *Gone With the Wind* and *A Tale of Two Cities*, at which point the children's librarian handed her off to the adult fiction section.

Now, as she closed in on the poetry section in the back of the store, the collected knowledge on the shelves comforted her. She shrugged off her down jacket and pulled out her syllabus for Middle Eastern Literature. She was an English major at the University of Chicago. Her father, a scientist, had not been pleased with her choice.

"What sort of job can you get with an English degree?" he sniffed when she told him. "A teacher? Do you have the patience to teach spoiled American teenagers who are only thinking about the next rock concert or marijuana cigarette?"

She didn't argue. She had no good answer except that she suspected a grounding in literature, especially that of other cultures, would give her a solid base for whatever she eventually pursued. Sometimes it was anthropology, and she saw herself authoring a breakthrough study of some obscure Native American tribe. Sometimes it was law, and she imagined herself a female Clarence Darrow. Other times it was film. She would be a highly sought after director, the American Lina Wertmuller, whose *Swept Away* Anna had seen three times, each time reveling in the brutal but magnetic sexuality of Giancarlo Giannini.

She scanned the books on her syllabus. The first few books she'd need were *The Selected Poems of Rumi; Ghazals from Hafiz;* and *The Poetry and Philosophy of Omar Khayyam.* She plucked the Rumi book from a shelf of brightly colored volumes and thumbed through it. The introduction described Rumi's background as a Sufi and mystic, his erotic energy, how reading his poetry was like making love. A smile curled her lips. This would be fun.

"I gaze at the porcelain of your face and my heart lights up..." A male voice cut into her thoughts.

She spun around. A young man was watching her. He was tall—taller than she—and slim. Straight black hair, curling below his ears. A flat chin and aquiline nose balanced his face, and his skin was as pale as hers. But it was his eyes that took her breath away. Pools of rich brown, they flashed with hints of amber and were surrounded by thick black lashes.

"Your gentle nature teaches me to float into your embrace..."

Her insides went warm.

As if he knew his effect on her, he smiled. "It is from the *Divan*, the collected works of Rumi in his middle years."

She noticed how the bulky blue sweater under his jacket emphasized his shoulders, how his tight jeans did the same for his buttocks.

"There is no better poet to fall in love with."

He bowed and gestured with a flourish. "I am Nouri." He straightened up, smiling. "And you?"

She tucked the book under her arm and extended a hand. "Anna."

He took her hand and held it a beat too long. His skin was soft. Not a speck of dirt under his nails. "Anna is a beautiful name."

Her cheeks felt hot. She knew he was trying to pick her up, and she knew she should be wary. But she also remembered how, in *The Godfather*, Michael Corleone was hit with a thunderbolt when he met his Sicilian wife for the first time. Was this what it felt like?

She watched him take her in. She considered her own looks average, but he seemed pleased with her long blonde hair—that could hide her face with a shake of her head—her frank green eyes, sharp chin, and athletic build. "May I see your syllabus?"

She handed it over, aware that apart from her name, she hadn't yet spoken a word.

He studied it. "Rumi, Hafiz, Khayyam, Ferdowsi." He nods. "Yes, these are all masters. Is your professor Persian?"

"I…I'm not sure." She grimaced mentally. Her first words should have been more confident, more assertive.

He didn't seem to notice. "I am from Iran."

"Are you a poet?" she asked shyly.

He laughed. "I'm studying engineering. At UIC."

The University of Illinois at Chicago campus was a few miles north of Hyde Park. "What are you doing down here?"

He gestured toward the shelf. "This is one of the only bookstores with a decent collection of Persian literature."

An engineer with a love of literature. She smiled a little. She couldn't help it.

His dazzling grin made up for her puny effort. "Will you have tea with me?"

She considered it. The wintry, frigid afternoon was threatening snow, and light was already slipping away like a thief in the night. She could think of nothing she'd like more.

§

"Nouri Samedi," Anna said, stirring her tea thirty minutes later. They were in the lounge of the student union, a nondescript university building with brick walls, linoleum floors, and plastic furniture.

He looked pleased that she'd spoken his name as he picked up his cup. "Anna Schroder," he said. "Samedi and Schroder. You see, our names have their own rhythm. It is a sign."

She swelled with pleasure. She had never met a boy like Nouri. American boys were either preening Marlboro men or disco rats. "Are all Iranians this romantic?"

"If they're Persian."

"Of course. I'm sorry."

He waved a dismissive hand. "Romantic, poetic, and fatalistic."

"Fatalistic?"

"We Persians have a tragic view of life. The rose withers. The butterfly dances its way to death. We love to mourn. We wallow in misery and martyrdom."

"Why is that?"

"It started with Husayn ibn Ali, Mohammed's grandson. He is as important to Shi'a Muslims as Moses is to the Jews. But he was beheaded. You will learn about him in your class."

She tapped her spoon against her cup. She hesitated before asking her question. "Are...are you observant?"

He shook his head. "I am Muslim in name only. I reject all orthodoxy, no matter what its source."

A surge of relief ran through her. She was a Christian but a nonbeliever.

"The fatalism..." he continued. "It also comes from the fact that Persia was conquered so often. It is ironic: Persian culture has survived because the conquerors assimilated *our* culture, rather than the other way around. Still, we always worry."

"The other shoe theory of life," Anna offered.

"Pardon?"

She explained. She always waited for, indeed expected, the other shoe to drop. For things to go bad.

"Exactly."

"But Iran is quite modern now, isn't it?"

"Oh yes. The shah has made sure of that." A shadow moved across his face.

Anna caught it. "You don't approve?"

"The shah has modernized quickly. Some say too fast. But his regime is repressive. If you disagree with anything, SAVAK will find you. Many have disappeared. It is, in some ways, a reign of terror." He pressed his lips together. "And the US does not help. They continue to support a dictator."

She paused. "I am an American citizen—I was born here. But that doesn't mean I always agree with my government." She told him about her anti-war days. Taking over the principal's office with twenty other students, all of them puffed up with arrogance and self-righteousness. It wasn't that long ago.

The shadow on his face disappeared, and the amber in his eyes flashed. "I am glad you feel that way. You know, with a civil engineering degree, I can help rebuild democracy in Iran. Put structures in place— electricity, running water, bridges, and roads—that will improve lives. Give people a sense of community and entitlement. Like Mosaddeq."

"Mosaddeq?"

"He was prime minister of Iran's only popularly elected government. He nationalized the oil companies to plow profits back into the country. For the people instead of the privileged few. But your CIA and the Brits didn't like that. They accused him of being a Communist. In fact, they staged a coup to overthrow him and brought back the shah." He blew out air. "Poof. The flame of democracy was extinguished."

He was lyrical even when he was critical. Still, she bristled. "It's not *my* CIA." She told him about her intellectual journey from Hegel to Marx, and then Marcuse. How she was anxious to come to Chicago, in part because of Saul Alinsky. Over the past few years, though, she had backed away from social action, focusing more on observation and analysis. On good days she called herself a chronicler. But she left unsaid the nagging fear that on bad days she was nothing more than a blank slab of stone.

Nouri was swept up in the conversation, his eyes so intense they seemed to be lit by tiny candles from within. His voice sank to a conspiratorial whisper. "I too have read Marx. The shah has banned his books, you know."

Anna leaned forward. "Tell me, Nouri. Why engineering? You are so knowledgeable. And articulate. Why not politics? Or teaching?"

He snorted. "My parents expect me to become a *Mohandes*."

"Mohandes?"

"It's a title of respect for an engineer. Like a doctor. They insist. And I am good with numbers. I like to make things."

"What does your family do?" She suspected they must be wealthy if he was able to study abroad.

His expression turned sheepish. "My father is a senior officer with the National Iranian Oil Company."

Somehow she was not surprised. "So he supports the shah."

"They know each other. Socially." A flush crept up his neck. He cleared his throat. "What about yours?"

She chose her words carefully. "My parents are…European. But they met in the States. I spend summers abroad. My mother lives in Paris. She pretends to be an artist. They're divorced."

"And your father?"

"He is…" She paused. "…a scientist."

"Ahh." His smile was equal parts sunshine and desire. For Anna, it was a heady mix.

She sipped the last of her tea. "Tell me. How did Persia come to be named Iran?"

"It is from the word 'Aryan.'"

She looked up, startled.

"It comes from Sanskrit originally and means 'honorable,' or sometimes 'hospitable.' Iran literally means 'Abode of the Aryans.' But your parents are from Europe. Surely, you knew that."

She stared at her teacup.

Three

A few days later Anna nervously cooked dinner for Nouri. She'd never been taught to cook, and she only knew a few dishes. She'd prepared a chicken recipe she'd cut out of the newspaper that included bread crumbs, cheese, and cream. After she slid the pan into the oven, she ran a worried hand through her hair. What if he was a vegetarian? She should have asked.

She set the coffee table with the mismatched plates and utensils she'd collected. She lived on the third floor of a greystone in Hyde Park. The apartment had only one bedroom, but it featured a long hall and hardwood floors, and the kitchen opened onto a back porch with stairs going down to the backyard.

The buzzer sounded. Her stomach tightened. She released the lock, heard the vestibule door click open. Boots clumped up the stairs. She opened the door. A light snow was falling, and snowflakes dusted his hair and jacket. She felt the urge to brush them off but restrained herself. They greeted each other awkwardly. His cheeks were red, his eyes bright. She inhaled the smell of wet wool. He bent over to take off his boots, and set them by the door. She took his jacket and hung it over the bathtub. When she returned, he handed over a bottle of wine. It was red, not white, but she pretended to be thrilled. She dug out two jelly jars from the cabinet and poured.

"To you, Anna." He took his glass and held it up. "Thank you for inviting me to dinner."

She sipped her wine.

He sniffed. "It smells wonderful."

"I hope…I should have…do you eat chicken?"

He laughed. "Of course."

Her attack of nerves eased.

He gazed around. Her father paid the rent, but Anna was thrifty and had cobbled together the furniture from second-hand stores and garage sales. A green worsted couch—shabby but serviceable—shared the space with a black recliner, a couple of straight-backed wicker chairs, and a coffee table made from a giant telephone company spool. Her books, albums, and stereo rested on shelves supported by cinder blocks. Two small dhurri rugs covered the floor.

"Your apartment is so…well…my place is a hovel in comparison. Just a dorm room."

Secretly pleased, Anna gestured to the couch. "Make yourself comfortable. Dinner will be ready soon."

But instead of sitting, he went to the stereo. She tensed. She'd spent twenty minutes deciding whether and what music she should have on when he arrived. She didn't want to appear as if she was orchestrating the mood, but she didn't know his taste: rock, classical, jazz? The choices were too overwhelming so she ended up putting nothing on.

He inspected her meager collection of records and 8-tracks. They were mostly classical, except for two Moody Blues albums and one Dolly Parton she'd bought on impulse. He tipped his head to the side. "I wouldn't have taken you for a Dolly Parton fan."

She felt herself blush. She didn't know what to say.

He put on one of the classical tapes. Beethoven's Ninth, performed by the Philadelphia Orchestra, Eugene Ormandy conducting. She would have preferred something lighter, but she kept her mouth shut and went into the kitchen.

He followed her in. "I got a letter from a friend today."

"In Tehran?"

Nouri nodded. "Hassan. We were at school together, on the same soccer team. He is the best defender I ever met."

She smiled. She liked that he was telling her about his life. Ordinary details, like letters and soccer.

Nouri continued. "He says things are heating up. People are openly accusing the shah of repression. Writing letters, declaring resolutions. Calling for the restoration of constitutional rule."

"Really?"

"Yes. And there's this cleric—his name is Khomeini. He's in exile in Iraq, but he's calling for the overthrow of the shah. He's starting to get a following."

"Is he religious?"

Again, Nouri nodded.

"Religion and revolution are not always a good mix," she said.

"This time it's different. Everyone is working together. Hassan says it is the first time he has seen so much unity. He is with a group of students who are planning demonstrations. I wish I was there."

"Isn't that dangerous, given SAVAK?"

Nouri was quick with an answer. "Sometimes there is no alternative. Anyway, Hassan says the demonstrations will be peaceful."

"Even so…"

He eyed her speculatively. "You worry too much, Anna."

"I would make a good Persian, wouldn't I?"

He laughed then, a hearty musical sound, somewhere between a viola and a trombone. She loved the sound of it. "That's right," he said. "You would."

She served dinner. He must have been hungry because he ate two helpings of chicken, rice, and salad. Afterwards he was effusive in his praise. A warm glow came over her.

They did the dishes together, slipping the plates into the dish rack. Afterwards, they curled up on either end of her couch, their legs and feet overlapping in the middle. Nouri sighed contentedly. They finished the wine, and even the dim lamp in the living room seemed too bright. Beethoven's Ninth was long over, but Anna felt too sluggish to put on anything else.

Nouri laced his hands behind his head and watched her.

She smiled tentatively, uneasy with the silence. "What?"

He sat up and looked around, spotting her Rumi book on the shelf. He got up and retrieved it.

"More poetry?" Was this is an Iranian seduction technique? she wondered.

"Just a few lines. They are famous. I'm sure they are here." He thumbed through the book. "Ahh." He smiled and cleared his throat. *"The minute I heard my first love story I started looking for you, not knowing how blind that was. Lovers don't finally meet somewhere. They're in each other all along."*

Her toes curled. A smile tugged the corners of her lips. If it *was* a seduction technique, it was working brilliantly. He put the book down and came to her end of the couch. Kneeling down, he traced the line of her jaw with his fingertips. A shiver ran through her body. He kissed her, tender at first, then more urgently. She felt slippery and warm. At the same time a slow-building tension tightened her muscles. She opened her mouth, her arms, her insides. They moved into the bedroom.

Afterwards, she said, "No one has ever read poetry to me before."

"Stick with me. You will ace your course."

§

Anna did ace the course, but she had no idea how. She hardly spent any time out of bed that semester, much less in class. Thick sweaters, jeans, and boots ended up in a pile on the floor of her apartment. She and Nouri were addicts, obsessed with each other's bodies. Sometimes they spent the entire day making love. After a week she began to feel incomplete without his weight on her, his breath in her ear. Even his smell, a sweet musky sweaty scent, was a narcotic.

The times they did go out, for food or shopping—though Anna was never hungry—they couldn't keep their hands off each other. After a while they didn't even try. By the time winter slid into spring, they had made love on the rocks by Lake Michigan, near the lagoons at Jackson Park, and once on the Midway behind some trees.

Anna was surprised at the bold, wanton creature she'd become.

Not that she was a virgin. She'd had a lover or two, but this was a new experience. Nouri grew to be as much a part of her as an arm or leg. He burrowed his way into her marrow. She grew so attuned to him that the mere blink of an eye or the arch of his eyebrow incited her to passion or angst, depending on his mood. She decided she finally understood Rumi's poetry.

At the end of May Nouri gave up his room and moved in. The night he brought his things over, they fired up a celebratory bowl of hashish. Then, they tore their clothes off and made desperate love. They were both feeling an impending sense of doom. Nouri was due back to Tehran for the summer, and Anna was going to Paris. They decided to cut their vacations short and reunite in Chicago at the beginning of August. They would only be apart for eight weeks, but Anna didn't know how she would survive.

Four

The time Anna spent in Paris visiting her mother that summer was torture. Her mother lived on the Left Bank, off boulevard Saint-Germain not far from the Sorbonne. Anna wandered the neighborhood, past Notre Dame, the cafés, the tiny farmers' market that popped up as if by magic on Wednesdays and Saturdays. She often ended up in the Jardin du Luxembourg where, despite the riot of flowers and blossoms, she felt colorless and drab. She was jealous of every couple whose arms were wrapped around each other, who shared secret smiles and giggles.

She and Nouri spoke on the phone twice a week, frantic calls in which they professed undying love, but once they disconnected, she was wracked by doubt. He was an only son, and although he had a sister, he was the heir to the family name. No doubt they treated him like a prince. The brave hero who'd returned from the front. He was probably having the time of his life. Though he claimed to miss her more than she did him, and he alluded to intimate parts of her body only he knew, Anna couldn't help wondering whether he might be eyeing Iranian girls the same way he once looked at her. Iranian girls were dark and fiery and beautiful. Her pale blonde coloring couldn't compete.

After one such call, she met her mother in a small café on the rue des Écoles. Julianne Schroder divorced Anna's father when Anna was five and moved back to her native France. Though Anna flew to Paris every summer, and sometimes for Christmas too, her mother was more like an aunt, or a cousin, than a mother. She was a painter, and spent most days in a bright, sunlit studio. Anna was allowed to spend time with her in the studio, but her mother never pried. She kept her distance. Whenever Anna revealed a piece of herself in conversation, her mother would nod or purse her lips. Anna guessed her mother had decided she'd surrendered her right to judge Anna when she abandoned her so many years ago. She didn't want to believe her mother just didn't care.

She slipped through the door of the café. The smell of coffee mixed with cigarette smoke saturated the air. It was early afternoon, but the place was crowded and cramped, at least for her American sensibility. But Americans had an exaggerated need for room, her mother insisted. Here in France everyone rubbed elbows, apparently not bothered by the invasion of their personal space.

Her mother was already there, a Gauloise dangling between her lips. Anna had cautioned her about smoking many times, but her mother always made that dismissive blowing out "pee-ue" sound the French do so well. Anna was a less beautiful version of her mother, who had enormous blue eyes and thick blonde hair she wore in a twist. Her body still looked like a teenager's, and she could wear a scarf over a black sweater and jeans and look like she'd just stepped out of a house of couture. Next to her, Anna felt clumsy and big, and, well, American.

Her mother waved her over to the tiny table. "*Bonjour, ma petite.* Gerard is going to meet us here. I didn't think you'd mind."

Anna sat. Gerard was the latest of her mother's lovers, all scruffy men with beards and vague intellectual pretensions. Many of them were Communists, her mother confided, but some were existentialists who lived dreary, disappointing lives at the same time they sought happiness and contentment.

"I thought we could go to the cinema later," her mother said.

Anna nodded. Despite her faults, her mother was the one who kindled Anna's love affair with film. Her mother would take her to see Antonioni, Bergman, Chabrol, Truffaut—sometimes two films a day. Anna suspected it was a way for them to pass time together without really communicating. Perhaps because of that, Anna had fallen in love with the celluloid stories played out on the screen. She loved the larger-than-life characters, who, with just a flick of a finger or the narrowing of an eye, spoke volumes. She loved the editing which could take her from a Paris village to New York, or from the present to the past in less than a second. They went to films in the early evening, after which her mother typically brought her back to the flat, said goodnight, and went out again. When dawn was creeping over the rooftops of Paris, her mother returned, her long blonde hair hugging her shoulders, smelling of men and sex.

Once Anna asked her mother why she left her father. "It was a marriage of convenience," her mother said after a long pause. "We were—are—very different people." She was quick to add that Anna was the only worthwhile thing from the marriage. But if that was true, why did her mother live seven thousand miles away? And why, Anna thought, with a frisson of resentment, did she seem so happy? Anna used to wonder if she would be as vibrant and alive as her mother if she moved to Paris. Now she knew it was Nouri who fueled her energy and joy. Stripped of his body, his smell, his hands on her, she was a pale shadow of a woman.

Her mother ordered a Croque Monsieur. "What about you, darling? What will you have?"

Nouri's absence was so visceral and raw it scraped the inside of her stomach. "Nothing."

Her mother frowned. "You've been eating poorly since you arrived."

Anna shrugged.

Her mother stubbed out her cigarette in an ashtray. Then she looked at Anna, a knowledgeable glint in her eyes. "You are in love."

How did she know?

As if she had spoken the words aloud, her mother said, "I know the signs." She waved down the waiter. "Henri, a carafe of wine for us today." She looked back at Anna. "Tell me about him."

Anna smiled and told her mother everything. She didn't mind. Talking about Nouri made him seem closer.

Her mother listened keenly, perhaps for the first time in Anna's life. When Anna finished, her mother lit another Gauloise and slowly exhaled a stream of smoke. "I know some Iranians here. They are exiles. Mostly Communist."

Anna nodded. "Nouri says the Communist Party was expelled by the shah."

Her mother tapped her cigarette against the ashtray. "There are other Iranians as well. Muslim clerics."

"I didn't know."

Her mother hesitated. "Is your Nouri...religious?"

"Oh, no," Anna said. "He's studying engineering. He'll go back to Iran once he has his degree."

Her mother inclined her head. "And will you go with him?"

Anna had asked herself the same question. She didn't know.

"I see," her mother said. "So. Do you have a photo of your lover?"

Anna fished in her bag and extracted a shot of Nouri she'd snapped one night after sex. His hair was tousled, and his heavy lidded eyes said he couldn't wait to go again. She handed the photo to her mother.

Her mother examined it. "Ahh. Now I understand." She gazed at Anna as if she was seeing her for the first time. As if her daughter had suddenly become a woman. Though her cheeks got hot, Anna felt a perverse sense of pride. She had just become a member of a sorority she never knew existed. She took the photo back from her mother and smiled.

But her mother didn't.

Five

Nouri lay on Anna's bed in August—their bed now, he reminded himself. A small fan blew desultory air across his body. Anna, who, like Nouri, had just returned from abroad, was lying beside him, so still he wondered if she had fallen asleep. He turned his head. She was staring at him. She was always watching him. As if she was afraid he would disappear if she looked away.

He rolled over and cupped her chin in his hand. She was so blonde and waiflike, so different from anything he'd known before. Like one of those yellow-haired porcelain dolls his parents used to bring his sister from Europe. From the best shop in Geneva, his parents would crow.

He kissed Anna's nose—it was small and straight with a slight tilt at the tip. She nestled into the crook of his arm. Her scent drifted over him. Since they'd reunited, he was never without the smell of her on or near him. Sometimes it caught him unawares; he would shift or turn around, and a hint of her wafted over him. He loved it. He was only half teasing when he called the similarity in their names a sign. They belonged to each other, body, soul, and scent.

Anna rolled on top, her long hair trailing across his chest. Since their return, she had grown more sexually assertive. Sometimes she even took charge. She gave him a half-smile, another new habit she'd adopted. Part come-on, part mystery, it hinted at depths and secrets and untold pleasures, and it drove him crazy. Whatever she'd picked up in Paris he liked. He let her do her magic.

Afterwards they napped. When they woke, it was dusk but still steam bath hot. August was a tricky month in Chicago, and sometimes even the setting sun offered no relief. Still, when people in Chicago complained, Nouri turned a deaf ear. Until you'd lived through a Tehran summer, when the air scalded your throat so relentlessly it was hard to breathe, you didn't understand what heat was. He went into the bathroom to shower. Anna joined him. He admired her pale body, lithe and slim. There was not an ounce of fat on her.

Anna made a cold eggplant dish for dinner, which she served with salad and flatbread. Although she tried to hide it, he spotted the Middle-Eastern cookbook she brought back from Paris. She was making an effort to prepare food he knew. But when he thanked her, she waved a dismissive hand and said it was healthier. He tried to show his appreciation, but her cooking was uneven, and he was still hungry much of the time. Sometimes he snuck into McDonalds for a Big Mac.

By the time they finished eating, it was dark, but the heat had finally lifted. They decided to walk toward the Point on Lake Michigan. He laced his fingers through hers. "I need to finalize the topic of my thesis."

"Oh? What are you considering?"

"I haven't decided. But I know the criteria."

"What are they?"

"I am to describe the problem to be solved, analyze why previous solutions to this problem are unsatisfactory, propose a better solution, and then compare its benefits and drawbacks to what has gone before." He swatted at mosquitoes. They had to be nearing the lagoons.

"Civil engineering is broad, isn't it?" Anna said. "There is structural, construction, environmental, municipal. You have so many choices."

He slipped his arm around her. She'd been studying his field. It was so like her. To make sure she understood *his* world. "I know. The proposal is due next month. I have twenty minutes to present it to the heads of the department."

A fishy smell permeated the air. They were definitely near the water.

"You've said you want to contribute to your country. Help modernize it. Like the shah."

"Not like the shah. He buys weapons, expands the army, enforces cultural edicts people do not like, and calls it modernization. That is not my plan."

"Okay." She was quiet for a moment. Then, "What if you wrote a thesis about bringing electricity or running water to a specific rural village? If you do it right, it might even serve as a template for the real thing. When...," she paused, "...you go back."

He thought about it. Of course.

"You could choose a place where you already know the condition of the soil. Or the closest water supply," she added.

An idea jumped into his mind. "You know something? My parents have a summer home on the Caspian Sea. There are villages nearby. Some are in the mountains, but others..." He stopped. "The Caspian is salt water, but only slightly. If I could figure out a way to desalinate the water—it wouldn't have to be as rigorous as the methods they're developing for the ocean—perhaps the water could be pumped from the sea into the village." He felt mental cylinders clicking into place. His enthusiasm mounted. "Oh, Anna, what a wonderful idea!"

Even in the dark he knew that half-smile was on her lips. "It is perfect! You are perfect!" He kissed her on the nape of her neck, a spot he knew was one of her favorites. He couldn't believe his good fortune. This girl, this marvelous American girl, completed not only his body but his mind, too. At that moment he knew, without a doubt, that Anna was the woman he would marry. They would go back to Iran. She would teach; he would be a famous engineer. They would serve their country and live a perfect life. He would bask in the respect accorded him for choosing such a progressive, desirable woman. They would call him Mohandes.

§

The fall semester began on a sunny September day, and the pace of their lives quickened. Anna's three seminars required hours of reading. She also did the shopping, cooking, and laundry. Nouri saw her only at night. Nouri's schedule was more flexible—he had blocks of time supposedly devoted to researching his thesis—but he was busy. He had discovered a new pastime.

Over the summer in Tehran, Nouri and Hassan had engaged in long discussions about the shah and the state of the country. They agreed that the shah's massive military buildup had caused economic and social dislocation. They also agreed that the corruption, the inflation, and the gap between the rich and poor were potentially disastrous. Although the shah did try to fix some things, his clumsy actions alienated the very classes who supported him. Even a new prime minister didn't help. Iran's economy was in shambles.

Hassan also deplored the encroaching westernization. "There are over sixty thousand foreigners in Iran," he said. "And forty-five thousand of them are Americans. We see only Western fashions, music, films, and television. What has happened to our culture?" He confessed to Nouri that he had joined a group of students with similar complaints.

Their discussions continued via letters. In his latest, Hassan wrote that more people were speaking out. Amnesty International had condemned the number of political prisoners in Iran; even the American president was making noise about human rights. The opposition was strengthening. Hassan encouraged Nouri to get involved.

"You are in the belly of the beast," he wrote. "If you can convince the American people to join our cause, their leaders will not be far behind."

Nouri took Hassan's letter into the bedroom.

Anna looked up from her book. "What is it?" Was her voice sharper than usual or was it just his imagination?

He sat on the edge of the bed and ran his fingers gently through her hair.

She put the book down and her body went slack. She seemed tired, but she was still ready for him. He swung his legs up on the bed and lay down.

"I've had another letter from Hassan."

"Oh?"

"Opposition to the shah is building. People are organizing. Speaking out."

"What opposition?"

He propped himself up on his elbow. "Lawyers, judges, university professors. Professional groups like the National Front, the IFM, and—"

"The who?"

"The Iran Freedom Movement. Anna, the revolutionary spirit is spreading. People are writing open letters demanding the restoration of the constitution. For the first time I think there is a real chance we might get rid of the shah."

She ran her fingers up his arm, letting them sweep across his skin.

"You miss being there, don't you?"

He nodded. "I have been lucky to lead a privileged life when there are many who do not. But America could do so much, if people just understood how evil the shah is."

"But you're supposed to be here to study. What about your thesis?"

Nouri waved a hand. "Sometimes there are more important matters than academics."

Anna's eyebrows arched. "Your family has prospered under the shah. Your father supports him. They socialize together. What are they going to say?"

"The oil industry will do well no matter who's in power. And my father's support is one of convenience. Believe me, he wasn't happy when the shah declared war on profiteers and exiled those industrialists. You should have heard him."

"But you're just a student. What can you really do?"

"How can you say that, Anna? You know how powerful a student movement can be."

"That's true." She sighed. "Looking back, though, I'm sure we believed we were more powerful than we really were."

"That is not the case for us. The Iranian Students Association has a chapter in Chicago. I'm going to a meeting."

Anna dropped her hand from his arm. She frowned slightly, as if she wanted to say something.

"What, Anna?"

She hesitated, then looked down at her book. "Nothing." She pressed her lips together.

Six

By the time winter settled in Nouri had attended several meetings. They were held in one of two Iranian students' apartments near UIC. About ten people usually showed up, mostly men, although two women dropped in occasionally.

Nouri learned that there was a vast network of Iranian student organizations in the US. Several years previously, though, the movement had splintered. Many of the Islamists broke away, leaving moderates and Marxists to vie for control. All three factions wanted the shah gone, but apart from that, their agendas were quite different. The Marxists gradually overpowered the moderates on some campuses, but internal tensions still ran high. As a moderate, Nouri sensed the others didn't fully accept, or trust, him. And when, one night, he mentioned the short window of democracy that Mosaddeq opened twenty-five years before, one of the students challenged him.

"What makes you think whoever replaces the shah will improve the lot of our people?" he asked in a strident voice.

"Because, hopefully, the people will elect a leader who is committed to doing just that," Nouri replied. "Iran must become democratic again."

The other student started to reply, but Massoud, their leader, cut in. "Internal squabbles will not help our cause. We have the opportunity to make a significant impact on US perceptions, perhaps even policy. But first we must show Americans how bad things are back home."

"How?" Nouri asked.

"We've studied the tactics of the anti-war movement, and the American civil rights movement—protests, demonstrations, speeches, pamphleting, manifestos. All of these tools are part of our plan."

"What is the most important task?"

Massoud gazed at the group. "To make sure we are united. After all, we come from all parts of Iran, and all segments of Iranian society."

Nouri was skeptical. Even though the shah now subsidized education abroad, you still needed money to study in the US. Most of the students in the US were, in all likelihood, from wealthy families. But he kept his doubts to himself. "What are you planning for Chicago?"

"When the weather is better, we will demonstrate at Daley Plaza."

"For what purpose?"

The student who challenged him cut in. "Why are you asking so many questions?"

"I want to understand."

Massoud and the other student exchanged glances. The student glared at Nouri. "Let me see your identity card."

He pulled out his student ID and handed it over.

The student inspected it, then passed it to Massoud. They retreated to a corner and whispered. The others stared at Nouri as if he'd developed leprosy.

Nouri shifted his feet. "You can't think I'm an informer?"

"Are you?" the student asked.

Massoud came back to Nouri. "This is not a game, Nouri Samedi," he said solemnly. "We are not playing at politics."

Nouri thought it *was* theatrics, but he wanted to do his part. "I understand."

"You see, we are being watched."

"By whom?"

"Supporters of the shah. The CIA. FBI too. They monitor us. Tap our phones. Their photographers take pictures of us and send them back to Iran. Once students return home, they are rounded up by SAVAK and questioned. Their family members, too. That's why we insist our members wear masks or paper bags during demonstrations."

"I am not afraid," Nouri said.

"Maybe you should be." The militant student shot him a patronizing smile and handed his ID back. "We will be keeping an eye on you, brother."

§

At Christmas Anna planned to visit her father, who lived near Frederick, Maryland, but Nouri would stay in Chicago. Anna apologized but said it wasn't yet time for him to meet her father. Still, it was clear she didn't want to leave him alone, and Nouri knew she felt guilty. He told her not to worry, that, in fact, he would relish the solitude. Over the past year, except for those eight weeks during the summer, they had not been without each other for more than a few hours.

Still, after she left, he felt the emptiness. Without Anna, the apartment seemed less his, more hers. Objects he usually took for granted, like Anna's stereo, her books, even her toiletries left in the bathroom, assumed a foreignness, a strangeness around which he didn't feel comfortable. He spent his time going to the movies, eating junk food, and trying to ignore the forced materialism and sentimentality of the American holiday.

The evening before Anna came home, a woman from the Iranian Students Association invited him for dinner. Several other Iranian students were there as well, and they made a party. The hostess cooked chelow kababs with ground beef, which Nouri had not eaten since he'd been in Tehran. She apologized that she had only pita bread, not lavash, but no one seemed to care. They stuffed themselves. After dinner they broke out the liquor, and Nouri, who rarely drank, had too much. He stumbled home after midnight and collapsed on the bed.

§

"Nouri, Nouri, wake up."

He came awake slowly. Light spilled through the window. He tried to answer, but his throat was like sand, and nothing came out.

"Nouri, wake up!" The voice was insistent.

He opened his eyes. Anna was standing over the bed. He tried to grin, but his lips felt like they were sewn together.

"You are home," he managed to croak. He spread his arms, but she stepped back from the bed. He blinked.

"I called last night," Anna said. He heard the ice in her voice. "I left a message." She pointed toward the other room where the answering machine sat. "You didn't hear it?"

He shook his head.

"I told my father about you. He wants to meet you."

Nouri realized what an important development this was. Anna had told him repeatedly how difficult her father was. How she had to time her announcements and requests just so. Nouri should have thanked her. They should have celebrated. But Anna was still scowling.

"Why didn't you answer?"

He sat up. He was still wearing his clothes from last night, and he had a monster of a headache. "To be honest, I had too much to drink." He got up slowly, shuffled into the bathroom, gulped down some aspirin with a glass of water. When he returned, she was sitting on the bed with a blank expression.

"Where were you?"

He told her.

She crossed one leg over the other. She was still wearing her coat. "You went to another woman's apartment? An Iranian woman?"

"Yes. There were six of us...no, seven."

Anna's leg started to jiggle. Whenever she was worried or upset, she couldn't sit still. Something—an arm, a leg, a finger—was always in motion. She would have made an excellent whirling dervish.

"It was not what you think," he said quickly. "It was just a dinner party. You know we don't celebrate Christmas. It was a way for us to be together."

"Why didn't you tell me about it when I called?" Anna had called every day.

"Fatimah...she just called yesterday afternoon. It was—how do you say it—spur of the moment."

Anna's leg was still jiggling. He should have soothed her. Taken her in his arms. Whispered how much he loved her. But he didn't. She was the one who'd left him. He'd had to fend for himself while she was with her father. The unfairness of it all gnawed at him. "That's not who you should be concerned about, anyway," he blurted out.

Anna's face went white. "What do you mean?"

As soon as it came out, he realized it was the wrong thing to say. He tried to roll it back. "Nothing."

"No, it's not nothing." Worry lines creased her forehead.

Nouri's head was throbbing. He felt nauseous.

"Nouri. Tell me. Who *should* I be concerned about?" Her eyes bored into him, and she looked like she might cry

What box had he just opened? He'd never seen her like this. He wished he hadn't had so much to drink last night. He wished Anna had never left. He wished he could turn back the clock. "It is not important."

"Let me be the judge of that."

He took a long breath. He had no choice, she wouldn't let it go. "All right." He exhaled slowly. "There are still some arranged marriages in Iran. Not as much now, since we are quite modern. But when I was little..."

Anna's voice was as sharp as a blade. "What are you telling me, Nouri?"

"There is a girl. She is nothing to me...really. Her name is Roya. She is friends with my sister. Our parents are friends. We always thought... well, it was assumed..."

"That you would marry her? That you'd get your fancy American education and go back to little Roya?"

Nouri's eyebrows shot up. Anna sounded bitter. It was an emotion he'd never heard from her before. He took another breath. "It was never a formal arrangement. Just a..." He shrugged and let his voice trail off.

"But now that I've met you, it will never happen."

Anna tilted her head. "How do I know that?"

"Anna, you are the only woman I want. Our souls are meant to be together."

"What about Roya?"

"Anna, I have not talked to her, or even thought about her, in years. I care only about you. You must believe me."

Anna's leg stopped jiggling. She peered at him for a long time. Then she rose, took off her coat, and nodded. "All right."

Just like that, it was over.

That night Anna did things to him she hadn't done in a long time. Nouri decided maybe a little jealousy was good for the soul.

Seven

How is your research on the thesis coming along?" Anna asked one night in January.

Nouri didn't want to talk about it. It was not going well. The desalination proposal had turned out to be more difficult than he'd anticipated. For one, it was not realistic to build a plant in the rocky soil of a mountain village. Even if it could be built, and the water treated, there was no existing infrastructure through which to pipe the water from the plant into homes or wells or cisterns. He might have to abandon the topic, but he wasn't ready to admit it yet.

A few days later an article in an Iranian newspaper attacked Ayatollah Khomeini, which sparked a mass demonstration in Qom, perhaps the holiest city in the world for Shi'ite Muslims. Several demonstrators were killed. A little over a month later, more anti-shah protests, this time in Tabriz, Iran's fourth largest city, turned violent. It took two days before order was restored.

Nouri went to a hastily called meeting of the student organization. Just getting to the meeting was proof of his commitment: snow was piled in banks over six feet high, with more blanketing the city almost every day. The harsh Chicago winter was unprecedented. On some streets Nouri's feet were level with the roofs of cars—cars which wouldn't be dug out until spring. Anna joked that it was the start of Armageddon.

At the meeting, the students made plans to show solidarity with their Iranian brethren. They agreed that letters, resolutions, and declarations aimed at restoring constitutional rule were not enough. The system—and the shah—had to go.

"We need to purify and purge Iran of corruption and repression," said one student.

Nouri agreed. "We need to empower workers and farmers. They need to share in Iran's wealth. It is not just for the privileged few. The first—"

"But that's only part of it," another student cut in. "We need to purify ourselves of Western influences and imperialism. That will only happen if we create a government based on Marxist principles."

"No!" another student protested. "We need to create a structure based on Islamic law. An Islamic republic."

Nouri frowned. "Wait!" His hand shot up. "Not everything should be cast out. The shah is evil, and he needs to go. But he did build roads, and he brought electricity and water to many villages. Education too. We need to make sure that progress continues. That is what will enrich our people."

"What about the land he stole from the mullahs and farmers?" one of the students shouted. "Is that enriching the people? His so-called reforms have brought nothing but misery. Meanwhile, he and his cronies get rich at our expense. And anyone who disagrees with them ends up in prison to be tortured. Or worse." The student spoke with passion. Others joined in, and a frenzy of shouting erupted.

Nouri remembered Anna saying how politics and religion didn't mix. He raised his voice above the din. "I'm not defending the shah. I'm just saying—"

"Not defending the shah? Your father works for the oil company," a student spit out. "He is nothing but a lackey."

Nouri was taken aback. How did they know that?

As if reading his mind, the student went on. "Do you think we don't know who you are? We make it a point to identify everyone who comes to our meetings."

Nouri swallowed. "Surely you would not denounce me because of my family. Many of us come from wealthy families, but we are not our fathers."

"Prove it," a student cried, his voice dripping with scorn. "Prove to us that you are not a spy for the CIA or SAVAK."

Nouri didn't know how to respond, but to his surprise, the leader, Massoud, came to his defense. He held up his arms in a placating gesture. "Nouri is no spy." He turned to the others. "He may come from privilege, but he understands things must change." He looked back at Nouri. "And you are correct. I, too, am from a family of means. My father works for the government." He turned back to the others. "If you honor me with your trust, you must honor Nouri as well. We must work together to destroy the evil and repression caused by the shah. We must bring freedom to our people. Of course we cherish our Islamic traditions, just as we cherish our Persian culture. Whether we are mullahs or Marxists, engineers or workers, rich or poor, we want the same thing."

His speech seemed to mollify the students, and the bickering subsided. They changed subjects and started to discuss plans for the spring, when Iranian students from all over the Midwest would converge on Daley Plaza for a massive protest. Some students were told to organize campus demonstrations, others to write speeches, and still others to distribute leaflets. Finally, the meeting ended, the participants exhausted but fueled with fervor.

When he arrived back home, Nouri told Anna about the meeting. "I still have no idea how they knew about my family."

"Perhaps they are better organized than you thought."

"But still..."

"It isn't unusual. If I were studying abroad, I'd check out any Americans I ran across. You know, ask around."

"But who? Who would have that information?"

"It could come from anywhere. Maybe one of them works in the university's admissions department. Or maybe someone recognized your last name." She frowned. "Is your father well known?"

Nouri shrugged and changed the subject. "What do you think about the protest? Should I do it?"

He was surprised by her response. "Of course you must. And I'll help."

Nouri gazed at her.

"You seem surprised. Did you think I wouldn't support you?"

Maybe he didn't know her as well as he thought. "I...I wasn't sure." He paused. "Do you really think it's okay to oppose the shah so...so openly? What if it causes problems back in Iran?"

"Nouri, sometimes there is no choice. You *have* to do what you think is right. I'm proud of you." Anna beamed. "You know, if the group needs a place to meet, you can use the apartment."

"Really?"

She laughed. "Tell them it's their safe house."

Nouri gathered Anna in his arms, aware of how much he loved her. And needed her. He pressed against her. He wanted her. Right then. Right there. He was just about to lift off her sweater when she whispered.

"There is something we need to talk about."

Nouri was still kissing her neck. "Your skin tastes so sweet."

"No, really." She pushed him away. Just a little, but it was enough. Frustration spilled over him. "What is it?"

"We need to make a few changes." Anna needed help around the apartment, she said. She could not do all the housework and still have time to study. She would cook and shop and clean the kitchen, but he would have to do the laundry and clean the rest of the apartment.

"Is that all?" Relief coursed through him. "You are becoming a liberated woman," he joked.

She peered at him as if she didn't see the punch line. "Liberated or not, I'm exhausted. Even my father commented on how washed out I look. I just can't do it all." She hesitated. "If I didn't have so much work for school it would be different. I would be happy to cook and clean and make our house...," she motioned with her hand, "...the perfect refuge. But right now...it's just too much."

Nouri tilted his head. When they first met, her only goal was to please him. Nothing was too small or troublesome. Since she'd returned from Maryland, however, a subtle change had come over her. She wasn't as subservient. Plus, the apartment, which she'd always kept compulsively neat, was less so. Nouri decided he didn't mind if it made her feel and look better. Tonight, in fact, she did. With her bright eyes, her hair like spun gold, and that half-smile that drove him crazy, she was ravishing. He pulled her close, inhaling her sweet smell.

"I will do whatever you want."

She curled up in his arms. "Thank you, Azizam," she murmured, using the Persian word for sweetheart.

§

Over the next few weeks, the Iranian students created their flyers and signs, and the manifesto that Massoud was to deliver at the demonstration. Although they declined to meet at Anna's apartment, Nouri offered to help draft the manifesto, and because her English was more idiomatic, Anna ended up writing most of it.

The demonstration at Daley Plaza came just before the Iranian New Year, which coincided with the first day of spring. The crisp March day was sunny but cold. Anna cut class, something she was usually loath to do, so she could go with Nouri. Nouri grabbed a few paper bags, and Anna made holes in them for their eyes. They packed up their signs and leaflets and rode the El to the Loop. When they reached the plaza, a crowd had already gathered. Nouri guessed there were over two hundred students.

Anna's eyes grew wide. "Where did they all come from?"

"Downstate, Indiana, Iowa, Wisconsin, even Michigan," Nouri said. He spotted Massoud and the Iranian student group from UIC. He and Anna worked their way through the crowd toward them. "Hey!" Nouri shouted. He was reluctant to shout out Massoud's name; SAVAK could be watching.

Massoud spun around, saw Nouri, and waved. Nouri took Anna's arm and pushed closer.

"Massoud, this is Anna. She helped write the manifesto."

Massoud's eyes tracked her up and down.

"Hello," Anna said. "I'm impressed with the organization. How did you get so many people to participate?"

"We had help. People like Nouri here, but others too. We have—"

A tall brassy-looking blonde with an armful of signs grabbed Massoud's jacket. "Massie baby," she interrupted. "Where do you want these signs?"

He turned around, scanned the area, then pointed in the general direction of Clark Street. The woman smiled, planted a passionate kiss on his mouth, then trudged in the direction he'd indicated. Massoud turned back to Nouri, who was still eyeing his blonde American girl-friend. They exchanged awkward smiles, each recognizing themselves in the other.

Massoud cleared his throat. "Thank you for your contributions," he said formally to Anna. She replied with a cool nod, but her gaze was following the blonde, too. What did she think of her? Nouri wondered.

"As you can see, we have all sorts of alliances." Massoud gestured to the police. "Except with them."

Nouri craned his neck. There had to be over fifty uniformed cops edging the plaza's perimeter. Some held shields in front of their bodies. Nouri tried to spot the spies he'd been warned about. He saw a TV news crew and several men with cameras, but he couldn't tell whether they were journalists or something less benign.

The protest began a few minutes later. The students put on their paper bags, waved their signs, shouted, and chanted. Anna and Nouri slipped on their bags and joined in. Someone handed Massoud a mega-phone. He unfolded a piece of paper and began to speak.

"We, the Iranian Students Association, wish to make known to the American people the sins of Muhammad Reza Shah Pahlavi. He has created a military state that brutally oppresses and persecutes his subjects. He has stolen millions of dollars in oil revenues that belong to the people. His secret police have imprisoned and tortured and killed thousands of people, whose only sin was to speak out against his policies. He has…"

Every sentence Massoud spoke was followed by clenched fists and cheers, each round louder and more intense than the last. Nouri stole a glance at Anna. He couldn't be sure, but he suspected that, beneath the paper bag, she approved. When Massoud finished, another speaker took the megaphone and picked up where Massoud left off. A third speaker followed him.

As the speakers proliferated, the sun climbed higher in the sky, and the day grew warm. It was becoming hard to breathe under the bags. Nouri kept fidgeting with his. So did Anna. Finally, Nouri tapped her on the shoulder.

"I can't breathe. I'm taking it off."

"You can't. It's too dangerous."

"I don't care." In a sweeping gesture, he tore the bag off his face and gazed around defiantly.

Anna froze. He knew she wasn't sure what to do. A moment later another student nearby stripped off his bag. Nouri and he exchanged nods. A third student, then a fourth slowly took off their bags. Soon, everyone around Nouri had ripped off their bags. Some congratulated each other and clasped hands. Others hugged. They all cheered Nouri. He dipped his head.

As the crowd cheered and pushed in, Nouri and Anna were separated. When he realized she was not behind him, he whipped around. He spotted her, four or five people away. He gestured to her. He could see her trying to slip through the throng to get to him. As she did, she slowly removed her bag as well. Her eyes were wet, but she was smiling. Nouri sucked in a breath. She was telling him how much she loved him. How proud of him she was. He didn't think he could love her more.

His joy was short-lived, though. A moment later a scuffle broke out on the other side of the plaza. A student and an on-looker, Nouri thought. As if it was a signal, the police started to move in. Shouting erupted, followed by more scuffles. The police grabbed some of the protestors. Nouri, in the middle of the crowd, couldn't get away. The police were closing in, heading straight toward him. He turned around and saw Massoud slinking off in the opposite direction with his brassy, blonde girlfriend. Nouri wanted to yell at him to stop. Everything was coming apart, and Massoud was their leader. He should do something.

Nouri turned back to see a beefy police officer brandishing his club ten yards from where he was standing. He was going to be arrested. Then what? He would be thrown in jail. His life would be over. He swallowed nervously, edging toward panic.

Suddenly, Anna was beside him. She snatched his hand and pushed through the crowd. Nouri followed, stumbling at first, then steadier. Together they wove through the hordes of people, Anna still clutching his hand. He couldn't tell how far they'd gone, but he lost sight of the police. By the time she guided him to the other side of Washington Street they'd left the demonstration behind.

Eight

The warmth of spring eventually came to Chicago, and cars that had been buried in snow for months were finally dug out. The warmer weather brought with it hot political rhetoric, and a female politician decided to challenge the mayor in the next Chicago primary. Anna thought it was long overdue.

"There's no reason in the world a woman shouldn't be mayor," she said to Nouri at dinner one night. "Israel had Golda Meir. India, Indira Gandhi. And Margaret Thatcher may be the next prime minister of Britain. As usual America lags behind."

Nouri sliced his chicken and took a bite.

"What do you think, Nouri? Would you vote for a woman?"

He chewed and swallowed his meat, then laid down his knife and fork. He clasped his hands together. "I don't think I will have the opportunity to vote for the mayor of Chicago."

"Well, of course not. The election is over a year away, and you're not a US citizen, anyway."

"Even if I was a citizen, I would not vote."

Anna frowned. "Why not? Don't you believe a woman can do the job?"

He smiled broadly. In fact, he looked like he was going to burst. Anna frowned, puzzled. "What is it, Nouri?"

Nouri backed his chair away from the table, scraping the floor with its legs. He stood up. "I've been waiting for the right moment to tell you.

I was offered a job in Tehran. It's an engineering job with the company that's building the Metro."

"I didn't know they were planning a metro," she said cautiously. She wanted to share his joy, but her stomach was suddenly queasy. This meant he'd definitely be going back to Iran. She'd always known it would happen, but she'd preferred not to think about it.

He came around the table and grabbed both her hands. "Anna, this is my chance."

She ran her tongue around her lips. What was he really saying? "What about bringing electricity and running water to rural villages?" she asked. "All your plans to help your countrymen? Get rid of the shah?"

"That hasn't changed. Not at all." He rubbed his thumbs over the backs of her hands. "But I will need a job, and this is an excellent place to start. My father knows the man in charge. He's a good man. Assuming I pass the engineering exam back home, it is the chance of a lifetime." He paused. "But that's not what I want to say."

Anna steeled herself. In just a couple of months she'd graduate and Nouri would have his master's. It was clear she hadn't prepared herself.

Nouri started to laugh.

He was behaving in a highly inappropriate way, she thought. She was about to tell him so when he knelt at her feet.

"Anna Schroder, I can't live without you, and I don't want to. Will you give me the greatest honor a man can possibly have? Will you come with me to Iran? Will you be my wife? Bear my children? Live with me forever?"

Her mouth flew open. She couldn't speak.

He rose and pulled her to him.

She slipped into the crook of his arm. Her eyes filled.

He brushed her tears away. "Why are you crying? This is supposed to be a happy time."

She sniffed and wiped her nose. This had been her dream. To marry a wonderful man. Raise a family. Live a life surrounded by warmth and love and security. It was a life she'd never known, a life she didn't think she deserved. Now it was coming true.

"Is that a yes?" he asked.

A tear rolled down her cheek and she hugged him tight. "Yes, Nouri." She sobbed. "Oh, yes."

§

But Anna's joy was short-lived. Over the next few weeks, her anxiety came back. What if it *was* a dream? A mirage that would disappear the closer it approached? "Didn't you say your parents aren't sure you should come home right now? Didn't they say things are deteriorating, with all the demonstrations and riots?"

Nouri made a dismissive gesture. "We live in the safest neighborhood in Tehran. Nothing will happen."

Anna sat on the bed. "What neighborhood is that?"

"My parents live in north Tehran. We will live near them in Shemiran. It is all arranged. You will see—it is very beautiful. And safe."

"But I don't speak Farsi, except for the few words you've taught me." He'd taught her hello, goodbye, and how to write his name using the Arabic alphabet.

"You won't have to. There are so many Americans in Iran that most Iranians speak at least some English. Believe me, you'll hear it on TV, in music, in the shops. You'll feel right at home."

She gulped. "Nouri…" She bit her lip. "What if your parents don't like me?"

"Don't be silly. They will love you, just as I do." A puzzled look came over him, as if he wasn't sure why she was so wracked with doubt. "And in Tehran you will be closer to Paris and your mother. You can visit her anytime you like."

Anna started to jiggle her foot.

"Look," Nouri said. "If it makes you feel better, consider our visit there temporary. If you don't like it, we'll come back to the States."

Her foot stopped jiggling. "You'd do that? Come back to America for me?"

"I would do anything for you, Anna." But his expression was not quite as certain, his voice not as sure. "What is it? Why are you so upset?"

She couldn't keep it from him any longer. "There is something I need to tell you. Let's go for a walk."

§

The Midway Plaisance, a strip of park sandwiched between 59th and 60th Streets, had been built for the Columbian Exposition in the 1890s. As Anna and Nouri strolled down it, the setting sun was molten gold. Stately university buildings flanked both sides of the park, and flowering bulbs shared the dirt alongside trees and shrubs. But Anna wasn't focused on the architecture, or the flowers, or the lush carpet of grass.

"There is something I haven't told you," she said. "About my father." She hesitated. "It might make a difference in...well, everything."

"Nothing could make a difference in how I feel about you, Anna."

"Don't...until you've heard me out."

They passed a statue of Carl Linnaeus, the father of modern taxonomy, which Anna knew was the method of classifying organisms by categories such as genus and species. With his long, curly marbled hair and bookish appearance—although he looked rather pale—he resembled a young Benjamin Franklin.

"Even if your father was a mass murderer, I couldn't love you less."

Nouri was closer than he knew. Anna halted at the base of the statue. They had been holding hands, but she withdrew hers and squeezed her palms together. "My father is a physicist. He works for the government at a secret lab in Maryland that doesn't officially exist."

Surprise crossed Nouri's face.

"He started out in genetics. Studying and deciphering genomes within cells. You've probably heard about it. They're calling it gene therapy. When the techniques are perfected, it will supposedly cure cancer and everything else."

They started walking again. "It sounds like a noble occupation," Nouri said.

Was he trying to be helpful? If so, it wasn't working. Anna swallowed. "The thing is, I don't know exactly *what* my father does. He won't tell me. It's classified." She made a little snort. "For all I know he's working on some genetically engineered virus or bacteria that will wipe out the human race."

Nouri frowned. "Why would you say something like that?"

"Because of his background. He was...this is hard for me to talk about, Nouri."

Nouri kept his mouth shut.

"My father was born, raised, and educated in Germany. During World War II he was conscripted and forced to join the Nazi Party. He...well...he worked with scientists who were trying to engineer the Master Race. You know, the pure Aryan."

Nouri's eyebrows shot up. He started to say something, but she cut him off.

"Yes. *Aryan*." She rolled the word on her tongue with only a trace of contempt. "The same word that the name of your country comes from. The same race, too." She let out an uneven breath. "You see, eighty years ago the eugenics movement was considered a promising science. Everybody was interested in improving human beings. Wiping out the flaws that cause disease. But Hitler turned it into something else."

Nouri nodded.

"There were massive sterilizations. Especially of the mentally and physically disabled. What they called the mongrel population. Then, Hitler decreed that Jews possessed 'bad' genes and were a threat to racial purity. You know the rest."

"What part did your father play?"

Anna hesitated. She had seen the films, read the books about that time—at one point she'd been obsessive about it. She had to know every detail, decision, and incident of the war. After a while, though, the need faded. Whether it was the natural consequence of maturity, or some psychological block that prevented her from absorbing more, she never knew. Nor did she make an effort to find out. Her impressions of that era faded into the hazy residue of knowledge most students retain once the course is finished, the exam over. She could now watch *The Diary of Anne Frank*, *Casablanca*, even *Triumph of the Will*, which her professor screened during a course in Twentieth Century European History, with a curious, almost ironic, detachment.

Now she said, "I can only guess. Probably some kind of medical or chemical experimentation, because toward the end of the war, he was sure he would be caught by the Allies and tried. Maybe even executed. Then an American came to see him. It was all very secret—my father had to go to three separate locations before he actually met the man."

"What man?"

"I don't know. Someone high up in the OSS, maybe. Or the War Department. At any rate, he wanted to know if my father was interested in bringing his work to the US. The government wanted to revisit eugenics—not to create a Master Race—but to manipulate genes for other purposes."

"What purposes?"

"I told you. I don't know. But given my father's background, and what they're talking about today, I suspect it was some kind of germ warfare program." Anna nervously cleared her throat. "This man offered to smuggle my father out of Germany and bring him here. He would avoid prosecution and imprisonment. In fact, there would be no consequences. None at all." She paused. "Of course, my father said yes."

Anna stopped walking. They had almost reached the western edge of the Midway. "So you see, Nouri, my father was a Nazi."

Nouri was silent.

"I was in middle school when I discovered it. One of my teachers left an article on my desk. I took it home and my father admitted it."

"Is that why your parents divorced?"

She shaded her eyes against the setting sun. "I'm sure of it. They met at an embassy party in Washington after the war. I don't think my mother knew who he was or what he was doing, but when she found out—which had to be when I was quite young—she left."

"And you? What do you think?"

44

"I was just a little girl. I didn't know why my mother left and didn't take me with her. I still don't. But she did leave, so my father was the only parent I had." She was quiet for a moment. "I never had many friends, you know. It wasn't that they shunned me..." her voice trailed off. "Or maybe it was. People tend to keep their distance from the daughter of a Nazi. My father was the only person who understood. And accepted me. At least on some level." Her throat tightened. She faced Nouri. "So. Now you know. I can understand if you want to call it off. I wouldn't blame you. After all, I am—what do they say?—'damaged goods.'"

They turned around and walked back east up the Midway. Nouri didn't say anything. Anna hung her head. She was afraid to look at him, afraid to breathe. It occurred to her that this must be what an innocent person accused of murder felt like just before the jury rendered a verdict. They walked past the statue again. Past leafy trees stirring in the breeze. Finally, Nouri turned to her. She froze, unsure what she would do if he said the wrong thing. She steeled herself for the worst.

"Well, then, it's a good thing we're moving to Iran." He smiled down at her and squeezed her hand. "You will have a *real* family to care for you."

Nine

Anna graduated in June. She skipped the ceremony, but she and Nouri celebrated by going out to dinner. It was, in fact, a double celebration: Nouri would be granted his master's degree after he handed in his thesis. He told Anna he planned to finish it back in Iran and send it over. Anna didn't pursue it; she was busy shopping and packing their things, which would be shipped to Iran. She bought a set of steak knives in a wooden block, jars of peanut butter, and boxes of tampons—all items she'd been told were hard to find in Tehran.

At the beginning of August they flew to Baltimore, rented a car, and headed west to Frederick. Once off the highway, they drove through rural Maryland farmland. Nouri, who had never been in this part of America, was surprised by the gently rolling hills and acres of crops. Anna explained that the land had been continually farmed since the 1700s, well before the American Revolution.

"What are those mountains in the distance?" Nouri asked.

"The Blue Ridge. They are part of the Appalachians." She remembered a trip to Catoctin Mountain with her father where the view had been spectacular.

"They are so…blue." Nouri marveled. "In Iran, our mountains are brown and rocky."

"It has to do with the trees and the hydrocarbons they release into the atmosphere. My father could tell you exactly how and why."

Eventually they pulled up at an old white clapboard farmhouse surrounded by several acres of land. It was comfortable looking, but not opulent. As she slid out of the car, the bright August sun, the heat-baked smell of the dirt, and the chirr of insects triggered a sharp memory of her childhood. The memory, both tender and full of longing, was so intense it took her breath away. She leaned against the car.

Her father was not home, but Anna had a key. They went up to her old bedroom. She'd attended boarding school after she turned fourteen, only coming back for vacations, but the room was much the same, with a huge, four-poster bed, crisp white spread, an antique armoire, and lace curtains. She took Nouri into the guest room across the hall, which was utilitarian more than decorative.

"You'll have to sleep in here," she said apologetically. "My father is very traditional."

"That's fine." He grinned. "As long as you keep your door unlocked."

She kissed him lightly on the lips. After unpacking, they went outside. The memories were less overpowering now, and she showed him where she used to play hide and seek, where she'd fallen out of a tree and broken her arm, where her cat had kittens. As the afternoon wore on, though, she grew more agitated. She was in constant motion, arms pinwheeling, tongue licking her lips. Even Nouri noticed.

"Anna, don't be nervous. He is your father, but he doesn't control your life. Not anymore."

She flashed him a grateful smile. Nouri was right. Nouri was her frame of reference now, her refuge, her joy. She could go about life without her father's approval, without the doubts as to whether he loved her. Without fear about the secrets of his past. In Iran she would have a happy, fulfilling life. She would not have to yearn for a normal family, the kind on those silly TV shows she'd watched as a child, like *Father Knows Best* or *Leave it to Beaver.*

Anna was making tea when a long, black car sailed up the driveway. Her father had used a driver for as long as she could remember. She and Nouri went outside and watched him climb out of the car. She wondered what Nouri saw. To Anna, Erich Schroder was a distinguished looking man well into his sixties. His flowing white hair was long but neatly combed. His piercing blue eyes could burn a hole in Anna's soul if she allowed it. He had a strong chin, which Anna inherited, and shaggy eyebrows, which, thankfully, she did not. He was not tall, but he was sturdy. If he hadn't become a physicist, he might have been a boxer. Although people dressed less formally now, her father wore a suit, crisp white shirt, and silk tie.

He embraced her and dropped a perfunctory kiss on her forehead. He clasped Nouri's hand, smiled, and introduced himself. They trooped into the house. Inside, her father took off his jacket and loosened his tie. They sat in the room Anna always called the front parlor—the formal room. Anna served tea. Her father took two sugars, she remembered. Nouri liked three. Her father quizzed Nouri about his family, his education, his interests. He nodded after every response. Nouri seemed subdued, and Anna wondered what he was thinking. Was he having doubts? Reconsidering?

"And what of your future, young man?" her father asked. "What will you do back in your country?"

Nouri told him about the Metro job. "It is the chance of a lifetime. To be at the center of the shah's progress and modernization."

"I see." Her father took a sip of tea, placed the cup and saucer back down on the tray. "And how do you feel about the shah?" Her father's eyes were bright and measuring. Anna's stomach twisted.

Nouri's response was nuanced. Anna wondered if her father could tell. "He's done good. A lot of good, actually, in bringing modern life to Iran. But at the same time, his record on human rights...," Nouri had adopted the term from observing American politics, "...is a failure. SAVAK is an abomination."

Her father bent his head. "Do you not believe that the end justifies the means? If poverty is erased, and the people are better off, does it really matter how it came to be?"

A frown line appeared on Nouri's forehead. Was this a trick? Anna wondered.

"If people cannot express themselves without fear of reprisals by the state," Nouri replied, "what good is prosperity?"

"But your shah is promising a car for every Iranian."

"Exactly. I stand by what I said."

Her father's smile was speculative. "If I didn't know better, I might think you're a progressive—perhaps even a Marxist—in capitalist's clothing."

Nouri grinned.

Her father pressed his fingertips together. "Then again, everyone is a Marxist when they're young."

Anna was miffed. Nouri kept a neutral expression on his face.

"Of course…," Anna's father said, "history has shown Iran to be quite…flexible. The father of your shah tilted toward Hitler during the war. At least until the British and the US stepped in. Then his son tilted just as easily the other way. Did you know that?"

Nouri shook his head.

"They probably deleted it from your textbooks. Persians rival the French in their…elasticity."

A plume of anger flared in Anna. Her father's comment was a dig not only at Nouri, but also at her mother.

"Well…," her father concluded, seemingly oblivious to Anna's discomfort, "…we have an eight o'clock dinner reservation. Until then, I bid you…" he paused, then flashed them a conspiratorial smile, "…adieu."

§

The town had only one decent restaurant, a country-style café that served thick soups and hush puppies, but it sported white tablecloths, courteous waiters, and a well-stocked bar. The maître d' welcomed her father and pretended to recognize Anna, although they hadn't seen each other since she was twelve. The servers were unfailingly polite to Nouri, and even offered him the wine menu, which he declined.

Anna's father wore the same suit but had changed into a fresh white shirt. He ordered baked mostaccioli, which Anna considered an odd menu item for a country restaurant. She ordered fish, Nouri chicken. The food was surprisingly tasty. They made small talk while they ate but, once the entrées were cleared, her father took off his Ben Franklin glasses, pulled out a linen handkerchief, and started to polish them. He put his glasses back on, then clasped his hands together.

"Nouri," he said. "I find myself in a somewhat awkward position. Anna is my only daughter. While I did expect she would ask permission to marry one day, I must admit I didn't anticipate it would come so soon. As you know, she just graduated from college."

A flash of irritation flickered through her. Since when did she need permission to marry? But she held her tongue. Her father wanted to make a point.

"But Anna has chosen you," her father continued.

"As I have chosen her. I love and honor your daughter. I will cherish her forever."

A smile tugged at Anna's lips.

"I believe you." Her father cleared his throat. "But unfortunately, my advancing age, plus my work schedule, will not permit me to come to Tehran for your wedding."

"We hope to persuade you otherwise."

"I don't think so." Her father paused. "I assume you will have a Muslim ceremony? And that Anna will be required to say she will convert?"

Anna wondered how her father knew that. She and Nouri had already discussed it and came to a compromise. For her it was a non-issue.

Nouri answered. "Please understand, sir…it is just a formality. No one takes it seriously. At least, I don't. And neither does my family. We understand Anna is a Christian. We respect people of all faiths in Iran. No one will force her to embrace Islam."

A strange expression—half smile, half grimace—unfolded across her father's face. "I appreciate your candor, Nouri. As her father, how-ever, I must be sure Anna has no objection to marrying you under any conditions, lenient as they may be."

Anna jumped in. "We're not religious. Never have been. You know that. I couldn't care less."

"Good." Her father nodded. "Then I have but one other request, in which I hope you'll both indulge me."

Anna and Nouri exchanged glances.

"I would like you to marry here—in the States—before you leave. Nothing elaborate. A civil ceremony will be adequate."

"Marry here? Why?" Anna asked.

"Isn't it enough that I want to 'give away' my only daughter to her intended?"

Anna sat back. Her father had never demonstrated any sentimentality. In fact, she'd always thought he had the emotional quotient of a frog. She called him on it. "Papa, what are you really asking?"

At first he looked chagrined that she dared to question his motives, then he shrugged. "I would like to ensure that your marriage is certified in the US, as well as in Iran."

"Why?" Anna couldn't quite keep the suspicion out of her voice.

Her father peered at her, then Nouri. "Please. Indulge me."

"But we're supposed to leave in three days. Our visas stipulate that. We don't have time."

"There is no blood test required in Maryland. You can pick up the license and be married forty-eight hours later. Or you can go to Virginia, where there is no waiting period at all."

Anna sucked in air. "You want us to elope? I thought—"

Her father cut her off. "It is all quite legal."

Anna's jaw dropped. She was confused. "But you just said…I mean… you actually want to give me away at a wedding chapel or City Hall? I don't get it."

His voice was assured and strong. "Anna, I don't ask you for much. Please do this for me. Consider it a parting gift."

Nouri cut in. "Dr. Schroder, sir, I beg you to reconsider and come to Tehran. You would be an honored guest. But, if you are absolutely certain you can't, of course, we will do what you ask."

"But Nouri…" Anna cried out.

Nouri shook his head.

Anna bit back a reply.

Her father smiled.

§

The next morning the three of them drove south to Leesburg, Virginia, the seat of Loudoun County. The colonial red brick courthouse in the center of town bore graceful white columns. Anna and Nouri applied for, and got, a marriage license. An hour later they were married by a circuit court judge during his lunch hour. Even though they agreed that the "official" ceremony would take place in Tehran, Anna felt a thrill as she and Nouri exchanged vows. She was Mrs. Nouri Samedi. She couldn't stop smiling. Her father looked pleased, too, and pumped Nouri's hand.

Anna's father made copies of the marriage license, and they headed back to Maryland. Two days later, Anna and Nouri drove to the airport and boarded a plane for Tehran.

Ten

Anna's first view of Tehran was from the air. She saw a sprawling metropolis as large as, or larger than, the five boroughs of New York. Endless rows of small buildings and high-rises lined streets laid out in no apparent pattern. In the distance were the rocky Alborz Mountains, which hugged three sides of the city. The Alborz range defined Tehran much like Lake Michigan did Chicago.

Most everything was in shades of brown—the mountains, the soil, even the haze of pollution. As the plane descended, though, objects came into sharper focus, and the brown lightened to beige, cream, even white. It was a distinct contrast to the sturdy gray of Chicago.

A blast of heat rolled over Anna as she walked down the steps of the plane, hot and dry and dangerous. Beads of sweat broke out on her neck. Fortunately, the air-conditioned Mehrabad Airport building was only a few steps away. Inside the terminal, they walked toward customs. Anna noticed the rounded arches and bright mosaics in the halls. It was early afternoon, but the airport was bustling with people, many of them Westerners. Her presence didn't attract much attention.

Customs was problem free—the officials didn't even open their luggage. Outside they hailed a cab. Nouri had called his parents from Frankfurt and told them not to come to the airport; everyone in the family would have come, and there would have been no room for their luggage. Anna was grateful for the temporary reprieve; it gave her time to acclimate herself.

The taxi driver spewed forth an eager stream of Farsi. Nouri replied, then said, "Please speak in English. My wife...," he grinned at Anna when he said the word, "...doesn't understand."

Anna almost giggled. Nouri was trying to make her feel welcome.

The driver shrugged. "Not too much English speak." He went quiet.

Soon a multi-arched tower loomed in front of them. It had gracefully curved walls, as well as an elegant design of recurring diamonds in blue and gold under the arches. A fountain burbled in front. "This is the Shahyad Aryamehr," Nouri pointed out. "'The Remembrance of the Shahs.' We call it the gateway to Tehran. The shah built it for the 2500th anniversary of the Persian empire."

The driver slowed down and piped up, again in Farsi.

Nouri translated. "He says it is built from eight thousand blocks of white marble."

Anna craned her neck to see better. Imposing and stately, it resembled a Persian Arc de Triomphe.

A few minutes later the streets became choked with traffic and people. They navigated what Anna assumed was the business district, passing ten- to twelve-story buildings, a department store, and hotels. It looked much like any other large city.

They swung onto a wide boulevard flanked by trees. Western-style buildings with sharp geometric angles lined the street, but sprinkled between them were structures with graceful curves and domes, terraced roofs, and intricate grill work on the façades. Many were textured with colorful recurring patterns. In addition to white, Anna saw flashes of bright blue, green, even lavender. It all worked to soften the architecture. As they wound around, every so often she got a peek at the mountains.

They drove around circles with an occasional fountain in the center. "We are heading to north Tehran," Nouri said. "It is the better part of the city. You won't want to go south."

"Why not?"

"It is just...well..."

"The ghetto?"

He nodded.

The cab driver launched into a fresh stream of Farsi, gesturing and looking at Nouri through the rear view mirror. Nouri listened, then replied in a sharp voice. The driver was suddenly silent.

Anna laid a hand on Nouri's arm. "What just happened?"

"He was talking about riots against the shah. Asking whether we heard about them in the States. And what I thought about them."

"But you didn't want to talk?"

"No." He patted Anna's hand. "He could be SAVAK. Or an informer. Hoping I will say something, so he can turn me in. Or force me to pay a bribe."

Anna stared at Nouri, then the taxi driver. Should she be concerned? She decided she had too much on her mind to worry about freedom of expression at the moment.

Nouri changed the subject anyway. "Now we are on Pahlavi Avenue. One of the longest streets in the world. It runs all the way through Tehran."

Anna gazed out at the street. They could talk later.

"Well, what do you think of my city?"

She peered out the windows on both sides. "I love it."

He laced his fingers through hers. "I'm so glad. Oh, Anna, what a life we will have together."

"It has already begun." She smiled. "You are everything to me."

A few minutes later, they veered off Pahlavi Avenue into a residential section. The streets were narrower here, and it was quieter. Most of the homes were secluded behind walls; sometimes a canopy of leaves peeked out above. They were entering the affluent area of Tehran, Anna thought. The taxi wound around several streets and stopped at a stone wall that ran the length of the block. The street was on a gentle rise; they were at its highest point.

Nouri spoke to the cab driver who blasted his horn long and loud. A moment later a gate opened, and several people spilled out: a woman, small and round, and a girl, who had to be a few years younger than Anna. Behind them a man and a woman hung back. They must have been the household help. Before she knew it Anna was being hugged and kissed and surrounded by exclamations of joy.

§

Behind the wall was a huge house that looked like it had been recently remodeled. Anna headed toward it, passing a patio flanked by fruit trees and a garden with blossoms in full bloom. A small pool sat in the middle of the yard. The others barely noticed, but Anna slowed her pace as she walked past. The fact that someone had a private space where they could dip their feet into cool water, read poetry, or contemplate nature seemed like paradise.

Inside the house were high ceilings, thick Persian carpets, and brightly colored tapestries. Silver and gold accessories flashed in the light, which poured in through a floor-to-ceiling picture window. Abstract oil paintings framed in ornate gold designs covered the walls. The furniture was upholstered in what Anna assumed was silk and the walls were white. The entire effect was light and airy, but not quite comfortable. As they strolled from room to room, Anna grew overwhelmed. She had grown up in comfort, never wanting, but this opulence was beyond anything she'd imagined.

Nouri's mother barked an order to one of the servants. The woman, wearing a scarf over her hair, murmured something back and picked up Anna's suitcase and duffel.

"No, I'll take them," Anna said to the woman.

Nouri's mother raised her palm and shook her head. The woman picked up Anna's bags. Nouri's mother smiled, looped her arm through Anna's, and led her up the stairs. Parvin Samedi was small and round, but Anna could tell that she was once a beauty. Her dark hair was threaded with strands of gray, but Nouri had her eyes: rich brown with flecks of amber, fringed with dark lashes. She wore a simply tailored beige dress accessorized with gold jewelry. She spoke only broken English, but between her smiles, gestures, and pantomimes she made herself understood.

Upstairs she led Anna down a long hall lined with a series of doors. Opening the second on the right, she mumbled something in Farsi and motioned Anna into the room. Floor-to-ceiling windows offered a view of northern Tehran, mostly a mass of buildings, many of them still under construction. They looked like they stretched all the way to the Alborz. The mountains seemed to have changed color in the past hour, Anna noticed. They were pinker now, not so brown.

The furniture in the room was Western and included a queen-size bed, a bureau, and bookcases filled with leather-bound books. A few trophies sat on the top shelf, along with framed photos of the family. There was even a shot of Nouri in a soccer uniform.

The female servant with the head scarf struggled into the room with Anna's luggage. She lifted the bags onto the bed, unzipped the duffel, and began to take out Anna's things.

"Please. I can do that," Anna said. But Nouri's mother said something in Farsi, and the servant kept unpacking. Anna was relieved to see Nouri come into the room. A male servant lugged his bags to a room farther down the hall.

"This is our number one guest room," Nouri said.

Anna bent her head. She was surprised Nouri's mother put them in different rooms. She was surprised they were staying here at all. "I thought we were going to the apartment."

"My father says it is not quite ready. They are painting and cleaning. We will see it tomorrow."

"How long will we be staying here?"

"I'm not sure."

"But…" She stopped. She'd only just arrived. She didn't want to be difficult. She looked around. "Nouri, why are we in separate rooms? We're married."

Nouri looked at the floor. He didn't answer.

"Nouri…" She crossed her arms.

When Nouri finally looked up his neck was flushed. "I haven't told them."

She stepped back. "You didn't tell them we got married?"

"Maman is so excited to be planning the wedding. For us, weddings are the most important event in a family's life. I didn't know how to break it to her."

"Nouri, we have to tell them. We shouldn't have to maintain a… fiction."

Nouri's voice took on a placating, almost whining tone. "Please, Anna. It's only for a few days." He eyed her sheepishly. "I will join you here. After everyone is in bed."

"What about when we move into the apartment? The wedding's not for another month. Do they expect us to sleep in separate rooms there, too?"

"You know how parents are." He waved a hand. "They'll ignore it. Appearances are what's important. Saving face."

Nouri had told her it was not unusual for couples of different nationalities or religions to be married twice, once in the States and once in Iran. In fact, Islamic law required that a Muslim ceremony be performed. So why was Nouri keeping their American marriage a secret? Anna felt just the tiniest bit betrayed. And excluded. Exhausted from traveling, her patience strained, she nearly told him exactly how she felt. But Nouri's mother was watching, a curious expression on her face. With a great effort Anna controlled herself. She was about to say they would talk later when Nouri's sixteen-year-old sister bounced into the room.

Laleh had Nouri's eyes, precise features, and dark, lustrous hair, but in a smaller, more feminine version. In fact, with her tight jeans, skimpy t-shirt, and artfully applied makeup, she was stunning. Even though she was five years older, Anna promptly felt intimidated; Laleh's beauty was coupled with the self-confidence that her entrances would always be noticed.

Laleh immediately went to Anna and gave her a hug. "I am so excited you are here, Anna. I can't wait to show you around Tehran." Her English was almost as good as Nouri's. "We shall be best friends, as well as sisters." She flashed Anna a dazzling smile.

Anna managed a wan one in return.

Nouri beamed proudly. Then his mother said something in Farsi, and Nouri nodded. "Anna, let the servant finish unpacking. We will go down for tea."

Anna would have preferred to unpack herself. But this was not her home, and she reminded herself to be a good guest. She threw a grateful look at the servant who was busy putting her things in the bureau, and followed the family downstairs. She was annoyed at Nouri.

From the living room, Anna heard the clink of plates and cups in the kitchen. A moment later, another servant—how many did they have? she wondered—carried in a tray bearing a slender teapot, five narrow glasses, and a plate of sliced fruit. Iranians drank their tea in glasses, Anna remembered, sometimes with a cube of sugar between their teeth. Nouri patted the upholstered sofa next to him.

Nouri's father entered and sat in what was obviously his chair next to the sofa. He had only recently arrived home from his office. Bijan was light-skinned, tall, and slim. Nouri had inherited his shape. His hair was grayer than his wife's, and his almond-shaped eyes looked jade green. He sported a well-trimmed mustache, and wore a tailored, expensive looking suit, silk tie, and cuff links.

Parvin sat in a chair across from her husband and poured tea. Laleh slumped on a loveseat.

Nouri's father leaned forward. "Your travels were satisfactory, I hope?"

"Long, but fine," Anna said.

"If you are tired, you must nap." He spoke English with a crisp British accent.

"I never sleep during the day. I'll go to bed early."

Parvin offered Anna a glass of tea. She took it carefully. "You have a beautiful home, Mrs. Samedi."

"Oh, but you must call us Maman-joon and Baba-joon," Nouri's father said with a smile.

"Dear Mother and Father," Nouri explained.

Anna nodded shyly. Then, "Oh, that reminds me." She put down her tea, got up from the couch, and went to the stairs.

"Where are you going?" Nouri asked.

"You'll see."

She climbed the stairs back up to her room. The servant was almost finished unpacking. That was a problem, Anna thought. She had no idea where the woman had stored her things. She flipped up her hands in a questioning gesture, then realized the servant had no idea what she was after. She tried to sketch a box in the air with her fingers.

"The present. The gift," she said. "Where is it?"

The servant shook her head. Anna searched the room. She didn't see it. She knew she'd packed it in her big duffel. Then she opened the door to the closet. There it was on the top shelf: a pale blue box with a dark blue ribbon. She reached for it, but the shelf was too high. The servant was taller and retrieved it.

"*Khayli mamnoon.*" Thank you very much. It was one of the few Farsi expressions Anna knew.

The woman dipped her head. "*Khâhesh meekonam.*" You're welcome.

Anna took the box back downstairs and handed it to Nouri's mother. "This is for you, Maman-joon."

Nouri's parents exchanged glances.

"Open it," Nouri said.

Anna watched as Parvin opened the box. She had obsessed over the gift for weeks. It couldn't be too lavish, but it couldn't be cheap or shoddy. She'd finally settled on a pair of Lalique crystal candlesticks. They'd cost a small fortune. She hoped it was an appropriate choice. "I know the name Nouri means light. As his wife, I hope to bring a bit more light into your lives. I am honored to be part of your family."

Nouri's father translated. Parvin examined the candlesticks carefully. A slight frown furrowed her forehead. She spoke in Farsi.

"What did she say?" Anna asked nervously.

Nouri translated. "She said she can't accept them."

Anna's stomach flipped over. "What do you mean? Why not?"

"Maman says they are beautiful. So beautiful we should keep them for ourselves."

"But it is a gift for her," Anna said. "Tell her."

Nouri did, but Parvin shook her head.

"Please…" Anna's stomach tightened into a knot of anxiety. "I don't understand. Have I done something wrong? Doesn't she like me?"

Nouri's father barked out something in Farsi. Parvin answered him.

They went back and forth. Bijan had the last word. It sounded decisive. Then Parvin looked at Anna. "Okay," she said in broken English. "Is okay."

"What's okay?" Anna was totally confused.

Nouri piped up. "It is an Iranian custom. *Ta'arof.* Iranians always decline a gift before we accept. It is our way. But Baba knows this is not the custom in the West. He was explaining that to Maman."

Parvin rose, went to Anna, and gave her a hug. "*Khayli mamnoon.*"

"They are beautiful," Bijan said. "And thoughtful. But the honor of having you join our family is ours."

Anna sat back, tired but relieved. Immersing herself in Persian culture was going to be more challenging than she'd anticipated.

Bijan changed the subject. "I have called the head of the company with the Metro contract. They would like to meet with Nouri in two days. I assume that will be suitable?"

"Of course," Nouri replied. "Thank you, Baba."

"And you, Anna. I know you will be busy with the wedding and your new home. But after you're settled, will you want to work?"

She was pleased he'd been thinking of her. "I would like to. Until we have children, of course." She smiled shyly.

"Ah." He grinned broadly. "You want children?"

"Oh yes. At least three or four." She had always wanted a brood of children, their sweet baby smell in her nose, their noise and laughter filling the house. She couldn't wait to shower kisses on them when they skinned their knees and elbows, or woke up frightened from nightmares. She'd vowed that her children's lives would be vastly different from her cold, antiseptic childhood.

Baba-joon laughed. "I suppose you and Nouri will be quite busy."

Anna felt her cheeks get hot. She hoped she hadn't made a faux pas. But Baba-joon was still grinning. "Well, until that blessed day arrives, what do you have in mind to do?"

She spread her hands. "I don't know. I was hoping to take some time and figure it out."

"The company I work for is always looking for people who speak and write English. Writing letters, translating, making phone calls, and what not. I realize you need to learn some Farsi, but if you're interested I can make inquiries."

The oil company? Especially the one where Nouri's father worked? Just how involved would Nouri's family be in their lives? Anna hesitated. She knew better than to refuse. "I appreciate the offer, Baba-joon. Can we talk more after we're settled?"

"Of course. Take your time."

Anna swallowed. She'd only been in Iran a few hours, but she wondered how long it would take to feel at home.

Eleven

Nouri snuck into Anna's bed late that night, and they made muffled, secretive love, all the more erotic because of the need to be quiet. He fell asleep in the crook of her arm but woke at first light and crept back to his room.

The next morning the family's chauffeur drove them to Shemiran, a district at the northern fringe of Tehran's city limits. One of the most beautiful areas of Tehran, Shemiran was once the summer residence of the Qajar and Pahlavi shahs, who built ornate palace complexes and villas. Now, though, with the population of Tehran exploding, Shemiran was slowly becoming part of Tehran's northern suburbs. It was growing into an upscale neighborhood with stores, high-rises, and traffic. As always, the Alborz Mountains towered over everything. Although it looked different, Anna decided Shemiran was equivalent to Chicago's North Shore.

Eventually the car turned onto a narrow residential street where high walls surrounded everything. Anna was expecting an apartment building, but as they pulled up to an open gate, she saw a small house with a narrow brick front and columns flanking the door.

Nouri climbed out and held the car door for Anna. She stared at the house. "This is our new home?"

Nouri grinned. "I wanted it to be a surprise."

"You knew?"

"Yes, but this is the first time I've seen it."

Anna shook her head. "I don't believe it," she sputtered. "We can't... I mean...what are..."

Nouri placed his finger on her lips. "Shh." He took her hand, and they walked through the gate. The first thing Anna saw was a tiny garden with an even tinier pool. Next she passed a chenar tree, then leafy green shrubs, between which there were bright flowers and grass.

The house was three stories high, although the top floor was little more than a closet and loft with a sliding door that opened onto a roof. There were three bedrooms, two baths, hardwood floors, and elegant countertops. The smell of fresh paint hung in the air, and two workmen were nailing baseboards to the downstairs walls. Someone else was waxing the floors. Anna went into the kitchen. Aside from the new stove and refrigerator, there was a dishwasher. And a garbage disposal. Anna felt slightly dizzy, as if she'd walked into a dream.

"So what do you think?" Nouri asked with a sly grin.

She ran her hand over the snow-white kitchen counter. Every-thing was pristine, sleek. "This...is magnificent. But how can we afford it? Even if I get a job, the rent must be astronomical. There's no way—"

He cut her off. "That is the best part."

"What?"

"This...," he spread his arms, "Anna, this is a wedding gift from my parents."

"They're giving this to us? The entire house?"

"My father bought the land and built the house himself."

"No. He can't. It's too much."

"Anna, they want to do this."

"*We* should be building it. And paying for it. You know, start small and work our way up."

"My parents want us to get off to a good start. This is their way."

Anna bit her lip. "We can't accept it. We have to tell them."

He laughed, but it sounded hollow. "Oh, now *you* are practicing ta'arof?"

"I'm serious, Nouri." She tried to formulate the right words. "It's a matter of independence. Living within our means. Building something together. Do you want…"

Nouri's smile faded. "Anna, did you pay rent on your apartment in Chicago?"

"No, but we…I…was a student. That was different."

"How? We are barely out of school. And you know that first jobs are always underpaid. We are lucky to have a family that cares enough—and has the resources—to help."

Anna's lips pursed into a thin tight line. She didn't want to alienate Nouri or his family, but her instincts told her this was wrong. She'd pictured life with Nouri as the two of them building their future step by step. Feeling the joy of achievement after tilting against windmills. It was clear now that wasn't going to be the case. She knew Nouri's family was wealthy. But this was much more than she'd imagined. Why did he downplay his wealth? Was he afraid of her reaction? The very one she was having now?

She should have known. America was expensive. Any foreign student who came to the US had to have means. She remembered Nouri telling her about the first protest meeting he'd attended. How suspicious they were of him because of his family's wealth. Why didn't she pay more attention? Connect the dots? She wasn't thinking straight. She ran a hand through her hair, wondering what to do. She couldn't refuse to live in the house. Nouri's family would be insulted.

She walked out of the kitchen. Maybe she should try to be positive. There was much to be positive about. Everything in the house was sparkling, new, and very Western. Even the bathrooms. The master bedroom had walk-in closets. The second bedroom could be an office, the third a guest room. She went into the living room, wondering how she would ever decorate it, when the doorbell rang. The door promptly opened and Laleh waltzed in, surrounded by a swoosh of perfumed air.

"Yoo hoo!" she called out. Anna suspected she'd come to check out the house, and their reaction to it. Nouri met her and they talked in Farsi. From her breathless tone, Anna could tell Laleh was thrilled. "So, what do you think? Isn't it wonderful?"

Anna managed a smile. "It's amazing."

Laleh clapped her hands. "I knew you would love it. I helped Baba with the design."

"I didn't know."

"I am a student of architectural design." A knowing smile crossed her face. "Until I get married, of course."

Anna wasn't sure what to say.

Laleh didn't appear to notice. "I have a boyfriend, you know. His name is Shaheen. He's the same age as Nouri. He's handsome and rich and wonderful. I think we will marry."

"How lovely." Laleh was only sixteen, Anna recalled. Nouri was twenty-three. Seven years was a huge age difference, but she kept her thoughts to herself.

"But until then, I hope you will allow me to visit often."

Anna shrugged. "*Mi casa es su casa.*"

Laleh frowned.

"Sorry. It's an expression. Of course you're welcome. Any time."

Laleh smiled and looked around with a satisfied expression. "So, have you thought about decorating yet? Better get started."

Anna inclined her head.

"The *mahr*. Your dowry."

"Dowry?"

"Iranian custom says the husband pays for the wedding, while the wife provides the furniture and household goods. The families also agree on a figure to be paid in case of a divorce." Laleh waved a hand. "You didn't know?"

Anna felt suddenly chilled. She didn't have a dowry, and she had no idea how much she would be worth if they divorced. She didn't want to start a marriage by thinking about how it could end. She didn't have any money for a prenuptial agreement, anyway.

Nouri scowled at his sister. "Don't pay any attention to Laleh, Anna. That is an old, outdated custom. My family is more than pleased to supply whatever we need. And we will never get divorced, so you don't have to worry about mahr."

Before Anna had a chance to reply, Laleh jumped in. "Good.

Well, then. I know all the best stores. We will go together. Tomorrow. So the furniture arrives by the time you are married. How is noon?"

Anna swallowed. She felt like a princess who'd been taken to an enchanted kingdom. Her father had given her what she needed, but nothing to excess. It was the German way. And while her mother wasn't as pragmatic, she wasn't around enough to have made a difference. Now, though, because of her decision to marry Nouri, people—no, she corrected herself, her new family—were showering her with attention and gifts. They *wanted* to care for her. She took in the living room, kitchen, and hall of her new house. Why shouldn't she live in luxury? It wouldn't hurt anyone. She should banish her nagging doubts. Learn to enjoy for a change. After all, it was the start of a new life. She turned to Laleh.

"Noon will be perfect."

§

Anna climbed into the Samedis' Mercedes the next day. The chauffeur drove them to a furniture store in the heart of the city. Tehran was trying to be as modern as New York or Paris, and Anna saw Western influences everywhere: in shop windows and office buildings. Even the pollution and snarl of traffic were familiar.

Turning off the broad boulevards, though, they entered a different world. A donkey calmly munched away on a narrow street; on another, a weather-beaten shop displayed boxes and jars on the sidewalk. In yet another, foodstuffs hung from the ceiling. A picture of the shah sat in each shop's windows.

The people made for sharp contrasts as well. Persians were Caucasian, and Anna saw many with fair skin and light-colored eyes, but there were also those with darker, more Arabic looks. Some of the women, dressed in fancy clothes and makeup, strode confidently along the street looking like they were headed for Rodeo Drive. But others wore black robes—chadors, she learned—that covered them from head to toe. The chador-clad women seemed to glide down the street like black angels. The men mostly wore suits, or sports shirts and pants, but once in a while Anna saw a mullah with a flowing beard, clad in long robes and a turban.

The driver pulled up in front of an upscale store that featured European-style furniture in the window. "It's the best in Tehran," Laleh said. "We know the owners."

Inside, Anna found the store daunting; there were too many choices. With Laleh's help, she eventually settled on a queen-size bed, two dressers, and end tables. For the living room, she chose a sleek, contemporary sofa and two chairs in a dusty earth tone. She also ordered a glass-topped dining table, with matching chairs, and bookcases. When it came time to pay, Laleh told them to charge it to the Samedis' account. The salesman happily dipped his head so low it was almost a bow. Why not, Anna thought? He'd probably never had such a good day.

Next, they went to an appliance store where Laleh made sure Anna bought a color television, a stereo unit, lamps, a toaster, and a coffee maker. When that was done, they were driven to a restaurant that catered to Americans and Brits. They took their time eating salads, scones, and tea, and by the time Laleh picked up the check, it was almost four o'clock.

"Perfect timing," Laleh said with a smile.

"For what?" Anna hoped they were going home.

"You'll see."

Back in the car, Laleh ordered the driver to head north to the Bazaar Tajrish. Laleh told Anna it was the place to go for all sorts of goods, and once they were there, Anna saw why. A combination variety store and flea market, the bazaar was a seemingly endless series of covered stalls selling everything from food, to clothes, to jewelry, to music. It reminded her a bit of Maxwell Street, the open-air market in Chicago she and Nouri used to visit.

As they wove through the narrow aisles of the bazaar, Laleh was a force of nature, so knowing and confident that waves of energy seemed to radiate out from her. She pointed out dishes, silverware, rugs, and more, all at wholesale prices, but cautioned Anna not to buy too much. "People will be giving you many wedding gifts."

The bazaar was filling up, entire families making an event of after-noon shopping. Anna brushed up against sweaty bodies. The smells, too, were foreign: pungent spices, grease, perfume, and a peculiar cloying scent she couldn't identify. Some of the bazaari—mostly men—tried to wave them over, but Laleh didn't stop.

The smells, the heat, and the mass of people took their toll on Anna. Between the furniture, appliance store, and now the bazaar, she was exhausted. She couldn't possibly shop for anything else.

"Laleh, I'm sorry, but can we go home? I…I'm so tired. I need a break."

Concern splashed across Laleh's face. "Oh dear, I've overdone it, haven't I? Maman tells me I'm like a wild horse that must be tamed. I'm so sorry. Of course we will go." She hugged Anna. "You should have said something."

Anna tried to smile. "It's been fun." She almost meant it.

Laleh backtracked through the bazaar, stopping at a stall that sold 8-track tapes and records. "Just one more minute."

Anna nodded tiredly.

Laleh pored through the selection, chatting in rapid-fire Farsi with the bazaari. Anna made out the words "Michael Jackson" and "Eric Clapton." Laleh turned to Anna.

"Who is your favorite rock musician?"

Anna hesitated. She preferred classical. She wasn't even sure who was popular now; they slipped in and out of favor so fast. Luckily, a name came to her. "I like Steely Dan."

"Oh, I love them, too. In fact, they play a lot of Steely Dan at the disco I go to. You and Nouri must come with me. Maybe tonight, eh? After you rest, of course." Laleh scooped up half a dozen tapes, one of them with a black, white, and red cover bearing the word "Aja." She pulled out her wallet, fished out a few bills, and handed them to the bazaari. He slid the 8-tracks into a bag and passed them back to Laleh, who thrust them into Anna's hands. "Now when your stereo arrives, you will have something to play."

"Laleh, this is too much. I can't accept these. Keep them for yourself."

"No, no. These are for your new home. A house warming, isn't that the American expression?"

"I can't...I..." Anna stopped her protest. Laleh would think she was practicing a form of ta'arof and just keep going. She resigned herself to the irony, thanked Laleh, and tucked the bag under her arm. Laleh took Anna's other arm, and guided her out of the bazaar. Anna marveled at their shopping spree; she'd never had a friend who spent so freely. Then again, she'd never had many friends at all.

Twelve

Tehran's traffic was chaos in motion—four or five lanes of autos surged forward, switched lanes, suddenly braked. There were few traffic lights, and Anna gripped the edge of her seat, wondering how the driver could navigate through the mess. Within a mile, traffic was so congested they were forced to stop. Horns blasted, taxi drivers shook their fists and, despite the air conditioning in the Mercedes, sweat pasted Anna's t-shirt to her back.

A siren blared, in the shrill European sing-song tone Anna had heard in films, the ones that foreshadow the Gestapo's arrival in the middle of the night. She shivered. Flashing lights passed the Mercedes. Ahead on the right was a park in which a mass of people were chanting. Many were young and looked like students. Some of the men were bearded. The crowd did not appear to be moving but, like some giant amoeba, it mysteriously swelled. Many waved sticks. Some held up placards. One said, in English, "Down with the shah!"

Laleh rolled down the window. "Oh, no." Her tone was scornful.

"What?" Anna squinted through the front windshield.

Laleh shook her head, clearly irritated. "Why don't they just go home? Don't they realize they're blocking traffic?"

Anna didn't say anything. A police van threaded its way through the traffic and swerved to a stop at the edge of the park. Uniformed officers spilled out, waving pistols. They hauled off a few protestors, but many remained, yelling and punching their fists in the air. Then army troops, brandishing

71

rifles and bayonets, arrived. The soldiers, dressed in green fatigues, hit more of the protestors and dragged them away.

Anna recoiled at the violence. She'd seen it before, but it never lost its power to shock. Still, most of the pedestrians seemed oblivious to the demonstration, and casually jaywalked between the blocked cars. On one side of the road was bedlam; on the other, apparent normalcy. It was unnerving. "What do you think of all this? Why do some people ignore it?" she asked.

Laleh shrugged. "Someone is always demonstrating these days."

Anna recalled Nouri's activities back in Chicago. "So you—and the people crossing the street—don't have a problem with the shah?"

"The shah is not perfect, but he's better than the people who complain about him."

"What do you mean?"

"You see how crowded Tehran is? Especially in the southern part of the city? Most of them come from small villages. They're illiterate, and they have no skills. They have nothing to do but make trouble." Laleh's lip curled. "I wouldn't be surprised if they were Arabs."

Anna remembered the joke Nouri told her early in their relationship. She'd looked up the derivation of his name and found that it came from the Arabic word for "light." *Arabic*, not Persian. Nouri laughed and said, "Forty percent of all Persians have Arab blood, but a hundred percent of them will deny it."

Laleh went on. "Most of them are strict Muslims and think anything modern is decadent. The women wear chadors, even though the shah has banned them. *Hijab*, it's called. They smell bad too."

Anna motioned toward the park. "Some of the demonstrators looked like students."

"They're playing at politics." Laleh sniffed. "Imagining some kind of alliance with the masses. Baba-joon says it is all theatrics. It is against the law to be a Communist, you know."

Theatrics or not, Anna thought about the masses and the role they'd played throughout history. Especially when there was a big gap between rich and poor. What's more, Laleh was exactly the type the masses would like to get their hands on.

§

By the time they arrived back at the Samedis' Anna was ready to lie down. But Nouri was in the living room drinking tea with a young woman. Anna stopped, taken aback. The young woman was tall and sturdy-looking. Her long, wavy auburn hair was tied back with a blue ribbon. She had clear brown eyes, thick eyebrows, and a spray of freckles across her nose. She looked pleasant, if not pretty, and if Anna mustered up one word to describe her, trustworthy. She wore a simple white blouse and a dark blue skirt that covered her knees.

Laleh followed Anna into the room, and when Anna saw Laleh's arched eyebrows, her stomach churned. She knew who the girl was. Nouri, who stood up and motioned her over, confirmed it.

"Anna, I am so glad you are back. I want you to meet an old family friend, Roya Kalani."

Roya was the girl to whom Nouri was informally engaged until he met Anna. Anna stifled her discomfort and extended her hand. Roya took it and offered a weak, clammy shake. They eyed each other.

Nouri seemed unaware of the subtle dynamics, but Laleh, who sat on the couch, watched with a knowing expression. "Roya's parents and ours are good friends," she said. "Her father runs the giant sports complex in Tehran."

Anna forced herself to smile and sat down. The tea tray was next to Roya, and she poured tea for Anna and Laleh as if she was the mistress of the house. Anna wanted to squirm. Shouldn't she or Laleh be pouring?

Roya passed her a glass. "What a long journey you have had," she said. Her English was passable, but not as good as Nouri's, or Laleh's. "You have much courage to move here from America." She pronounced it "Amreeka" with the emphasis on "Am." "You must love Nouri very much."

Anna didn't know how to reply. This was the girl who'd thought she was going to marry Nouri. She settled for a simple, "I do."

Roya smiled. Anna had no idea whether it was sincere. Was she full of jealousy and disappointment? Hiding behind a veil of calm?

Nouri spoke to Roya in Farsi and then translated. He was asking after her family, but his tone sounded slightly patronizing, as if he was playing the role of family chief. As if by dint of being engaged, he had risen to a new level of adulthood. Anna wondered if Roya sensed it.

They muddled along for a few minutes in broken English and Farsi until the door opened and Baba-joon came in. When he saw Roya, he flashed the same arched eyebrow expression as Laleh, then suppressed it with a polite smile. He grasped her arms in a kind of half-hug, and asked, in English, after her family. She replied in Farsi. For the first time Roya seemed animated.

Anna felt a stab of jealousy. She couldn't compete with decades-old family ties.

Baba-joon and Roya continued their conversation, as Nouri translated. "Roya is going on Hajj with her grandmother."

"Hajj?" Anna asked.

"A pilgrimage to Mecca. Roya is looking forward to it."

Anna knew Muslims were required to go to Mecca at least once in their lifetime. It was one of the five pillars of Islam. Roya and her grandmother would spend three or four days in a variety of activities, all designed to cleanse them of their sins and deepen their submission to Allah.

"Roya's grandmother has been on Hajj before, but not Roya," Nouri explained.

"Have you?" Anna asked.

"Not yet." Nouri winced. Just a bit.

Roya said something in Farsi, then motioned to Nouri. She wanted him to translate.

"She says her grandmother is very observant. For example, despite the shah's edict to wear Western clothes, her grandmother wears a chador—at least in the house—and seems a bit...confused...by modern life. And yet she has the purest, most spiritual soul of anyone Roya knows. Roya hopes by going on Hajj, she will learn her grandmother's secrets."

Anna had never met her own grandparents. As far as she knew, none of them were alive. But Nouri's lineage was long and deep, and interwoven with other families. She might not have liked it, but together the family formed a bond, a shield against outsiders. And despite the difficulty of assimilating, she would become a part of it. She would be protected.

Roya said something and Nouri translated. "Roya hopes Allah will bless us with long, healthy lives. And many children."

Baba-joon kissed Roya's cheek and said, "It has been a pleasure to see you again, my dear. I hope you will visit us again soon. Now I must go and listen to the news."

Anna beamed. Maybe Roya wasn't so bad.

A few minutes later Nouri walked Roya to the door. Anna wanted to ask him how Roya came to be at the house. Was it an unexpected visit or was it planned? Liking Roya didn't necessarily take away her twinge of jealousy. Before she could ask, though, Laleh jumped in.

"Roya and I were never best friends. She's your age, you know. But she's changed."

"How?" Anna asked.

"She's getting too religious. Like the people I was telling you about before."

"What people?" Nouri asked.

Anna told him about the demonstration they'd passed and Laleh's reaction to it.

Nouri frowned. "You shouldn't be so irritated, Laleh. The protestors have real issues."

Laleh's voice dripped acid. "How would you know? You haven't had to deal with them. You've been in America, having a fine time."

Anna jumped in. "People change. Surely, there's room enough for all of us on this earth." She tried to steer the conversation back to Roya. "Even Roya."

"I'm telling you. Roya...well, it's strange...I'm not even sure it's genuine." Laleh shrugged.

Anna was about to reply, but Nouri put his arm around Anna, effectively ending the conversation. "I don't understand Roya, either.

But then I don't have to. I have you."

The doorbell chimed. "That must be Shaheen," Laleh said, scurrying toward the door.

"Who's Shaheen?" Nouri asked.

"Shaheen Khandil. My boyfriend."

"I thought you were to become engaged to Jangi, the son of Maman and Baba's friends."

"Have you seen him recently?" Laleh sniffed. "He's fat and smelly and his teeth are bad. I could never touch him, much less marry him."

"But it has been arranged."

"If you can break the rules, so can I," Laleh said petulantly.

Anna was surprised. She thought Nouri already knew about Shaheen. Before she could ask, though, Laleh opened the door and ushered a young man into the living room. She clutched his arm and wore a triumphant smile.

"I'm delighted to make your acquaintance," Shaheen said, after Laleh introduced him. Like most of the other Iranians Anna had met, his English was excellent, spoken with a British accent. "Laleh has not stopped talking about you since you arrived."

Anna smiled. Shaheen was handsome and tall, with light brown hair and deep brown eyes. He wore tailored clothes that looked expensive, and carried an air of confidence that made Anna think there was nothing he couldn't do. No wonder Laleh was smitten.

Shaheen turned to Nouri. "And so nice to meet you finally, Nouri. Laleh talks about you as well. So much, in fact, that I would be jealous if I didn't know you were her brother."

Nouri's weak smile said he wasn't so sure about Shaheen.

§

That night Anna said to Nouri, "Shaheen is charming, isn't he?"

Nouri grunted. "Laleh met him just a few months ago. And yes, he is charming. In fact, he's known to be a playboy."

"Really?" She perched on the couch.

"He travels to London and Geneva. One of the jet set. Laleh says she's in love, but Maman and Baba disapprove."

"Because he's so much older?"

"No, not at all. Girls marry quite young in Iran." A frown flitted across Nouri's face. "But Laleh was promised to someone else."

"So were you."

"Yes, but I am a man."

Anna stiffened.

Nouri seemed to realize he'd said the wrong thing and covered himself. "And Shaheen...he's—what do you call it in English?—nouveau riche. His parents were basically peasants. Very poor. Shaheen made a killing in foreign real estate and now he thinks he's royalty. Maman thinks he's using Laleh."

"For what?"

"Respectability."

"He seems to care for her."

Nouri made a derisive sound.

"What does your father think?"

Nouri hesitated. "Baba cannot say no to Laleh. He spoils her."

Anna jiggled her foot. She was thinking about fathers and daughters and loyalty. Baba-joon—she'd started to think of him that way, she realized—hadn't asked about *her* father. Given what she'd told Nouri about his history, she was surprised. She wondered if—along with their wedding in Virginia—Nouri had forgotten to mention it.

Thirteen

One afternoon, two weeks later, Anna was reading in the living room with Maman-joon, when Nouri returned from a trip downtown. "You are looking at the newest engineer for the Metro project!" he announced proudly.

Anna looked up. "You got the job?"

"I start next week."

Anna cried out, jumped up, and wrapped him in a big hug. Nouri picked her up and twirled her around. It had been a long, arduous process—three interviews, intense briefings, as well as studying for the exam that would make him a member of the Iran Society of Engineers.

"So," she cried breathlessly, once he set her down, "now you can finish your thesis and get your master's degree."

Nouri had been given an extension of six months, but still hadn't completed his thesis. Now, though, he shrugged. "They're a French company, and they don't care about a thesis from an American school. Only that I pass the exam, which they're helping me study for. One of the other recent hires just took it. He said it's easy."

Anna bent her head as if she wanted to say something, but Nouri turned to his mother and repeated what he'd told Anna in Farsi. His mother flashed a broad smile and hugged him as well. "We must celebrate," she said.

"I'd like that, Maman. Oh, and Hassan will be joining us for dinner."

"Wonderful." His mother headed into the kitchen.

Nouri twisted back to Anna. "We are on our way, Anna!"

"Congratulations, again." She started up the stairs. "I should change for dinner."

Nouri stretched his arms contentedly. His life in Iran was turning out just the way he'd hoped. His beautiful American fiancée was settling in well with his family, his career was beginning to take off, and he would be moving into a new home in Shemiran. It was a good life.

He followed Anna up to the guest room. Anna was taking off her t-shirt. At the sound of the door closing, she spun around, automatically covering her breasts with the shirt. When she saw that it was him, she let the shirt fall to the floor. He gazed at her bare breasts, her tousled blonde hair. He wanted her. He went to her and cupped her breasts in his hands.

She giggled. "Nouri, it's the middle of the afternoon."

He pulled her close and buried his face in her neck. Her arms encircled him. He unsnapped her jeans. He breathed in her smell—sweat, mingled with the essential essence of Anna. She had become part of him now. He was no longer sure where his body ended and hers began. Together they moved to the bed.

§

By the time they pulled themselves together, it was evening. They intended to make a casual entrance, although Nouri suspected his family would know exactly what they had been doing. He'd prepared an excuse, but when they snuck down, his mother and sister ignored them. They were staring at the television. His father, who had just come home, watched with a worried expression.

"What is it?" Nouri asked, as he glanced at the TV.

Laleh answered. "There's been a horrible fire. At the Cinema Rex, in Abadan. Over four hundred people were inside. They all died."

Anna gasped. Nouri reared back. Abadan was in the south of Iran, hundreds of miles from Tehran. Still.

"They are saying Islamic terrorists set the fire, but the police were the ones who locked the gate so no one could get out."

"That makes no sense." Nouri frowned. "Why?"

"Some are saying the shah and SAVAK are behind it," Baba said.

"No!" Anna cried softly.

"The film that was playing was *Gavaznha*, 'The Deer,'" Baba explained. "It is critical of the shah. Some people claim the firemen—intentionally—waited too long before going to the theater because they knew the audience would be anti-shah."

They peered at scenes of fire trucks, crowds gathered outside the theater, the faces and cries of grief.

"Police believe the terrorists set a small fire in the theater, intending to escape with the rest of the audience," the TV announcer reported. "So police closed the gates to prevent that from happening. But the fire quickly burned out of control."

Nouri sucked in a breath.

"There are rumors that most of the bodies were still in their seats," the announcer continued, "which indicates they were unable for some reason to get to the doors. Obviously, many questions remain. What isn't at dispute, though, is that this deliberate arson is the worst terrorist attack ever recorded in Iran—or anywhere else."

"Why were they still in their seats?" Laleh asked. "Isn't that strange?"

"Maybe someone sprayed some kind of poison. Or gas," Nouri said.

Maman got up, clearly upset. She looked at Baba, but he shook his head and kept staring at the TV. Maman went into the kitchen. No one said anything.

§

"Mark my words, this is a turning point," Nouri's best friend, Hassan Ghaffari, pronounced after dinner that night. Hassan was thick and squat, like a bull. His black eyes glittered and, while they seemed to take everything in, they didn't give much back. His skin was the color of melted caramel, he had a pointed chin, and he wore a thin mustache. Before he grew it, Laleh said he looked like Michael

Corleone in *The Godfather.* Hassan took it as a compliment, although Nouri wasn't sure Laleh meant it as one.

Hassan was unusually quiet during dinner, answering Maman and Baba's questions about his family, but not offering anything more. Nouri tried to keep the conversation cheerful by talking about the Metro—how quiet and modern it would be, how there would be art on the walls and sculpture in the tunnels. No one talked about the fire. Or the shah.

After dinner, the four young people went out to the patio to dangle their feet in the tiny pool. Though it was dark, a spotlight threw a pattern of light and shadow on the fruit trees. A slight breeze carried the scent of flowers and leftover grilled lamb.

"It really is a turning point," Hassan repeated, kicking his feet in the water. He was animated now, so much so that Nouri wondered if Baba's presence had intimidated him earlier.

"A tragedy, yes," Anna said. "But a turning point? How?"

"Don't you see? No one can pretend the situation doesn't affect them personally. Five hundred families are the proof. It is time to take sides."

"I don't know what you mean, Hassan," Laleh said. "I don't know any of those families."

Hassan stopped kicking the water. "You can't believe the shah is blameless. SAVAK's fingerprints are all over this. Right, Nouri?"

Nouri hesitated. "I'm not sure what to believe. My father—"

"Your father works for the oil company," Hassan interrupted. "He is a good man, but have you asked him what's happened to oil revenues over the past few years? The price of oil has quadrupled. Yet peoples' lives are no better. The shah keeps most of the profits. And what he doesn't keep, he doles out to foreigners who woo him with all sorts of projects. Like the Metro."

Nouri suppressed his irritation. "A French firm *is* building the Metro. But it will give Tehranians clean, fast, and inexpensive transportation. That is a good thing."

Hassan snorted. "Especially since they're not going to have their own Paykans."

Nouri pressed his lips together.

Hassan explained to Anna that the shah, in one of his speeches about progress, assured the people that everyone would soon be able to afford their own Paykan, the national car of Iran. "It was an empty promise," he added. "Just like all the others. No one gets anything...except the military."

"Are you saying Nouri shouldn't take the Metro job?" Anna asked. "That he should be doing...something else?"

"That is for him to decide," Hassan said. "But the neighborhood in Abadan where the fire occurred was working class. The film was anti-shah. The fire trucks didn't arrive until the building was engulfed in flames. And the police barred the door. I call that a clear case of mass murder. The shah is putting his own citizens' lives on the line to protect his regime."

"Hassan, be honest," Nouri said, "there are Shi'ite Muslims who think every film is an affront to Allah. They abhor Western decadence. Their militants could have set the fire."

Hassan shot Nouri a curious look. "You wouldn't have said that a year ago. You have changed, Nouri." He turned to Anna. "And what do you think, Anna?" There was an implicit challenge in his tone.

She dipped her fingers in the pool. "I think any kind of oppression, whether initiated by a government or a religion, is wrong." It was a prudent answer, Nouri thought. "But I also think true revolutionaries don't have room for religion."

"What about your Martin Luther King? Or Martin Luther? Or Jesus?" Hassan fired back.

"They were reformers, not revolutionaries," she said. "The state must be separate from religion. When it isn't, it ends badly. Even your Persian culture believes that. Look at Rumi and Hafiz. Their Islam has no tolerance for orthodoxy. It is spiritual, not dogmatic. It would be...unfortunate...if that wasn't the guiding principle going forward."

Nouri smiled inwardly. Anna might be more intelligent than Hassan. She was certainly more eloquent.

Hassan lifted his chin. "Rumi and Hafiz never had to see the country overrun by the British. Or watch the CIA depose the only democratic leader Iran has ever had."

Anna and Nouri exchanged glances. Nouri knew she would like to continue the argument but wasn't sure it was a good idea. Nouri changed the subject. "My father has offered Anna a job at the oil company."

"Really? And will you take it?" Hassan asked.

"I don't know."

"If you don't what will you do?"

"I was thinking of teaching English. There must be many people here who want to learn."

Hassan sat up straighter. "There is the Iran-American Society."

Laleh chimed in. "That's a wonderful idea, Hassan. I was going to suggest Abbott Labs. The have just opened up an office here. Shaheen's sister will be working there. But the Society is better."

"Who is Shaheen?" Hassan asked.

Laleh explained that Shaheen was her boyfriend.

"Really? Where's he from?" Hassan asked.

"He used to live in Shiraz. But he lives here now."

"What is the Iran-American Society?" Anna asked.

Laleh twisted around to Anna and explained that the IAS was a center where Iranian and American citizens taught students about the US—its history, customs, and above all, its language. "It's the perfect place for you, Anna."

"It does sound interesting. Thank you, Hassan. I will look into it."

Hassan left a few minutes later, and Nouri was relieved. He felt as though he had been walking a tightrope. He glanced at Anna. He suspected she felt the same. As they went back inside, he asked, "What do you think?"

"Hassan has strong opinions."

"But is he right? Do you think I've changed?"

Anna peered at him. "Do you?"

"Perhaps. I still think the shah is wrong in many ways. But…"

"It's easy to be a critic when you're not in the middle of things, isn't it? When you are far away in America. But now that you're home, you have a stake." She brushed her hand across his cheek. "Not so easy."

He grabbed her hand and kissed her fingers. "You have changed too, you know. You are getting accustomed to our ways. And becoming quite the diplomat."

She smiled. "Tell me something—at dinner, Baba-joon asked after Hassan's mother and sisters. But he never mentioned his father. Why not?"

"Hassan's father was imprisoned and tortured by SAVAK. They let him go after a few months, but he was never the same. He took his own life soon afterwards."

Anna winced. They headed upstairs in silence. At the top of the steps, she said, "Speaking of fathers, Nouri, have you told your family about mine?"

Nouri wouldn't meet her eyes.

Anna nodded as if that was the response she'd expected, walked into the guest room, and closed the door.

Fourteen

As the fiery summer blazed into fall, the shah behaved uncertainly. In late August, he replaced his prime minister and announced that he would honor Islamic traditions. Less than two weeks later, his troops opened fire in Jaleh Square during a massive demonstration. Depending on who you talked to, Nouri realized, somewhere between fifty and two hundred people were killed. Dozens of arsons were reported, and numerous banks, cinemas, police stations, and shops were destroyed. Martial law was imposed and opposition leaders were jailed. "Black Friday"—as it came to be called—made many despair of compromise between the protest movement and the shah.

Despite the turmoil in other parts of the city, the streets of north Tehran remained peaceful, and the planning continued for Nouri and Anna's wedding. The celebration would be in mid-September, after the end of Ramadan. They would go to Esfahan for a honeymoon. Maman-joon and Anna spent hours, sometimes entire days with the seamstress who was making her bridal gown.

The wedding ceremony and banquet would be held at a new luxury hotel, the Azadi Grand. The shah was not invited, but other important government ministers would be there. Parvin and Anna pored over the seating arrangements, the meal, the flowers, and the favors guests would take home. They spent two days rehearsing the ceremony so Anna would be prepared. Various members of Nouri's family planned to host parties after the wedding, so the celebration would stretch over an entire week.

Although he'd started his job and wasn't around much, Nouri was grateful the wedding had focused the family on something other than the future of the country. His mother and Laleh were consumed by the planning, and even Anna seemed swept up in the events. Only one problem remained, and one evening after dinner, after Laleh left with Shaheen for the disco, Nouri screwed up his courage. "Maman, Baba, there is something we need to tell you."

"What is that?" His parents were watching a variety show on television. They looked more relaxed tonight, a welcome respite. The frown line on his father's forehead had become a permanent fixture, and the cheerful energy he normally associated with his mother surfaced only when she talked about the wedding.

Nouri glanced at Anna who sat quietly on the sofa. She looked like she wanted to disappear into the upholstery. He took a breath. "Before we came here, while we were still in America, Anna and I were married." He spoke in Farsi, but he could tell Anna understood.

His mother reeled back as if someone had slapped her. His father didn't move. Anna nervously fingered her arm. Nouri wanted to melt into the floor. The shocked silence lasted an eternity. Finally, Baba spoke.

"Why?"

Nouri swallowed. "Her father requested it. He isn't able to come for the wedding, but he wanted to see his daughter marry."

His mother regained her voice. "I don't understand. Does he not trust us? Does he think we are peasants with no knowledge, or culture, or—"

"Parvin." Nouri's father cut her off. "Let me handle this."

His mother blew out a breath and clasped her hands together. She reminded Nouri of those women in old movies who nervously fan themselves during moments of crisis.

His father's eyes narrowed. "He gave you no other reason?"

Nouri shook his head. "Baba, I'm sorry if I made a mistake. I spoke with other Iranian students in the US. Apparently, many who marry

Americans do it twice—once in the States and once here. I didn't think it would be an issue."

Maman let out a stream of Farsi, emotional and tense. She gestured in Anna's direction.

At length, Baba sliced his hand through the air. "Enough."

Maman went quiet.

Anna cringed. She couldn't possibly understand, but she knew it wasn't going well.

Baba turned to Anna and spoke in English.

"Forgive us, Anna. We were…taken aback. That is all. We would like to have known this was happening. But it is not terribly serious. As you already know, many American and Iranian couples do what you and Nouri have done. With your permission, I will call your father and tell him that."

Anna felt relief wash over her. "Thank you, Baba-joon. If I had known the distress it would bring, I would have made sure you knew in advance. I didn't know the protocol. Forgive *me*."

"There is nothing to forgive. And do I have your permission to call your father?"

Anna's face darkened. Nouri knew it wasn't over.

Baba leaned forward. "What is it, Anna dear?"

Anna seemed flustered. "I don't know…I mean, I don't know if Nouri told you…" her voice trailed off. "But you—you and Maman-joon—need to know who my father is."

Baba steepled his hands. "Who he is?"

Anna blurted it out. "His background. He…well…it might make you reconsider having me in your family."

Baba glanced at Nouri, then back at Anna. "You mean the fact that your father is a physicist who worked for the Nazis before he was brought to the US?"

Nouri's mouth dropped open. So did Anna's. "How did you…"

Baba's smile told Nouri he was enjoying their confusion. "Did you think I would not investigate the family of my son's fiancée?" He chuckled. "I know that your father lives in Maryland, and your mother—

who divorced him years ago—is in Paris."

Anna's cheeks turned crimson. She wouldn't meet Baba's eyes.

"Anna, my dear, you should know there has always been a close relationship between Iran and Germany. The father of the shah changed Persia's name to Iran, largely because of the Aryans who dominate our culture. The same Aryans who were so important to Hitler."

Anna and Nouri exchanged glances. Anna looked shell-shocked, Nouri thought.

"In fact, Reza Shah wanted to ally Iran with Germany during the war but was prevented from doing so by the Allies. So, please, feel no shame. Your heritage is a proud one. You will always be precious to us."

Anna sat motionless, her hands folded in her lap. She must still have been absorbing Baba's words, Nouri thought. She had been carrying the weight of her father's supposed villainy for years. It was the guilty secret that tainted her, that made her less American. No one had ever expressed tacit approval of her father before. To have that weight lifted so quickly and easily must be cathartic. Nouri offered an encouraging smile. She needed to know he understood.

At length, Anna jumped up and threw her arms around Baba. Then she hugged Nouri's mother. Although his parents seemed flustered, even a bit awkward, Anna flashed Nouri a radiant smile. Nouri felt her release. Or was it his?

Fifteen

Nouri woke on the morning of his wedding with a massive weight crushing his chest. The day that had been heralded since he was a child was here. He took a deep breath, pondering its enormity. He was straddling the line between boy and man. For the first time, his actions would have real consequences.

He laced his hands behind his head. It would be too easy to assume it started when he stepped back onto Iranian soil. In truth, it began when he decided to marry Anna—soon to be his wife, the mother of his children. Their children would go to the best schools. He would have a distinguished career. They would live in a magnificent house. There was nothing they could not accomplish together.

Nouri got up and went into the bathroom. His father had held political aspirations once upon a time, but despite his connections to high-ranking ministers and the royal family, Baba's hopes were never realized. Nothing was ever said, but Nouri knew his parents saw him as their second chance. If he did well on the Metro, and parlayed that into other successes, he would be well-positioned. Perhaps one day he would be asked to help run the government.

He splashed cold water on his face. No. The shah was corrupt. He had abused his power. He must be replaced. Still, there would always be a need for Western-educated engineers, no matter who was in power. There were still many villages that lacked electricity and running water, people who could not read, too many with too little. He gazed at himself in the mirror. It was time to put away his childish ways. He would play an important role in the future of his country. And today was the first step.

He bathed and shaved, while the servants laid out his tuxedo. He was not allowed to see Anna until the ceremony, but Laleh and his mother were already tending to her. Anna's mother had been invited, and they'd expected her to fly in from Paris, but the violence of the past week had frightened her, and she canceled at the last minute.

The day passed as slowly as rock turning to desert sand, but finally Nouri dressed, and he and his father drove to the hotel. Many of the guests had already arrived and were seated in an auditorium with huge chandeliers. The soft hum of conversation filled the air. Nouri recognized faces he hadn't seen in years. He hoped he remembered their names.

On the floor, at the front of the room, was a white silk spread edged with vases of fresh flowers. On top of the spread lay the items for the *Sofreh Aghd*, the formal part of the ceremony, which was based on ancient Zoroastrian rituals. The ceremony required specific objects: a large mirror which represented light; a pair of elegant candelabras which signified fire (one for the bride, one for the groom); an enormous loaf of decorated flat bread; gold coins symbolizing prosperity; *esfand,* a smoky incense, which would be lit to ward off the evil eye; tiny bowls containing honey and rosewater; and small baskets filled with sweets, fruits, eggs, and nuts. Later, a ceremonial cloth on the spread would be lifted to represent Nouri and Anna's union. The spread itself faced the direction of the sunrise.

Nouri sat on the right, in one of two chairs near the spread, and at the other end of the room, the band struck up a version of "Bada Bada Mobarak," a happy tune often played at weddings he'd attended. Its lyrics congratulated the couple on their joyful event. His stomach flipped as he realized that today was his turn.

A moment later, Anna entered the room, trailed by Laleh and Nouri's mother. The crowd, which had gone quiet as the music began, emitted a collective gasp.

Anna looked ravishing. Her gown, a rich white satin, was fitted at the bodice and flared gently to the floor. The top of the dress was covered with lace, and threaded with tiny jewels that sparkled in the light. Her skirt and train repeated the jewels. The gown was strapless, and Anna's skin retained a rosy summer glow. A veil, attached to a thin headband, hung over her face, but Nouri could see her eyes. Lit by an inner fire, they blazed like green emeralds. Her long, blonde hair was coiled in braids around the head piece, and her ears were pierced with delicate diamond studs. She looked like a magic princess, Nouri decided. Or a movie star: Jessica Lange or Olivia Newton-John. He wished they were alone.

Anna sat down on the chair beside him, and the ceremony began. The officiating mullah was a distant cousin, and was known to be quite liberal—some clerics would not marry couples if they were not both Muslim. He recited some introductory blessings. The esfand was sprinkled on a bed of glowing coals in a brazier. Nouri's aunt and uncle walked around Nouri and Anna seven times. The smoke from the esfand made Anna quietly clear her throat.

After speaking about the sanctity of marriage for what seemed like an eternity, the mullah asked if Anna and Nouri wished to proceed. The idea was to make Nouri wait for Anna's answer, and Anna was asked three times whether she wanted to marry Nouri. Anna did not respond, and after each question, Nouri's mother placed a gold coin in Anna's hand, symbolically encouraging her to say yes. After the third time, Anna said in a clear voice. "Yes. *Baleh.*"

The mullah recited more verses from the Qur'an, after which Anna and Nouri and their witnesses signed the marriage contract. The mullah pronounced them man and wife, and Nouri lifted Anna's veil. They kissed and exchanged rings. Nouri heard Anna's intake of breath when she saw the ring Nouri slipped on her finger. Made from beautifully wrought gold, the diamond was enormous. Anna gave him a simple gold band.

During the ceremony, two of Nouri's female cousins had been holding the ceremonial cloth over Anna and Nouri's heads. Now a third cousin rubbed together two cone-shaped pieces of sugar and let the grains fall onto the cloth, to sweeten the couple's life together. Nouri and Anna dipped their fingers into a small pot of honey, then into each other's mouths.

They kissed again. It was done.

The guests moved into another room for the banquet. The room was lavishly decorated with flowers, fruit trees, and, in one corner, a pool with a tiny waterfall. The band was already playing but, between courses and during breaks in the music, guests sauntered through the artificial garden to enjoy the babbling water.

Nouri's mother had imported a chef from Paris to supervise the menu, which included escargots, followed by courses with names like *Quail in Puff Pastry Shell with Foie Gras and Truffle Sauce*. Different wines were served with each course. There was a nod to Persian food too, and the haute cuisine was paired with sweet rice, chelow kababs, vegetable dishes, and flatbreads.

As course followed course, the noise, the smells, the heat—despite the air conditioning, it was a hot September night—took their toll. Nouri slid into a daze. A blur of men, most of whom he only vaguely recognized, pumped his hand or took him aside to whisper how lucky he was to have snared such a beautiful blonde. The women overwhelmed him with hugs, perfume, and giggles as he danced them around the room. The relentless flash of the photographers' lights blinded him. It was all too much. His smile felt sewn on. And this was just the first of several parties, called *paghosah*, that would occur after the wedding.

He tried to be polite, the perfect host, but by midnight his patience had worn thin. Finally, they cut the cake, and were able to make their exit. They took the elevator to the hotel's honeymoon suite, where they fell into bed and were soon asleep.

§

Esfahan, about a six hour drive from Tehran, depending on traffic, was at one time the capital of Persia. It was also one of Iran's most beautiful, romantic cities. The five days they spent there reminded

Nouri of their life in Chicago. It was only the two of them, free to say and do whatever they pleased.

They stayed at the Abbasi, a luxurious five-star hotel with magnificent gardens, walkways, restaurants, even a teahouse. For the first two days they hid out in their room, doing what newlyweds did. By the third afternoon, though, they were ready to face the world, and got dressed, and strolled from the hotel to the Zayandeh River. The riverbanks, with their wide, sloping lawns, were crowded with families picnicking and drinking tea. Children frolicked at the water's edge. Nouri gave them a tolerant glance. "That will be us soon," he said to Anna.

Anna squeezed his hand and offered up a shy smile. Since the wedding she'd been different. Nouri couldn't quite define it, but something had changed. In bed she was less passionate, more tender, vulnerable. It was as though a catch had been released. She seemed... happy. Now he bought her an ice cream, and they admired the bridge with its series of pointed archways. Young people joyously paddled around the river in swan boats.

They found their way up to Shah Square, a complex of two mosques and a palace that were almost painfully beautiful. The bigger mosque, designed for men, was covered by a turquoise dome rising above a towering façade with elaborate mosaic patterns. Although seven different colors of tiles were used, shades of blue predominated. A huge reflecting pool sparkled in front. Nouri explained that the color blue was thought to calm the soul and promote spirituality.

Humbled by the architecture, they were subdued as they wandered the grounds. The smaller mosque had been built for the women of the seventeenth century shah's harem. Twenty stately columns protected a golden honeycombed façade and dome. Inside, thousands of tiny mirrors twinkled from the ceiling, and intricate mosaics and frescoes saluted the king, who'd built the complex during perhaps the most noteworthy of Persia's golden ages. Nouri told Anna about Shah Abbas and how he'd decided to move the country's capital to Esfahan in 1598.

"Which calendar?" Anna joked.

Nouri laughed. Iranians operated with two calendars, the Persian solar calendar and the Western one. It might be 1978 in the West, but it was only 1357 according to the Jalali calendar. "Which one would you like?"

"The one that will stop time altogether," she said.

Nouri stole a glance at her. Her expression was pensive, almost sad. "What's wrong?"

"This is all too beautiful, Nouri."

He brushed his hand down her cheek.

"Everything. This city. Our wedding. Your family. It is almost more than I can bear. You have filled the hole inside me—the one that has been there since I was a little girl. I think my heart might break from joy."

Nouri gathered her in his arms. At that moment he loved Anna more than life itself.

Sixteen

Anna couldn't remember a time when she was so content. Parched for affection most of her life, her marriage to Nouri had slaked her thirst, and like a desert flower, she was blooming. In the mornings she woke with a smile, eager to greet the day. As a wife, a daughter, a sister. She was loved. Finally, she belonged.

Their furniture eventually arrived, and she and Nouri moved into their house in Shemiran. Laleh was right; they received a mountain of gifts. Still, there were always odds and ends a home needed, and Anna was determined to provide them. Despite the traffic, she walked everywhere. She didn't mind; it was the best way to explore her new neighborhood. She fell in love with Persian architecture, and she was thrilled to find glimpses of the colorful tiles, mosaics, and intricate designs she'd seen in Esfahan. It was a sign, she decided, of hope and beauty.

As usual, the Alborz Mountains dominated the landscape, but sometimes it was difficult to tell where the buildings ended and the mountains began. Other times, the mountains changed color, transitioning from shades of ochre and brown to pink, all in sharp contrast to the rest of the landscape. Anna liked it best when they turned gray. She tried to guess when, and how, and why, that happened: was it the time of day or the weather or pollution? For now, the mountains were keeping their secrets.

Anna found Iranian shopkeepers quite eager to help her part with her money. Many assumed their few words of English made them fluent, and they chattered on incomprehensibly. Still, Anna nodded and smiled as if she understood. She picked up a few words in Farsi for food items, furniture, and simple directions. She also learned that the price of everything was negotiable, and she discovered that she loved to haggle.

Despite her happiness, a darkness was inexorably gathering, like a storm massing on the far side of the mountains. At first both Anna and Nouri refused to acknowledge it. It was Hassan who picked at the cloudy wisps of trouble.

Anna invited him for dinner one night in mid-October, when the warmth still clung to the city, as if summer was reluctant to depart. She set a small table on their patio so they could eat outside. A gentle breeze stirred the air, bringing the soft whispers of distant traffic. She worked all day on the meal: *tah-chin-e morgh*, a saffron chicken dish with yogurt, rice, tomatoes, hummus, and the Iranian flatbread called *sangak*. Hassan lifted a piece of chicken to his mouth, chewed, and swallowed. Anna held her breath.

Then he grinned. "This is good, Anna." He dug in, shoveling the chicken into his mouth as if he hadn't eaten in weeks. "You have become quite the Iranian cook."

Anna beamed. So did Nouri.

After dinner they went inside. While Anna made tea, Nouri got out a bottle of whiskey and two shot glasses. He poured a shot and handed it to Hassan. Hassan seemed reluctant to take it, Anna thought.

Nouri noticed too. "Is something wrong?" Nouri gulped his down and smacked his lips. "It's real Kentucky bourbon."

Hassan stared at the glass, then shook his head. He took a small sip.

"So, my friend," Nouri said, in the tone he had adopted recently, one that some might construe as patronizing. "How goes your life? Any interesting job prospects?"

Hassan had been looking for work for a long time, Anna knew. He'd wanted to become a doctor, but his father's death, and his responsibilities as the eldest son, forced him to quit medical school. He was working as a sales representative for a medical supply company. Anna hoped Nouri would help Hassan, perhaps even find him something at the Metro, once Nouri himself was settled.

Now, though, Hassan peered at Nouri with puzzled irritation, his silence almost deafening. Anna winced. Nouri should have been more sensitive, she thought, and made sure not to condescend, especially toward his best friend. Perhaps it was just the pressure of his new job. She let it go.

But Hassan didn't. "Nouri, help me understand," he said after a long pause. "There is rioting in the streets, people are being killed by the shah's men. Revolution is coming. But all you can think to talk about are my job prospects?"

Nouri tilted his head as if *he* was confused. "Revolution? That's a strong word. Certainly there is bitter opposition to the shah. As well there should be. But revolution? I don't see it."

Surprise flitted across Hassan's face. "I understand that you and Anna just celebrated your wedding. Perhaps you are still on your honeymoon." He emphasized the word *honeymoon*. "But you cannot be oblivious to what's happening. You have seen the riots on Shah Reza Avenue and at Tehran University. You have seen the cars set on fire, the attacks on the banks and government buildings."

"Of course." Nouri glanced at Anna, almost apologetically. As if he was trying to shield her from what was going on in central Tehran. She frowned. He didn't need to.

"That is not just opposition, Nouri," Hassan continued. "It is revolution, and it is sweeping the country." Hassan set down his glass of whiskey. He'd hardly touched it. "Just who do you think will take over after the shah leaves?"

Nouri twirled his glass. Was this an attempt to look thoughtful, Anna wondered? Or was Nouri hiding a budding sense of unease? "An interesting question. I favor a parliamentary democracy. Perhaps a democratic republic."

Hassan folded his arms. "What about the Imam?"

Anna listened to their discussion warily. Earlier that month, Saddam Hussein had expelled Ayatollah Khomeini from Iraq, where he'd been living for fifteen years. Khomeini promptly moved to Paris where his fiery rhetoric had been broadcast back to Iran far more frequently than it was from the dusty Iraqi village to which he had been confined. His influence had exploded, sparking even more upheaval.

"Khomeini is only one voice," Nouri said. Anna noticed he deliberately didn't repeat the word "Imam," which meant "Islamic leader." "There are also Socialists, Communists, Democrats—all of them want to depose the shah."

Hassan leaned forward. "Listen to me, Nouri. The Ayatollah could have gone to any Arab country when he left Iraq. But where did he go? To a place where freedom of the press assures he can continue to call for the overthrow of the shah. To a place where many more will hear him than did before. The man is a master strategist. You need to prepare yourself."

"For what?"

Hassan just looked at him. Anna's stomach clenched. In any other time, with any other person, she would have said—perhaps flippantly— that for every religious leader Hassan could name, she could raise him a Sartre, a Karl Marx, or a Marcuse. But she had seen the protests in the streets, the fervent chants for Khomeini, the tears streaming down women's faces. Hassan had a point. Discomfited, she changed the subject. "My mother lives in Paris."

Hassan looked at her curiously. "Is that so?"

She nodded. What's more, her mother was the type of person to befriend extremists, outlaws, and outcasts. But she kept that to herself.

Hassan stroked his mustache. "A mother in Paris. A German father in America. Who are you really, Anna Samedi? What do you want?"

She looked him straight in the eye. "I am Nouri's wife. I want what makes him happy."

Hassan flashed an enigmatic smile. "Spoken like a good Iranian wife. Perhaps there is hope for you."

Anna wasn't sure how to respond. A few minutes later, Hassan bid them good night. "*Marg bar Shâh*, my friends. Death to the shah."

§

Strikes had erupted sporadically over the past few months, but at the end of October a general strike closed down most of the country, including the oil fields. Over the next few days, mobs burned down large areas of the city. The British Embassy was set on fire, and rioters tried to attack the US Embassy. Some reports said that the shah's troops refused to act against the protestors and allowed the riots to escalate. The prime minister resigned. Baba-joon stayed away from his office and insisted that Anna come to their house while Nouri was at work. Although the riots had not spilled into north Tehran, and the streets were quiet, the Samedis' chauffeur picked her up every morning. Nighttime was another matter. After dark, the cry of *"Allâho Akbar!"* was shouted from rooftops across the city.

One afternoon in early November, only days after the resignation of the prime minister, Anna and Laleh lounged on sofas in front of the TV. Laleh was sulking because she couldn't leave the house to meet Shaheen. Maman-joon was in the kitchen. A soap opera was blaring away—pabulum for the masses, Anna thought. The state couldn't afford to let its people watch coverage of the riots all day. But the unrest was having an effect. The household help, including the woman who'd taken Anna's suitcase upstairs when she first arrived, the one who wore a scarf over her hair, had become hostile and quiet and refused to make eye contact.

Baba-joon stayed in his study, his shortwave radio tuned to the BBC. Anna watched part of the soap opera with Laleh. She'd picked up more Farsi, but the actors spoke too fast for her. Still, she got the general idea from their body language and expressions. Bored, she wandered into Baba-joon's study. He was behind his desk reading the newspaper. The radio hummed softly in the background.

"Baba-joon?"

He lowered the paper and peered at her. "Yes, my dear?"

"I'm sorry to disturb you."

"Think nothing of it." He smiled tolerantly.

"Baba-joon, do you think there will be a revolution? Will Khomeini come back to lead Iran?"

She wasn't sure how she expected him to respond: with a vigorous denial, perhaps, or a sardonic laugh that implied the question was ridiculous. Certainly not with the answer he gave. He leaned back in his chair. "I hope not. If there is, we are lost."

Anna felt as if her moorings had suddenly come loose. She sat down heavily. "So you think it could happen?"

His lips tightening, Baba-joon folded the newspaper into precise quarters and put it down on the desk. "Six months ago I would have said 'never.' I am no longer as confident. The shah is losing support—and quickly."

Anna knew Baba-joon's background. Nouri had explained that he had been in the military, and his upbringing had been spartan. There wasn't a lot of money, but there had been discipline, hard work, and determination. For him to express doubt about the shah was huge.

"And as far as Khomeini is concerned..." He explained that the riots and protests appeared to run in a forty-day cycle.

Puzzled, Anna frowned. "Why?"

"Islam requires forty days of mourning after the death of a family or loved one. It has always been so. Now that ritual has become a political act."

"I don't understand."

"After the forty-day mourning period, crowds gather to commemorate those who were martyred in the previous riot. Their despair and anger are still raw, so it often triggers a new riot, invariably bigger, and more destructive, than the one before. This is happening all over Iran, these forty-day cycles."

"But what does that have to do with revolution? Or Khomeini?"

"When peoples' lives are at the breaking point, when they can no longer stand the oppression of a despot, they seek shelter anywhere they can. Iranians do not have a physical space in which to hide, so they seek shelter in a different time. They revert to the past, where familiar rhythms and customs bring relief."

"The good old days."

He nodded. "Especially because the shah has tried to be so modern. If you continue to be modern, they say, we will be old. The result is the rebirth of religious Islamic laws, laws that are centuries old. *Shariah*, it is called."

"Which is what Khomeini preaches," Anna said.

"Exactly," Baba-joon said. "For those who have nothing, Khomeini's words and Shariah law are seductive."

"You sound almost sympathetic."

"I understand. There is a difference."

In the silence that followed, Anna heard the squeak of drawers opening in the kitchen, a blade chopping, the thwap of meat being pounded. Despite the warmth and familiarity of the sounds, she felt a chill.

Seventeen

It was in early November that events gathered speed, seeming to hurtle toward a still unknown end. The shah gave a speech in which he called the unrest a revolution for the first time, and seemed to extend an olive branch to the protestors. But this gesture was reversed when he appointed a military coalition to replace the civilian government. In Paris, Ayatollah Khomeini demanded that the shah abdicate the throne in favor of an Islamic republic. At home, Shi'ite religious leaders rejected the military government and urged the faithful to continue the struggle. But the government managed to break most of the strikes, and some people returned to work.

Meanwhile, the rainy season arrived. It was cold and damp, with periods of steady rain or intermittent sprinkles. Occasionally, a cheerful sun broke out, as if apologizing for the dreariness, and life seemed almost normal. Going out, Anna encountered the jubes—man-made gullies that ran beside the sidewalks. Running from north Tehran down to the city center, they smelled of damp concrete, and at first she thought they were sewers, but Baba-joon told her they were built to handle the excess rain and snowmelt from the mountains. Sometimes, little boys and dogs played in them.

Now that their house was more or less in order, Anna decided it was time to pursue a job. She took a taxi to a quiet, tree-lined street in north central Tehran, not far from the Samedis' home. Taxis in Tehran were an adventure. They could be private or shared, and today Anna was squeezed between a man who, despite the cool weather, was sweating, and a woman whose hair gave off a sweet, fruity aroma.

The taxi deposited her in front of the Iran-American Society, which occupied a modern, two-story building. Inside, on the first floor, were white-painted halls lined with oil paintings. Directly in front of her was a theater. She peeked in and saw seats for about two hundred. She took the stairs to the second floor and started down a hall flanked by offices, each with a nameplate on the door. The executive director's office was at the far end. The door was open, but Anna knocked anyway.

"Come in," a voice called.

Behind the desk sat a woman with dark hair, pale skin, a strong chin, and bright blue eyes, which probably looked bluer because of her turquoise suit. She wore little makeup, but her jewelry was something else. Bracelets tinkled, earrings bobbed, and Anna saw several rings on both hands, including a wedding band.

The woman came out from behind the desk. "I'm Charlotte Craft, but everyone calls me Charlie." She offered Anna her hand.

Anna took it. "Anna Samedi."

Charlie waved her into a chair. "So, tell me about yourself. Your father-in-law said only that you are an exceptional young woman and that you want a job."

Anna jiggled her foot. A few days ago she'd finally confessed to Baba-joon that she didn't want to work at the oil company, whereupon Nouri immediately told him about Hassan's suggestion that she try the IAS. It turned out that Baba-joon knew people there, too, and he'd arranged the interview.

"He is too kind," Anna said.

"Do you know what we do?"

"Not exactly."

"We're a cultural center. We try to strengthen the bonds between Iranians and Americans by exposing them to each other. We've been around for over twenty years, and I became director two years ago. I, myself, am married to an Iranian."

"I am, too." Anna folded her hands in her lap.

"Yes, I know." Charlie smiled. "I understand you lived in Chicago." When Anna nodded, she said, "I went to Notre Dame. Right around the corner, so to speak. But I'd visit friends at U of C. I miss Harold's fried chicken."

Anna grinned and felt herself relax. "I miss Medici's pizza."

Charlie laughed, and the sound was infectious: low, throaty, and raucous. "Oh, my god. Iranians are great chefs, but they have no clue about pizza."

Anna laughed too. "I know what you mean."

"At any rate," Charlie went on, "we have a dynamic organization, if I do say so myself. It's friendly, it's substantive, it's creative. We showcase some of the most exciting work being done by Iranian and American artists. We stage theater events, plays, concerts—you saw our gallery downstairs?"

Anna nodded. She liked Charlie, even if she did talk at eighty miles an hour.

"We also teach classes in English and American culture—mostly for professionals or Iranians moving to the States. As you might imagine, interest in the US is at an all-time high, so we have programs for young people, too. Especially students with promising careers. Do you have a teaching degree?"

Anna's stomach turned over. "I graduated with a degree in literature. No teaching."

Charlie leaned forward, plopped her elbows on her desk, and studied Anna. "Most of our teachers are instructors at Tehran University or someplace comparable. They moonlight here."

Anna looked at the floor.

Charlie was quiet for a moment. Then, "But given the current demand, we have more students than we can accommodate."

Anna looked up. "Even with all the unrest?"

"Because of it." She smiled again. "Don't believe everything you hear. The floodgates have opened. Everyone wants to learn English. Right away. I suppose, in one way, we can thank the shah for that." She smiled. "Tell me something. Would you like to teach young people?

Teenagers? We don't currently offer classes to Iranians that young, but we've had a number of calls. If you can handle it, I think we can make room for you."

Anna sat up. "Are you kidding? I would love it."

"It's just part time, you understand."

"That would be perfect."

"Because you need time to devote to your husband and family."

"Exactly." Anna grinned. They were complicit, she and Charlie. In fact, for one of the first times since she'd been in Iran, she felt comfortable. Charlie was the kind of woman she would like to become. Dare she think this woman might one day be her friend?

"Charlie, thank you so much. This is so much more than I expected!"

Charlie peered at her. "It's just a job." But she looked pleased as she rose and strolled to a set of file cabinets in the corner. She rummaged in a drawer and pulled out a folder. "Here are some sample curricula from past classes. They were designed for adults, so you'll have to adapt them. Can you do that?"

Anna nodded eagerly.

"Good." Charlie handed them over. "We'll gear up in January. December is a month of mourning here, and, of course, all the Americans are consumed with Christmas. Does that sound workable?"

Anna nodded, thanked Charlie again, and took her leave. She practically skipped down the steps. She was already dreaming up a syllabus. Poetry, she thought. She would track down an English translation of Rumi. And e e cummings. She was so absorbed she barely remembered the trip home. She couldn't wait to tell Nouri.

"How much will you be paid?" he asked that night.

"Sixty tomans an hour," she said. About nine dollars.

"Not bad. In fact, it's quite good."

She wasn't doing it for the money, she wanted to reply. She was doing it because someone wanted her, and she could contribute. And maybe make a friend in the process. But she didn't tell Nouri that. She just dipped her head and beamed.

§

As November came to an end, Anna tried to cook a Thanksgiving dinner for her Iranian family. She couldn't find a turkey to roast so she made do with a chicken. But the ongoing unrest had reduced shopkeepers' inventories, and the bird was scrawny and tough. Anna hoped her rice and currant stuffing would hide its flaws.

The Samedis pretended to like the chicken, but the way they scarfed down the kababs and curried meatballs she also cooked, told her they were just being polite. Over dinner Anna chattered about her new job, the students she hoped to teach, the texts she was thinking of adapting. Nouri's family asked all the right questions, but after dinner—like an open wound that couldn't be ignored—the conversation turned to politics.

Baba-joon said he'd talked to the shah. There was a moment of awestruck silence, during which Anna decided Baba-joon must know everyone in Tehran.

Nouri asked what he said.

"He is moody and depressed and sees enemies everywhere. First he thinks his foes are the oil companies. Then he blames the CIA and Carter, because they stopped the secret subsidies paid to radicals and clerics. Then he decides it's the Communists, and, of course, Khomeini. Then it's the treachery of his own ministers." Baba-joon sighed. "One day he frees political prisoners. The next his troops shoot people in the street." Baba-joon shook his head. "I just don't know anymore."

Everyone went quiet. If someone as prominent as Baba-joon was despondent, what hope was there?

"Does the shah think he can weather the crisis?" Nouri finally asked. His tone seemed to beg for reassurance.

"I believe he does," Baba-joon said. It was clear Baba-joon did not.

Nouri didn't say anything. Didn't he believe his father? Anna wondered. Or was he unwilling to face reality?

Apparently, Laleh didn't want to face it either. "I hope he does survive. I don't like being restricted. I can't go to nightclubs, can't go shopping, can't take the car for a drive. What kind of life is that?"

Anna kept her mouth shut, but it was a relief when the family piled into the Mercedes to go home. As she cleaned up, Nouri turned on the news, which, like in the US, came on late at night. Troops in Shiraz had killed fifteen people who were rioting. More ominously, over two hundred high-ranking politicians and royal family members were discovered to have sent their savings, estimated at over two billion dollars, out of Iran.

Nouri sucked in a breath.

Anna came out of the kitchen. She watched the riot scenes for a moment, then said quietly, "You didn't expect this, did you?"

He ran a hand through his hair. "I didn't think it would be so... violent. Then again, when a government deserves to be replaced, I suppose violence is the most efficient way to do it. And when people have nothing to lose..." His voice trailed off.

Anna was quiet. Then, as if the thought had just occurred to her, she asked, "What about Hassan?"

"What about him?"

"Is he someone with nothing to lose?"

Worry lines popped up on Nouri's brow. "Why do you ask?"

"His father committed suicide because of the shah. That can be a powerful motivation for revenge."

"It's not that simple, Anna."

"Isn't it?"

"Hassan's politics aren't based on retribution. He truly believes things must change. He always has. You're insinuating that no one can advocate for change if they're not miserable. But what about us? We're not miserable, but we certainly want change."

Anna realized the hole she had just dug. "I didn't mean that. I just..."

"I love this country. I want to see progress. If the shah is not moving us forward, and he clearly isn't, then someone else should. I will gladly support them. Just like Hassan."

"Would you really?"

"What are you getting at, Anna?"

"What if you were required to give up something in order to move forward?"

His brow furrowed, and he looked around. "What would I possibly have to give up?"

Eighteen

Decomber marked the beginning of Muharram, which, next to Ramadan, was the most sacred month of the Islamic calendar. Fighting was supposedly prohibited during the month, but violent riots broke out in Tehran, and other cities, three nights running. Demonstrators seized government buildings, shut down businesses, and attacked government officials. Even in Esfahan, the city Anna recalled with so much affection, protestors attacked SAVAK offices, and burned down the cinemas. A number of people were killed. Chants for the return of Khomeini choked the air. Foreigners, including many Americans, fled the country.

Anna decided the whole world had gone crazy. Three weeks earlier, over nine hundred people in Jonestown, Guyana, had committed mass suicide on the order of one man. And November 27th saw the assassination of San Francisco gay leader Harvey Milk. Maybe there was something to the concept of Armageddon.

It got worse. On December 7th, US president Jimmy Carter was asked at a news conference whether he expected the shah to survive. He replied that it was a decision the Iranian people would have to make, not the US. This stunning about-face, coming after months of proclaiming the shah one of his staunchest allies, sealed the shah's fate. His remaining support was now in tatters.

On the 11th of December, the Day of Ashura—a sacred Islamic day of mourning and fasting—nearly a million people gathered in Tehran's

Shahyad Square to call for the shah's ouster. The protest spilled over to Shahyad Tower—the "gateway to Tehran"—the landmark Anna had marveled at as she and Nouri drove from the airport only four months before. The shah refused to use force and did not order his troops to disperse the crowd. His military government resigned. The unrelenting pace of events distorted Anna's perception of time; it felt like four years, not four months.

As the new year began, the shah appointed yet another government, but that did little to stem the turmoil. Demonstrations and riots persisted, each more violent than the one before. On the 16th of January, the shah flew his own plane to Egypt for what he told the country was a vacation. Everyone knew he would not be back.

Millions of Iranians poured into the streets, this time in jubilation. From Paris, Ayatollah Khomeini said the shah might be gone, but the need to create an Islamic republic still existed. Two days later, despite the opposition of the new government, the crowds poured out onto the streets again, demanding just that. A flurry of communiqués passed between Khomeini and Bakhtiar, the new prime minister—who had only been in office a few weeks. On February 1st, Khomeini flew back to Tehran.

PART TWO

Nineteen

"Come, Nouri." Hassan called up the stairs. "We won't get close if we don't leave right now."

Anna zipped up her jacket and draped a muffler around her neck. She and Hassan were waiting for Nouri. They were going to the southern part of the city to see the Ayatollah, whose plane had just landed at Mehrabad Airport. He was now en route to Behesht-e Zahra Cemetery where he would give a speech. According to the radio over two million people were already lining the streets. It promised to be one of those days people would tell their grandchildren about.

Hassan shuffled his feet impatiently. "Where is he?"

"Probably still shaving," Anna said.

Hassan scowled.

Finally, Nouri clattered down the stairs, trailing the scent of aftershave and toothpaste. Anna loved the way Nouri smelled after he showered. She wanted to burrow into his arms but settled for a quick kiss.

They piled into Nouri's BMW, another wedding present from his parents, and drove south toward the cemetery just outside Tehran on the road to Qom. As they got within a mile of it masses of people swarmed the streets, making further progress impossible. They abandoned the car and started walking. Nouri looked around in wonder. "I've never seen such huge crowds."

"*Inshallah*, it is the beginning of a new dawn," Hassan said.

Anna wanted to roll her eyes at the cliché. It was a mild day for

February, and she unwrapped her muffler and unzipped her jacket. The atmosphere was festive; people sang and hugged each other. They even smiled at Anna. Some had cut the shah's picture out of their money, and they waved their shah-less rials and tomans. Shopkeepers flung candy and sweets into the crowd. Children scampered to retrieve them. Others distributed flowers. Every so often they saw soldiers, but they didn't appear to be menacing. At one point, a girl inserted flowers in the barrels of the soldiers' rifles. If not for the clothing, Anna thought, she might have been walking through Haight-Ashbury during the height of the Vietnam War. The men were, for the most part, in Western dress, but many of the women were wearing chadors.

"Look!" Hassan pointed.

Someone wielded an ax, and was chopping away at a statue of the shah. He'd clearly been at it for a while; the statue wobbled precariously.

Nouri took Anna's hand. She squeezed it.

The throng of people thickened as they approached the cemetery, but the gates were wide open, and the crowd poured through. Anna, who had never been inside a cemetery, wasn't sure what to expect. She was oddly relieved as she walked into a bucolic setting with tree-lined streets and broad plazas and terraces.

A big banner just inside the gates proclaimed something in Arabic. "What does it say?" Anna asked Nouri.

"The Communist Party welcomes the Ayatollah back onto Iranian soil!" He answered cheerfully. Other people waved Iranian flags. Some held up green banners.

"Why green?" Anna asked.

"Green is the color of Islam." Hassan grinned.

Nouri picked up on his mood. "I've never seen you so happy, Hassan."

Hassan clapped his hands. "We did it, Nouri! The shah is gone, and the Imam will lead us into a new age."

The trace of a frown came across Nouri's face. "The Imam is a learned man, and a holy one, but he is not part of the ruling structure. We have a constitutional monarchy. Shapour Bakhtiar is our prime minister. And the Army is still loyal to the government."

Hassan's smile lost some of its wattage.

As if placating him, Nouri continued in a reassuring tone. "But Khomeini has pledged to abide by the constitution of 1906 which means we *are* going to have a democratic government. And a free press. Political prisoners will be released. SAVAK will be shut down. So, yes, that is what we wanted." Nouri rubbed his hands together. "You are right, Hassan. It is exciting."

Anna couldn't help thinking that she and Hassan had just been given a civics lesson. She shook it off. They'd been inching forward slowly, but now the crowd was so thick they were forced to stop. They'd reached a large grassy area that reminded Anna of Chicago's Grant Park. A platform was erected at one end. Loudspeakers attached to poles were scattered around the field. Some people sat on the ground as if they were at a picnic. Others had their eyes squeezed shut in prayers. Still others were on their knees. Anna could taste the anticipation.

A motorcade turned into the cemetery. It was made up of surprisingly ordinary-looking cars: Paykans, even an American car or two. At the sight of it, a swell of shouts erupted. Everyone pushed forward. The crush of the crowd blocked Anna's view. The cries rose to a frenzy. Tears streamed down women's cheeks. Anna could barely see in front of her, much less the platform. Several years before she'd seen the Rolling Stones at the Chicago Stadium. The audience had been so mesmerized that Mick Jagger could have strutted across the stage stark naked and people would have cheered. It felt like that now.

As several men appeared on the platform, the noise reached a fever pitch. Anna caught a glimpse of an old man in a black turban and robes. He was surrounded by men, some wearing white turbans, others in Western-style dress. Khomeini was seated on a chair on the platform; others sat cross-legged at his feet.

A youngish man came to the microphone. The noise of the crowd subsided. The man, speaking in Farsi, exhorted the crowd. Many in the audience raised their hands, made fists, and shouted replies. Then there was a long moment of silence.

When Khomeini started speaking, his voice was remarkably

dispassionate. Anna wondered if he was reciting prayers from the Qur'an. His face was solemn, expressionless. If anything, he looked angry. As he continued, though, his voice gathered strength. At one point he raised a stern index finger. He seemed to be warning the crowd. They responded with cheers.

Anna tugged on Nouri's jacket. "What's he saying?"

"He says he will smash the mouth of the Bakhtiar government. He thinks the government is illegal and he's calling for more strikes and demonstrations."

Hassan jabbed his fist in the air. Nouri didn't.

Khomeini's voice grew more emotional, even passionate. Another round of cheers went up.

"Now what?" Anna asked.

"He's criticizing the US. And appealing to the army to join the revolution."

More speech. More cheering.

"And now?"

"He's saying there will be a popularly elected government and the clergy will not interfere. He promises no one will remain homeless and that Iranians will have free telephone, heating, electricity, bus service, and oil."

"He sounds exactly like the shah."

"Anna, you know nothing." Hassan cut in with a stern frown. "This is the dawn of the Islamic Republic. Faith and democracy linked together. We will be the envy of the world. *Allâho Akbar!*"

Anna remembered what she had once said about the danger of mixing religion with politics. She wondered whether to remind Hassan of it, but when she saw the look on his face, she knew to keep her mouth shut.

§

That night Nouri and Hassan were glued to the television, watching footage of the Ayatollah's speech and the crowd's reaction to it. The commentators were enthusiastic, and Anna had a sense that history was emanating from the tiny screen.

Still, she felt restless. She climbed the stairs to the loft and slid open the door to the roof. It was a clear, crisp night. Bars of silver moonlight cast stippled shadows on the shingles. She thought about her father in Maryland, her mother in Paris. They were both so far away. Were they seeing the same moon as she? Feeling the same soft breath of night against her face? Or had Iran changed so much that even the moon and air were different?

Twenty

R*ooz beh khayr!* Good afternoon."

"Good afternoon," the students replied in unison.

Anna smiled. It was the third week of class. She was teaching about fifteen students, mostly girls in their teens. Americans would have called their English high level; certainly they spoke far better than she did Latin and French, which she'd studied at their age. At times she felt like the pupil. Even though she asked them not to speak Farsi in class, she'd picked up many new phrases since class began.

The classroom wasn't ideal: cinder block walls, linoleum floor, a small chalkboard, and chairs with no arms. Although the heat was only on three months a year, the radiators at the Iran-American Society must have been compensating for the other nine months, because it was hot and stuffy enough to induce a late afternoon lethargy.

Anna wiped her brow with the back of her hand. "I thought we'd do something different today." Up until now, she'd stayed close to the syllabus Charlie had given her. In fact Charlie was with her for most of the first two weeks, no doubt to observe how Anna handled the students. Apparently, Anna had passed muster, because Charlie now left her alone, greeting her with a cheerful smile and, sometimes, a joke or two.

The IAS had become a beacon of stability for Anna. The new government was fragile; most Iranians had no idea which factions or groups would ultimately prevail. While demonstrations and strikes persisted, there was much hope and talk of democracy in the now free press. Everyone talked about a new beginning, a cleansing. At the same time, some warned of dark days ahead if the revolution didn't succeed. Still others were fearful of an Islamic republic and what it might do to Iran's economy and international standing. Anna was grateful she had somewhere to go and something to do while the government and the people sorted themselves out.

In the spirit of the times, Anna made copies of the Declaration of Independence for her students. She distributed them and asked for a volunteer to start reading. A hand immediately shot up. It was Miriam, an energetic brunette with mischievous eyes and an impish grin.

"Go ahead, Miriam."

"When in the course of human events it becomes necessary for one people to dissolve the political bands which have connected them with another and to assume among the powers of the earth…"

Miriam read the English words haltingly. She had most of the sounds down, but her accent was thick and difficult to follow.

"Very good, Miriam. Who wants to continue?"

Another hand waved at her: a skinny young man with glasses, pale skin, and a scholarly attitude. "Zubin."

"We hold these truths to be self-evident…" His English was smoother than Miriam's, and Anna wondered if he'd learned it from watching American movies. *"…that all men are created equal, that they are endowed by their creator with certain unalienable rights, that among these are life, liberty and the pursuit of happiness."*

"Very good, Zubin," Anna said when he finished the section. "Let's stop there." She looked around. "So what do you think?"

The students were silent.

"Oh, come on. These words were written by the Founding Fathers of the United States over two hundred years ago. And yet they are still recited. Which means they're still relevant to many Americans. But what about you? Do you see any relevance to them today?"

A girl tentatively raised her hand.

"Yes, Jaleh?"

"The shah was destructive of these ends."

Anna nodded. "And what happened?"

"The people abolished his government and created a new one," another boy chimed in.

"No." Zubin interrupted. "Not all the people. Just the people who no longer gave their consent to be governed."

The students shifted and began to talk among themselves. Anna heard wisps of conversation in both English and Farsi. "But we are 'azad' now. Free."…"The monarchists are wrong"…"shah supporters"… "Anti-revolutionary."

The students were mimicking the same hopes and fears Anna was reading about.

Zubin shook his head and barked out something in Farsi. Anna couldn't quite understand it, but it provoked more comments. Zubin switched to English. "I am nothing," he said to Anna. "But some people, like shah ministers and the rich, they do not want revolution."

Zubin must have meant "no one," Anna thought. Regardless of his word choice, Anna thought he was quite brave to have raised the issue. And to stick to his point. "All right, class."

They continued to chatter.

"Class!" She raised her voice. This time they went quiet. "So, what happens when not everyone agrees? When only a segment of the population wants change? Should change go forward?"

No one replied. The students looked confused. "It's not a trick question," she added. "But perhaps it's one that should be asked."

A girl who'd been silent slowly raised her hand. "My parents say Khomeini will start a reign of terror. Like the French Revolution. My father says we will move to Canada."

Another student piped up. "My parents say Khomeini has saved Iran. That he is Iran's Messiah."

Once again the students buzzed, this time with passion and intensity. Anna wondered if she had unleashed something she hadn't intended. She decided to curtail the discussion. "I appreciate everyone's opinion, but it's clear we're not going to solve the future of Iran today. However, I will say one thing. The discussion we're having would have been difficult, perhaps impossible, just a few weeks ago. It can only take place in a democracy where there is free speech and freedom of assembly. For that we should be grateful." She hoped she'd struck the right tone. "Now, let's go back to the language of the Declaration, because parts of it are quite specific. And beautifully written."

She led them through an explanation of the preamble. The students asked about the "Laws of Nature," "Nature's God," and what "inalienable" meant. She did her best to reply, but she'd already discovered that teaching English was more than words, letters, and sounds. It was also politics, sociology, and culture. And while she tried to filter out her own judgments—the students should make up their own minds— she understood they were taking their cue from her. She discovered a newfound respect for her past teachers and professors.

Suddenly, one of Anna's students raced into the room. It was Dina, a girl Anna thought might be her brightest, most curious student. She hadn't been in class that day, until now. "The army has laid down its weapons!" she said breathlessly. "The revolution has succeeded!"

§

Laleh, who had finally obtained her driver's permit, was waiting in the Mercedes after Anna's class the next afternoon. Anna had agreed to go shopping with her at the bazaar. Nouri's parents hadn't wanted them to go out at all, certainly not by themselves. But Laleh, headstrong as always, dismissed her parents' fears and convinced Anna everything would be fine.

As they wound through the streets of Tehran with Laleh at the wheel, traffic crawled and eventually came to a standstill. They saw no policemen, traffic monitors, or troops. After ten minutes, Laleh angrily thumped her hand on the wheel. "This is ridiculous."

"Maybe we should go home," Anna said. "Or maybe your driver should have taken us. You heard about the army, didn't you? Bakhtiar is supposedly in hiding, and some parts of the city are in rebel hands."

Laleh waved a disgusted hand. "If this is what we have to look forward to, it will be anarchy. And our driver couldn't take us. He quit last week."

Anna sat back in surprise. "Why?"

"He said it was time for him to join the revolution." Laleh snorted.

"But what will he do for money?"

"Who cares?"

Anna pressed her lips together. A week or so before, Khomeini had named Mehdi Bazargan as prime minister of a new provisional government. The army's capitulation was basically an endorsement of that decision, but government services remained largely paralyzed. In some places local civilian committees, called *komitehs*, were starting to assume responsibility for things like neighborhood security and the distribution of fuel oil.

Laleh went on. "Everyone thinks Khomeini is the answer to their prayers. Wait until they find out what a fraud he is. How does that song go? 'Meet the new boss, same as the old boss'?"

Anna shook her head.

"The Who. That's who." Laleh smiled grimly.

By the time they approached the bazaar a steely winter dusk had set in, and the headlights of oncoming cars felt intrusive. The market itself looked grimier and messier than Anna remembered, as if no one had swept the ground or wiped down the counters for a while. Laleh led the way, winding around stalls whose occupants stared listlessly at the two women. Gone was the bustle and noise, the jaunty music, the merchants' eager come-ons. Even the smells were less fragrant, as if the spices and foodstuffs had gone stale.

Laleh stopped at a stall that looked vaguely familiar. Now, though, there was nothing decorative or distinctive about it. Just a slab of mostly bare counter. A pile of paper and plastic bags lay on the floor behind it. An older man, wearing a tattered argyle sweater vest over a white shirt, was hunched over the counter. His head was covered with a turban, and the stubble on his cheeks indicated that he was growing a beard. As they approached, he thumbed studiously through a newspaper. He didn't look up; it didn't appear as if he wanted customers. Anna recalled this was the booth that sold liquor. Laleh'd bought wine there a few months ago.

Laleh planted herself in front of the man. He refused to make eye contact with her, but Anna could tell he was appraising them from the corner of his eye. "I would like to buy a bottle of scotch," Laleh said in Farsi.

Again, Anna was surprised. She knew Laleh drank wine and the occasional beer, but hard liquor? Maybe it was something she'd picked up at the disco. Anna disliked cocktails and martinis and all the other drinks with fancy names. The taste was too grown up. They reminded her of a Cary Grant movie. He and Katharine Hepburn could hold a highball just right, tip it deftly towards their lips, but Anna could never imitate them. She was too unsophisticated and clumsy.

Laleh repeated her request. This time the man looked up. "I have nothing for you."

"What do you mean?" Laleh's cheeks reddened and her voice sharpened. She turned to Anna and spoke in English. "He'd sell liquor by the truckload if he could. I've seen him."

"No alcohol. Not anymore." He shrugged.

"Why not?" Laleh switched back to Farsi. "You sold some to my boyfriend last week."

"Do you not read the Qur'an? Intoxicants and gambling are Satan's handiwork." He'd answered in Farsi, but Anna understood the gist. He looked over his shoulder. "Consuming alcohol is a major sin. One of the roots of corruption."

Laleh's eyes grew round. "Since when?"

"Shariah law prohibits the sale of alcohol."

Laleh crossed her arms. "Just because the Ayatollah is back doesn't mean Iran is practicing Shariah law."

He smiled as if he knew a secret. "It will come soon enough, Inshallah."

Laleh pointed toward the pile of bags on the floor. "I want scotch. I know you have it."

"Come back next week. I will have spices and sweets. *Bamieh*. *Baklava*. You will like them."

Laleh didn't say anything for a moment. Then she dug in her purse and fished out a wad of rials. *"Ay Bâbâ,"* she said scornfully.

A man in a dark green uniform wandered towards them. A rifle was slung over his shoulder, but Anna was pretty sure the army wore brown, not green. With red caps. The man slowed as he got closer. Anna nudged Laleh.

"What?" Laleh snapped. She was still clutching the wad of bills. Anna pointed to the soldier.

Laleh whipped around. When she saw him, she glared.

He looked at them, then the merchant, then back at them. A proprietary smirk tugged at his mouth, as if he was in charge of the stall, the goods, the entire bazaar. "Women should not buy alcohol. Allah does not permit it."

Anna stepped back in surprise. He was speaking English.

"A new age is dawning. If you refuse to embrace it, you will be branded an infidel."

Anna's stomach knotted, and she tapped Laleh on the arm. "Let's go, Laleh. We'll come back another time."

"No." Laleh's chin jutted out. She stared him down. "Shariah is not the law of the land. Inshallah, it never will be."

The soldier shot her a withering look. Anna stiffened. What was he going to do? As if he had read her thoughts, he twisted toward Laleh looking like he was about to arrest her. Anna sucked in a breath, preparing herself. Then a flicker of doubt crept across his face. He adjusted the sling of his rifle, shot them a final scowl, then turned on his heel and walked away without a word.

Anna let out her breath. Laleh turned back to the shopkeeper and tossed the wad of bills on the counter. "You see?" she asked. "Now give me a bottle of Johnny Walker. Black."

The merchant eyed the money. He took a surreptitious glance around. The soldier was gone, and no one was watching. He grabbed the bills, stuffed them in his waistband, and ducked under the counter. Anna heard the sounds of paper rustling. Something being wrapped. When he reappeared, he handed Laleh a plastic bag. Something heavy was inside. "Go away. Quickly."

Laleh grabbed the bag, and they headed back to the car. She unlocked the front door, slid the bag in, then patted her purse. "Never forget, Anna. In Iran this will always speak louder than law."

Inshallah, Anna thought.

Twenty-one

Seven silver bowls sat on Maman-joon's dining table. Each was filled with something different, mostly grains. There was also a small mirror, two candles, a goldfish bowl, painted eggs, and all sorts of delicious food. It was Nowruz, the Iranian New Year. The holiday, a time of feasts, fire rituals, and little or no work, stretched over thirteen days, but the biggest celebration was on the first day of spring.

The Samedis always threw a big party, and this year was no exception. The guests—mostly relatives, colleagues, and friends—poured out of the house onto the roof and patio. Laleh complained that there were fewer guests this year, but Nouri told Anna that he didn't see much difference. Anna recognized faces from the wedding, the albums of which were finally assembled and lying on a table. People nodded and murmured as they flipped through the pages, no doubt wistfully remembering what had been only a few months ago, but now seemed like years.

Nouri had invited executives from the Metro project. They were French, but their English was good, and their Farsi was better than Anna's. Baba-joon's colleagues from the oil company came too, as well as some of Laleh's friends, and, of course, Shaheen. The girls, mostly in miniskirts and revealing tops, flipped and twirled their long hair, triggering sidelong glances from the male guests. Anna felt like an elderly aunt.

For her part, Anna had invited Charlie, her boss at the IAS and her one friend in Iran. Charlie brought her husband, Ibram. Charlie was dressed in a tailored green suit, with a low-cut tank top under the jacket. Anna also wore a suit, hers a baby blue linen with a white chemise.

Maman-joon scurried back and forth, making sure everyone had drinks and food. Although wreathed in smiles and good humor, she looked thinner, Anna thought, and the lines across her brow dug deeper.

The past six weeks had been difficult. Khomeini, who had decamped from Tehran for the religious city of Qom, condemned the idea of a democratic republic, claiming it would be unduly influenced by the West. Over two hundred army officers and SAVAK officials were executed by a new organization called the Islamic Revolutionary Tribunal. In addition, many shah loyalists were thrown in prison, some of them people Baba-joon and Maman-joon knew socially.

The turmoil sent shivers of apprehension through Iran's elite. Anna recalled how, in the eighteenth century, France's King Louis XV supposedly warned "après moi le déluge." It seemed to her as if Iran was indeed in the grip of a raging flood, its citizens trying to steer their flimsy lifeboats to safety.

Nowruz was supposed to be a day of celebration, but to Anna the gaiety seemed forced. Hassan stood in the corner of the living room, his hands flailing in the air in what looked like an intense discussion with a woman. Anna looked more closely. It was Roya, Nouri's childhood friend. Dressed in a long skirt that reached the floor and a simple blouse, she nodded eagerly. Anna wondered if there might be a spark of romance between them. She walked over.

"Hello, Roya." She smiled. "How was your hajj with your grand-mother? A good trip?"

Hassan raised his eyebrows as if surprised she knew what a hajj was, but Roya nodded politely. "Very nice," she answered. "In fact, I believe it was a harbinger of the future."

"How so?" Anna inclined her head.

"For the first time in many years there is hope. Now that the Imam is back."

Anna hugged her chest. She wished Nouri was with her, but he was on the other side of the room chatting with one of the Metro managers.

"You studied literature in university, yes?" Roya asked.

"I did."

"Then perhaps you saw the poem in the newspaper last month. I don't remember the poet's name but it said things like 'no one will tell lies anymore, people will become brothers, they will share the bread of joy, evil and treachery will be eliminated now that the Imam is back.'" Roya's face grew animated. "Did you see it?"

"I must have missed it."

"I saw it," a voice chimed in behind Anna. She turned around to see Charlie, holding a glass of wine.

Anna made introductions.

"The poet was some amateur no one's heard of." Charlie glanced at Anna. "It was a disaster, technically speaking."

Roya's expression froze.

"Well, it was," Charlie continued acerbically. "Chock full of sophomoric concepts and images." She shrugged and sipped her wine. "But obviously someone liked it."

Hassan's lips tightened. "You don't share the hope the rest of the country feels?"

Charlie took another sip. "To the contrary. I long for Iran to create a parliamentary democracy. It would be a blessing for the people of Iran, the Middle East, the entire world. But Khomeini has made it clear that's not his priority."

"You disagree with the idea of an Islamic republic?"

Charlie spread her feet apart. Her chest barreled out. "As I understand it, your *Imam*," she emphasized the word, "wants to suspend the law against bigamy, ban abortions, and end co-education. He also wants to require women in government ministries to wear hijab. As a woman, I find these positions unacceptable. Society can't go backwards."

Hassan waved a dismissive hand. "Ah yes, but you are an American. You wouldn't understand."

"Pardon me, but like Anna, I am married to an Iranian. I have lived here for more than seven years. These proclamations are not the signals of a moderate. They are a call to arms."

"There is much evil to be wrung out of society before we can be truly free," Hassan shot back.

Charlie planted one hand on her hip. The other clutched her wine glass. Anna had no idea what she would say next. Again she tried to make eye contact with Nouri.

"You are right, Charlie," Hassan said. "Religious and secular forces *are* in conflict. But, you see, the shah created the problem. By choking off democracy and free speech, the only place left where groups could gather and share ideas became the mosque. It's no wonder the movements born there have religious overtones."

"The shah is gone," Charlie countered. "So there is no longer a need for Muslims—or anyone else—to feel constrained. Iran should be flowering with discussions and plans and ideas. Instead, people are being shot by firing squads." She took another sip of wine. "This is not the Iran I know. The Iran I know is filled with hospitable, generous, open-minded people."

Roya stepped in. "I understand. But, you see, Hassan's point is that—"

Charlie cut her off. "And from what I gather, Khomeini is about to ban imports of foreign cars, alcohol, and pork, among other things. But the problem is you can't legislate religion. It never works."

"I'm sure it's just temporary," Nouri said with a smile. He had finally joined them.

Charlie looked over.

"Khomeini has more pressing problems anyway," Nouri went on. "He needs to get the country's economy started again."

Work on the Metro project had been put on hold. So far, it hadn't been disruptive. Nouri had been helping survey underground locations and finalize blueprints. But the planning couldn't last forever. They would need the funds originally promised to them by the shah.

"Khomeini must also deal with the problems in the north," Nouri said, as he slipped an arm around Anna.

"You mean the Kurds?" Hassan asked.

The Kurds were quasi-independent Muslims who lived in the mountainous regions of Iran and neighboring countries. Like the

Palestinians they were stateless, and like the Palestinians, they had been trying for decades to seize their own territory. Now that the shah was gone, fighting had erupted in the north. The problem was particularly sensitive, since the Kurds were mostly Sunni Muslims, unlike most Iranians, who were Shi'ites.

When Anna studied Persian literature in Chicago, she'd learned the difference. The professor gave them a simplified understanding of the two groups—to provide background for their readings—and had summed up the split between the two groups this way: Shi'ite Muslims felt nothing had gone right for them since they'd chosen Ali, Mohammed's son-in-law, as Mohammed's successor centuries ago, and then Ali had been assassinated. Fatalistic and melancholic, Shi'ites were quick to claim they were martyrs and victims of conspiracies. Sunnis, on the other hand, made up most of the Muslim world. They'd chosen Abu Bakr, Mohammed's adviser, as their successor. There had been friction between the sects ever since. Anna knew there was much more to the conflict and hoped that living in Iran would help her better understand the complicated history of Islam.

Despite the comfort of Nouri's arm, Anna felt pinched and tense, as if she was preparing to ward off a blow. What she wouldn't do for a carefree laugh, a funny movie, even a night out at Laleh's disco. The times were making people as dry as tinder. She hoped no one had a match.

Twenty-two

The knock on the door surprised Anna. It was a hot, arid evening near the end of May, and the heat hinted at the blistering summer to come. She'd kept the door open to fan the breeze; perhaps it had closed without her noticing. But when she went to the door, it was open, and Hassan stood outside.

Anna's eyes widened. She hadn't seen Hassan since Nowruz, almost three months earlier. Since then he'd grown a beard, and he wore a dark green uniform. A gun belt ringed his waist, and the gun in the holster was huge.

"Hassan! You look...so...different."

"I joined the Revolutionary Guards."

The month before, Khomeini had created his own army, men loyal to the revolution. They were not part of the regular Iranian Army, nor were they part of the police. Among other things, the Pasdaran, or Revolutionary Guards, were directed to go after leftist guerilla groups who were unhappy with Khomeini and the Islamic republic he'd created.

Her hand flew to her mouth although, to be honest, she wasn't that shocked. Hassan had been leaning that way for a long time. Still. "Why?"

He straightened up, looking proud. "It is the natural consequence of the revolution. The people who were powerless will finally have justice."

Anna's stomach clenched—she was wary of anyone who spouted polemics of any kind—but she said nothing. She opened the door wider. "Well, come in. Nouri's upstairs. I'll get him."

Hassan didn't move.

"I said, come in."

"Anna, I cannot."

"Why not?"

"I should never be with a woman alone, especially if she is another man's wife."

A flash of irritation streaked through Anna. "You're not. Nouri's upstairs."

Hassan still hesitated.

Anna clutched the edge of the door. "I guess you have become a devout Muslim too?"

He stared at her. "And if I have?" She heard the challenge in his voice.

Anna stared right back. "You were going to be a doctor, Hassan. Save people's lives. Make them whole. It's a noble calling."

"It is an even nobler calling to become the best Muslim possible. To help bring the gifts of Islam to our people."

Anna was about to reply when Nouri's voice floated down from upstairs. "Is that Hassan?"

"Yes, he's here," Anna replied. "Come down."

"Tell him to come up."

"He won't." Anna still clutched the edge of the door.

Nouri, his face filled with curiosity, appeared at the top of the landing. He hurried down the steps and did a double-take when he saw Hassan. "My god, Hassan. What's going on?"

Hassan repeated what he'd told Anna.

Nouri's brow furrowed. Then he cracked a smile. "Very funny, Hassan. That's a good one. You had me going for a minute."

Hassan jutted out his chin. "It is not a joke."

"But, of course it is…" Nouri's voice trailed off as he focused on Hassan, whose face was painted with a mix of pride and defiance. There was a moment of silence during which Nouri and Anna exchanged glances. "I see."

"Do you, Nouri? I am not sure. You ran off to America, and when you came back, you had an important job waiting for you. You never had to worry about where your next meal was coming from. Or whether you would make enough to support your family. You have never had to deal with a superior who withheld your salary because you did not sell enough supplies to doctors or hospitals. I do not think you *do* understand." He glanced over at Anna. "Nor does she."

Nouri winced. "I didn't know you were that bad off, Hassan. You never said anything. I would have helped. You know that. You're my closest friend."

"You never asked."

"I should have. For that I am sorry." Nouri gestured. "Please, come in. We will talk." He glanced at Anna who gave him a curt nod.

Hassan caught their exchange. He hesitated, then came inside. They sat somewhat awkwardly in the living room.

"Can I get you a drink, Hassan?" Anna asked.

He shook his head.

"I can't help feeling sad, Hassan," Nouri began. "You and I...we shared the same beliefs. All those discussions and plans to save the country. Yes, we opposed the shah. But our goal was a democratic government, not an Islamic republic. Don't you remember?"

Hassan gestured. "Idle chatter. The stuff of childhood. It is time to grow up. Especially since the referendum." Iranians had voted on the formation of an Islamic republic at the end of March.

"But what about our dreams?"

"It is necessary to wipe out the evils of the shah. To strip away Western influence. Iranians do not do well unless there is a strong leader. Democracy dilutes everything."

"Do you really believe that?" Anna asked softly.

Hassan stiffened. "Democracy breeds corruption, greed, and imperialism. Its culture is insidious. It has crept into films, music, clothing, even food. Shariah law will cleanse society. And keep our enemies at bay."

"Which enemies are those?" Nouri asked.

Hassan looked uncomfortable. "The Communist groups who are opposed to the Islamic republic. They have infected young people, especially at the universities. They are responsible for much of the unrest, you know."

Anna knew about the protests by leftists at Tehran University. There had been discussions about them among young Iranians at the IAS. But she didn't know how serious a threat the Communists really were. Maybe Hassan had fallen victim to the conspiratorial nature of some revolutionaries. It had happened before, during the activism of the Sixties, the French and Russian revolutions, movements throughout history, in fact.

"The students have a point, don't you think?" Nouri persisted. "The people who are running things now are not the people who led the opposition to the shah. This new government is made up of barely literate men with scruffy beards—you being the exception, of course. They have no idea how to run a country, to do what's needed. All they know how to do is call for revenge."

Anna remembered Laleh repeating the rock music line about the new boss being the same as the old boss.

Hassan crossed then uncrossed his legs. "It is true that power has shifted. But this is the future."

"It doesn't have to be," Nouri said.

"Do not be naïve, Nouri," Hassan said. "What's more, I'd advise you to be careful."

"Me?" Nouri sat up. "Why? What are you saying, Hassan?"

"It is known that you were once a Marxist. If you continue to identify yourself as one, you too might become an enemy of the Revolution." Anna heard an edge of warning in Hassan's voice.

Nouri's face darkened. "Is that a threat?"

"It is a suggestion. In fact, you might even consider growing a beard."

A wave of nausea climbed up Anna's throat. She stood up. "I'm sorry. I guess I'm not feeling well. I need to go upstairs. There is food in the kitchen, Nouri. Help yourself. You too, Hassan."

§

Though it had to be the warmest night of the year, Anna and Nouri held tight to each other in bed as if it was a frigid Chicago winter. Neither of them wanted to let go.

"What do you think?" Anna whispered.

"I don't know."

"It makes me nervous."

Nouri ran the back of his hand down her cheek. "Don't be afraid. I'll protect you."

Anna snuggled in closer. "We knew he was changing."

"Yes, but I never thought he'd go this far."

Anna stared at the liquid moonlight pouring through the window. "What did he say after I left?"

Nouri was quiet for a moment. Then, "Nothing of importance."

"Was it about me?"

"Why do you ask?"

"Because I thought I heard you mention my name."

Nouri didn't reply.

"Nouri…"

He cleared his throat. "Well, he did say something."

"What?"

"He thinks you are too outspoken."

A sour taste came into her mouth.

"He said it is not good for a woman to argue or contradict a man. Especially about politics or religion."

Twenty-three

How can they possibly expect us to call it '*Vali-ye Asr*'? It's *Pahlavi* Avenue, and always will be," Laleh fumed on a hot summer day. She and Anna were driving to a bookstore near Tehran University. Many of the streets in Tehran had been renamed in an effort to purge Iran of all traces of the shah. Anna remembered Nouri pointing the street out when they'd first arrived in Tehran. Still, whether they called it *Pahlavi* Avenue or *Vali-ye Asr* Street, it remained one of the longest streets in the world.

"I can't believe they're calling Shahyad Aryamehr, Azadi Tower." Laleh wiped her brow. The heat had crept inside, despite the Mercedes' air conditioning. "Freedom Tower! What freedom? What happened to all their promises of women's rights, democracy, and justice?"

Anna couldn't disagree. The new government had continued its crackdown on counter-revolutionaries, recently executing more than twenty people in just one day. The problem was their definition of "counter-revolutionary." It seemed to change depending on who was being targeted. As far as Anna could tell, it was anyone in a high position who was not an Islamic fundamentalist.

And yet life in Iran had a semblance of normality. People went to work. Ate in restaurants. Drove their cars. It was a parallel state of being, this new normal; like an eerie fun house mirror that distorted and bent reality. Anna knew she had to be careful, lest the edges came apart and the chaos just beneath the surface leaked out.

Some people were still suffused with the glow of victory over the shah. Like Hassan, they lavished unconditional praise on the new republic, excusing and rationalizing any decision—no matter how despotic—as necessary. Others, like Laleh, believed the situation was just temporary, that life would somehow revert to the way it used to be. Still others believed Iran would become a democratic society, and they persisted in protesting and pressing for free elections.

Anna still worked at the IAS, and Nouri at the Metro. In fact, the trip to the bookstore was Anna's idea. She was looking for a book of poetry by e e cummings to use in class, and the bookstores near the university were her best bet. She would have preferred to take a cab, so she could browse by herself, but Nouri refused to let her to go alone. She had to assure him that Laleh would be with her at all times.

They found a spot near Laleh Park, a few blocks from campus. "When I was little, Baba-joon told me the park was named after me." Laleh giggled. "For years I believed him."

Anna managed a wan smile. She and Nouri had been married almost a year now. She missed her own father.

They walked down Azar Avenue to the intersection of Azar and Enqelab-e Eslami Avenue, Laleh continuing to complain about the new street names. The heat was oppressive, and Anna didn't know which was worse: the muggy heat of the east coast back home, or the sweltering air of Iran. Either way, her t-shirt clung to her back, and her jeans felt heavy. A clearly pregnant young woman, her tummy protruding, passed them. Anna felt a pang. When would she have her own family—children to cherish, children who would fill the house with laughter, children who would need her and would never abandon her?

The English language bookstore was small and cramped. As they entered, the odors of mold and dust drifted over them. Books crowded the shelves and counters, and a tower of them on the floor wobbled precariously. Nothing seemed organized, and yet Anna instantly felt a powerful connection. All the books were in English. Her pang of homesickness swelled.

The proprietor came out from a room in the back. An elderly man with a flowing white beard, his face was as worn and faded as one of his books. He looked them over. "What do you want?" he asked in heavily accented English.

Anna explained that she was looking for poetry by e e cummings

The bookseller's eyebrows arched. He eyed her suspiciously. "Why do you ask for that?"

She explained. "Do you have any of his work?"

Another skeptical glare. Anna was uneasy, as if he knew a secret about her and wanted her to know that he did. But she continued to meet his eyes. Finally, his glare subsided, and his features morphed into a sad expression. He led her to a bookshelf against one wall and pointed a finger toward the top shelf. "You see?"

Anna followed his finger. There was a gap in the display of books.

"I no longer carry e e cummings. They took it away. My Shakespeare also."

Anna's jaw dropped. "Who? Why?"

"The komitehs." The local armed revolutionary groups sanctioned by Khomeini. In the weeks and months since the revolution, they had amassed broad power to weed out and punish immoral behavior. "Shakespeare is counter-revolutionary, they claim. Too Western."

"But that's absurd."

"Not to them." He flipped up his hand, then clasped his palms together. "But I still have some Robert Browning, which they haven't confiscated. And Emily Dickinson. Her poems should do nicely."

"Why don't you appeal the confiscated books? Let them know they've gone too far?"

If anything, the bookseller's expression turned even more morose. "You are young. And American, yes?" When Anna nodded, he said, "You think, if you demonstrate, everything will change." He snapped his fingers. "Just like that. Americans are like that."

Anna wanted to interject, but he stayed her with a raised palm.

"It is different here. We have been victims for years. Invaders, the shah, now the revolution. It is all the same."

Anna recalled what Nouri had told her the day they met: how

Persians craved their martyrdom; how they cherished the fatalism that accompanied it. But she couldn't accept it. It was so…well…un-American. "All the more reason to stop it. You have to do something."

"What I have to do is survive."

§

Thirty minutes later, Anna and Laleh emerged from the store, Anna carrying a book of Emily Dickinson's poetry. She was the recipient of ta'arof in reverse, she thought ironically. The bookstore owner kept pressing the book on her, but would not allow her to pay. She stowed it under her arm. They cut through the university campus on their way back to the car. Anna still felt uneasy. This was not the way it was supposed to be. After the shah was deposed, freedom was supposed to blossom with no restrictions, no limitations. Certainly no prohibition on literature.

"Confiscating anti-revolutionary propaganda is one thing," she said, more to herself than to Laleh. "But Shakespeare? e e cummings? They're about as political as that lamppost," she said, gesturing toward it.

Laleh's lower lip protruded in a pout. She was subdued as well.

The heat must have made sound travel farther than usual, because Anna heard a muezzin's far-off call for mid-afternoon prayer. The students bustling around them ignored it, seemingly oblivious to anything not directly in their path. Tehran University, like the University of Chicago, was a simmering cauldron of Leftists, Marxists, even Islamic fundamentalists. Indeed, the university was the source of most of the unrest Hassan had warned Nouri about.

Anna observed the young people swirling around her. The new government had mandated that women wear hijab, a head covering, but it didn't appear as if the mandate was being enforced. Most of the girls wore jeans and t-shirts, and some were in miniskirts. But more than one was wearing a head scarf, and she even saw a woman in a chador.

As they neared Laleh Park, they saw two young men in dark green uniforms slipping a piece of paper under the windshield wipers of the Mercedes. Revolutionary Guards.

"Oh no! What now?" Laleh hurried over and grabbed the paper. A ticket, Anna saw. Laleh launched into a rapid stream of Farsi. The men's eyes narrowed. When she took a breath, one of them snickered and asked a question. His hostile tone was evident. He was probably asking if this was her car.

Laleh waved her arms and talked even faster. Anna could only catch a few words, but it seemed as if she was challenging their authority.

Anna stiffened.

Laleh grew more agitated, the men more officious. Finally, Laleh threw up her hands in disgust, then dug into her purse. Pulling out her wallet, she extracted a wad of rials, separated them into two piles, and thrust one at each of the men.

Anna's stomach started to churn. Laleh shouldn't have done that.

The men's mouths opened. They stared at the money, at Laleh, then at each other. One of them flicked his hand in disgust, as if she'd handed them excrement. Laleh made a disparaging comment. The next thing Anna knew, the other man spit at Laleh.

Laleh's eyes widened in shock. She looked like she'd been slapped. Anna knew she had to intervene before the situation escalated. She forced herself to act and grabbed Laleh by the shoulders.

"Get in the car, Laleh. Right now."

Laleh glanced at Anna but didn't move. It was as if she was under a spell. The men loomed large and threatening, close enough that Anna could smell their body odor.

"Laleh!" Anna repeated. "Did you hear me? Get in the car!"

Laleh blinked. Anna half pushed, half pulled her over to the passenger door, threw it open, shoved her in. "Give me the damn key."

Laleh didn't react.

Anna grabbed Laleh's bag, fished inside, pulled out her car keys and the ticket. As she hurried around to the driver's side, the men were still in front of the car. One spread his legs and planted his hands on his hips.

Anna waved the ticket. "I am sorry. *Ma'zerat meekhâm.*" She threw out every polite Farsi term she knew. "Excuse me. *Bebakhshid.* Thank you. *Mamnoonam.*"

The two men eyed Anna skeptically. They had to know she was not Iranian. Did they know she was American, from the land of the Great Satan itself? She broke eye contact with them and looked down. Submissive. Obedient. Waiting for mercy. After a long moment, during which Anna was convinced they planned to arrest both her and Laleh, they stepped back.

Anna threw herself in the car, a wave of relief washing over her. Laleh stared straight ahead. Anna keyed the engine and put it into drive. As she pulled away she gave a little wave in the rearview mirror. "*Khodâ hâfez.* Good-bye."

"*Allâho Akbar!*" one of the guards shouted.

Twenty-four

It was horrid," Laleh complained to Maman-joon when they arrived back at the Samedis' home. "I was parked legally, but they gave me a ticket anyway. For twenty-five tomans."

Laleh seemed to have made a full recovery from her earlier distress. But Anna hadn't. For a few minutes at the park, she thought they would not be coming home. Her sister-in-law was clearly spoiled, but she wasn't an idiot. Given the situation, she should have toned it down, Anna thought. Not made herself a target. She debated whether to mention it, perhaps just in passing, but when she saw Maman-joon's face, she kept her mouth shut.

Of everyone in the Samedi family, Anna's relationship with Parvin was the most fragile. Parvin was unfailingly polite. She asked all the right questions and smiled at all the right times, but Anna sensed they had little in common. Maman-joon was raised in an observant Islamic family, where a woman's goals were to marry well, raise a family, and honor Islamic traditions.

All of which, of course, was fine with Anna, but put her at a disadvantage. Maman-joon was committed to doing the proper thing for the family. Like the wedding: invitations were sent to all the right people, and the seating arrangements and menu had demanded hours of planning. For Parvin, her family's place in society was her priority. That, and saving face. Parvin couldn't quite understand why Anna didn't share her values. In fact, sometimes she seemed surprised by what came out of Anna's mouth.

Parvin had changed since the revolution. More strands of grey were threaded through her hair. Her appearance, while still tasteful, was less precise, as if she no longer cared about choosing the perfect accessories. She wore a perpetually worried look, as if she'd lost her anchor and was drifting along an unpredictable current. Now, as she listened to Laleh whine about the men and the car, Maman-joon gazed first at her daughter, then Anna. Her lips thinned to a tight frown. "Are you sure you weren't parked over the time limit?"

"I'm sure, Maman. It was because I drive a Mercedes. I know it. No other cars on the street had a ticket. They wanted to harass me because of who I am."

And now they have her license plate number, Anna thought. She didn't say it aloud.

Laleh stood up and crossed her arms. "I've had it with this country. I want to leave."

Parvin leaned forward, her face registering shock. "What are you saying, Laleh? You can't leave your family. You're not eighteen." Eighteen was the age of maturity for women in Iran.

Laleh rolled her eyes. "If Baba gives me permission, I can." She turned to Anna. "You and Nouri ought to go too."

Maman-joon wrung her hands. "You don't mean that, Laleh. You're just upset."

"Sure, Maman." Laleh frowned and ran upstairs to change her clothes, leaving Maman-joon and Anna together.

Parvin stood up, nervous and agitated. "I will make tea."

Anna forced a smile. "Let me help you." But Parvin shook her head and disappeared into the kitchen.

Anna stayed in the living room, thinking about what Laleh had said. Things were deteriorating, but Iran was Anna's home now. Nouri and his family were her protection, her security. Things were bound to get better. After all, this was just the first wave of the revolution, and history taught that the first series of changes could often be extreme. It took time to moderate.

Anna picked up the newspaper from the couch. More executions had been ordered, and the faces of the dead were plastered across the front page. The paper was in Farsi, but she knew the men in the photos had been accused of treason. She wondered if there was any truth to the charges. She was skimming the pages waiting for Maman-joon to bring tea when the doorbell rang. She automatically got up. "I'll get it."

Opening the door, she was astonished to see a woman dressed in a chador. The only visible part of her body was her face, but that face was familiar. When she realized who it was, she gasped. "Roya? Is that you?"

Roya smiled. Anna's lips parted. First Hassan, now Roya. She suppressed her shock and pulled herself together. "Please, come in. We were just about to have tea. Will you join us?"

"*Albatteh*. Of course. That would be nice," Roya said. As she entered, Anna couldn't help thinking that Roya had put on a costume to audition for some still unexplained role.

"Maman-joon, Laleh," Anna called. "Roya is here."

When Maman-joon stuck her head out of the kitchen and saw Roya, her eyes widened too. She asked Roya a brief question in Farsi and received a briefer response. Then Maman-joon and Roya exchanged smiles. Anna felt self-conscious in her jeans and t-shirt. Laleh came downstairs wearing a skimpy miniskirt and tank top. When she spied the chador-clad Roya, her mouth opened. "What in the world are you wearing?"

Roya blinked and clutched the chador beneath her chin. "I want to be closer to Allah. This helps."

"I don't believe this," Laleh sniffed. "Has everyone in Iran gone crazy?"

"I can't speak for anyone else," Roya said quietly. "I just know it is right for me."

Laleh was adamant. She gestured toward Roya. "But what does it say about a woman's place in society? You're allowing yourself to be viewed as a subordinate. Maybe even opening yourself up to abuse, not to mention all the other barbaric laws they're talking about."

"The Qur'an says that 'wrongdoers shall be known by their looks.'

I am not a wrongdoer."

"Oh god." Laleh grabbed her head in her hands just as Maman-joon walked in with a tray of tea and biscuits. She put down the tray. She had clearly overheard the tussle between Laleh and Roya because she spoke to Laleh, and her tone was curt. Then she looked at Anna and waved her hand.

"What is it, Maman-joon?" Anna asked.

"She wants you to know that *her* mother wears a chador," Laleh said sullenly.

"I remember," Anna replied. "You know, Laleh, everyone should have the right to express their religious beliefs. No matter how much we personally disagree. Freedom means that Roya should be able to wear a chador and pray ten times a day if she wants. That's the mark of a true democracy."

"But the chador is a symbol of repression. Just like any form of hijab. Even the father of the shah realized that. That's why he banned it."

"It's unfair to label a woman who wears hijab repressed," Anna persisted. "In the same way you can't call a woman who wears a miniskirt liberated."

Laleh crossed her arms, but Roya flashed Anna a beatific smile. Even Maman-joon looked pleased. She leaned toward the tea tray and spoke in English, something she rarely did. "Let me pour tea for you, my daughters."

Roya shook her head. "Thank you, Maman-joon, but I am fine."

A moment of silence passed while Maman-joon gave glasses of tea to Laleh and Anna. Anna turned to Roya. "Nouri is still at work. Is there something special you needed, Roya?"

"Actually, I came to see you."

"Me?" Anna frowned. "Why?"

"I…I…" She peered at Laleh. "I was hoping we could talk privately."

Anna glanced at Maman-joon and Laleh, then stood up. "*Bebakhshid.* Excuse me. I'll just be a minute." She turned to Roya. "Come with me."

Laleh waved an indifferent hand. Anna led Roya out to the patio. The curtain of heat was so thick that Anna's t-shirt promptly went limp.

And it was made of a flimsy thin material. She could only imagine how Roya felt, wrapped in the heavy folds of the chador. They sat at the patio table in the shade of the fruit trees, which, unfortunately, offered scant cooling.

Roya cleared her throat. "There are many Iranians who do not like Americans. The mullahs, especially, think the US is meddling in Iran for our oil."

"They have reason to think so. Mosaddeq was overthrown by the CIA in 1953 for exactly that."

"Yes, I know." Roya ran her tongue around her lips. "But, Anna, I like you. And I want to thank you for defending my choice to wear hijab. You are a fair-minded person." She hesitated. "Unfortunately, your boss is not."

"You mean Charlie? At the IAS?"

Roya nodded. "She is very...opinionated."

"So what?" Anna's neck was ringed with sweat. She looked over at Roya. Her expression was solemn. "What are you trying to tell me, Roya?"

"I...I am afraid for what might happen to her."

Anna remembered the scene at the Samedis' Nowruz party several months earlier, when Charlie argued with Hassan—quite belligerently, she recalled. She wiped her neck with the back of her hand. "Afraid? In what way?"

"I...hear things, you know. What people are planning to do to make sure Shariah law is followed."

"Are you saying Charlie's in danger?"

Roya didn't answer.

"Is that why you've come? To warn me about Charlie?"

Roya looked at the ground. "As I said, I think *you* are a fair person. I am glad Nouri has you." She hesitated again. "He has made a wise choice."

For the first time Anna saw a wistfulness in Roya's eyes. Roya *did* care for Nouri, she thought. And yet she'd made an effort to befriend Anna. A panoply of emotions ran through Anna. She reached out to touch Roya's arm. *"Khayli mamnoon,* Roya. Thank you."

Roya nodded. "I know you are a Christian, but when you married Nouri you became Muslim, you know."

"Well…technically."

"I think you could become a good Muslim. A very good one."

Anna was suddenly uneasy. She chose her words carefully. "I appreciate your faith in me, Roya. I am honored. But Islam is not my way."

Roya smiled. "Perhaps not now, but one never knows what the future holds, does one? Who would have thought a year ago we would have an Islamic Republic?"

That much is true, Anna thought.

§

While her father-in-law drove her home, Anna mulled over what Roya said. Should she say something to Charlie? Charlie was a warm-hearted soul, and her intentions were good. But if she was drawing attention to herself, for whatever reason, it wasn't good for her—or the Iran-American Society. On one hand, Anna couldn't believe Charlie was in danger. She'd been married to an Iranian and living here for seven years. She was practically part of the landscape. On the other hand, times were different. Nothing was as it had been.

And what about Roya? Had she become a true believer, a Muslim missionary intent on spreading the Islamic gospel? Or was Roya a lost soul, substituting religion for the parts of her life that were lacking? It was not unusual for young people to join a cult—it certainly happened enough in the States. But Roya came from an observant family, and she willingly went on hajj with her grandmother. Did that make her more committed? Or more lost?

Anna thanked Baba-joon and got out at the gate to their house. She wondered what would have happened if Roya and Nouri *had* ended up together. She suspected that Maman-joon would have been thrilled. In fact, she wondered now if that was why Maman-joon was so cool towards her. Did she secretly wish things had turned out differently? That Roya had become her daughter-in-law instead?

Twenty-five

The evening air was tinted with the aroma of barbecued beef as Nouri walked up to the house. Anna must have been cooking *kabab kubideh*, one of his favorites. He recalled her telling him this morning that she planned to do so. He opened the door and went inside.

"Nouri? Is that you? How was your day?"

He ignored the smell, Anna too. He trudged up the stairs, opened the door to their room, and threw himself on the bed.

"Nouri?"

He heard Anna's light tread on the steps. He slid a pillow over his head.

"Nouri, what's wrong? Are you sick?"

He didn't answer. She came in and sat on the edge of the bed. "What's the matter, Azizam?"

Nouri said nothing. He knew he was frightening her, but didn't know how to begin. For once he wished Anna was less perceptive. She could tell in a heartbeat— without his saying a word—if something was wrong. He pulled the pillow more tightly over his face.

"Nouri, Azizam…" Her voice was tense. "Whatever it is, please, tell me. We'll work through it."

Maybe she was right. Anna was the type of woman who made everything seem lighter. He relaxed his grip on the pillow and lifted it off his face. Anna was staring at him, her face filled with concern. He reached for her. She snuggled in close, resting her head on his chest. He wondered if she could hear his heartbeat. He inhaled her special scent: sweet, musky, yet slightly metallic. It used to drive him wild. It still did when he let it. He could get lost in her. She made him feel whole. But now was not the time. He sighed.

After a moment, she raised her head and gave him a tentative smile. "So?"

Another sigh. "They cut me down to three days a week at work. They're not getting the funding from the new government that was promised, and they can't afford to keep staffing at capacity."

Anna's eyebrows arched. "Oh."

"They say it's just temporary," he hastened to add. "They say things should sort themselves out by the end of the summer."

"I'm sure that's true," Anna murmured.

"Yes, but what will I do if they don't?"

"Don't worry." Anna brushed her hand across his forehead. "It could be a blessing in disguise. We'll have more time together, you and I." She smiled. "To travel, see other parts of the country. Or...," she grinned, "whatever."

He forced a smile.

"Of course, you could look for another job if you want, but if it's just temporary, why not just relax and enjoy it?"

He gave her a halfhearted nod.

Her brow furrowed. "You know, you could always use the time to finish your thesis."

Nouri considered it. The thesis was from another time, another place. He was past academia. He had no interest in going back.

As if she knew what he was thinking, Anna shrugged. "It was just an idea." She hesitated. "Maybe your father has a suggestion."

He shook his head. "I can't keep asking Baba to make things right. It's time I learned to rely on myself."

"I understand."

But she didn't. Not really. Baba-joon would do anything for the family. In fact, he would like nothing better than for Nouri to ask for help. He considered it his duty to take care of his own. Which was why

149

Nouri couldn't go to him. He had his own family now. Or would have. He wanted to make his mark himself.

Anna continued to stroke his forehead. "You know, Nouri, you could work freelance. Everyone needs engineers. We can put the word out to friends and family and neighbors. You could become a consultant."

Nouri looked up, intrigued. "A consultant." He let the word roll off his tongue.

"Why not? In the States they make a fortune."

He brightened. "I like that. Maybe I can build a store, or remodel someone's home. Something like that."

"Exactly." Anna smiled. "If you want, after supper we can make a list of people you could call."

Nouri smiled again, a genuine one this time. He had a plan. A solution. The steel bands around his chest loosened. "Thank you, Anna. You are the perfect balm for my soul." He pulled her close again. This time he allowed himself to inhale her scent and wallow in it. Now he was ready. He rolled on top of her.

"We can't, Nouri. Dinner is cooking."

He raised himself on his elbows. "Let it burn."

§

The doorbell sounded a few hours later. Nouri was watching TV and Anna was washing the dishes. "I'll go," Nouri called.

When he opened the door, no one was there. He glanced left, right, straight ahead, but saw nothing. But the house was sheltered behind a brick wall so his view was limited. Someone could have been there and retreated through the gate. But the gate was closed and looked undisturbed.

"Who is it, sweetheart?" Anna said from inside.

"No one."

She came out of the kitchen, wiping a saucepan with a towel. "That's odd."

Nouri walked down to the gate, opened it, and peered up and

down the street. No one. He shrugged, turned around, came back. A small brown package was wedged between the door and the wall of the house. "Look."

Anna came out. "What is it?"

Nouri leaned over and picked it up. Something substantial was inside. He undid the wrapping. Inside was a leather-bound book. He pulled it out. Turned it over. "This is strange. It's a copy of the Qur'an. But it's in English."

Anna's eyes got big.

"I don't get it. The Qur'an in English? Who would do that? Why?"

Anna inclined her head. Then a knowing expression unfolded across her face. "Oh, my god. I think I know who dropped it off."

"Who?"

"Roya."

"Roya? But why?"

"It's a long story. Come in and I'll tell you."

Twenty-six

At the end of July, Shapour Bakhtiar, who had served as the last prime minister before the revolution, emerged in Paris, after six months in hiding, to claim there was no government in Iran, only feudal alliances that were breeding chaos. Around the same time, attacks by the Kurds in the north intensified, requiring the attention of the "feudal" government. Two weeks later, in retaliation for a leftist demonstration, Muslim militants attacked leftist headquarters, the library, and the law school at Tehran University. Classes were suspended, and because the Iran-American Society was so closely connected with the university, its programs were suspended as well.

Without classes to teach, Anna, like Nouri, was at loose ends. Instead of baking in Tehran's desert heat, they decided to go to the family's summer cottage on the Caspian Sea. The area was the vacation spot of choice for many Iranians, and the three provinces that bordered the sea were studded with homes and resorts. The Caspian coastal area, whose terrain and climate were different than Tehran's, had milder temperatures, lush vegetation, sandy beaches, and, of course, there was the water. In fact, Nouri told Anna the word "sea" was a misnomer: the Caspian was, in reality, a lake—the largest in the world, even larger than any of the Great Lakes.

The rest of the family stayed in Tehran to prepare for Ramadan, so Nouri and Anna took a long, meandering route northeast. They drove through the rocky Alborz Mountains. Steep reddish hills encroached on both sides of the pass, making the road seem fragile and temporary, as if it might disappear altogether if the mountains chose. Mount Damavand, the highest Alborz peak, loomed large and desolate, looking more sinister than it did from Tehran. Anna said the rocky soil reminded her of the Arizona desert.

The terrain flattened as they reached the steppes and forested foothills on the other side. The temperature was cooler, and the air was tinged with a slight fishy smell. Nouri's mood lightened along with the landscape. He rolled down his window and peered out at the horizon.

"Are we near the water?" Anna asked.

Nouri nodded and headed into town. Babolsar was once a major port on the southern tip of the Caspian, but was now known mostly as a resort town. He drove a few miles along the Babol River which was dotted with small boats. They stopped at the point where it flowed into the Caspian and gazed at the sandy beaches. Glints of cheerful sunshine danced on the water's surface. But there were fewer bathers than he remembered, and most of them were boys.

"This reminds me of the Chesapeake Bay."

"The bay is on your east coast?"

"Off the coast of Maryland. It stretches from Delaware down through Virginia. My father used to take me there every summer for hard-shell crabs. I never figured out how to crack them." She sounded wistful.

"You are homesick."

Anna's lip trembled. "Sometimes."

Nouri glanced over. Anna looked as if she had wanted to say something, then forced back whatever it was. They were both quiet as they got back into the car. Nouri drove to a cluster of houses hugging the beach a mile or so west of town. He threaded his way through newly paved streets. The trees flanking them were sparse and gnarly. They seemed to have stopped growing years ago, as if the continual struggle against water and wind had vanquished them. Many of the houses were just one story, but Nouri rounded a bend and parked in front of a two-story home.

"We're here."

He got the bags out of the trunk while Anna climbed out. She planted her hands on her hips. "Some cottage."

He heard the sarcasm in her voice and tried to see the house through her eyes. It was not as large as his father's Tehran home, but larger than theirs in Shemiran. It had three bedrooms, a large living and dining area, and a sloping back yard that led to a private beach. A dock, which they shared with their neighbors, sat to one side.

They went inside. The home was well-equipped, with modern appliances in the kitchen, a washer and dryer, even a TV. Anna stood in the kitchen and slowly turned around. "Sometimes I forget how wealthy your family really is."

Nouri wasn't sure how to interpret her comment. "Does it make a difference? Between you and me, I mean?"

Anna threw him a fleeting glance with an expression he'd never seen before. It was flat, almost detached; as if he were a specimen under a microscope. Then, as quickly as it came, it was gone, and she smiled warmly. "Of course not. But it helps me understand how much is at stake."

"What do you mean 'at stake'?" Nouri retaliated. "Your father is not exactly impoverished."

"True," Anna said. Again she flashed Nouri that detached, objective look.

He picked up their bags and carried them to the steps. "Come upstairs, and I'll show you where we'll sleep." He turned around. She was looking through the picture window at the water. "Well?"

She glanced back over her shoulder, as if unwilling to give up the view.

"You were the one who said we should enjoy our time, together. So…" Nouri gave her a sly smile. "Let's do that."

§

Although the resort town of Babolsar was more casual than Tehran, the tentacles of the revolution had stretched there as well. Nouri learned that the public beach had been forced to segregate—that's why there were fewer bathers. Furthermore, women bathers were frowned upon; bathing suits were an affront to Islam. As a result, he and Anna spent most of their time on their private beach, swimming, sunbathing, and running the Samedis' small motorboat across the harbor. Anna asked Nouri to keep the TV off, so evenings were spent reading or playing cards. One day they drove to Sisangan National Park and hiked through the forest.

By the fourth day, though, Nouri was restless. While he had no illusions that life would return to what it was, he sensed he was missing out on something. He wasn't sure what, but he wanted to go back to Tehran to find out. Anna didn't want to go back, but Nouri insisted. He tried to accommodate her by taking the long way home. They rode along the coast, then cut south on Chalus Road, one of the most beautiful roads in Iran. Like the one they'd come down, it was a twisty mountain pass hugged by the Alborz. On the Caspian side, a carpet of green covered the hills, made even greener by a glittering sun but as they approached Tehran the landscape reverted to barren brown rock.

Nouri decided to stop at his parents' house to drop off the key to the cottage. As they headed over, Anna pointed to something on the side of the street. "Slow down."

"What is it?"

"I don't know. But this is the third one I've seen."

Nouri slowed. Anna pointed to a blue box on a pole next to a newspaper stand. A yellow ornamental design ran along the sides of the box. Nouri pulled to the curb to study it. Up close, he could see the yellow was actually a pair of hands clasping the box around its edges. They were pointing up. A few words of Farsi were scrawled across the box. "I know what they are," Nouri said. "They're alms boxes."

"Alms boxes? What for?"

Nouri shrugged. "I assume the new government wants people to donate money to the less fortunate."

"Really?" Anna didn't bother to keep the edge out of her voice. "Who do you suppose the money really goes to?"

"Does it matter?"

"I guess not." As Nouri pulled away from the curb, she sighed. "Look. The posters are gone."

Nouri gazed at a brick wall, which until recently had been covered with movie posters, but was now pasted over with murals of Khomeini and other clerics.

Anna looked like she wanted to ask Nouri something. He looked away.

When they arrived at his parents' home, Nouri began to think they should have stayed at the beach. They'd only been away four days, but the atmosphere had changed. Baba-joon—usually a sharp dresser—was in wrinkled khakis, and the tails of his shirt hung out. His hair was more grizzled. In only four days, he'd aged dramatically.

He was glued to the TV, switching channels almost frantically. It didn't matter which he settled on. Every channel kept running photos of the "traitors" who'd been executed. Nouri wanted to tell him to turn the set off but, when he looked into his father's eyes, he hesitated. Those eyes were full of something he'd never seen. Not just worry. Despair.

An even bigger shock was his mother. Although it was mid-afternoon, she was still in her bathrobe. She hadn't combed her hair, and her skin looked pasty. She couldn't seem to sit still, and flitted nervously around the house. Nouri noticed a vial of pills on the coffee table. He arched his brows and flipped his hand in Laleh's direction. Laleh, who seemed to be the only one who hadn't changed, gave him a curt shake of the head that clearly meant "Don't ask."

He tried out a jovial greeting, but his parents, who usually welcomed him with open arms, barely acknowledged him. Nouri stood around for a moment, feeling awkward. At length Maman-joon darted to the TV and snapped it off. She turned back to Baba-joon.

"The pictures. Always the pictures. I can't take it anymore, Bijan." Her voice sounded taut and reedy.

Baba-joon got up, and slid his arms around her. She burst into tears.

A flash of fear shot up Nouri's spine. "What's going on, Baba, Maman? What happened?"

"I'll tell you—" Laleh started, but Baba-joon wagged a finger to cut her off.

"I'll do the talking, Laleh." His voice was brusque.

Nouri had heard that tone only twice before: once when he got into a car accident only a week after getting his permit; and again when he almost flunked his history course.

"Yousef, Aunt Mina's husband, was arrested and taken to prison," Baba said.

Mina wasn't really Nouri's aunt, but she and Roya's mother were Parvin's best friends. Nouri suddenly felt as if his feet were stuck in concrete.

"Why?" Anna asked softly.

Nouri was startled. He'd forgotten Anna was there.

"They say he is a traitor to the revolution."

"What did he do?"

Baba-joon spread his hands. "Nothing. He has a chain of movie theaters. Sometimes he showed Hollywood films, you know, with the sub-titles. Last week, they burned down one of his theaters, but apparently that wasn't enough. A few days ago they came to his house—his house, mind you—and arrested him for being an agent of the Great Satan."

"Why doesn't Aunt Mina just bribe someone to get him out?" Nouri asked.

Baba-joon shook his head. "She doesn't know who's in charge. Or where they took him. No one will tell her anything."

Maman jumped in. "It is Yousef today, but tomorrow it might be your Baba." She shuddered. She hurried over to the vial of pills, popped off the lid, shook one out, and dry swallowed it. Then she looked over at Anna. Anna's blonde hair had lightened from the sun, and her skin had a rosy glow. Nouri thought she looked like an angel, but Maman apparently didn't agree. The look Maman shot her was pure hostility. Why, Nouri had no idea, but he knew Anna felt it because she stepped back and seemed to shrink into herself.

But Maman-joon's hostility was short-lived, and her mood swung yet again. Now she began to wring her hands and wander around the living room. "We must put blackout paper over the windows," she said to no one in particular.

Baba-joon answered. "I told you before, no one can see in. The wall around the house protects us."

"Like it protected Yousef?" Maman's voice tightened even more. "Prying eyes are everywhere. We must put it up. Right away." She sat on the couch.

Baba-joon turned the TV back on. They saw shots of crowds at Friday prayers in the city of Qom where Khomeini now lived.

Laleh flicked a disapproving hand toward the TV. "Have you noticed the people who are now growing beards and dressing in chadors? A year ago they were at the disco in leisure suits and miniskirts. Currying favor with the shah. Now look at them."

Maman-joon made a shushing noise with her finger.

"It's true, Maman. And the guards are just boys playing with their shiny new toys."

"Machine guns aren't toys," Anna murmured.

"True," Laleh continued. "That's why we're forced to barricade ourselves in our house from dusk to dawn. You tell me. What kind of life is this?" She pursed her lips. "Shaheen left, you know. Went to London. He's smart. I'm going too. Just as soon as I can."

Maman-joon looked at her daughter and blinked.

Twenty-seven

Where have you been?" Nouri had a headache, and he knew he sounded cranky when Anna sailed through the front door the next afternoon. "I was worried."

"I'm sorry." Her cheeks were flushed, and there was a faint sheen of perspiration above her lip. "I was visiting Charlie."

He scowled. "I don't like you being on the street by yourself."

"I understand, Azizam, but it's been tough for her. With classes cancelled, there's not much to do."

"It's a tough time for everyone. Don't do it again, Anna."

"But she's my only real friend here."

"What if something happened to you? What if someone gave you a hard time? It's stupid. As for friends, you have Laleh."

"Laleh's family, and I love her. But Charlie is different. She's a friend I made myself. And I did think about it. I was careful."

Nouri gazed at her, still frowning. Then he changed the subject. Even though he knew she hadn't prepared anything, he asked, "What's for dinner?"

She threw him a look that said she knew what he was doing. But rather than challenging him, she went to the kitchen, opened the fridge and cabinets, and examined the contents. "I didn't have time to go to the market. Let's pick something up."

"All right. I'll go. You stay here."

"That's fine." She ran a hand through her hair. She looked like she wanted to tell him something.

"What?"

She shook her head. "It's nothing."

Nouri, edgy and anxious, wouldn't let it go. "It's not nothing. What?"

Anna blew out a breath. "I wasn't going to say anything, but… something happened today."

His stomach flipped. "What?"

"Charlie and I were at the fruit market near her house, and I bought an apple. I started eating it in the store, then walked outside. A man in a uniform was watching me. All of a sudden he snatched the apple out of my hand."

"Why?"

"He said I was eating it too seductively."

"What?"

"He said a woman shouldn't eat on the street. That it was a sin against Allah. That I could be taken for a whore."

Nouri rubbed his nose. In July, three women were accused of running a prostitution ring and executed. They were the first women ever to go before a firing squad in Iran.

"Then he told me I needed to wear a chador. That I would be forced to if I didn't do it voluntarily." She went back to the fridge and took out a wedge of cheese.

"Who was this person?"

"A Revolutionary Guard, I think. He wore the same uniform as Hassan."

"Are you sure?"

She took the cheese to the counter and set it down. "Sure about what? Whether it happened, or whether the man was a Guard?"

"Both."

She glared at him. "Nouri, don't you believe me?"

He backed off. "Of course I do."

"I was…well…it was creepy. I was shaken up." She took out a box of crackers from the cabinet, got a knife, and sliced the cheese. She placed everything on a plate and walked it out to the living room.

"So, what do you think?"

Nouri took a slice of cheese and a cracker, put them into his mouth, and chewed slowly. "It might not be a bad idea. At least temporarily."

"What? For me to wear a chador?"

"Not a chador. But some type of hijab. Something on your head. Everyone is crazy right now. And don't forget, Anna, you are an American. It's not wise to call attention to yourself."

"But what about my choice? I am not Iranian. Or a Muslim. Why should I do something I don't believe in?"

"It's just for a little while. It will keep people from bothering you. Things will ease soon."

"Do you think Laleh should wear hijab too?"

"It wouldn't hurt."

Anna planted her hands on her hips. "Don't you see a double standard here?"

He shrugged. "It's just outside the house. Inside, behind our walls, you can wear whatever you like." A sly smile came over him. "In fact, the less the better."

Anna didn't return the smile. "Charlie says there's a difference between 'foreign' wives and 'Iranian' wives—"

"Of course there is," Nouri cut in.

"Listen to me. She says it's in the *Shahnameh*. Iranian men want a woman to be childlike, obedient, and submissive. Only then can they be called 'pure Iranian.' I think that's nonsense, and I won't do it."

Nouri picked up another cracker and a piece of cheese. "I understand, Anna. I don't expect it of you here. But in the outside world…it would be safer."

Anna was quiet for a moment. Then, "Nouri, maybe we should leave Iran for a while. We can go to Paris and visit my mother. I haven't seen her in over a year, and she's dying to meet you. Our wedding anniversary is coming up. I'd love to show you Paris. Or we could go to the States for a visit. Until things calm down. What do you think?"

Nouri chewed his snack. "I don't know. I have the Metro project. And what about the family? Baba and Maman-joon need us."

Anna hesitated. "Maybe they should think about leaving too."

"Baba has an important job. Maman has never lived abroad. Iran is their home. They will never leave."

"A lot of people, especially the wealthy, are sending their money to Swiss banks. And then leaving."

"How do you know that?"

"Charlie."

"How does she know?"

"She's the director of the IAS. She travels in those circles."

"Baba-joon will never leave Iran," he repeated. He hoped his tone sounded as emphatic as he wanted it to.

"But you can."

Nouri frowned.

"Will you at least think about it?"

He sensed that was all she wanted. "Of course." He went to her, putting his arms around her and pulling her close. "Now, let's stop discussing such depressing matters."

She didn't react. He took it as acquiescence and started to massage the back of her neck with one hand. With the other he tipped up her chin and kissed her deeply. Usually he heard a quiet sigh from her when they connected. It was her signal that she loved how he loved her. That she had surrendered to the physical. But this evening it wasn't there. He kissed her again, his tongue probing hers. Then she did something she'd never done before. She pulled away.

"Not now, Nouri."

"Ah, but Anna, I cannot be with you and not want to make love to you. That Guard was right, you know. You are very seductive. Even when you are not eating an apple."

"Just hold me, okay?" She searched his face.

"But you are my wife."

"Nouri, please." She looked like she might cry.

"Don't worry, Azizam. I will put a smile on your face, I promise."

She let him lead her up the stairs.

Twenty-eight

The day Nouri was arrested began like any other hot August morning. He and Anna discussed their plans for the day over a breakfast of tea and fruit. Nouri would be going to the Metro offices. He expected to be back by mid-afternoon. Anna would stay home, and then they would go to Nouri's parents for dinner.

Nouri went upstairs to take a shower. He liked a vigorous flow. He imagined the gushing water was a noisy, pulsating waterfall. He was soaping his chest when a bearded man in a military uniform burst into the bathroom and tore aside the shower curtain.

"*Ay vây!*" Nouri yelled. "Oh my God!"

"You are Nouri Samedi?" the man shouted in Farsi.

Nouri quickly covered his privates with his hands. Water streamed down his back and legs. He blinked rapidly. "Who are you? What are you doing in here?"

The man ignored his questions and twisted off the spigot. "Get out and put on some clothes," he ordered.

Afterwards, Nouri didn't know how he summoned up the presence of mind to take a stand, but he refused to move. "Get out of my house, or I'll call the authorities."

"Who do you think we are?" The man laughed scornfully, then pulled out a gun and aimed it at him. "Now do what I say."

Slowly Nouri wrapped a towel around his waist, stepped out of the shower and the bathroom. A second bearded guard stood in the hall, also brandishing a gun.

"Who are you?" Nouri demanded.

There was no answer. He tried one more time. "You have no right to do this. Do you know who I am?"

A fist smashed into his face. Pain exploded across his nose and mouth. He staggered back. His towel dropped to the floor. His hand flew to his cheek. The room started spinning. He tasted blood in the back of his throat. As he fell, he thought he heard Anna scream, but it was coming from a distance. He curled into a fetal position.

Through a haze of pain, he heard one of the guards say, "Find his clothes." The other guard grunted.

"Tell us where your clothes are," the first guard barked. "Unless you want to come with us naked."

"In the closet," Nouri croaked. He was still curled up on the floor. A moment later, something was thrown on top of him. A shirt and pair of pants.

"Get dressed."

Nouri rolled over and sat up. A wave of nausea threatened to overwhelm him, but he tamped it down. His hands shook, his stomach cramped. "Where…where is my wife?"

"She has not been harmed."

Stiffly, painfully, Nouri got dressed and stumbled down the steps. Anna sat on the living room couch, held at gunpoint by a third guard. Her face was ashen and her fists were clenched. A look of terror contorted her face.

"Call Baba," he said.

She nodded. Then one of the guards pulled out a blindfold and put it over Nouri's head.

"What are you doing?" Nouri shouted. "Take it off. I am not a common thief."

The guard shoved him into the wall. Nouri crumpled to the floor. Anna screamed.

"That was just for show," the leader scoffed. "He is not hurt." To Nouri. "Get up! Now."

As Nouri struggled to his feet, he staggered forward. His head felt loose on his neck. One of the men grabbed him under his armpits.

"Get him out of here."

"Where are you taking him?" Anna asked. There was no response. "Please. I'm begging you. Where is he going?"

Their reply was to slam the door.

§

The car ride seemed endless. Without sight, Nouri concentrated on sounds and smells. The car's windows were down; horns blared, engines accelerated, angry drivers shouted. He was still in Tehran. With no air conditioning, he inhaled the rancid body odor of his captors. Every so often, he caught a whiff of hot asphalt and gasoline. Still, he was disoriented, and each swerve of the car made him nauseous. After a couple of sharp turns, he gagged. Bile rose in his throat.

"I'm...I'm going to be sick," he stammered.

"You'd better not," a hostile voice replied.

It was too late. Nouri vomited all over the back seat. The stench permeated the car's interior.

"*Ah...Mâdar ghahbeh! Estefragh kard!* Oh no!" one of the guards yelled. "The son of a bitch threw up!"

There was a brief silence. Then, "Show him what we do to traitors who damage the property of the Islamic Republic."

A blow slammed into Nouri's cheek. He cried out and slumped against the door. His ears rang, and his head felt like a whirling dervish. He gulped down air. Ironically, the blinding pain obliterated his other sensations and, for a moment, his stomach settled.

The men muttered to each other, but there was no real conversation. Drops of sweat ran down Nouri's back. He wondered what he'd done wrong. He wanted to beg them to let him go. He would have confessed to anything, just to make the nightmare end. What did they want?

Finally, the car stopped. He tried to estimate how long they'd been driving, but he'd lost all sense of time. He could still hear the drone of

Tehran traffic, which meant he was still downtown. A good omen. If they'd taken him to Evin Prison on the northwest side of the city, there would be far less noise.

The men dragged him out of the car and shoved him forward. Nouri lurched to one side. Someone grabbed the back of his collar and pushed him forward again. Nouri doubled over—whoever was yanking his shirt was also choking his windpipe. They stumbled up a few steps and entered a building with a squeaky door. They dragged him up a flight of steps. Then another.

The men paused to confer. Then someone propelled him down a hall. A door opened, and he was thrust into a room. It was at least ten degrees hotter inside, and the air reeked of stale, dirty humans. A hand clamped down on his shoulder. Nouri collapsed onto a hard surface. A bench? Shackles were put around his legs. His range of movement was only a few inches.

He leaned his head against the wall, which mercifully felt cooler than the rest of the room. Footsteps shuffled away. The door slammed. He couldn't hear or smell anyone; he thought he was alone. He tried to gather his thoughts, but they drifted over him in snatches of panic.

He had no idea how much time passed. His throat grew parched, his lips felt like gravel. He was desperate for a glass of water. At the same time, he had to pee.

He wondered what they'd do if he wet his pants. An image of Anna, her face ashen and tight, flashed across his mind. Did she call Baba? Was he coming? How would they know where he was?

Finally he heard footsteps outside. More than one man. The door opened.

"Nouri Samedi?" The voice was high-pitched and thin. He couldn't be sure, but he didn't think he'd heard it before.

He lifted his chin. "Who wants to know?"

Footsteps approached and someone slapped him across the face. Nouri recoiled. His cheeks stung.

"You will speak respectfully," the voice ordered. "Do you understand?"

Nouri nodded.

"I cannot hear you."

"*Baleh.* Yes, sir."

Someone cleared his throat. Then, "Nouri Samedi, we have evidence that you have betrayed the revolution and Islam."

Nouri was about to scream "No!" but remembered the pain that came when they struck him. He shook his head vigorously.

"So you deny it?"

He nodded.

Someone thwacked the side of his head. Nouri fell sideways. His head throbbed. Hands roughly propped him up. He thought he might be sick again.

"We have evidence that you are part of the Mojahedin-e-Khalq."

Nouri struggled to rise above the fog of pain. The Mojahedin were a leftist group. They were accusing him of being a Communist.

"I am not a Communist. I work for the Metro project. I am not—"

"Shut up!" a new voice shouted in Farsi. "You will speak only to answer questions."

"Our intelligence says otherwise," the high-pitched voice barked. "We have proof."

"It is not true." Nouri stiffened, preparing himself for another blow, but for some reason it didn't come. Still the anticipation made him sweat. It trickled down his face, stinging his eyes under the blindfold. He blinked.

"If you confess, the pain will stop. If you do not, it will continue."

Nouri was in a no-win situation. Maybe he should confess. He couldn't take much more. But confess to what?

"You spent time in the land of the Great Satan. The avowed enemy of Islam. You even brought home Satan's wife as your own."

So they knew about Anna. Had they been spying on him?

The high-pitched voice kept going. "You have made your choice clear. You and your family." Nouri's stomach twisted at the mention of his family. Had they arrested Baba and Maman-joon?

"You abandoned your homeland," the voice continued. "You consorted with infidels and traitors. Tell me why we shouldn't hang you for treason."

Nouri tried to think. How did they know about his studies abroad? When he was in the US there was no Islamic Republic. Just the shah. And the protests against him.

The protests.

The fog lifted for a moment. The demonstration at Daley Plaza in Chicago. He and Anna. Massoud and the others. He'd had a bag on his head, but he took it off. He'd been warned not to. SAVAK might be taking photographs. At the time he didn't care.

Now he understood. SAVAK was gone, its leaders either in prison or dead. But what if a few guards had been SAVAK agents before the revolution? What if they'd shot—or found—pictures? And decided to use them to bolster their new role as guards?

His theory felt oddly satisfying. Perhaps it was just that he could still think clearly but, whatever the reason, it fueled a flash of courage. "I am no traitor or infidel. I fought for Iran. Against the shah."

"We know the truth. We have been watching you. Do you know what the revolution does to traitors?"

Nouri went rigid. This time the blow slammed into his gut. He doubled over. He couldn't catch his breath. His bladder released and he wet his pants, but he was in too much pain to care. What did they have on him? And who gave it to them? Did someone denounce him? As he struggled to sit up, he recalled that Hassan had warned him. Did Hassan know more than he'd admitted? Nouri knew his friend had changed. The question was how much.

§

Nouri was alone. He had no idea for how long. No idea whether it was day or night. He was still blindfolded, his stomach in knots. His eyes, mouth and nose—his entire face, in fact—was hot and swollen. The rest of his body ached. Chills alternated with sweat. No one would save him. They were going to kill him. Yet he was surprisingly calm. Even detached. Terror cannot last forever. It was too powerful an emotion. This must be how a condemned man felt. He wondered what Anna was doing. Where his parents were. Whether they would miss him.

Footsteps tromped down the hall. This was a busy place. Occasionally he heard a muffled scream. Someone in another room was being tortured. He felt no compassion, no pity. Just resignation.

At length, a pair of footsteps stopped outside his door. Odd that he felt proprietary about "his" room, but he figured he'd suffered enough to warrant a sense of ownership. The door opened, footsteps closed in. More than one person. They were probably not more than a foot away, but no one spoke. Nouri cocked an ear. Was this the end? Were they about to shoot or stab him? He took what could be his last breath.

Instead, someone ripped off his blindfold. Light flooded his eyes and he squeezed them shut against the glare. A moment later he cracked them open. He was seeing double. Four men—no, only two—wore the dark green uniforms that had become so familiar. One scowled at him, but the other had a neutral, disinterested expression, as if Nouri was simply a speck of dirt on his sleeve. Slowly his vision cleared.

This man bent down and unlocked his leg shackles. "You are free to go."

Nouri wasn't sure he'd heard him correctly.

"Get out."

Nouri peered at one guard, then the other. He blinked several times.

"Are you deaf? Go. Get out." The man's voice was gruff.

Nouri took a tentative step towards the door. He was unsteady, dizzy. He leaned a hand against the wall until he could get his balance. Everything hurt. But no one stopped him. He took another step. Then another. When he reached the door he looked both ways down the hall.

"Turn left."

Nouri shuffled down the hall to a waiting room with a desk and several chairs. Sitting in one of them was Baba-joon.

Twenty-nine

As Nouri sank into his father's arms, tears welled in Baba-joon's eyes. He, Nouri, must have looked half dead; he certainly felt it. At the same time relief surged through every pore of his body. He was going home. Baba-joon slipped his arm around Nouri's waist, and together they descended the stairs and exited the building.

Outside Nouri found himself in the heart of downtown Tehran. The streets were choked with pedestrians and traffic. The slanting rays of the sun indicated it was nearly evening. Nouri was surprised. What seemed to him an eternity was probably no more than eight hours. It was as if nothing was amiss.

Before he climbed into the car, he turned around to gaze at the building in which he'd been held captive. His left eye was almost swollen shut, but he caught a glimpse. Again he was surprised. It was an innocuous five-story office building. The windows were covered; then again, most Tehran windows were, to protect against the sun. Still, no one would ever imagine the abuse going on inside. Had it always been this way? Or did the new government convert the building into a makeshift torture chamber?

Baba-joon led him to the car. There was no driver today, so his father drove. Baba was careful and solicitous as he settled Nouri into the front seat; still Nouri winced in pain. His father apologized, slid into the driver's seat, and started the engine. Once they were on their way, he looked over.

"Do you want to talk about it?"

Nouri shook his head. "How did you find me?"

His father hesitated. "It is not important. Praise Allah I did."

"How much did it cost?"

His father didn't answer. Nouri knew it must have been a lot.

"How is Anna?"

"She called as soon as they took you away. She's at the house."

"Do you know who framed me?"

His father grimaced. "No. Do you?"

Nouri pressed his lips together. "No."

Neither of them spoke. Then his father frowned. The skin on his face looked looser, the lines on his forehead deeper than they had just the other day. "Nouri, I am grateful I was able to rescue you. But I doubt I can do it again. I have used up all my favors. The people who are in charge...I do not know them. I no longer have any influence. I don't know what you've done or—"

"Baba, I didn't do anything," Nouri said, cutting him short. "I am no rebel. Or traitor. The only thing I did was protest against the shah."

"Where? When?"

"In Chicago. Before we came home." Nouri told him about the demonstration at Daley Plaza.

Baba-joon scowled "That should not have provoked the guards to..." His voice trailed off. "What about your wife?"

Your wife. Baba usually called her Anna. "She's done nothing either."

Baba ran his hand over the stubble on his chin. He needed a shave. Then again, so do I, thought Nouri.

"Nouri, I think you and Anna should leave Iran."

"Leave? How can we?"

Baba-joon gestured toward the street. "At first I thought this was an aberration. I thought this revolutionary...zeal...would subside. That sensible, competent men would regain positions of power." He paused. "I am no longer sure that will happen. Your mother..." Baba sighed. "Well, never mind her. The country is being torn apart. I cannot protect you. You should leave while you can."

Despite the pain of his injuries, Nouri's insides turned liquid. It had to be killing Baba to say this. His father was always in control, the fixer who solved everyone's problems. Admitting he could no longer protect his family had to be his biggest shame. Indeed, in a culture that prized appearance and saving face, it *was* failure. More disturbing, it meant Nouri was on his own. He could no longer count on his father to rescue him.

"I ask just one thing, my son. Whatever you do, wherever you go, do not dishonor the family."

A wave of panic rolled over Nouri. It sounded as if his father was saying goodbye. "But I don't want to leave."

Baba-joon gave him a sad smile. "Persia will always be your home. But things are different. Fortunately, you are still young. You have many good years left." He stared through the windshield, his expression pensive and anxious, as if he was surveying the destruction wrought by a bomb or natural disaster. "And your wife...well...it is not good for either of you to stay."

"But I need you. I mean, you need me. I am your son."

"Yes, you are, and they arrested you anyway. Just like Maman-joon's friends. Next time they may kill you. That is what it has come to."

Thirty

Afterwards, Anna realized that Nouri's arrest was the rip in the fabric of her life—the point at which everything veered off course, down the path to destruction. But the tear did not have a surgical precision; it took its time, it was relentless, and it sapped her. She came to feel as if she was drowning in a pool of quicksand.

For the first few days, as his wounds and bruises turned purple then yellow, Nouri was quiet. Too quiet. He barely ate, he didn't want to see anyone, go anywhere. He stayed in bed, but he didn't sleep. When he did manage to doze, he had nightmares and woke up screaming.

Anna tried to persuade him that the worst was over. He was home. And safe. But he didn't listen, and she felt as insignificant as the noise that blared from the TV when no one was watching. Aural wallpaper, she called it. Baba-joon telephoned twice a day, but Nouri wouldn't speak to him. Anna knew the memory of the arrest was raw, that he needed time for his wounds, both physical and mental, to heal. She wondered how long it would take. His suffering broke her heart.

Anna remembered the pills—tranquilizers, she thought—that Maman-joon was taking when they returned from the Caspian Sea. She suggested he go to the same doctor. Nouri did and stayed away all day. He finally came home with a prescription for something Anna couldn't pronounce.

"You were gone a long time. What did the doctor say?"

"After the doctor I went to talk to some people."

"What people?"

"Baba-joon thinks we should leave Iran."

"Really?" A butterfly of hope fluttered her stomach. "When? How? Do you really think—"

Nouri lifted his palms. "Stop. It isn't going to happen."

"What? Why not? We could just go for a while. You know, until…"

"Anna, I cannot leave. The authorities will not let me."

"Why not?"

"They…it has to do with the arrest. They will not give me permission to leave."

"But that's absurd. Crazy."

Nouri didn't reply. He wheeled around and started up the stairs. Anna followed. "But, Azizam, isn't there something we can do? Maybe Baba-joon—"

Nouri whirled around. "Stop. Baba-joon cannot help. Not anymore. Don't bring it up again. We stay in Iran. That's final."

Anna fought back tears. How could they stay in this place? Perhaps, in a week or two, when Nouri had fully recovered, she could bring it up again.

§

One night about two weeks later, there was a knock at the door. When Anna opened it, Hassan was there. He was in his uniform, the gun belt around his waist. Anna shrank back. In the days that had passed, she'd tried to work out who, or what, prompted Nouri's arrest. She couldn't help thinking Hassan had something to do with it. He'd practically warned Nouri the last time he was at the house.

She greeted him with barely disguised hostility. "Good evening, Hassan."

Hassan shifted uneasily. Did he know he was under suspicion? Did he feel guilty? "I heard about Nouri," he said quietly.

I'll bet you did, Anna thought. She said nothing.

He looked down. "I am sorry." Finally he looked up. "I would like to see him."

"He's not seeing anyone."

"Please, Anna."

Was he the one who'd betrayed Nouri to the authorities? Caused him to suffer? If he wasn't, did he know who did? This man used to be Nouri's best friend. Anna had to make a split-second decision. Either choice was fraught with risk. The only thing that swayed her was their childhood friendship. "Stay here. I'll ask him."

She went upstairs. Nouri was lying on the bed, staring at the wall. He'd started taking the pills, but they didn't seem to make much difference. When she'd commented on it, he seemed suspicious of her motives. Why did she want him to take more drugs? Couldn't she live with him the way he was? Anna admitted she might be judging him unfairly. He had been beaten. Tortured. She couldn't imagine the trauma he'd been through. She vacillated between coddling him, and going crazy with worry.

Now she said quietly, "Hassan is here. He'd like to see you."

Nouri didn't move.

"I can tell him you'd rather not."

He rolled over and looked at her. Was he thinking the same thing she was—that Hassan's visit might take Nouri even deeper into the maw of evil? Nouri's eyes left hers, flitted to the window. He sighed. "Let him come up."

Anna didn't move. She felt protective. "Are you sure? I told him you weren't seeing anyone."

He hesitated. "I will see him."

She went down the steps. Hassan was still standing outside the door, his hands clasped together. "You can go up. But only for a few minutes," she added.

§

Hassan stayed for more than an hour. The door to the bedroom remained closed, but Anna heard their murmurs. At one point Nouri raised his voice. Hassan's reply was strained but quiet. They were talking in Farsi, and Anna wished she knew what they were saying. Since she didn't, she made busy work for herself. She hadn't been cooking much since the arrest. Nouri wouldn't eat. Now she pulled out paper and pencil and made a list of his favorite dishes. She would shop for the ingredients tomorrow. Inside the house it was warm, but a chill of unease crawled up and down her arms. She felt out of control, powerless, with Hassan in the house.

Finally, the bedroom door opened, and Hassan hurried down. Anna came out of the kitchen. He was almost at the front door. He was trying to slink out without saying goodbye.

"Well?" she asked.

Hassan stopped, spun around. "Nouri will be fine." His expression was lighter than when he'd arrived. Almost triumphant, she thought.

"What does that mean?"

"He understands what he needs to do. Inshallah, all will be good." He turned to leave.

An icicle of fear pricked Anna's spine. She went upstairs. For the first time since the arrest, Nouri was out of bed. He was actually getting dressed in something other than shorts and a t-shirt. He turned around and gave her a smile, or what passed for one.

"How was your visit with Hassan?"

His smile faded, and she realized it wasn't a smile; it was a grimace.

"You talked for more than an hour. What did he say?"

Nouri shrugged.

Anna ran a hand up and down her arm, her agitation growing. "Nouri, have you considered the possibility that he was the one who set you up?"

He stared at her for a moment. Then, "That's what he said you'd say."

She jerked her head up. She felt like she'd been punched in the gut.

Nouri folded his arms. "Anna, I've known Hassan all my life. I've known you eighteen months. Who would you believe?"

Anna stiffened. Nouri was looking at her with perhaps the emptiest expression she had ever seen.

"In fact, how can I be sure it wasn't *you* who informed on me?"

"Me?" Anna staggered back, stunned. "Because I'm your wife, Nouri.

I left the States to be with you in Iran. I changed my life because of you. I love you. Why on earth would I try to have you arrested? That's crazy." Still, a wave of fear rushed up her spine.

Nouri's face softened, and his voice went quiet. "I know that, Anna. Never mind." Then, "Anna, would you make me something to eat? I will be going out."

Thirty-one

When their first anniversary arrived, Anna was bitterly disappointed. She'd imagined it as a day of celebration and joy. Maybe even teasing the family with the hint of an impending pregnancy. At least that they were trying. But none of that happened. If not for the gift Anna gave Nouri, she doubted he would have acknowledged the day at all.

She had thought about her gift for weeks. It was actually a series of gifts: she had assembled an "engineering kit"—a set of tools that included a fancy calculator, mechanical pencils, a drafting table, and several triangular scales. She shopped at three different stores, asking enough questions to make sure she bought the right things. She brought them home surreptitiously, wrapped them separately, and, except for the table, had kept them hidden until now.

Nouri unwrapped the gifts and inspected them, as if it was his due. Then he gave her a peck on the cheek. "I do not have your gift. Yet," he added hastily.

"It doesn't matter. Happy anniversary, Azizam." She slipped her arms around him. For a moment, Nouri relaxed into her body the way he always did, but then he stiffened and pulled away. Anna was left with her arms outstretched in mid-air. She felt foolish.

"What shall we do to celebrate?" she asked.

"I have no time to celebrate today. I have a meeting."

"But it's our anniversary. We should do something special. I thought..."

Nouri looked at Anna with the empty expression she had seen several times now since his arrest. She was starting to dread it. "I have commitments."

A jolt pulsed up her spine. Since Hassan's visit, Nouri had been going out almost every night. On one hand, she was glad he seemed to have bounced back from the arrest, on the other, she was disturbed. Where was he going? What was he doing? And why not celebrate their marriage, just this one evening? What could be more important?

"Where do you go when you go out?" she asked, her voice tentative. "Is it part of your Metro job?"

Nouri gazed at her, again with that dispassionate air. "You do not need to know where. Just that I am going out."

"But, Nouri, it's our anniversary. Your family—"

"I told you. I am going out." He turned on his heel and walked out of the house.

Anna spent the evening crying into her pillow. What was happening to her husband?

§

As another hot summer melted into fall, Nouri and Anna suffered another blow. Funding for the Metro project was not restored, and Nouri lost his job altogether.

Anna said she'd continue working—classes at the IAS had started up again.

"Or, I can look for another job," she said as she prepared dinner. "Perhaps I can make more money."

Nouri scoffed. "You are an American. And a woman. No one will hire you. Women aren't supposed to work anyway. They are supposed to stay at home. Where they belong."

"You don't really believe that."

He shrugged and rubbed his hand across his chin, which was now covered with stubble. He was growing a beard. "Whether I do or don't isn't the issue. We must acknowledge the reality."

Anna started to pace the kitchen, stopped, twisted around. "Nouri, I've been thinking. I still believe we should leave the country for a while. Please. Can't we find a way to go back to the States? Or Paris? Anywhere but Iran."

"Anna, I told you. We are not leaving. Iran is my home. And yours."

"I don't feel at home. What happened to the brilliant world of Cyrus and Darius? The world of Zoroastrian tolerance? Iran has changed."

"Change is unavoidable if Iran is to assume its rightful place as a world leader. We stay."

Anna was stricken. When had he started to mouth platitudes? "Nouri, ever since the arrest I feel like I hardly know you. Please. Explain it to me. I want to understand."

Nouri's eyes narrowed, suddenly suspicious. "Why?"

She spread her hands. "I'm your wife, Azizam. Your partner. In good times as well as bad."

He squinted. "You're thinking about leaving on your own, aren't you?"

"Never!" Anna's distress mounted. "I would never leave without you."

"That's not what I hear."

She was close to tears. "Nouri, who is talking about me? What are they saying?"

He covered his mouth with his fist and said nothing.

"Nouri, this isn't fair. You can't accuse me of something and not tell me what it is. How can I defend myself?"

Nouri still didn't answer.

"I don't understand, Nouri. I get that you're probably going to religious meetings. I get that you're becoming more observant. Is it Hassan's doing? What has he been telling you? Are you planning to join the Guards? Tell me. I can live with just about anything. Except your silence. You're pushing me away. I feel like I've turned into your enemy. Please, Azizam."

Nouri just looked at her. Then, "There is only one thing you need to know. You cannot leave the country without my permission. I must give written approval. And I refuse."

Thirty-two

On a crisp morning in early November four hundred Iranian students stormed the US Embassy and took nearly a hundred staff members hostage. Outside, hundreds more students burned American flags and shouted "Die America." The students demanded that the US return the shah to Iran to stand trial. He was currently battling cancer in a New York hospital.

At first everyone thought the crisis wouldn't last, that it was mostly for show. Even Khomeini suggested the students withdraw. But they dug in and, as time passed, the government sensed an opportunity to transform the situation into a victory over the Great Satan. Khomeini changed his mind and gave tacit approval to the hostage-takers. Shock waves resonated around the world. America had been humiliated.

Anna, who was glued to the TV, discovered that she had a personal stake in the incident. As students paraded the blindfolded hostages before TV cameras, she reeled back. She was certain one of the women was Charlie, her boss at the IAS. Her friend. A call to Ibram, Charlie's husband, confirmed it.

"What was she doing at the embassy?" Anna asked.

"She was there often," Ibram said softly. "For meetings."

Charlie had never mentioned any meetings with embassy officials. In fact, she had never mentioned the embassy at all. Anna had heard rumors about American intelligence operatives—CIA or military— working undercover in bland, innocuous jobs. Hassan claimed it was part of the Great Satan's efforts to sabotage the revolution. Now, Anna wondered if there was some truth to those rumors. Was Charlie a spy? Had she been playing Anna for a fool? Or, as someone who had a lot of interaction with Iranians, was she simply reporting what she knew to the government? Either way, her relationship with the embassy had clearly put her in peril.

But there was another problem. Like Charlie, Anna was an American. Who worked at the IAS. Did that make Anna suspect as well? Her stomach knotted. It was all becoming too much. She couldn't work. She couldn't go out. Nouri wouldn't talk to her. Her best—her only— friend in Iran had been captured by a gang of student thugs. And now she might come under suspicion. Her husband's family, once her source of comfort and support, was falling apart before her eyes. Her life was becoming a nightmare.

When Nouri came home, she tried to raise the subject with him. "Do you think there's something we can do to get Charlie out?"

"You want to intercede for an American?" His tone was contemptuous. "I support the hostage-takers. The embassy—and the people who inform for it—are nothing but a nest of spies."

Anna tightened her lips. Nouri was spouting this kind of propaganda more and more. She suspected Hassan was coaching him, but she was hesitant to say anything. He'd become so temperamental. Even though she wasn't sure about her loyalties, she felt the need to defend Charlie. "She's been a guest in our house. She is my friend."

"She is an enemy of the people."

Anna tried a different tack. "What about Baba-joon? Maybe he can help."

"Baba-joon?" Nouri's laugh was scornful. "I think not."

Anna cringed. "Why not?"

"Baba must cut his ties to the Great Satan as well. We all must."

Anna ran a worried hand through her hair. "Nouri, do you realize what you're saying? You are married to an American. If you cut your ties to Americans, you will destroy our marriage." She paused. "Do you understand that?"

For a moment Nouri's expression shifted, as if he knew he'd gone too far, and a remorseful look unfolded across his face. Anna held on to it, her heart swelling with hope. She wanted to run into his arms, to feel him encircle and protect her. He loved her. She knew it. All he needed to do was show her. Just one small gesture. She waited, realizing any move on her part might break the spell. She was almost afraid to breathe.

Nouri's features rearranged themselves into the perpetual scowl he had started to wear. He drew himself up, his eyes narrowed. "Stop whining, Anna. You know nothing."

§

Anna was not the only family member concerned about the crisis. That night, for the first time, Anna's mother called her from Paris. Anna picked up the phone in the kitchen, and when she heard her mother's voice, a flood of longing she didn't know was bottled up inside her came unleashed.

"I'm worried about you, darling. I want you to come to Paris. I don't think Iran is a safe place for Americans right now."

Tears sprang to Anna's eyes. Someone actually seemed to care about her. "I…I can't, Mother," she said softly.

"Why the hell not? Don't tell me you—"

"Nouri must give written permission in order for me to leave the country. He won't."

"Well, for heaven's sake. Have him come too. He's never been to Paris, has he? It would be—"

"He won't leave."

"Why not? Is he crazy?"

Anna kept her mouth shut.

"Then you need to leave without him." Her mother's voice sounded resolute.

"I can't. I told you."

"Anna, you need to get out. You're a smart cookie. Forge his name on the permission form."

"Mother, I would like nothing more. But I made a—" She spun around. Nouri was standing at the door to the kitchen. Her voice trailed off and a spike of fear raced up her spine. How much of the conversation had he heard?

"Anna, are you still there? What's going on?" her mother demanded through the phone.

Evidently Nouri had heard enough, because he grabbed the phone from Anna. "You didn't come to our wedding," he barked into the receiver. "You haven't visited your daughter in years. You have no right to interfere in our life. Anna is my wife. She is happy here. Leave us alone. Do not call again." He hung up the phone, pulled it out of the wall, and glowered at Anna. "From now on, I will keep the phone hidden. You are not permitted to make calls or answer them. Even when I am not home. If I find out you have, there will be consequences."

Thirty-three

It was hard for Anna to imagine how life could get worse, but as the cold rainy season swept away the crisp autumn days, her life deteriorated even further. A few days after the hostages were taken, Khomeini had threatened to put them on trial for espionage unless the US sent the shah back to Iran. Bazargan, Iran's current prime minister, resigned.

With Charlie a prisoner in the embassy, classes at the IAS were suspended again. Anna was relieved. Since the start of the revolution, anti-American texts had been added to American and European literature courses at the university. Charlie had told her it was only a matter of time before the IAS would also be required to add them. At least now Anna would not have to teach anti-American propaganda.

New laws were proposed by the Islamic Revolutionary Council, which had assumed the de facto role of government. Among them were restrictions on the public expression of emotion. Men and women were not permitted to kiss, hold hands, or walk together on the street. Most music was outlawed, along with dancing, liquor, movies, bright colors, and games like chess. Even laughter was punishable by a fine.

It seemed to Anna as if anything that brought pleasure had been banned. Everything was interpreted in political terms. A too colorful headscarf was seen as a symbol of Western decadence. A poem was only worthwhile if it reinforced Islamic ideology. Even the wearing of the veil was considered a revolutionary triumph, since it was the shah's father who'd banished them in the 1930s.

A few days after her mother's phone call Anna was making the bed when she saw something on the floor underneath it. Sliding it out, she discovered a book. It was a Qur'an—in Farsi. She opened and rifled through the pages. Some passages were underlined in red. She took it down to the living room and rummaged through their bookcase, where she found the English version of the Qur'an Roya had given her. She thumbed through it; maybe she could figure out the corresponding passages in English. She hoped they would give her some insight into Nouri's transformation. But after a few minutes she realized she couldn't make any sense of the Arabic script and gave up.

She sat on the living room couch and ran her fingers back and forth on the nubby upholstery. She remembered when she'd bought it with Laleh, little more than a year ago. They were on a carefree shopping spree. They ate lunch at an exclusive club. Since then their world had collapsed. She stared out the window for a long time.

§

Death and martyrdom had always played an important role in Iranian culture. Persian poets like Rumi, Hafiz, and Omar Khayyam spoke eloquently about the divinity of the spirit. Death was seen as a natural step toward that goal. Life and death coexisted.

But the carnage that descended on Iran bore little resemblance to Persian spirituality. Anna shuddered as she watched the constant TV chatter about torture, executions, and beheadings. The government seemed to revel in doling out death sentences, twisting the philosophy of the past into something ugly and frightening. When she saw the phrase "The more we die, the stronger we become," plastered on the walls of the US Embassy, she couldn't help wondering what the purpose of that strength was, if it was only achieved by killing.

She ventured out only when she had to, and when she did, she tried to blend in. She kept her head covered with a long black scarf, and made sure her clothing wasn't tight or revealing. She didn't make eye contact with anyone. One afternoon she hurried to the market to buy ingredients for *beriyani*, another of Nouri's favorite dishes. They had discovered it on their honeymoon. She would stew lamb with sliced onions, then mince, fry, and serve the mixture on sangak bread. Part of her clung to the fragile hope that, if it turned out well, the scents curling out of the kitchen would entice Nouri to change his behavior. The other part of her knew better.

She did her shopping and left the store with lamb, turmeric, and fresh bread. Next to the newspaper stand was a rack of pamphlets. Usually it contained ads and circulars, but today she spotted something new. She had trained herself to ignore the photos of the condemned in the newspaper, but this pamphlet, stacked next to a circular for health and beauty aids, included photos of men and a few women who had been recently executed. Anna backed away in dismay and headed for home.

It was a mild day, so she unbuttoned her sweater and turned her face into the breeze. Afternoons like this seemed to promise that life would be easier, maybe even happy one day. She was enjoying the play of sun and wind on her face when the blast of a car horn made her jump. A white Toyota swerved out of the traffic and parked just ahead of her. Inside were three people, two women and a man.

The women jumped out of the car and hurried towards her. The man stayed in the car, its engine running. The two women wore chadors, the man a khaki uniform.

Her nerves jangling, Anna picked up her pace, but the women matched her. Who were they? A Guard would wear a dark green uniform, not khaki. And would never work with women. Her pulse beat like a caged bird's.

The women called to her in Farsi. "Wait. Come back, sister. We want to talk to you." Anna slowed. She wasn't sure why. Probably instinct, an inbred impulse to be polite. The women came abreast of her. They were sizing her up, feet to toe. Anna bent her head. If she spoke in Farsi, her accent would tag her as an American. Not a good idea. She thought quickly. *"Qu'est-ce que vous voulez?* What do you want?" she asked in French.

A rag suddenly appeared in one of the women's hands. Where had it come from? The other woman grabbed Anna from behind and pinned her arms to her sides. Anna struggled to break her hold, but the woman was stronger. Anna was trapped.

"*Lâchez-moi!* Let me go!" she cried.

But the woman held fast, and while Anna thrashed and squirmed, the woman with the rag started to scrub her face.

"*Lâchez-moi! Toute suite!* Let me go! Right now!" Anna sputtered. The woman continued to scrub. The rag was damp and foul smelling. Anna grimaced. Her voice was muffled. "*Je ne comprends pas.* I don't understand. *Pourquoi?* Why?"

The woman replied in Farsi. "Your face is that of a whore's. Do you want to be flogged? Taken to prison? You must give up your decadent Western ways. The Imam has decreed. You are violating the revolution."

Anna *was* wearing makeup, as she did every day. Not a lot. Just some blush, mascara, and eyeliner. Many women—at least most upscale Iranians—wore much more. Why were they objecting to her?

"Stop. *Lâchez-moi!*" Anna craned her neck. She saw pedestrians in front and behind her. "*Aidez-moi!*" she shouted. "*Quelqu'un! S'il vous plaît!*"

But no one came to her aid. Passersby gazed at the spectacle, then scurried away with grim, frightened expressions. Some actually crossed to the other side of the street. Anna tried to wriggle out of the woman's hold. "*Lâchez-moi ou je vais à la police!* Let me go or I'm going to the police."

The woman with the rag laughed harshly. She waved her free hand, gesturing toward the people on the street who had refused to intervene. "Go ahead!" she said in Farsi. "You will see. They will do nothing." She turned back to Anna. "You must wear chador from now on. For the sake of independence. To show up America."

Anna was so enraged she almost blurted out she *was* an American, but stopped short. There was no telling what effect that might have. Still, her silence alerted them to something, some mind-set that was not in accordance with their beliefs. The woman with the rag narrowed her eyes. "The Qur'an says the finest of all robes is the robe of piety. Inshallah, may you see the piety of Allah in your soul. As well as your body."

The car horn bleated. The two women looked over their shoulders. The man behind the wheel was beckoning them. The woman who'd been clutching her from behind suddenly released her with a shout. *"Allâho Akbar!"*

Anna staggered backwards. The two women hurried back to the car and piled in. The man in the khaki uniform pulled out so fast the Toyota's tires squealed. The car was soon lost in traffic. Seconds later a police car cruised by without stopping.

Anna slowly took a mental inventory. She hadn't really been injured. Just some tenderness where the woman had grabbed her arms, and rawness where her face was scrubbed. But her bag of groceries had split apart. The lamb lay on the sidewalk, covered with dirt. The bread too. She scraped them up and dumped them in a garbage bin. She wanted to dissolve into tears. But home was still four blocks away.

She had heard about instances of vigilante justice: people inspired with revolutionary zeal who patrolled the streets enforcing Shariah law. Was this one of those cases? Or was someone targeting her, making an example of her? And if that was the case, who was behind it? Hassan? One of her students at the IAS? Or, god forbid, Nouri?

Thirty-four

For the first time in her life Anna didn't celebrate Thanksgiving. Nouri forbade it, and the Samedis had no interest. Her hopes dimmed. If he wouldn't let her celebrate Thanksgiving, which wasn't a religious holiday, Christmas would be out of the question.

In December, Iranians voted to accept the new constitution and named Ayatollah Khomeini their Supreme Leader. Although sporadic resistance from opposition groups was reported, the outcome was never in question. A few of the US Embassy hostages were released, but most of them, including Charlie, were still held prisoner. Later in the month, the Soviets invaded Afghanistan, Iran's neighbor to the east. Although it didn't affect Iran directly, it reinforced the perception that this part of the world was a powder keg.

By the turn of the year, Nouri was practically a stranger. He spent most of his days—and evenings—away from home. It appeared he was not becoming a Guard like Hassan—he had not brought home any uniforms. So what *was* he doing? Anna asked him repeatedly, but he refused to tell her and claimed she did not need to know. On the few occasions he did stay home, he wouldn't talk except to demand food and clean clothes. And then he was curt and churlish. When she tried to ask him about his behavior, he replied that it was *she* who'd changed. Alternatively, he criticized everything she was *not* doing: not practicing Islam, not wearing a chador, not being an obedient Muslim wife.

Eventually, Anna stopped talking at all. She wasn't allowed to use the telephone, and even if she was, there was no one to turn to. Her one friend was a hostage, she and Nouri were estranged, and the Samedis had their own problems. She had started to build a new life in Iran. At first, she'd had a loving husband, a welcoming family, even a friend. But now, one by one, her support systems had disappeared, like hazy dreams that vanished in the morning light.

Indeed, life had come full circle. Her strength was depleted, and the old familiar isolation of her childhood settled like a weight on her shoulders. But this time it was almost intolerable—because she'd tasted the other side. So she did what she'd always done to survive. Like a prisoner suffering from Stockholm Syndrome, she tried to please. She kept the house spotless. She spent hours cooking. She even started reading the Qur'an, although she found it violent and rigid. Allah was not a forgiving god.

As the days passed, and Nouri remained distant and hostile, Anna tried to think of what, if anything, would improve their relationship. There was only one thing. A last resort. She had been loath to do it, her refusal perhaps to give up the last vestige of her independence. Now though, she had no choice. She would try. And if that didn't work…she shuddered at the thought.

The next morning, before Nouri left the house, she asked him to make a call for her.

An hour later the doorbell rang. Anna answered it. "Good morning, Roya."

Roya, in her black chador, flashed Anna a warm smile. "*Khodâ râ shokr*, Anna. I am full of joy that you called."

§

The chador shop—you couldn't really call it a store—was tucked away in a tiny building somewhere in downtown Tehran. Anna was lost; she and Roya had come by cab, and the taxi made too many twists and turns.

At the top of a steep set of stairs, an open door led to a small, cramped room. Every available inch of wall space was lined with shelves that appeared to be warped and rickety. Most of the shelves teemed with bolts of materials. Dark colors predominated. On the other side of the room, the shelves were jammed with books, pamphlets, and magazines.

In front of the door stood three female mannequins, or rather the heads of mannequins, attached to black metal poles. Their faces had simple, cartoonish features with empty expressions, the kind of faces Anna might have doodled on a piece of paper. Each head was draped in black material, but each drape had a slightly different style around the face. One headdress was a traditional round border; one was an upside-down V; the third sported two flimsy v-shaped wings that protruded slightly over the forehead.

"That's a *maghna'eh*." Roya gestured cheerfully. "You see, you have choices."

Anna swallowed and managed a nod.

Roya called out in Farsi. A moment later an elderly man, bent over with arthritis, came out from a back room. Roya told him why they were there, and the man studied Anna. When he smiled, Anna noted he was missing two front teeth, and the remaining ones were yellow. He pulled out a tape measure from his pocket, and handed it to Roya, who measured Anna around the head and shoulders. As she did, the man spoke to Anna in Farsi, but his accent was not clear, and Anna shook her head.

"He wants to know how many you want," Roya translated.

"How many would you suggest?"

"I would buy two. You do not have to wear them at home."

"*Do*," she said in Farsi.

The shopkeeper asked another question.

"He wants to know which *rusari* you want."

Anna gazed at the mannequins. She pointed to the traditional round border. "That one...," then she pointed to the one with tiny wings, "...and that one."

Roya grinned. "Like mine."

Anna hadn't noticed. She did now.

As they rode in the taxi back to Shemiran, Roya nattered on about teaching Anna how to drape and clasp her chador when she was on the street. Anna felt like she had surrendered the last bit of her freedom.

§

That night after dinner, she said to Nouri. "I have something to show you."

He scowled. "I do not have time."

"It will just take a minute." Anna got up and went into the kitchen. She took one of the chadors out of the bag and draped it over her. She grasped the material under her chin, the way Roya had shown her, and glided back into the dining area.

Nouri looked up. Anna pivoted one way, then the other, modeling the robe. Nouri was silent.

"Well, what do you think?" she asked. "Roya helped me pick it out."

His face smoothed out at the mention of Roya, and he looked as if he might say something. Then he sucked in a breath, as if reminding himself to be angry, and his frown lines reappeared. He rose from the table, scraping the legs against the floor, and headed to the front door.

"Nouri, please. I did this for you. What do you think?"

He slammed the door on his way out.

Thirty-five

Two weeks later Anna was cooking dinner on a chilly night when Nouri came home. His nose was runny, and his cheeks were flushed. He was holding a canvas bag tied at the top. For a moment, she smiled, remembering the chapped lips and achy fingers of cold days when she was a child. The blanket of warmth that enveloped her when she finally went inside.

"I'm hungry," Nouri barked, interrupting the memory.

"Dinner will be ready in a few minutes." She was preparing a *khoresh-e*, Iranian stew. Tonight it was *khoresh-e qeymeh,* split pea and beef, with onions, potatoes, tomato paste, and limes.

"Why is it not ready now? You've had all day to cook."

"Ten minutes. What's in the bag?"

Nouri didn't answer. He wheeled around and mounted the steps to the third floor. Anna didn't go up there much. There was nothing up there except a closet and the door to the roof. She heard a squeak as the closet door opened, followed by a thump or two. She wondered what he was using it for. Maybe that's where he kept the phone. She'd check when he wasn't around. Then he came back down to the living room and turned on the TV. Anna finished seasoning the stew, ladled it into a serving bowl, and set the table. "OK. It's ready."

Nouri went to the table, peered at the food, then at her. He folded his arms. "Why are you wearing jeans?"

She shrugged. "I'm at home. I can wear whatever I like."

His scowl deepened, but he sat down. Anna sat at the other end of the table. Dinner was rarely pleasant these days, and she had little appetite. Often she ate her meal after he finished. Nouri broke off a chunk of sangak and put it on his plate. He dished some stew onto his plate, dipped the bread in it, and brought it to his mouth.

Midway through chewing, he stopped and spit the food back on the plate. "Something is wrong."

"What do you mean?"

"I can't eat this. It tastes like dirt. What did you do to it?"

Anna's stomach clenched. She picked up the bowl, scooped a spoonful onto her plate, and tasted it. It seemed fine to her. She said so.

"No. Something is bad. You've done something different."

"Well, I didn't have any saffron, so I used extra turmeric. Gives it more of an Indian flavor. Maybe that's what you're tasting." Saffron was probably the most common spice in Persian cuisine.

Nouri was not mollified. "Why would I eat anything Indian? It's a country full of ignorant, dirty, uncultured heathens. You tricked me."

Anna just looked at him.

"You can't even cook anymore. What good are you?"

Something inside Anna snapped. She stood up, grabbed the serving bowl, and threw it on the floor. The shatter of china was the most satisfying sound she'd heard in weeks. The stew oozed out between the shards of the bowl.

Nouri's eyes widened. He jumped to his feet. "What do you think you're doing? You've gone crazy. Evil jinns have taken over your soul!"

She planted her hands on her hips. "Enough, Nouri. This stops! All of it."

Nouri edged closer. "Don't talk to me that way. Clean it up. Now!"

Anna refused to move. Nouri raised his hand as if he was going to strike her. She didn't give him the chance. She bolted and raced up the steps. When she reached the bedroom she hurled herself inside and locked the door.

§

Nouri didn't come home that night. As she cleaned up the mess, Anna told herself she didn't care. She even managed a few hours of sleep. By the next morning, she had made a decision. She hunted for her passport. She hadn't thought about it in months; she hadn't needed it. It was supposed to be in the wall safe built into the bedroom. She knew the combination and opened it, but the passport wasn't there. A wave of panic rolled over her. Her passport was more than her identity. It was the formal record of her existence. Without it, she was nothing. She searched her dresser and closet. No passport.

Maybe he'd put it in the closet on the third floor. The one whose door she'd heard him occasionally open and close. She went up the steps and opened the door. The only things inside were items like linens that she'd stored. No passport, and no telephone. Why did he keep opening the door if he wasn't storing anything in it? She frowned, but couldn't dwell on it at the moment. She went back downstairs and searched for her passport in the kitchen, behind the bookshelves, in the closets. It wasn't there. Where was it? Had Nouri done something with it?

She started to pace the living room. Her stomach churned, her breath came in tight gasps, and she thought she might be sick. What would she do now? Then, suddenly, she stopped. There had to be a way around this. People lost their passports all the time. She couldn't let that discourage her. She'd figure it out. As she talked herself into it, anger replaced fear. Anger at Nouri, anger at herself, anger at her own helplessness. She was wasting time.

She put on her chador, grabbed her purse, and ran out of the house. At the corner she hailed a taxi and gave the driver the address of the Swiss Embassy, which, now that the US had broken diplomatic relations with Iran, was handling any issues that involved Americans. During the trip, her anger mounted. This time she welcomed it—it was better to be pissed off than to fall apart. The sensation of her pulse throbbing against her temples was perversely satisfying. The anger crystallized her thoughts, strengthened her resolve, channeled her toward action.

It was a surprisingly short ride to the embassy in the northern part of Tehran, not far from the Samedis' house. The building, an imposing structure with elegant columns in front, looked a little like the White House, but like most upscale buildings in Tehran, it was surrounded by high walls. Winter was gradually relinquishing its grip, and a bright sun glinted off the white stucco.

She discovered that the "Foreign Interests" section of the embassy occupied a separate building a few blocks away. She walked to a small concrete structure, vastly different from the grand embassy. Bars protected the entrance, and a man in a Tehran police officer's uniform guarded the gate. She pressed an electronic buzzer on the wall. A metallic voice asked what her business was.

"I'd like to see someone who can help me go back to America."

She was buzzed in. After a cursory body search, a man speaking English with a thick accent asked for her passport.

"I…I don't have it."

Frown lines appeared on his face. He appraised her, then apparently decided she was legitimate and ushered her down the hall to a small office. He knocked on the door and entered. Anna waited in the hall, hearing the murmur of conversation inside. A moment later the man gestured her in, walked out, and closed the door.

A second man sat behind a desk in the nondescript office. His skin was sallow, his hair was receding, and he had a paunch. Wire rim glasses perched on his nose. He looked harried and in need of a vacation.

He cleared his throat. "Good morning. I'm Peter Deutsch. What can I do for you?" He too had an accent, but Anna recognized it as Swiss.

"Good morning, Mr. Deutsch. I am an American. I've lived in Iran about a year, and I want to go home. As soon as possible."

"Are you married to an Iranian?"

She nodded.

"Do you have children?"

"No."

"I see." He cleared his throat again. "I'm glad there are no children. Complicates matters. Even so, there isn't much I can do."

Anna crossed her arms. His tone was crisp, almost mechanical, as if he'd said this many times. "But I'm an American citizen."

"Yes, you are American as far as the US government is concerned. But not according to Iran."

"What are you talking about?"

"You became an Iranian citizen when you got married."

"No. I have dual citizenship. I...I still have my US passport."

Deutsch took off his glasses, opened his desk drawer, and fished out a handkerchief. He wiped first one lens, then the other. He put them on again. "The Iranian government does not recognize dual citizenship. US nationals who are married to Iranians are treated as Iranian citizens. You became a naturalized citizen of Iran when you married. And as long as you are in Iran, you will be treated as one."

"Meaning what, exactly?"

"Meaning that under Iranian law—despite the fact that you still hold US citizenship—you must now enter and exit Iran on an Iranian passport."

"But I don't have an Iranian passport."

"You must get one." He paused. "Did you marry here?"

"Here and in the States."

"If you married in Iran, your American passport would have been confiscated by the Iranian authorities at that time. Didn't your husband tell you?"

Anna was quiet for a moment, trying to take it in. "It must have slipped his mind," she finally said.

Deutsch laced his hands together on the desk. "You know, of course, that women must have the consent of their husbands in order to leave the country."

"And if the husband refuses?"

"I am sorry." He opened his hands.

The walls were closing in. A seed of desperation bloomed inside Anna. "Sorry isn't good enough. You have to help me."

"As I said, the law is the law. When you add in the absence of diplomatic relations at the moment, we can only give you limited assistance."

"But that...that's unacceptable. I have to leave. I can't stay another week."

He intertwined his fingers again. His tired expression suggested this wasn't the first time he'd heard that, either.

Anna refused to accept defeat. "What about my mother? She lives in Paris. Surely, there's a way for me to visit her."

"Again, if you have your husband's written permission, you may go anywhere you like."

Anna blinked rapidly. "If you were me, what would you do?"

"Madame, I can't advise you. What I can tell you is that if you divorce, or if your husband dies, you then will have an opportunity to renounce your Iranian citizenship. However, if you have any children, they are automatically considered Iranian citizens, and their citizenship is irrevocable. They will be required to enter and depart Iran on Iranian passports."

Anna couldn't imagine having any children with Nouri at this point.

"And you will still need permission from the local authorities to leave."

Anna's misery returned, smothering her earlier energy. She didn't know what to do. She didn't want to break down in front of a stranger. "So," she asked shakily, "what *can* you do for me?"

"We can call or write your family and tell them you're being held against your will. Of course, I imagine they already know."

"My husband won't let me call my mother, and I haven't spoken to my father in months."

"I can mail a letter for you. Maybe get you some clothes if you need them."

"Can you call my father? He's a physicist. He works for the government in Maryland."

When Deutsch nodded, she gave him her father's phone number and address.

"And your mother?"

"I told you. She lives in Paris."

"Ah. The city of lights."

Anna couldn't believe he was making small talk at a moment like this. Despair seeped through her body like poison. She couldn't leave Iran unless Nouri gave his permission, and that was something he said he would never do. She was trapped.

Thirty-six

A few mornings later, Nouri and Anna were finishing tea when the phone rang—Nouri would magically retrieve it from wherever it was hidden when he was home. Anna, still reeling from her visit to the embassy, tried to behave normally, to keep Nouri from taking any particular notice of her. She barely reacted as Nouri took the call. It was only when his tone sharpened that she looked up.

"Who is this?" he barked into the receiver. "Why are you calling us?"

Anna quietly carried their glasses into the kitchen. It had to be Deutsch from the Swiss Embassy. Had he talked to her father? She was desperate to find out. She wanted to beg for the phone.

Nouri's face darkened. "She does not want to talk to you. She has no interest in communicating with her parents." He spun around and focused on Anna. The rage in his eyes assaulted her like a spray of bullets. "No, you may not. And do not call here again or I will report you to the authorities for harassing my wife." He slammed down the phone.

Anna's stomach clenched.

Nouri took a step toward her. "That was someone from the Foreign Interests Section of the Swiss Embassy. Why did they call here, Anna? What have you done?"

Anger shot up her spine, but she couldn't deny it. Nouri had stepped over the line. She remembered the old adage about a good offense. "Where is my passport?"

"Why? Are you thinking of going someplace?"

"You didn't tell me that Iran doesn't honor dual citizenship. Not a word. You kept it a secret and surrendered my passport to the authorities when we got married, didn't you?"

"And if I did?"

"You told me I was going to be a Muslim. I accepted that. I wanted to honor your traditions. But you never said that in the process I would lose my rights as an American."

"You should have known." He shrugged. "You are not only disobedient, but stupid." Then something shifted in his expression. It was subtle, but Anna saw it.

"You didn't know either, did you?"

Nouri drew himself up. "What…what are you talking about?" he sputtered. "Of course I did."

His posturing gave him away. "No, you didn't. You had no idea. It was Baba-joon, wasn't it? He knew. He was the one who handled it. He took my passport."

Nouri tried to argue, but Anna knew she was right. Her anger mounted and she was about to tell him what she thought of his family's duplicity when an idea occurred to her. She smoothed her hands down her slacks.

"Nouri, listen to me. If you let me leave Iran, I'll make sure you save face. You can divorce me. Tell everyone it was my fault. That I was a bad wife. That you don't love me anymore. Whatever you want. Just let me go."

"You *are* a bad wife. But divorce is out of the question. It is a disgrace to divorce in Iran. Instead I will take a second wife. Islam permits it, you know." He paused, then inclined his head as if considering the notion. "Yes, that is exactly what I will do. Then you will realize how little you matter. Surely Roya will be interested. Or maybe a young girl. I can marry a girl as young as thirteen if I choose."

Anna seethed and her hands curled into fists. She wanted to hit, strike out, as if that would knock some sense into him. She was about to retort when something dawned on her. Suddenly, Anna understood why her father had wanted her to get married in the States. If Nouri

201

wouldn't divorce her, *she* would divorce *him* when she got home. Which was something she desperately wanted to do, she now realized. She mentally blessed her father for his wisdom. At the same time, she wouldn't rise to Nouri's bait. "Maybe you *should* marry again. Then you won't care about me, and you'll let me go home."

Nouri threw her a withering look. "You will never leave as long as I am alive."

Anna glared at him. He should only know what she was thinking.

"In fact," he went on, oblivious, "since it is clear I can no longer trust you to be out by yourself…," he went to the front door, slammed it shut, and locked it, "…from now on, you will not leave the house alone. Someone must go with you. Either me, or someone of whom I approve."

Anna's jaw dropped. "You couldn't be that cruel."

"Americans are deceitful. Untrustworthy. Everyone knows that."

"You didn't think so when you lived there."

"I was taken in by your trickery. But I learned. You will be punished. Maybe then you will learn."

§

Nouri called his parents and told Laleh to come over. Anna started to cry, ran upstairs, and locked herself in the bedroom. Half an hour later she heard someone at the door. A deep male voice called out. It was Baba-joon, not Laleh. He and Nouri exchanged harsh words. A moment later, the door slammed, and for the first time in days the house was quiet.

Still, Anna stayed in the bedroom. Although she'd been visiting Baba and Maman-joon regularly, she didn't want to see him now that she knew he'd surrendered her passport without her knowledge. He'd duped her. She no longer trusted him. She wasn't sure what to do, all she knew was that she wanted to get out of Iran.

Presently, she heard someone's tread on the stairs followed by a light tap on the door. "Anna, it is Bijan. Can we talk?"

He had called himself Bijan, not Baba-joon. What did that mean?

She mulled it over. Nouri and Baba-joon had argued. It was Nouri who'd stomped out of the house. She opened the door a crack.

When he saw her, Bijan's lips tightened, and he looked embarrassed. "Will you come downstairs? We will make tea."

She was somewhat surprised, but not much. Anna had always liked Baba-joon. She thought the feeling was mutual. She could only imagine what she must look like, her eyes rimmed in red, her skin blotchy and pale. She nodded.

By the time she'd washed her face and come downstairs, he'd found a tray, a sugar bowl and glasses, and was heating water. A hand-painted teapot sat nearby. A wedding gift.

She watched him spoon sugar into the glasses. "I am sorry your life has come to this, Anna."

Anna didn't respond. She needed to be careful. How much did he know?

He continued, as if he hadn't expected an answer. "This country is on a path to destruction. It's difficult to imagine anything surviving."

"Including my marriage," she said.

He turned around, his back against the kitchen counter. "There is something you need to understand about Nouri. Maybe you already do. We raised our children—well, as you Americans say, we spoiled them. But it is part of our culture. We treasure our children. Nouri has always been taken care of, petted and spoiled, almost like one of the peacocks the shah used to raise. He was a beautiful child. Proud, confident, handsome. Afraid of nothing."

"I know." Anna almost smiled. She remembered that Nouri. The one who swept her off her feet, who read poetry to her in Chicago, who made love to her with such tenderness. She remembered how perfect he seemed. How sensual, how sensitive, infallible. How happy she was when she first moved to Iran. How joyful she was to become his wife.

"Like the peacocks, he struts, beautiful and proud," Baba-joon went on. Then he stopped. "But the reality is that he is dependent on others—usually us—for everything. He has no inner compass. And if the world collapses around him, as it is doing now, he is lost. That is what is happening to my family. They are all trying to withstand the assault, but none of them are armed with the right tools."

Anna swallowed. Somewhere deep inside she'd known this from the start. In Chicago, Nouri had moved into *her* apartment, let *her* take care of him. She was the one who encouraged him to write his thesis, to reach out to other Iranian students, to become politically active. He depended on her.

"Nouri thought that he would study at a fine American school," Baba-joon said, "and then he would come home as an engineer, and play the role of a young businessman in the elite, privileged class."

Bijan was right. Once they moved back to Iran, Nouri shifted his reliance from Anna back to his father. Baba-joon would find him a job. Pay for his house. Solve his problems.

"But then, this revolution, this chaos, descended, and now there is a new order. A new elite. Nouri's dreams have been ravaged and he doesn't know what to do with his anger and frustration. So he takes it out on you. It is not right—not at all—but it is, perhaps, understandable."

Anna thought about it. Baba-joon was right. Since the revolution began Nouri had transferred his dependence yet again, this time from Baba-joon to Hassan. He was trying to survive. To play a role that someone else had carved out for him.

"It is my fault, of course," Bijan said. "Parvin and I should have raised them to be more independent."

Anna frowned. "Why are you telling me this? Why now?"

"Because I want you to understand. Nouri is not a bad person. But he is immature and he is afraid. You are more centered. Indeed, I think you are—and have been—the perfect wife for him. I know it is not easy, but perhaps—you can wait it out? I know you were happy at one time. And I do believe all this...," he waved a hand, "...is just temporary. This...chaos...cannot last forever."

Anna leaned over and gently kissed him on the cheek. "You are a good father."

Bijan grasped her hand. He looked like he might tear up.

"I have a question."

He blinked.

"Did you confiscate my passport? And if you did, why didn't you tell me?"

"You didn't know?" His expression was one of concern. She tried to detect any duplicity in it. She couldn't find it.

"Nouri was supposed to tell you. I told him before the wedding. It is the law. Whenever a couple weds, if the wife is not Iranian, she must surrender her passport."

"I was not told. I thought my passport was in the safe upstairs, here at the house."

Baba-joon sighed and shook his head. "I am so sorry, Anna." He looked off into the distance. "I kept waiting for you to apply for an Iranian passport. I should have realized you didn't know." A deep sadness came into his eyes.

Anna believed him. It was Nouri who'd failed to follow through. Always Nouri. Baba-joon apologized again, then gathered his things. She walked him to the door and saw him out. She understood his motivation. A father had to defend his son. And he was right about Nouri: he might seem bossy and temperamental, but it was all bluster. Nouri was panicked. He was struggling to stay afloat in uncharted waters, and the only way he could navigate them was through rage.

Perversely, that knowledge gave Anna a sliver of hope. If he was that malleable, maybe she could persuade him to her point of view. Because what she couldn't, and wouldn't, tell Baba-joon was that she would be leaving Iran soon. She had to. Somehow.

§

Hassan came to the house that night, which was unusual for him. He'd made himself scarce recently. Anna suspected he'd been embarrassed to visit, given how he'd brainwashed Nouri. Not that she saw him when he arrived. She'd been banished to the bedroom and told repeatedly not to come downstairs.

At first she was happy to be alone. Nouri's continuous humiliation of her grated. She picked up a book and tried to read, but her mind wandered. She wanted to know if Deutsch had contacted her father. Her father had government connections. There must be something he could do to get her out. The alternative—to be trapped in Iran for the rest of her life—was unacceptable.

She tried to go back to her book, but the murmur of conversation downstairs aroused her curiosity. Nouri never told her where he went or what he was doing when he went out. For all she knew, he was drinking, carousing, maybe even seducing other women. Aside from Hassan, Nouri didn't have many friends. His associates at the Metro were gone. If she knew where he was going, what he was doing, it might help her to convince him to let her leave. She crept out of the bedroom.

Hassan and Nouri were talking in Farsi. For a while their chatter sailed over her head. They might have been speaking in tongues. Then she scolded herself. She'd been hearing Farsi for over a year. She should be able to understand if she concentrated. She closed her eyes and homed in. She managed to pick up a phrase here and there, but it was largely meaningless until Nouri mentioned her name. Then the word "Deutsch." And "Switzerland." She leaned forward.

She couldn't quite make out Hassan's reply, but his tone was clipped. Curt.

Nouri's reply sounded defensive. Anna was puzzled. Didn't Nouri sense Hassan's arrogance? Or did he choose not to? Hassan was probably telling Nouri how to handle her. How to humiliate her even more, show her how little she mattered. She blinked back tears, some of Bijan's sorrow washing over her. All that wasted talent and energy.

Hassan's voice grew slower, more distinct, and Anna began to understand his words. When Baba-joon's name was mentioned, Anna stiffened. Her pulse shouted in her ears. They were talking about doing something to Baba-joon. And the house.

"They need to know you are with them," Hassan said.

Nouri's reply was emphatic. Was he refusing to do it?

Hassan's voice grew sympathetic. "Nouri, I understand that you must provide for your loved ones. But never forget that today's blessing can become tomorrow's curse."

Nouri said he didn't have the energy. "I can't fight any more. All the hate and anger and cries for revenge. It's exhausting."

Good for Nouri, Anna thought.

But Hassan's reply was honey sweet. Anna couldn't quite catch it, but she thought he was saying that Nouri must focus more. "As I said, the right choice is critical." He paused. "I am sure you will be a good Brother."

§

Anna couldn't sleep. Nouri was downstairs. Drawers opened and closed; the kitchen door squeaked. Finally, she heard his tread on the stairs. He went up to the third floor and opened the door to the roof. Or was it the closet? She heard a thump as the door closed. Then he came into the bedroom and undressed, making no effort to be quiet. The mattress sagged as he fell into bed. He rolled first in one direction, then the other. The sheets whispered as he pulled them up to his chin.

Anna stayed very still. Then she said, "I'm still awake."

Nouri grunted.

She reached across the bed for him. "Nouri, Azizam, I heard what you and Hassan were discussing downstairs. About Baba-joon."

Now it was Nouri who lay very still.

"That was…just talk, right? You aren't going to follow through with it."

"What?" Nouri asked

"What you and Hassan talked about…the house. Baba-joon."

He pushed her arm away and rolled over on his side. He didn't say anything for a moment. "You have the nerve to listen in on my conversation? To eavesdrop like a common thief?" When she didn't answer, he rolled back and grabbed her shoulders.

Anna winced. "That hurts."

"I hope it does," he snarled. "Once again you have disobeyed me.

You had no business listening. I am through with you. You are no more than a piece of trash."

She was about to utter a retort when she remembered her conversation with Baba-joon. She decided not to retaliate. Instead she said, "Nouri, I love you. I always will. But this isn't working. I'm miserable, and so are you. We'll both be happier if you let me go. Please."

Nouri stubbornly shook his head. "How many times do I have say it? I make the decisions. And I have decided you will never leave."

"Nouri, we're drowning. You're not working. I'm not working. If we don't do something soon, we'll run out of money. Then what?"

Nouri's eyes narrowed as if he suspected her of a crime. "Why do you care? Allah will provide."

"As long as his name is Baba-joon."

Nouri's breathing grew more shallow. "You dare to criticize me? And Baba-joon? You were the one who went behind my back. Who deceived me. Your lies and treachery are a crime. Do you know I can report you? You could be arrested. You could be beaten, taken prisoner, maybe even stoned to death."

Anna tried to rein him in. "I know you don't mean that, Azizam."

But Nouri was working himself up. His body went rigid, his voice raw. "I am not your Azizam. Never again." The moonlight streamed in, sowing his eyes with beads of rage.

Anna tried to wriggle out of his grasp. "I'm going to sleep downstairs on the couch."

"No. You won't. Not unless I give my permission." He rolled on top of her. His smell was a combination of rose water, smoke, and sweat. She used to crave it, but now she found it repugnant. She tried to push him off, but he was stronger, and her attempts only made him settle on her more firmly. He seemed heavier than usual. Anna struggled to breathe.

"I should never have married you. I should have listened to my family," he seethed. "They warned me."

Anna's stomach twisted. Was he making that up just to be cruel? He started moving on top of her. To her shock, he was hard. She thrashed her legs and arms about, trying to shove him off, but he had her pinned.

"Nouri. Please. Don't."

He ignored her. He was behaving like a stranger. A rageful, vengeful stranger. How could he? She was Anna. He was Nouri. They were supposed to love each other. The gentle, intimate love that Rumi described so eloquently. Not this harsh, hurtful…act.

He started to pant and bore down on her, forcing her to spread her legs. He rammed himself inside her, thrusting hard and deep and fast. The pain was intense, but she wasn't strong enough to fight him off. He started to grunt like an animal.

"Nouri, stop! You're hurting me!"

But it wasn't the pain that made her cry out. For the first time, she thought she knew what hate really felt like, and the depth of his rage terrified her. What if he lost control altogether? What if, in the midst of some future outburst, he killed her?

He kept going until he was finished.

Afterwards, a tear rolled down her cheek. Nothing would ever be the same.

Thirty-seven

Nowruz, the Iranian New Year, began on March 21st and, for the first time, the Samedis did not host a party. The Ayatollah disapproved of secular celebrations, so festivities throughout the entire country were subdued.

A few days later, Anna noticed a vial of Nouri's pills in the bathroom wastebasket. When she asked him about it, he said he didn't need them anymore. She fished through the trash and pulled them out. The label was written in Arabic, and she couldn't understand anything on it, except Nouri's name, which he'd taught her back in Chicago.

Nouri followed through with his threats. He made sure Anna could not leave the house by herself. Consequently, he was home more, and made life miserable for Anna. He took to changing his clothes several times a day, and ordered her to iron his shirts and pants. A tiny wrinkle sent him into spasms of rage. Anna suspected it took more energy to demean her and keep her isolated than to do whatever it was he did outside the house. Even so, her home had become a prison.

One morning Laleh came over. She now wore a manteau—a sort of overcoat—on the street, but underneath she was dressed in a tank top and hot pants. Nouri scowled, but Anna was thrilled to see her; it meant Nouri would be going out.

"Laleh will stay here while I'm gone," he said as he went to the door. "I have given her strict instructions. If you disobey her, you will pay the price."

Once he was gone, Laleh turned to her. "What did you do to him?

I've never seen him like this."

"It's not me, Laleh. I swear it," Anna said. "He's keeping me prisoner."

Laleh planted her hands on her hips. "I don't believe you. Why would he do that? You are lying."

Anna's jaw clenched. Had Nouri turned the entire world against her? She weighed the risk of explaining, decided she had to try. At this point Laleh was her only hope. "Laleh, please. You must believe me. I've done nothing. I need help. I'm desperate."

Laleh sniffed. "Nouri told me you'd say that. He said you'd try to convince me to help you escape." She looked around, as if seeing their house for the first time, and sighed. "But I suppose I can't blame you. This country is a hellhole. I am leaving myself."

"How is that possible? Don't you need written permission?"

"Until I am eighteen Baba must give it. But after that…" She flashed a conspiratorial smile. "My birthday is quite soon."

"Where are you going? How will you live?"

"I'll go to London. To join Shaheen."

"But your mother…she'll go crazy."

Laleh shrugged.

A sharp pain throbbed in Anna's temples. If Laleh could leave, why couldn't she? It wasn't fair. She had no one to fight for her, no one in her corner. The family she wanted to cherish had become her enemy. She'd never felt so alone.

"I'm going upstairs." She stopped on the second floor and paused. Then she continued up to the third floor. She opened the door to the roof and stepped out. She walked to the edge and peered down over the cement patio, the chenar tree, the alley beyond. She could end it right now. Just one leap and it would be over.

As she took in a breath, the phone inside trilled. Evidently Nouri trusted Laleh not to let her, Anna, use it in his absence. She heard Laleh pick up. The conversation was muffled, but a moment later, Laleh raced up the stairs to the roof. Her face was white, her eyes wide with panic.

"What's wrong?" Anna asked.

"That was Maman-joon. We must go home. They've taken Baba!"

§

"We...we were having tea outside, enjoying the spring morning." Maman-joon sobbed, huddled on the living room sofa. Anna hadn't seen Parvin in months. Her hair was much grayer, the lines on her forehead deeper, her face more gaunt. "A car swerved up to the gate. Three men got out and banged on it. I went to open it. They...they were in uniforms. And...and they were aiming machine guns at me." Her face was tight with anguish. "They could have killed me."

"What color were their uniforms?" Anna asked.

Parvin ignored Anna's question, and swiveled towards Laleh. She spread her hands. "I had to let them in. I had no choice."

Laleh pointed to Anna. "The uniforms, Maman. She wants to know if they were Guards. Were their uniforms dark green?"

"Yes. No. Two were green, I think. One brown. I really don't remember." Parvin wouldn't make eye contact with Anna.

Laleh nodded. "Then what?"

"They were scruffy. They had beards. And they smelled bad. They demanded to see Baba. I told them to wait. They said no, that I must let them come with me. They warned me not to tell Baba they were here or they would shoot me." She shivered.

"They were afraid he would escape."

"They said they would take us both unless I cooperated." Parvin covered her face with her hands. "What could I do?" Her tears tracked tiny rivulets down her cheeks.

Laleh put her arm around her mother, but Parvin shook her off.

"So they...they stalked up to the house. Baba had gone inside. I didn't know why until he came back out. He was carrying a knife."

Laleh gasped. Anna swallowed.

"Then they shouted, 'You are Bijan Samedi?' 'Who are you' he shouted back. They trained their machine guns on him. *Ay vây!* They were going to shoot him! I begged them to stop. 'We have orders to arrest you for crimes committed against the Islamic Republic,' they yelled. 'Drop the knife now. If you make even one move against us, you are a dead man.'"

"Oh, god. What did Baba do?" Laleh asked.

"He froze. The men racked their guns." Another shudder ran through Maman-joon.

Anna imagined Baba debating what to do. Weighing whether he could take them. Knowing it was impossible. Deciding whether to make the attempt anyway and die trying.

"Finally Bijan threw down the knife," Parvin said. "One of them picked it up and stuffed it into his waistband. I hope it slashes his guts." She spit on the floor. "Then they put handcuffs on Bijan and dragged him out. That was the last I saw of him." Her face crumpled again, as if the pain of recounting the story was too overwhelming. Her body was wracked by sobs.

"Where did they take him?" Laleh asked.

"I don't know." Her voice cracked. She got up, and went into the kitchen. She came back with a glass of water and a pill, which she swallowed. She drank the water. "Whatever shall we do? Where is Nouri?" Her voice was shrill.

"We left a note at home," Anna said. "I'm sure he'll be here soon."

Again Parvin ignored her.

"Did they take anything?" Laleh asked. "Besides Baba?"

"Isn't that enough?" Maman-joon started to mutter. "The evil eye is all around us. It has cursed us. I knew it would happen." She glared at Anna.

Laleh, sitting beside her mother, laced and unlaced her fingers. Anna wanted to tell her to put her arm around Parvin again. Her mother needed comfort. But Laleh just sat, and Anna couldn't say anything. If Anna tried to soothe her mother-in-law Parvin would probably slap her. The three of them were silent for a moment, each lost in their own thoughts. Then a clanging sound rang out from the patio.

Parvin jerked back. "Now what?" Anna and Laleh exchanged looks. Parvin slumped against the sofa.

"I'll go," Laleh said.

"No." Parvin gestured towards Anna. "Let her."

Of course, Anna thought. If anyone was to be put in danger, it should be her. She went outside, crossed the patio, and walked to the gate. Three men were training machine guns on her. They all had beards, and they wore brown uniforms. Not Guards. Still, they yelled at her to open the gate.

"*Chee Shode?* What's wrong?" she asked in Farsi.

"We are from the Martyrs' Foundation. We command you to open the gate."

Anna had heard of this organization. Created by Khomeini a year earlier, its mission was to confiscate property belonging to the shah's family and his associates. The idea was to help people who had suffered under the shah. Kind of an institutional Robin Hood. In and of itself, it wasn't a bad idea, Anna thought. It appealed to her sense of justice. But she had never been the target of their activities. And there was the question of whether the largesse really did go to the poor or ended up in the pockets of the mullahs. Whatever the reality, she had no choice. She had to open the gate.

The men tramped into the house. Laleh and Parvin cowered on the sofa. "We are here to confiscate the property in this house. You will stay in this room while we work," one of the men pronounced.

"What's going to happen to us?" Anna asked.

"Your family was allied with the shah. Your possessions are therefore corrupt. We must cleanse the house and return your stolen wealth to its rightful owners."

"*Ay vây!*" Parvin's hands flew to her head. "They did this to the Golzars the other day. The Hemmatis too. They had to leave Tehran!"

"Are we going to have to leave the house?" Anna asked one of the men.

"We will see. If you renounce your wicked ways you may be allowed to remain."

Anna's nerves throbbed with dread, but she tried to stay calm. She turned to Laleh, whose face was now ashen. Parvin bowed her head, refusing to make eye contact with the men. Anna attempted to reassure the women. "Don't worry," she whispered. "I'm sure they won't hurt us." She hoped it was the truth.

As the men climbed the stairs, Laleh grimaced and raised her chin toward the staircase. Anna knew what she was worried about. Her records, makeup, books, and magazines. All things that were now forbidden. What would they do when they found them? For the first time since Anna had known her, panic unfolded across Laleh's face. Her body went limp, as if she was waiting to be punished. Or worse. Parvin still wouldn't look up, but her shoulders heaved with silent sobs.

The men clomped from room to room occasionally issuing a cry of triumph as they ransacked the Samedis' belongings. Anna wished she could monitor what they were taking. It was impossible to stay in the living room as though she and her in-laws were simply drinking afternoon tea.

Twenty minutes later, two men descended the steps. The arms of one were loaded with several bags, each overflowing with clothes, books, and shoes. The other man carried Parvin's jewelry box. It wasn't entirely closed; gold chains and bracelets spilled over the top.

Laleh looked horrified. "You're stealing our things! Put them back!"

The men laughed and carried the loot out. Then they came back in and went to work on the first floor. They confiscated gold-framed photos of the family: Bijan with Parvin, the family together. They took the paintings that hung on the walls; most of them abstract oils the Samedis had purchased in Europe. They raided Baba-joon's office and came out with files, documents, and more photos. Back in the living room they seized books from the shelves, most of them first editions. They pocketed some of them, and flung the rest on the floor. They grabbed the turquoise peacock that sat on the mantle. One of them inspected it, then smashed it on the floor. He picked up the pieces and threw them into his bag. They stole candlesticks, cloisonné bowls, even the family's silverware.

"Please!" Laleh jumped up from the sofa. "This is all we have."

One of the men waved her away. "Don't give me this *chert-o-pert*. Bullshit. People like you have already sent your money to Swiss bank accounts. Maybe you've even bought a house in America."

Laleh raised her arms in supplication. "No. You're wrong. *Lotfan.*

215

Please. Where is my father?"

"He conspired against the Supreme Leader and the revolution. He will be tried and, if he is convicted, he will be executed." The man sneered.

Parvin gasped. "*Nakhayr!* No!"

Anna chimed in. "My father-in-law is a well-respected man. By people from all walks of life. *Komak!* Help us!"

"Your father-in-law helped the shah exploit the people. Tell me. Where was he during the revolution?" The man's tone was scathing.

"But…," Anna gestured to the bags of loot, "…what are you going to do with all this? Where are you taking it?"

"It is none of your concern." He glanced around. "We will be back. Maybe tomorrow."

The man started toward the door, but stopped at Anna and Nouri's wedding album, which was still lying on a shelf. He picked it up and started thumbing through the pictures. The second man joined him. They thumbed through the photos, glanced at Anna, then back at the album. The first one snapped it shut and shoved it under his arm.

"*Lotfan.* Please." Anna begged them. "They're from our wedding."

"Lots of big shots there, no?" The men cackled.

Anna didn't know whether to be embarrassed or enraged. Even though she had a copy of the album at home, they were invading her life. Stealing her memories.

When they finally left, Laleh and Parvin remained on the couch, huddled together, looking shell-shocked. Anna tried to pull herself together and made tea. Parvin refused to drink.

"I have an idea," Laleh said. "Come with me." Anna followed her into Bijan's office where Laleh pushed against a section of wall behind the desk. A panel sprang open revealing a hidden compartment, in which, among other things, a bottle of bourbon was stowed. Laleh took the bottle, poured a shot, and tossed it down. She poured another and offered it to Anna, who shook her head.

"When was that built?" she asked Laleh.

"The secret wall? Oh, Baba had it done a long time ago. Lots of Iranian families have them. They're better than a wall safe for valuables.

Especially these days. You need—" She suddenly stopped, as though she'd just realized she'd said too much.

Anna caught the slip. "Need to what?"

"Nothing."

"What were you going to say?" Anna persisted.

Laleh shook her head, closed the safe, and took the bourbon back into the living room. She offered some to her mother but, as with the tea Anna had offered earlier, Parvin refused.

Anna tightened her lips.

They were still huddled on the sofa when Nouri arrived. Parvin immediately jumped up and started babbling about Guards, jewelry, and jinns. Anna couldn't understand her, and apparently, neither could Nouri. He and Anna made eye contact, and he rolled his eyes as though he and she were complicit. For an instant, Anna dared to feel hopeful. Then Anna remembered what Nouri had done to her just a few nights earlier. Did she really want to bond with him now? Was she that desperate for a connection? She looked away.

Parvin saw the look pass between them and pointed a finger at Anna. "It's *her* fault. If you hadn't brought her into the family, none of this would have happened. She's evil."

To Anna's surprise, Laleh defended her. "Maman, you're wrong. I think it was the maid we had last year. You know, the one who always wore hijab? After she quit, I heard a rumor she became active with the komitehs."

Anna had a vague recollection of a sullen woman who'd taken her bags upstairs when she first arrived at the Samedis. Laleh could be right. But Parvin denied it and gesticulated wildly. "No. Shahrzad would never betray us. But *her...*" She motioned to Anna again.

Nouri's eyes went cold and he tended to his mother.

But Parvin couldn't stop. Without Baba-joon to temper her, her self-control had evaporated. "You've ruined my son. Destroyed his life. Ours too. We should never have allowed the marriage to take place." Her shrill attacks pierced Anna like broken glass. Eventually Parvin sputtered, trailing off into incoherence. She collapsed on the sofa.

Nouri slid an arm around her. "Maman, do not worry. I am the man of the house now, and I will take care of you. You can move in with us until Baba comes back."

Laleh snorted in contempt. "You? The man of the house? After what you've done with your life? I think not."

Nouri glared at his sister. "Baba was always too lenient with you. From now on, you will do as I say. Do you understand?"

Laleh kept her mouth shut but her face radiated hostility.

"But Nouri," Anna asked. "What if the Foundation comes to our house next?"

Nouri brushed it off. "They won't. They've had their fill for a while." He glanced around at the mess. "I'm sure of it."

§

At home that night, Anna took out their copy of the wedding album and paged through the photos. Only eighteen months had passed, but that had been a different era. Innocent. Nothing but possibilities. Nouri had said she looked like an angel. He would never say that now. She studied the photos of the two of them with his parents. It was subtle, but Parvin seemed to be leaning away from Anna in the photos. Did she disapprove of Anna even then?

She flipped through photos of the guests at their tables, recalling the hours Parvin spent on the seating arrangements. She didn't remember many of the guests' names, but she did remember each seemed to be more important than the next. The minister of this, the chief of that. All of them well-heeled, sophisticated, wealthy. All of them associates of the shah.

Suddenly, she inhaled sharply. The Golzars. The Hemmatis. All friends of the Samedis. All had their property confiscated. And yet Nouri said the Foundation wouldn't bother *them*. She snapped the book shut, recalling his conversation with Hassan a few nights earlier. They had been talking about doing something to Baba-joon and the house. Hassan had said they needed to know that he, Nouri, was with them.

Is that what Nouri was doing? Working for the Martyrs' Foundation? Identifying people whose houses and wealth should be confiscated? He knew many wealthy Iranians—Iranians who were associates of the shah—he'd grown up with them.

Like a snowball that gets bigger as you roll it along, the idea gathered force. Anna got up and started to pace. Her husband could have become an informant. Hassan might have goaded him into it. She could almost hear Hassan: either inform or be branded a traitor. An enemy of the revolution.

She kept pacing. So Nouri had turned on his own parents. Allowed their things to be stolen. How could he? She tried to be charitable. What would have happened if he'd refused? Would he have been hauled off to Evin Prison? Maybe his arrest last summer was a warning. Either shape up or else. Maybe Nouri didn't have a choice. She tried to imagine what she would have done in his position. He was in a no-win situation. Like Odysseus choosing to sail between Scylla and Charybdis.

Still.

How could a son betray his father? She stopped pacing and raised her palm to her forehead. When had their lives sunk to this level?

Nouri was still at his mother's, but the television was on. A couple accused of adultery was being beaten in a Tehran square. Hundreds of onlookers cheered. Anna shut the TV off and slowly climbed the stairs.

Thirty-eight

By May Tehran was seared with the now familiar summer heat. The morning sun blazed through the window, waking Anna. Nouri was already gone, but a note told her that Laleh was on the way over. Nouri was spending more time with his mother, helping her adjust to their altered lifestyle. Men still barged in unexpectedly to take items from the house, but for some reason, they allowed Parvin and Laleh to remain. Anna thought she knew why.

As she climbed out of bed, a wave of nausea overwhelmed her. She stumbled to the bathroom and threw up. Afterwards, she tried to remember what she'd eaten the night before. Nothing unusual. In fact she hadn't had much of an appetite for some time. When she opened the bathroom cabinet for a sponge, she came across her tampons and realized she hadn't had a period for several months. She jerked back.

Oh god, not now, she thought. She didn't move for a moment, then finished cleaning up, showered, and dressed. She felt jittery and unsettled. How could she be pregnant? She and Nouri barely had sex. She was chewing a bit of lavash when she remembered the night he'd forced himself on her. She'd begged him to stop. He hadn't. A muscle in her jaw pulsed. She'd wanted children of her own for as long as she could remember. But not like this, not from a rape.

She slumped on the sofa, watching long rectangles of sunlight creep across the room. She lost all sense of time, and when someone knocked on the door, she didn't know if two minutes, or two hours, had passed.

She rose to her feet, feeling sluggish and thick. She went to the door, thinking it was Laleh. She couldn't tell her. It had to remain a secret, until she figured out what to do.

She opened the door to Hassan.

"Is Nouri here?" he asked.

Anna was carrying so much tension in her neck and back she felt bowed over. At the same time, her gut roiled with emotion. She gripped the edge of the door. "He's at his mother's. She's going crazy, you know. Ever since Bijan was taken. She still doesn't know which prison he's been taken to. And the house had been stripped of all their valuables. For the Foundation." Her eyes bored into Hassan, defying the decree not to make eye contact with a man.

Hassan returned a circumspect gaze. "I am sorry to hear that. But I really must talk to him. It's…it's important."

Enough, Anna thought. This two-step of duplicity had to end. "Stop pretending. You're not sorry, Hassan. Not one bit."

He flicked his eyes away from her and shifted his feet.

"You're the one who persuaded Nouri to betray his father. To make sure all their belongings were confiscated. You hated the fact that Bijan was wealthy, didn't you?"

"It is not true. You are wrong, Anna."

"I don't believe you. You were…are…jealous of Nouri, because he hasn't suffered like you. You wanted retribution. So you threatened him and forced him to denounce his family." She paused. "What did Nouri—and his family—ever do to you except show you love?"

Hassan's gaze returned to Anna. His eyes were veiled, but Anna sensed deep emotion. "You seem very sure of yourself," he said softly.

She was. For the first time, she was ready to cast off the wariness, the worrying, the measuring. She relished the opportunity to speak the truth, to let her spirit fly, limber and free. "You wanted to ruin my marriage. Well, you succeeded. You wanted to get back at Nouri. Congratulations. You've turned him into a monster."

"You are quick to blame me, Anna. Do you not think you should look elsewhere? Perhaps you should examine what your role has been in…," he waved a hand, "…all this."

"I don't need to. We both know Nouri is…impressionable. Malleable. You took advantage of that." She folded her arms. "Better than I did, in fact."

"You give me too much credit," he said again in a soft voice. His dark eyes went flat.

Now it was Anna's turn to be suspicious. What was he trying to say?

"You should not make wild accusations," he persisted. "You have not had trouble because you are Nouri's wife. But you should be careful. That could change."

A bolt of fear streaked up her spine and, for an instant, her composure slipped. She forced it back. "You know something, Hassan? You don't scare me. Get out of my house. I never want to see you again."

§

A few days later, Farrokhroo Parsa—the only woman ever to serve as an Iranian cabinet minister—was executed by firing squad. Parsa, a champion of women's rights, had been Minister of Education before the revolution. She was arrested for "spreading vice on Earth and fighting God," a trumped up charge, one of many the Council of the Islamic Revolution was fond of inventing. Shortly afterwards, the government announced that all the universities would close in June to purge academia of Western and non-Islamic influences.

Anna remembered Charlie talking about Parsa, how dedicated she was, what a fine example she set for Iranian women. Now she was dead, and Charlie was still being held hostage.

A cloud of despair settled over Anna. Her morning sickness was persisting, and her breasts had grown tender. Without a doubt she was pregnant. But she didn't know if she wanted it. She needed someone to talk to. Someone to advise her. Charlie would have known what to do. She bit her lip. She prayed Charlie was still alive.

Anna tried to think who else she could turn to. Laleh was obviously out of the question. She remembered Peter Deutsch, the man from the Swiss Embassy. She doubted he could, or would help. He would probably tell her that, once the baby was born, it would be an Iranian citizen, subject to the same rules about leaving the country as she. It didn't matter in any event. She had no way to contact him. Someone was always watching over her.

Laleh arrived and went up to the third floor. She was probably going out on the roof. Anna didn't follow her; she had no desire to chat. Instead she walked out to the patio and dipped her toes in the tiny pool. She made circles with her feet, first in one direction, then the other. She was a prisoner in a foreign country, a country that was marching backwards in time, a country that hated Americans. She'd thought Iran would be the answer to her prayers, her dream come true. But now, once more, she was alone.

She stopped circling her toes. What about Roya? At first it didn't seem like a good idea. Roya had embraced Shariah law. Anna wasn't sure, but she suspected abortion was taboo for Muslims. Probably a mortal sin. Roya wouldn't consider it. Even Anna was unsure how she felt about it. Right now she'd probably do it, but what about later? Maybe as the baby grew and came alive in her belly, she'd be more willing to be its mother. She didn't want to do something she'd regret. Still, if there was even a slim chance Roya could help her in some other way, perhaps to leave Nouri, or hide her until the baby was born, shouldn't she take the chance? It was not like she had any other options.

She decided to ask Nouri to let Roya visit. His threat to take another wife had, so far, been just that, but he would approve of Roya's visit. He might even think Anna herself was finally coming around, ready to assume the role of the meek Islamic wife. She prepared what to say to Nouri. How to smile shyly and beg his indulgence. Appeal to his ego. It might work. She stood up, dried her feet, and went up to her room, feeling a tiny sliver of hope.

Anna was napping when she was awakened by loud voices from downstairs. She crept to the top of the staircase. Nouri and Laleh were arguing. Bitterly. Both their faces were crimson. They were speaking very rapidly in Farsi, so Anna couldn't pick up much. She could tell

Laleh was cursing, and Nouri replied by calling her a whore. Anna was so tired of the incessant fighting that she clapped her hands over her ears. She could still hear the shouts. Finally she yelled out.

"Stop it! Both of you! Stop arguing!"

Nouri spun around. He was scowling, his eyes hard, and his face was unusually creased. Anger seemed to pour off him. "How dare you interfere? Stay out of this."

While he was yelling, Laleh slipped out the front door, her bag on her shoulder. Anna couldn't blame her. Nouri looked wild, out of control.

When Nouri realized Laleh had gone, he ran to the door and yelled after her. There was no response. Then he turned and raced up the steps two at a time. At the top of the staircase he grabbed Anna's shoulders with both hands and squeezed them so hard it was painful. "And *you!*" He emphasized the word. "Why are the women in this family so insolent? What did you say to Hassan?" His voice was laced with fury.

"What do you mean?"

He sucked in a breath, as if he couldn't believe she had the nerve to ask the question. "The other day," he seethed, "you accused him of brainwashing me. You forbade him to come to the house. Do you have any idea what you've done?"

Anna was exhausted. His rage was like a deep pool with no bottom. She let it float over her. "No. Tell me."

Nouri squeezed her shoulders harder. She tried to shake him off, but his fingers dug into her skin. "Let go. You're hurting me, Nouri."

"Do you know how much power Hassan has? You have done enormous damage. You have ruined my relationship with him. Jeopardized our safety. And the family's."

"Me? I've put the family in jeopardy? Ever since Baba-joon was arrested, your family has fallen apart. Maman-joon has gone crazy. Laleh is useless. Tell me something, Nouri. Why was Baba arrested? Of the thousands of people who were associated with the shah, why him? Why now?"

Nouri glared at her, but the pressure on her shoulders lessened. She shook him off and backed up.

"I know you've been working for the Foundation. I know you betrayed your father. Your own father, Nouri. The man who gave you life."

For an instant Nouri looked stunned, and Anna knew she was right. But then his eyes bulged out, his lips tightened, and his features twisted into a mask of rage. He grabbed her again and dragged her to the steps. She felt hot breath on her face. He was so frenzied he was panting.

Her pulse raced, but she wouldn't stop until she'd said it all. "As for Hassan, he's no friend of yours. He engineered your arrest. And your job for the Foundation. He might have power, but he's used that power to turn you into something ugly and cruel. The evil jinns you are so quick to say are inside me? They live in your soul, Nouri. You've become a monster."

Nouri seized her again and shook her back and forth. Her head swung back and forth like a rag doll. He yanked her to the top of the staircase. She was sure he was going to push her down the steps. She would break her neck.

"You deserve to be put to death for your lies," he shouted. "Arrested and killed or executed or…" He glanced down the steps, then back at her.

Her heart hammered in her chest. Somehow she summoned up the strength to stay calm. "Or what? Go ahead. Kill me, Nouri. But you should know if you do, you will be killing your own child."

He froze, his hands still clutching her shoulders.

"It's the truth. I'm pregnant, Nouri. Kill me and you'll be two for two. Your father and your child."

He raised his hand. He was either going to strike her or shove her down the stairs. Either way, she wouldn't survive. She watched his hand. He saw her watching. He hesitated for an instant, then lowered his arm. "You will say anything to get what you want."

He pulled her into the bedroom and threw her down on the bed. He pinned her down with one hand and pressed down on her chest. With the other he started tearing at her shorts.

She struggled to escape. "Stop. Nouri. Don't!"

He ignored her. Her shorts ripped. Then he went to work on her panties. As they tore, he grunted and unbuttoned his pants. Panic lodged in her throat.

"It's over Nouri. There's nothing left."

"It is over when I say it is," he hissed.

When he was finished, he rolled off her, spent, and fell asleep. She picked herself up off the bed and went into the bathroom. Afterwards, she went down to the kitchen. At that time of the day she'd normally be cooking dinner, but tonight she couldn't even consider it. Husband or not, she would not feed a man who had raped her. As she left the kitchen, she noticed one of her steak knives was missing from the wooden block on the counter. She made a half-hearted attempt to find it, but it wasn't in the drawers or the dishwasher. She couldn't worry about it now. She was too miserable.

§

Nouri woke two hours later and came downstairs in pants and an undershirt, demanding dinner. Anna told him there was none. He glared at her, then ordered her to iron his shirt. She refused.

"There is something you need to understand, Nouri. I don't want this baby. I do not want a child to endure this…hell. Not in this house. Not in this family. Not in Iran. Do you understand, Nouri? Do you?"

For an instant his shell cracked, and Anna saw a profound sorrow spread across his face. Then the crack disappeared and his features realigned themselves into his usual mask of sullen indifference. He rose from the table, grabbed his shirt, and stormed out.

It was the last time she would see him, but she didn't know it then. She washed the dishes from breakfast, stacked them in the drain board. She rested her head in her hands. Felt the tears roll down her cheeks. Then she went upstairs. She was glad for the silence and peace, however fleeting. She changed into her nightclothes and went to bed.

PART THREE

Thirty-nine

Whenever the words "Evin Prison" were mentioned during a conversation, a hush descended. Iranians fidgeted, looked anxious, tried to change the subject. Years ago, the property occupied by the prison had belonged to a pro-Western prime minister. After his death, the estate passed to the shah, and SAVAK turned it into a prison for criminals and political prisoners. Evin officials were known to treat inmates harshly, doling out punishments that included torture. Many went in, few came out. It became the most feared place in Iran. After the overthrow of the shah, the management of Evin fell to the Revolutionary Guards and it became even more brutal.

Still, Evin was a study in contrasts. Nestled in the foothills of the Alborz Mountains, the prison wasn't far from Shemiran. Anna had driven by many times when returning from central Tehran. And the fact that it was once an estate gave it a patina of elegance. Of course, the buildings were "remodeled," with a thick wall now surrounding them. But the grounds, sprawled across a few acres, were known to be dotted with trees, and the prison yard was clean.

When the Guards came in the middle of the night to arrest her for Nouri's murder, Anna knew without asking that she would be taken to Evin. It was the closest prison to the house, and it was the place that everyone had nightmares about. The Guards who came to the door were armed not only with machine guns but wore knives on their waistbands. One brandished the steak knife from America. They wouldn't let her touch it, but they claimed the rusty brown spots on the blade were Nouri's blood.

They ordered her to get dressed and cover herself with her chador. Then they cuffed her wrists and dragged her out to the black Mercedes. Anna followed their orders without protest. For some reason she couldn't summon up the fear she knew she should. She wasn't sure whether she was in shock or if it was something else, but once they were on their way, her hands rested placidly in her lap. She almost smiled, anticipating how she would tell them that the steak knife was from the Great Satan's factories. She wondered if they would drop it like a red-hot poker. At the same time, she noted the irony of her plight—given what was probably coming, this might be the last time she found anything humorous.

It was a short ride. They turned onto a narrow twisting road, then drove through a gate. Night painted the property in a swath of black. In daylight the walls were sandy, Anna recalled. Now the blackness was slashed by the sharp white beam of spotlights, strategically placed near the prison buildings. Armed guards were stationed every few yards. The enormity of her situation settled over her. She was going in. The question was whether she would ever come out.

The men who brought her slipped a blindfold over her eyes, and hauled her out of the car. One seized her arm and marched her across an open space. A courtyard, perhaps? It was the height of summer and still hot, but the night breeze raised goose bumps on her skin. Anna tried to count the steps to the entrance, and, once inside, down the hall. But they made too many twists and turns, and she lost count. Finally, they pushed her against a wall and pressed down on her shoulders. She dropped awkwardly to a stone floor. She could just make out a thin ribbon of light below the blindfold, and she had the impression of boots. Someone ordered her not to move. They spoke in Farsi, but that much she understood.

She leaned her head against a wall and tried to get her bearings. The smells—body odor, urine, and, for some reason, onions—assailed her, but another odor, acrid and salty, was layered over them. The smell of fear. She breathed through her mouth. What tightened her stomach, though, were the sounds. The shuffling of boots. The snap of a whip followed by a piercing scream. Mysterious thwacks, doors being slammed, the cries of people begging for mercy.

Anna shivered. Unfamiliar sensations coursed through her. The cool hard floor was comforting one instant, unbearable the next. Was she sick? Was it the pregnancy? She wondered if this was how Nouri felt when he was arrested. Her earlier bravery vanished. She'd been a fool to imagine she could survive this.

Nouri. Nouri was dead. Living with him had been hell for the past six months, but before, when they'd first connected, she'd never loved anyone more. And been loved in return. She remembered how they'd met in the bookstore. Their year in Chicago. How he couldn't keep his hands off her. How she felt the same way. She doubted she would ever love anyone with the same abandon. God, or Allah—or whoever decided these things—had given her a chance. But then he'd destroyed it. She lowered her head. Despite the anger—no, the hate—she and Nouri had shared, Anna felt a hot tear roll down her cheek.

She had no sense of time passing, but the pitch of the noise around her changed. It wasn't quieter. Just different. The screams didn't seem as raw. Or was she getting used to them? Her thoughts tumbled out, jumbled and chaotic. It was clear someone was framing her. Just like they'd framed Nouri. But unlike Nouri, someone had gone to a lot of trouble to make *sure* she would be blamed.

There weren't a lot of possibilities. It had to be someone who came to the house. Who had the opportunity to steal the knife. Which meant Hassan, Laleh, Roya, Maman, or Baba-joon. Some of Nouri's associates from the Metro had been to the house for dinner, but that was a long time ago. She would have noticed a missing knife. Charlie and Ibram had been at the house, too, but obviously Charlie wouldn't have done it. She doubted Ibram would, either. When she thought through her relationship with each person, she kept coming back to Hassan. Hassan had always hated her—for marrying Nouri, for being American, for not being submissive. She imagined how he might have stolen the knife while she was in her room, or watering the chenar tree, and Nouri was in the bathroom.

A sudden shout sliced into her thoughts. "Anna Samedi! Get up!"

Between the blindfold and her hands, which were still cuffed, her balance was off. She lurched awkwardly to her feet, using the wall as a brace.

"Take three steps forward," the voice shouted. She did. "Now turn to your right and walk." She obeyed. Eight steps later, she stumbled into a wall and knocked her head against it. She staggered back. A current of air wafted toward her. A door had opened. Another male voice called out in English. "Enter."

She stretched her hands out in front, like a child playing blindman's bluff, and shuffled into a room. Someone grabbed her and pushed her into a chair. Hands snatched the blindfold and tore it off. The bright light pouring in blinded her, and she squeezed her eyes shut. When she opened them again, she squinted.

Three men were in the room, two seated at a table. They were not the ones who'd brought her here. All three had scruffy looking beards. One had pitted skin where his beard hadn't grown—he must suffer from a bad case of acne. The second looked older and wore glasses. Usually she liked men in glasses—they gentled a person—but this man's eyes were cold steel. There would be no mercy from him. The third man stood behind the others. He fidgeted, shifted his weight, and seemed embarrassed. They made eye contact. He looked familiar. She knew this man. He looked away. Who was he?

The man with the glasses tossed a pad of paper down on the table. And a pen. "If you make a confession, it will go easier on you," he said in English. No introduction. No name.

She pursed her lips. They were dry and cracked. She needed water. "What am I confessing to?"

His eyebrows arched. "Please, do not take us for fools. We know you killed your husband. We know why. We know how. There is nothing more to investigate. Inshallah, justice will be served."

The men's body odor drifted across the table. She forced herself not to react. "I didn't kill him. I don't know who did. I'm being set up."

The eyebrows arched higher. A knowing look came into his eyes.

"I would never kill my husband." She considered telling them that she was pregnant, but decided it might backfire. They could accuse her of killing Nouri so she could take the baby back to America once it was born.

"Of course you will deny it. Murder is a capital offense in Iran. You will pay the price with your own life."

Anna gazed steadily at the man. "I told you. Someone is framing me."

He didn't answer her directly. "We have the words of a brave Iranian mother and daughter against an American. Whom do you think we will believe?" He fixed her with a penetrating glare. "You should know that your husband's death has made him a martyr. As much as anyone, he has been a victim of the Great Satan and his minions. His death will be inscribed as that of a brave soldier, fighting against the oppressors."

Anna's spirits sank. It was no use. This was a kangaroo court. She glanced at the other two men. The man with the pitted face wore a predatory leer, as if he couldn't wait to get his hands on her. But the third man, the man who was standing, still refused to make eye contact. Who was he?

In a flash it came to her. Massoud. Chicago. Daley Plaza. The man who'd headed the Iranian Students Association. She stared at him. Yes—despite the beard and the uniform—it was him. He'd been with an American girl, Anna recalled, a blonde who helped him distribute flyers. Anna opened her mouth, about to address him by name, then hesitated. Something told her not to. But he knew she knew. She could see it in his eyes. She turned her gaze back to the man with the glasses. For some reason, she felt more confident.

"I moved to Iran to marry Nouri. He was my husband." She gave him a sad smile. "I never loved anyone like I loved him."

The man flicked his hand dismissively. "You wanted to go back to America. He wouldn't let you. You failed to become a good Muslim wife. He had every right to divorce you or take another wife. But he did not. He gave you every opportunity to prove yourself. Still, you wouldn't obey. You refused to wear the chador, to submit to Shariah law. You were plotting to escape. He discovered it. And so you killed him."

Who had he been talking to?

"Do you deny it?"

Anna laced her hands together to keep her temper—and fear—under control. "I didn't kill him. And I won't sign anything that says I did."

Meanwhile, her thoughts were racing. How had Massoud ended up as a Guard at Evin Prison? He must have moved back from the US not long after they had. And decided to take the path of least resistance. He *had* been an anti-shah activist. Anna wondered briefly what happened to his blonde girlfriend. She probably married a doctor and was living on the North Shore.

Then another thought occurred to her. Perhaps Massoud and Nouri had been in contact. No, Nouri would have said something. Perhaps, perhaps not. But even if they were, what good would it do now?

The man with the glasses seemed to know her mind had wandered. He cleared his throat. "If you will not confess willingly, we must 'encourage' you to change your mind."

Her focus snapped back.

He stood, lowered his voice, and murmured to the others. They went to her, flanking her on both sides. They slipped her blindfold and cuffs back on, grabbed her under her armpits, and walked her out of the room. Was Massoud's hold just a little gentler than Pitface's? Or was she imagining it? Either way, she tried to shake them off. "It's all right. You don't need to do that. I'm coming."

They tightened their grip.

§

The men walked Anna out of one building and into another. This one had a linoleum floor. Her shoes thudded on the tiles. They walked down a set of stairs, making so many turns that she lost her orientation. She wondered if they did that on purpose. Finally, they stopped. Something swung open with a metallic squeak. They unlocked her cuffs and shoved her inside. The gate shut with a clang.

The first thing that assaulted her was the fetid smell, a combination of urine, feces, and vomit. She took off her blindfold. She was in a small cell, no bigger than a closet. Barely enough room to stretch. She spotted a tiny slit at the top of wall. A feeble light struggling to break through told her that she was in a basement. There was no sink or toilet. No bed or blankets. Nothing except a cement floor. The walls were concrete.

At first it seemed quieter here, but the silence was deceptive. As she acclimated to the space, Anna picked up whimpers and soft cries. Other people were nearby. People in misery and pain. Had they been tortured? Was that what was in store for her?

She bit her lip and looked around. Did anyone even know she was here? Maman-joon and Laleh must know, as they were apparently the ones accusing her. They would be no help. They would be preoccupied with their own grief, anyway, and were probably planning Nouri's funeral. Muslims buried their dead within twenty-four hours. Tears welled up. She would not be there.

She thought about her parents. They had no idea that Nouri was dead. Unlike in America, here there was no opportunity to make a phone call when you were arrested. Indeed, unless her jailers allowed her to contact them, there was a good chance no one would ever know what happened to her. She would simply disappear, like so many others, just swallowed up. Her jailers would say that she'd died trying to escape, she had an accident; maybe she'd committed suicide. No one would dispute it, because no one would know the truth.

The isolation swelled and became overpowering. Anna pulled her legs to her chest and rocked back and forth. She suspected it was only a matter of time before her own sobs joined the quiet chorus of grief around her.

Forty

The only way Anna could detect the passage of time was by the slit at the top of her cell. It became brighter. She assumed that meant it was daylight. But her internal clock was off kilter, and she was exhausted. The man with the pitted face made it a point to come to her cell—probably every hour, she guessed—to shine a bright light on her face and wake her from the little sleep she'd managed to grab. Each time he intruded he demanded to know whether she was ready to confess. Each time she said no. He would leave, only to return again later.

During one of the visits a new Guard appeared. He brought with him a cup of tea. She drank it greedily, then realized she had to pee. "Where is the bathroom?" she asked in Farsi.

"You're in it." He laughed.

She suppressed her disgust.

The light from the slit at the top of the cell faded. The sun must have been setting. She had been in jail almost twenty-four hours. Her stomach agreed. It had been growling in hunger, but now it felt like it was being squeezed by a steel band. Was there something in the tea? Did they put something in it to make her more miserable?

The Guard with the pitted face returned. This time Massoud was with him. They repeated the charade with the light, demanding to know if she was ready to confess. She shook her head. They didn't retreat. Massoud unlocked the cell. They came inside, put on her blindfold, and walked her upstairs.

When they ripped off the blindfold, she saw that the other man who'd interrogated her had joined them, but she'd been taken to a different room. This one had a metal cot in one corner. A thin, tattered spread covered it, but Anna could see the crisscrossing of a metal frame underneath. Attached to the four corners of the cot were chains, which in turn were attached to metal cuffs. In the corner, she saw a thick black pole with a group of wires at one end. A whip. Fear streaked up her spine.

The Guard with the glasses saw her looking at the whip and smiled. "Did you think you were exempt from Shariah law because you are American? When you married your husband you became Muslim and an Iranian citizen. You are accountable to the laws of Iran."

Anna kept her mouth shut.

"Chain her," he said to Massoud and the man with the pitted face. They pulled her over to the cot. She tried to wriggle out of their grasp, but it was useless, and they seemed to know it was just a pro forma effort. She glanced at Massoud. He still would not make eye contact. They slammed her down on the cot. The metal frame bit into her skin. They clutched her arms and forced them over her head, then cuffed them to the bed, one on each side. They did the same with her feet.

The man with glasses peered over her. "Last chance to confess to your crimes."

"I didn't kill my husband."

The man shrugged, picked up the metal whip, and came back. She turned her head to the side and saw Massoud. This time he was looking at her. His face was a mix of sorrow and shame. The man with the glasses flicked the whip back, then forward. She heard it swish, followed by a staccato crack as it lashed her feet. Her feet stung. At first she thought it wasn't so bad, but then a wave of unbearably hot, sharp pain rushed up from her feet. She screamed.

He whipped her again. This time the pain took her breath away. She couldn't take in enough air to scream. The man with the whip lashed her again, and somehow, she found enough air to shriek. Massoud bolted into the hall. Between her cries, the sounds of him retching, and the howls from other rooms, it was too much. Mercifully, a powerful force rose up and enveloped her in a soft black silence.

§

Anna was running on a beach, but the sand was so hot it burned her feet. The cool, blue water was just a few feet away. She jogged toward it, knowing it would bring relief, but the closer she got, the farther the ocean receded, as if it was low tide in warp speed. "Stop!" she yelled to the sea. "I need you!"

Slowly, she came back to awareness. She was still strapped to the bed. Her first impression was that she was alone. The second was that her feet were on fire. Burning, blazing, pulsating flames licked her skin. She thought maybe someone had screwed her feet in backwards. She groaned and tried to lift her head, but she felt heavy and sluggish. She doubted she would ever walk again.

A dull pain throbbed against her temples. She needed to turn off her brain. Withdraw. She couldn't be vigilant and aware—the pain was too agonizing. Where was the switch, she thought? Please, God. Turn it off. Turn *me* off. Maybe she *should* confess. It wouldn't make much difference. They were going to kill her one way or another. Wasn't she already half dead? The door opened. A Guard she hadn't seen before eyed her, gazed at her feet, and flinched. He retreated, then came back with rubber thong sandals and dropped them on the floor. He proceeded to unfasten her arms and legs from the cuffs. Anna didn't move. She didn't know if she could.

"Come," the Guard said. He looked young, maybe as young as Laleh. And embarrassed, as if he would rather have been anywhere on earth than here. She slowly raised herself. Her head whirled with dizziness, and she fell back on the cot. The metal bed frame felt like sharp spikes stabbing her back.

"Please," she croaked. "I need help."

The Guard nodded. It was the first acknowledgement by anyone that she was a human. She felt unaccountably grateful. He grasped her arm and helped her up. The world slowly settled upright.

"We need to go," he said urgently, as if there was a schedule to which they had to adhere.

Anna blinked. With a great effort she bent over and checked her feet. She wasn't sure what she expected—her skin in shreds, or a bloody pulp—so she was surprised to see it wasn't. The most noticeable thing was that her feet were swollen, almost twice as large as normal. They were blue and purple, too, but there was no blood. The whip had not broken her skin. She had trouble actually believing it—the pain had been so excruciating.

She slipped the thongs on, slid off the bed, and shifted her weight onto her feet. A fresh wave of pain engulfed her. She cried out and rolled her feet to their outer edges. But the young Guard's support was firm, and she managed to hobble to the door. The Guard opened it, but then froze, as if he'd forgotten something, and shut it. For an instant Anna wondered if this had all been a ruse, and something even more horrible was about to happen. But it was only the blindfold. He retrieved it from the floor and slipped it over her eyes.

Together they shuffled down halls that seemed endless. They exited a building and crossed the courtyard. A soft rain was falling. Anna lifted her arms and face into it. She caught a whiff of her own unwashed body. She hadn't showered in days.

A moment later they were inside yet another building.

"Where are we going?" she asked in Farsi.

A grunt was his response.

He led her down a hall with linoleum floors into a small room. He took off her blindfold. Anna blinked. The office was bare, save for a desk and two chairs. Behind the desk sat a woman in a chador. She was thin, almost gaunt, and her face was shaped like a triangle, with a broad brow—above which not a strand of hair escaped her rusari—and a narrow, pointed chin. Bushy eyebrows framed a stern expression. She nodded at the Guard and he retreated. Anna clutched the back of a chair for support. The woman gestured her into it.

As Anna sat, the woman folded her hands. "I am Sister Azar," she said in English. "You will be under my supervision until you are sentenced."

"Sentenced? What sentence? There has been no trial," Anna said.

Sister Azar's gaze turned calculating. "Oh, but there was. The night you were brought here. You were not present, but you were found guilty of murder."

Anna's jaw dropped. "They can't do that! I didn't kill him. I have a right—"

The woman laughed. "This is not America, with your endless system of justice that protects the guilty. Here, justice is swift. And final."

"I want to lodge a protest." Even as she said it, though, she understood how naïve she sounded.

Sister Azar didn't bother to reply. "I will take you to the ward."

She got up and went to the door. Anna sank back in the chair. "How long until I'm sentenced?"

She shrugged. "Everyone is preoccupied with the hostages. And you are American. They will be careful." She waggled a finger. "Do not give them a reason to hurry." It was a warning.

She marched down the hall, with Anna limping behind. She blew out a breath, seemingly impatient that Anna couldn't keep up. They made a few turns, and eventually came to a door. Sister Azar unlocked and opened it, and they continued down the hall.

The room they came to wasn't much larger than the Samedis' living room, Anna guessed, but at least forty women, maybe more, were crammed into it. Most sat on the floor in small groups reading or talking quietly. It was so crowded that they were practically on top of each other. A few sat by themselves. One rocked back and forth, muttering in silence. Sister Azar gave Anna a little shove, and she stumbled in. Anna heard a metallic click as the door was locked behind her.

Curious glances came her way. She shuffled awkwardly to a corner of the room and gingerly lowered herself to the floor. She slipped off the thongs, and extended her feet. They touched the back of another woman who twisted around with a scowl. Anna bent her knees and placed her feet on the floor so they were no longer touching the woman, but a fresh stab of pain shot through her. Trying to breathe through it, she distracted herself by looking around.

The first thing she noticed was the women's clothing. They were dressed in t-shirts, jeans, and dresses. No hijab or chadors. The next thing she noticed was that despite the lack of space, there was a sense of order in the room. Blankets and spreads were folded in one spot, books and shoes in another. Chadors and bags hung on hooks. She leaned back against the wall. She wasn't sure she wanted to see more. She knew what was ahead. Interacting with this place, and the people in it, would bring her closer to death. She squeezed her eyes shut.

She wasn't sure how much time passed when she felt a gentle tug on her chador. Her eyes snapped open. A young woman with riotous auburn curls tamed only by a yellow headband was smiling at her. It was the first real smile Anna had seen since she was arrested. She examined the girl. Widely-spaced eyes the color of ochre, lashes so light they looked invisible, and a spill of freckles on her nose and cheeks. She held strips of cloth and dangled them in front of Anna. "Let me help you bandage your feet," she said in English.

This simple kindness was the breaking point. Anna couldn't hold it together any longer. She started to weep, long wrenching sobs. She thought maybe she would cry forever.

Forty-one

Nousha was a political prisoner, she explained when Anna's tears finally stopped. She'd been found guilty of spying for the enemies of the revolution. When Anna asked which enemies, she shrugged. "I am a Kurd. And a Sunni Muslim. The Ayatollah has declared a holy war against us."

Anna knew about the problems between Iran and the Kurdish people. The Kurds were mostly Sunni Muslims and lived in Northern Iran. They wanted independence from Iran and, since the shah's downfall, they'd been bitterly fighting for it. Iranians, on the other hand, were mostly Shi'a Muslims and considered the Kurds a threat.

"Even so," Anna asked, "hasn't there always been a Kurdish community in Persia?"

"That is true. Sometimes they persecute us, sometimes they leave us alone. Now, though…" Nousha blew out a breath. "We are not a part of the new society—even though we fought for the shah's downfall. They think we are being exploited by foreign powers, that we want to destabilize the new regime. So they are trying to crush us. Many Kurds have left Iran."

"Why didn't you?"

"My fiancé was teaching at a Kurdish school. He pledged to stay as long as the school remained open. I chose to stay with him." She sighed. "They closed the school a month ago. We tried to leave for Mahabad, then Turkey, but they stopped us outside Tehran. They accused us of conspiring to bring down the Islamic government. We weren't, of course, but it didn't matter. My fiancé was executed, and I am sentenced to death."

A swell of anger rolled over Anna. How could Nousha sound so calm? Why wasn't she fighting the trumped up charges? Scratching, clawing for justice and a chance to stay alive?

As if she knew what Anna was thinking, she said, "I have no way to fight back. This is my life now. For as long as it lasts. It will go better for me in Paradise."

Anna understood. She felt that way herself. "I am a Christian."

Nousha nodded. "They will pressure you to convert."

"Technically I did. When I got married."

Nousha studied her, then tilted her head. "Why are you here?"

"They say I murdered my husband."

"And because you are an American, and there are Americans being held hostage, it has become political."

Anna nodded.

Nousha touched her shoulder. "Be brave, my American friend. I will say a prayer for your feet." She stood, faced the wall, and whispered words Anna didn't understand. Only afterwards did Anna realize that Nousha had never asked her if she *had* killed Nouri.

§

Over the next few days Anna's feet healed. They were still stiff and sore, but it no longer hurt so much to walk. As she settled into the ward, a routine of sorts emerged. A bell woke the women before dawn for prayers, but since she was not Muslim, no one forced her to participate. Tolerance came at odd times and places, she thought. And yet the only books in the room were the Qur'an and religious tracts, and they were all in Arabic.

After prayers, breakfast—or what they called breakfast—was served. Usually it was tea and bread. The first time she drank the tea, it was tinged with a distinct taste. It took a moment to identify. Vicks Vapo-Rub.

"This tastes like the salve they used when I got sick as a child," she said to Nousha.

"It is camphor. They add it to the tea."

"Camphor? Why?"

"It will stop your period."

Anna frowned.

"They don't want to spend money on sanitary napkins."

Anna stiffened. If camphor stopped periods, what would it do to someone who was pregnant? She wanted to ask, but she didn't know Nousha well enough. What if she was a spy or an informant? She spit the tea out.

"Some of the girls don't mind," Nousha said. "They say camphor is soothing. It dulls pain."

"What do you say?"

"It's hard not to drink it. It is the only beverage we have. I think it makes me lethargic. Sometimes it causes swelling. Others say it makes them depressed." She shrugged. "Then again, what does it matter?"

Anna eyed the tea suspiciously.

After breakfast the women made an effort to tidy up, stacking blankets and other things, and washing up with cold water. Nousha told her they got hot showers only once every two to three weeks, and then only for a few minutes.

The rest of the morning was spent reading, talking, and gossiping, except for the "crazies," as Nousha called them, women who had lost their sanity and were comatose or talked gibberish. Lunch was sometimes soup, sometimes stew, but was always thin and watery. Once in a while someone found a chunk of meat in her bowl and showed it off to the others.

More prayers, and then, most days, the women went out to the courtyard for an hour of air. Inmates from each cellblock were taken out separately; there was no interaction between wards. Or, of course, the sexes. Which meant Anna had no idea how many prisoners were housed here. Or if, like her, Baba-joon might also be imprisoned at Evin.

Anna noticed some women seemed to have more than others:

clothes, cigarettes, even bits of extra food. She asked Nousha about it.

"Most of the girls who have more than the rest of us are prostitutes, thieves, con artists. They know how to work the system and get what they need." Nousha rubbed her fingers together.

"How do they get the stuff?"

"From family. During visits. Then they hide it and only bring it out when it's time to bribe the Guards."

"Where do they hide it?"

"They sew it into the lining of their chadors."

Anna's eyebrows arched. She had much to learn.

Dinner was usually fruit, more tea, and sometimes cheese. Anna had to drink the tea; no other beverages were offered. The lights were turned off at eleven, but with fifty girls in a room designed for twenty, sleeping space was at a premium. They jammed together on the floor or in the hall. Sometimes they took turns lying on their backs. Nousha carved out a tiny space for Anna next to her.

The third night Anna was there, a series of loud cracks woke her. "What was that?" she asked shakily.

Nousha swallowed. It took her a moment to answer. "Executions. They are shooting prisoners."

Anna couldn't go back to sleep.

Forty-two

The only thing Anna had was plenty of time. Time to ruminate, to regret, to relive the past. She tried to pinpoint the moment she knew her life was in tatters. Was it the first night that Nouri had deserted her for one of his endless meetings? Was it the morning when he woke up, rolled over, and stared at her with disgust? Was it when he refused to let her stay alone and kept her a virtual prisoner?

She recalled a book written about the five stages of grief, and decided she was passing through them now, except she was doing so out of order. She'd already passed denial—she went through that when Nouri first started to change. Then she'd skipped to bargaining—if she tried to please, if she tried hard, everything would still work out. But of course, it didn't, and she sank into a depression, the fourth stage.

From there she was supposed to find acceptance, the same resignation as Nousha. Except she couldn't. Anna's lifelong dream—to be part of a real family and have one of her own—had been destroyed. And that infuriated her. Indeed, her anger had bloomed like a hothouse flower, casting off petals of rage. But with it came clarity and a sense of purpose. Someone was framing her for Nouri's murder. She could not permit that to continue. She must try to save herself. Or die trying.

Anna came to trust Nousha and one day she talked about Nouri's death. "The day the Guards took Baba-joon, Laleh and I raced over to the house. I wonder now if that was the setup. Maybe that was when someone broke into my house and took the knife."

"Yes, but who? Who wanted to kill Nouri? And who wanted to frame you?"

"Maman-joon never liked me, I know that now. But I don't believe she had anything to do with this. She just doesn't seem capable of it. Why would she kill her own son? Surely she could think of another way to get at me. And Laleh wanted me to be her best friend. Of course, that was before things started…" Her voice trailed off.

"What?"

Anna shook her head. "No. I can't believe Laleh is responsible. The most important person in Laleh's life is Laleh. And she was determined to leave Iran for London to be with her boyfriend."

"So?"

"If anything, Laleh would want to keep on Nouri's good side. In Baba-joon's absence, he would be the one to grant her permission to leave."

"If she is not married, she only needs a *ghayyem*—guardian—until she's eighteen. After that she can get her own passport and go."

"She just turned eighteen," Anna said, remembering that they'd marked the day about a month ago. Nouri had given Laleh a beautiful gold bracelet he'd bought in downtown Tehran.

"Then there is no reason for her to care what her brother thinks."

Anna mulled it over.

"Didn't you say you thought your husband was working for the Foundation? Confiscating the assets and property of others?"

Anna nodded. "Most were friends of the family."

"Well then." Nousha flipped up her hands and flashed a triumphant smile. "There it is."

"What?"

"It was one of them, taking revenge for what Nouri did to their family."

"You think so?"

"What would you do if someone—who you knew and trusted your entire life—came to your house and stole everything of value? Perhaps arranged for one or two family members to be put in prison too, just for good measure?"

Anna frowned. She hadn't considered that. "But why would they frame *me*? Why not Nouri?"

It was Nousha's turn to frown. "Retribution. You know. An eye for an eye. The Qur'an exhorts Muslims to wreak vengeance on one's enemies."

"It's possible," Anna said. But she still suspected Hassan. "Even after Nouri denounced his father, Hassan considered him a threat. Probably because he was married to me, an infidel." She told Nousha her theory that Hassan had waited until he knew they were gone, come in, stolen the knife, then had one of his compatriots stab Nouri. "Murder is just another part of life in Iran today."

Nousha played with her lips, as if she was thinking it over. Then she shrugged. "Well, there is one thing."

"What's that?"

"They won't do anything to you until your baby is born."

Anna blanched. "How did you know I was pregnant?"

"You get sick in the morning. Your skin has a rosy glow. And you have a bump on your stomach. With the food here, there is no way you are putting on weight."

Anna laid her hand on Nousha's arm. "Please, don't say anything. I haven't told anyone."

Nousha's eyebrows arched. "Oh, but you must tell them. How far along are you?"

"I'm not sure. Three...no...maybe four months." She was unwilling to recall the times Nouri had raped her.

"But you *must* remember. You are carrying Nouri's child. An Iranian child. If they know that, they will not kill you. It is against the law. In fact, they will take better care of you."

"Really?" Anna clasped her hands together. For the first time since she'd been in Evin Prison, she felt a surge of hope. Then she noticed Nousha would not make eye contact. She was looking down, as if something of acute interest had materialized on the floor.

"What is it, Nousha? There's something you're not telling me."

Nousha looked up. Sorrow lined her face. "They will probably take the baby after it is born."

Anna stiffened.

"They might give him to your in-laws. Or to a childless couple."

Anna imagined Maman-joon or, even worse, a stranger raising the baby growing inside her. No, that would not, could not happen. It wasn't until that very moment that she'd realized that, conceived in rape or not, she wanted this baby.

"Then I will escape. Somehow. And take the baby with me."

Nousha smiled sadly, as if she knew Anna was simply spinning fantasies. "If the baby is born while you are still in Iran, it will be Iranian. You will not be permitted to take it out of the country."

"No!" Anna cried. At her outburst the other women turned and stared. She drew herself up. The baby was hers, she thought fiercely, and she would do whatever was necessary to keep it.

§

Two days later the ward hummed with anticipation. The women washed and dressed in clean clothes. It was visiting day, the one day a month when prisoners could see close family members. Anna tried not to pay attention to the buzz. She would not be entertaining any visitors. Laleh and Maman-joon would never come to Evin willingly, unless it was to her execution.

She sat on the floor as women's names were called. One by one they put on their chadors and left the room. They returned about an hour later. Many were crying, their earlier anticipation replaced by grief or a gnawing look of anxiety. Anna was almost grateful she didn't have to go through it.

When they called her name, she sat up in surprise. Who could be visiting her? She rose slowly, put on her chador, and went to Sister Azar's office where she was blindfolded. "You are going to a special place." Anna went rigid. Where were they taking her?

Nousha had told Anna about the visitation building. It was divided by a thick glass partition, with family members on one side, prisoners on the other. There was no phone through which to talk, and families communicated through sign language or reading lips. When Anna was finally told to sit down, she expected to be on the prisoners' side of the glass. But when they removed her blindfold, she was in a small room, much like the room they'd interrogated her in when she was first brought to Evin. The Guard cuffed her hands and shackled her feet.

Her pulse started to race, and her breath grew short. Were they going to interrogate her again? Lash her feet? Or something worse? Maybe Nousha was wrong about their policy of not executing pregnant women. Her mouth went dry. Terror seeped under her skin.

The door opened and someone entered. Dressed in a Guard's uniform, he kept his back to her. When he closed the door and turned around, Anna gasped.

Hassan walked to the table and sat across from her. He did not smile.

It took Anna a moment to regain her composure. "Have you come to gloat? You must be pleased how everything's turned out."

He hesitated. Then, "I know that you hate me, Anna."

She didn't answer him.

He waved a hand. "You think I am responsible for this."

She still didn't answer.

"Anna, I am not your enemy."

Anna pressed her hands together so hard that her nails sliced into her skin.

"I have come at Bijan's request."

She reeled back. "Baba-joon?"

"He has been released from prison. He is back home."

"What? How? When?"

"They tell me that you already know that Nouri's death is being treated as that of a martyr. Because of that, they took pity on the family and released Bijan from prison."

Anna's anger welled up, strong and pure. "Are you saying that's the price the family paid for Nouri's death? That good came from it? Is that the way you fool yourself into thinking you didn't commit murder? You disgust me, Hassan." She would have spit on him, wheeled around, and stormed out of the room if she could have.

Hassan remained remarkably calm. "There are things you do not know, Anna."

"I know you're a killer."

"I didn't kill Nouri." Hassan's words were slow and deliberate. "But it is true he and I argued."

"You were angry because I threw you out of the house."

"No," he said after a long pause. "Not that."

She glared at him. How dare he try to dissemble? To manipulate the truth?

Hassan cleared his throat. "Nouri *did* work for the Foundation. And I *was* instrumental in getting him the job. At the time I thought it was a good fit. Because of his family's connections, he knew many wealthy people. He knew what to look for, what to take."

She snorted. "Including his parents' home? Did you help Nouri betray his own family?"

"No." He paused. "I tried to stop it. But the Foundation demanded he prove himself."

And he did, she thought. "So I was right."

"But not about me. Nouri and I argued because..." He swallowed. "...Nouri was embezzling what he collected."

Anna felt like someone had suddenly slammed her head against the wall. Her voice cracked. "What?"

"The Foundation does not pay much. Certainly not enough to support you and the family. Most of the Samedis' assets were gone. So Nouri kept some of the bounty he collected. The Foundation does not care. If a bracelet disappears, or a diamond necklace doesn't end up in inventory, they look the other way."

"Are you saying Nouri was a thief?"

"We fought bitterly about it. I told him he had to stop. He told me he had no other means to live. I told him it was exactly the thing we had been struggling against, exactly what the revolution was designed to purge." A painful look came across Hassan's face. "We were like brothers when we were young, you know. Nouri and his family always helped me out. Whether it was books for school, clothing, meals, even the occasional movie. I probably spent more time at his house than my own. I thought that helping him get the Foundation job was a way to pay him back." Hassan fidgeted. "It isn't a bad idea, what the Foundation does. But I did not know that Nouri would end up stealing from the people he was supposed to be helping."

"So *you* killed him."

"Anna, think clearly. Why would I kill him? I could have had him imprisoned. And I would have if—" He suddenly stopped.

"If what? If someone else hadn't stabbed him? Do you really expect me to believe that, especially after what you've just admitted?"

"Anna, I was appalled at what Nouri was doing. But being appalled doesn't mean I killed him. I didn't. I swear it upon Allah."

"Well then, who did?"

"I don't know. But I know it wasn't you."

Anna jerked back. Her mouth fell open.

"You loved Nouri. You hated him too, the same as I. But you are too gentle to have harmed him. You were framed, and though I doubt you will believe it, I am trying to free you. So is Bijan. I understand that he has contacted your father in America. He has decided it is time for the family to leave Iran. Laleh will be leaving within the month, Nouri's parents soon after."

Despite everything, Anna felt the faint stirring of hope.

"I do not know when it will happen, or how. I do not have strong contacts in the new judicial system. Neither does Bijan. All I can say is that you must not despair. You have friends."

Anna just looked at him.

"I know you are not Muslim, but a few prayers would help."

Forty-three

The next day Anna and Nousha watched as the Guards dispensed packages brought by family members during their visits, mostly clothes that the women paraded for the others to see. A bitter edge crept into Nousha's voice. "Of course, the Guards confiscated the best items for themselves."

"Curious you mention that," Anna said.

Nousha's eyebrows arched into a question mark.

Since Hassan's visit, Anna had been confused. She wasn't sure whether to believe him. She told Nousha what he said.

"Why would Hassan come all this way to lie to you? He's a busy man. What possible gain could there be?"

"I don't know," Anna admitted. "But if Hassan—or his surrogates—didn't kill Nouri, who did?"

"I told you. It was someone whose wealth—whose assets—Nouri confiscated."

"But how would they have known the precise times we weren't at home so they could break in and steal the knife? And why frame me? It still doesn't make any sense."

Nousha frowned and hugged her knees, rocking back and forth. "You said his father is out of jail now?"

"Yes, but the family is ready to leave the country. Laleh is leaving this week."

"The sister who just turned eighteen?"

Anna nodded. They watched as one of the women showed off her new underwear.

"How did she get enough money to leave?"

"I assume Bijan gave it to her."

"But you said they didn't have anything left."

"That's true."

"So how are they paying for their emigration?"

Anna looked blank. "How much do they need?"

"Enough for airline tickets, plus the bribes to make sure they get the tickets, plus enough money once they get where they're going. You can't live on air."

"In Laleh's case, maybe her boyfriend Shaheen is helping. But as far as the others, I really don't know."

Nousha's eyebrows went up again. "Well then, don't you think you should find out?"

§

A Guard took Anna to Sister Azar's office the next morning. She knocked tentatively on the door.

"Come in."

Sister Azar was behind her desk. Dressed in her black chador and headgear she reminded Anna of a nun. But, in most of the world, becoming a nun was a choice. And nuns were rarely jailers. Sister Azar was wearing glasses and, ironically, they softened her face.

"Please, Sister, I would like a word."

She watched as Sister looked up from her papers, removed her glasses, and looked Anna up and down. "Yes?"

Anna swallowed. "There is something I need to tell you."

Sister Azar tilted her head.

"I am pregnant."

Sister Azar didn't seem surprised. "How many months?"

"Over three months, I think. My husband and I..."

Relief flooded Sister Azar's face. At first Anna thought it was an odd reaction. Then she got it. The women often whispered about being raped by the Guards. But Anna had only been in Evin for about a month. Not enough time. It was clear Sister Azar had made the same calculation.

"Well, congratulations. Inshallah, you will have a beautiful Iranian son."

Anna gave her a brief nod.

Afterwards, Anna noticed a subtle shift in the Guards' attitudes, especially the females. They were never nice, but they seemed slightly less abusive. They even brought her tea separately from the others. Without camphor. But Anna remained edgy. What if she was still in Evin when the baby was born? Would they take it away? She rubbed her palm in little circles over her bump. This was the baby that was conceived in rage. The baby she didn't want. Yet the irony was that this baby was the one sure thing keeping her alive. In a way Nouri was saving her life.

Perhaps as a result of that irony, the rage Anna had been harboring towards him when he was alive largely evaporated. She wanted to remember the Nouri she'd met in America, not the Nouri he'd become after the revolution. Her rage now was directed toward finding Nouri's killer. She wondered if that was the case with most people who'd survived a loved one's murder. Even if they loathed the individual when they were alive, in death that person assumed a decency, perhaps even a sanctity, they never had in life. It was all becoming very complicated, she thought. There were no absolutes. Except the three she herself had mandated—she wanted to live, she wanted the baby, and she wanted justice.

§

A few days later after breakfast, two female guards came into the room and tapped Nousha on the shoulder. "Gather your things and put on your chador."

Silence descended. The women prisoners stared at the floor, the wall, each other, anywhere but at Nousha. But Anna watched as Nousha gathered her clothes, chador, and personal items. She squared her shoulders, and pasted on a brave smile. Anna put her arms around her friend. At the last minute, Nousha rummaged through her things, pulled out a book and placed it in Anna's hands. "Remember me," she mouthed. The female guards took her by the arms, and they exited the room.

Anna thumbed through the book. It was a Qur'an, written in Arabic. As Anna flipped through the pages, she blinked back tears. She passed the rest of the day in a haze of misery, unable to focus. That night she slipped the Qur'an under her makeshift pillow as a talisman, but sleep did not come. She was waiting for the sharp spits of the rifles. When they came, a single tear rolled down her cheek.

When she woke the next morning pain slashed through her stomach. At first Anna thought she was having menstrual cramps, then realized that couldn't be. She tried to ignore it, but the pain sharpened, digging so deep into her belly she had to struggle for breath. She attempted to stand, but her head started to spin, and her muscles felt rubbery. A fog descended, and the floor rushed up to meet her.

Forty-four

The next twelve hours were studded with moments of clarity, but most of it was like a fugue state from a Fellini film. Bright lights. Bare walls. Doctors in white coats. Nuns at her side. The smell of alcohol and iodine. Flashes of excruciating pain. Blessed blackness. Guttural cries she learned later were her own. Orders barked at her in Farsi, then English. Gentle voices pleading with her. Sweating until the sheets were soaked, then numbing chills on the same sheets.

At one point someone lifted her up, and there was stabbing pain. Then a rumble, the smart slam of doors, and her entire body began to vibrate. The sense that she was in a vehicle of some kind. More lights, voices, doctors, nuns. Sharp pokes and sticks. Masks over her nose and mouth. Plunging back into darkness.

There were dreams, too. Nouri angry. Nouri kind. Nouri and she making love. Swimming in the Caspian Sea. Someone was with them. The baby. But how did it know how to swim? She had an image of a whale with its offspring, but when she twisted her head around to check, the image vanished, and she was driving through the desert back from Esfahan with Nouri. The sun blasted down, and the sand whipped them with such force it stung, like thousands of fire ants. She had an enormous thirst. Her father appeared with a glass of cold water. She thanked him. It didn't seem strange that he was in Iran. Had he been here all along? Before she could ask, she sank back into darkness.

§

A voice urged her to wake up. Anna reluctantly climbed up to consciousness. It had been so pleasant, the darkness. She had been warm and comfortable. She didn't want to leave.

"You have been very sick," a voice said in thickly accented English.

Anna cracked her eyes. A blurred image swam before her. She blinked slowly and turned her head toward the voice. A nurse was holding her wrist. Taking her pulse. Anna blinked again, and her vision began to clear. The nurse looked like a nun in a habit, with black head gear that reached to her waist. Under the cloak was a white manteau that looked like a raincoat.

"Who—" Anna croaked, but stopped after just one word. A profound sense of weariness washed over her.

"Don't talk," the woman said. "You are weak. You are in hospital in Tehran." She pressed her lips together. "You...collapsed...in Evin Prison. I am Sister Zarifeh. Your nurse."

Anna frowned. Hazy memories flashed through her mind: her feet being lashed; Sister Azar examining her over her glasses; a Kurdish girl named Nousha. Was she really there? Was it real, or just another dream? Then it came—Nousha had been executed. Anna couldn't sleep. Then the stabbing pain in her belly.

"The baby? Is it all right? What happened?"

The nurse blinked, then turned her head away. "I am so sorry. You miscarried. There was much bleeding...we didn't...they didn't know if you would live. That's why they brought you here."

Anna sank back onto the pillow. She let her eyes close. There was no reason to stay awake. Not anymore.

§

The next few weeks were a blur of sleep and wakefulness, during which doctors and nurses prodded and poked. Gradually Anna's intervals of awareness lengthened, and she took stock of her surroundings. She was alone in a small hospital room. White walls, black bars on the window. The view through the window was of a brick wall. The door to her room was closed, probably locked. There was a small glass panel at the top. The antiseptic smell of the hospital was strong, but at least there was no scent of disease. No oily hair smell either. Or saffron.

Sister Zarifeh attended her during the day, but another nurse, a surly woman who rarely spoke, had the night shift. Still, they seemed to be taking good care of her. The tea was good and strong and camphor free. The food, although soft, was surprisingly tasty.

One morning she asked Sister Zarifeh why she wasn't back in Evin Prison.

"It is as I told you. You needed emergency treatment that wasn't possible at Evin. You were transported here."

Anna motioned toward the bars. "Am I in another prison hospital?"

Sister shook her head. "You're in a special ward of the government-run hospital in north Tehran."

"What ward is that?"

"The ward for criminals and prisoners."

Anna was crestfallen. Once she had recovered, they would send her back to Evin. She had been dreaming that, by some fiat or dictum or magic, she might have been freed, her ordeal over. She slumped back against the pillow, a fresh fog of misery threatening to swallow her.

The nurse seemed to know what she was thinking. "Be grateful we did not strap you down. Most prisoners are shackled to the bed, even in hospital."

Anna didn't reply. She might as well be chained. She couldn't go anywhere; there was nowhere to go. She rolled into a fetal position and stared at the wall. She was doomed to die in Iran. Like Nousha, she would spend the rest of her life in prison, waiting for the day the guards appeared and told her to gather her things. How ironic to make her healthy just so they could kill her later.

She turned onto her back and gazed out the window. She could just spot a tiny bit of sky above the brick wall. She stared at the patch of blue, wondering if it might hold the key to her freedom. Out there, in the free world, the hot Iranian summer was coming to an end. People were still wiping sweat off their brows, anticipating the cool rainy season.

The Tehranians who had spent thick summer nights on their rooftops would soon go back to their beds. The markets would stock a profusion of fruits and vegetables. Anna recalled the mornings she'd spent ferreting out the freshest, most tender produce. Her eye had become so sharp that even the shopkeepers couldn't trick her into buying inferior goods. But the simple pleasure of buying fruit was something she would never do again.

She drifted into sleep. For some reason her dreams were particularly vivid. It was as if her subconscious was mourning the loss of the baby by reliving her childhood. She was with her mother and father on the playground of her grade school. They pushed her on a swing, laughing as she rose higher and faster. Anna was ashamed to admit she was afraid. If she went too high, it would break up the family, and her mother would move to Paris. So she smiled bravely and pumped the swing, all the while terrified that she would swing too far. It occurred to her, in that eerie way dreams evolve into something else, that God was punishing her because she hadn't wanted the baby at first.

A few hours later she woke. A doctor had come in to examine her. After he finished, she asked, "Doctor, will I still be able to have children?"

Frown lines popped out on his forehead, and he took his time answering. Did he know something she didn't?

"I don't know," he finally said.

She searched his face and decided he was telling the truth. She concluded his response was better than an unqualified "no."

"How long have I been here?"

"You developed a staph infection after the miscarriage. Probably from the Evin infirmary. That's why you were brought here."

"Yes. So how long has it been?"

"About a month."

Anna was surprised it had been that long. Then again, she had been delirious for much of the time. "Is there any chance I could get some books in English? I would love to read."

The doctor said he would ask, but something in his tone made her think he wouldn't follow through. She was just a prisoner, after all. Inconsequential. After he left she fell back against her pillow.

She recalled Hassan's visit to Evin—it seemed like just last week, but must have been almost a month ago. He said they were trying to get her out. That Bijan had contacted her father. That the family was planning to leave Iran. Laleh was leaving in a month. A burst of anger flashed through her. Laleh was free to leave, but she was not.

She was dozing later that afternoon when an argument erupted outside her door. The row was in Farsi, the bitter raised voices those of a male and female. It was probably a squabble between a Guard and a nurse. Nurses wanted to nurture. Guards wanted to punish. The argument subsided, but it roused Anna. She drowsily recalled another argument not so long ago. What was it about? Who was fighting? Where? She couldn't quite place it, but something told her she should. She tried to concentrate, but it wouldn't come. She let it go.

It wasn't until after her evening meal of soup and toast—they had started to give her solid food—that the memory came unbidden. A contentious argument between Laleh and Nouri. An argument that, like the one this afternoon, woke her. She couldn't understand much of what they said, but they were both furious, spitting out what she knew were nasty insults.

She recalled how Nouri, hostile and red-faced, had turned on her when she came out of the bedroom. How Laleh quickly scurried out of the house, hoisting her bag on her shoulder. How Nouri shouted that all the women in the family were disobedient whores. She frowned. Then another memory surfaced: Laleh prowling the third floor of their house while Anna was cleaning. The third floor that had nothing but a closet and a door to the roof.

The closet.

The closet that Nouri opened and closed. Anna had looked inside it the day she was hunting for her passport, but it had been empty. At least it appeared to be. She continued to ponder it. When she suddenly put it together, the air left her lungs in a gasp. She looked around her hospital room. She needed to get well. She needed to get out. She knew who'd murdered Nouri. And why.

Forty-five

A few days later, during the nurses' shift change, Sister Zarifeh said goodbye to Anna. Anna frowned. Usually she said good night. It was probably just a slip of the tongue.

"See you in the morning," Anna replied. She finished her meal, wondering how to spend the long hours until bedtime. She was feeling stronger. She thought she was ready to leave. But with her recovery came a feeling of dread. Once they knew she was well, they would send her back to Evin. It would be smarter to pretend she was still sick.

She thrashed around in the bed. As she had recovered, so too had her realization that the hospital bed was uncomfortable and hard. The pillow too. Finally she dozed. She was dreaming about jogging down the Midway Plaisance in Chicago when she felt a tug on her arm. She ignored it, thinking it was part of her dream. Someone wanted to jog with her, even though she'd never jogged a block in her life. Was it Nouri? There was another tug. She wanted to say, "Leave me alone. I'm trying to jog," when she heard someone whisper her name.

"Anna, Anna, wake up. Hurry."

The whisper, though soft, sounded urgent. She cracked open her eyes. The night nurse stood at her bedside. Why was she whispering her name? Anna frowned in irritation.

The nurse leaned closer. "Anna, do you know who I am?"

Anna opened her eyes wider and stared at the nurse. She saw the nun-like habit, the white manteau underneath. Then she focused on the nurse's face. The light was dim, but suddenly it dawned on her. The figure at the side of her bed wasn't the night nurse. It was Roya!

Anna sucked in air. "How did...what is going on?"

Roya shushed her with a finger on her lips. "We're going to get you out of here."

"What time is it?"

"It is three o'clock in the morning. Can you walk?"

Anna ran her tongue around her lips. "I...I think so."

"Good. I have a uniform for you. Put it on. Quickly."

Anna was fully awake now. Her pulse started to race. Slowly she swung her legs to the edge of the bed and stood. She had been walking to the bathroom regularly; still, she felt shaky. Roya gripped her arm and handed her the white manteau. Together they slipped it over her head.

"Now this." Roya unfurled a headdress from the folds of her manteau. She helped Anna put it over her head and fasten it. Finally she handed Anna a pair of rubber-soled shoes and helped her put them on. They were too tight but Roya said, "They will have to do."

"How did you get these—"

"Later," Roya said softly. "We only have a minute. Listen carefully. I will walk out of the room but I will make sure the door stays unlocked. I will turn left down the hall. At the end of that hall I will turn right. There is a door to the outside at the far end of that corridor. You will count to twenty and then follow me. That will be the most dangerous part. Do not speak to anyone. Not a word. If someone talks to you, just nod and continue down the hall. I will wait for you outside the door behind the flowering bush. If you do not come in ten minutes, I must leave. Do you understand?"

Anna nodded.

"Good. We go now."

Without another word, Roya opened the door and edged out of the room. Anna heard the soft thud of her footsteps. Then they disappeared.

Anna's mouth went dry. Her hands trembled. How had Roya managed this? She longed to escape, but what if someone stopped her? What if she was recognized? Then she remembered that she was supposed to be counting to twenty. She guessed she should already be at ten. She counted out ten more beats.

She went to the door and twisted the knob. As Roya had promised, it was unlocked. She took a breath. This would be the first time she had been out of her room since they'd brought her here. She cautiously opened the door. The nurse's station was down the hall on the right. To the left was a series of closed doors. No one was in sight. No nurses, no doctors, no Guards. Then again, it was the middle of the night.

Anna took a tentative step to the left. It was difficult not to run—to gallop as fast as she could down the hall, and throw herself against the exit. But that would give her away. She padded down the hall, following a blue stripe that ran down the center of the floor. She was almost afraid to breathe.

After what seemed like an endless length of time she reached the end of the corridor and turned right. Ahead of her was another hall. At the far end, the shadow of a figure disappeared through a door. It had to be Roya, leading the way outside. To freedom.

Anna followed her. The scent of iodine permeated the air, as well as a gummy smell that reminded her of adhesive tape. Someone behind one of the closed doors murmured. Were they chanting prayers? She tried to tread lightly but heard soft footfalls—her own—on the linoleum floor. The fluorescent light, flat and shadowless, bathed everything in blue.

She reached what she guessed was the halfway point. She had about one hundred more feet. She kept walking. She began to see the outline of the door leading outside. Now there were only eighty feet. Although each step seemed as long as a city block, she began to think she might make it. She picked up her pace. Sixty feet. That was all.

Suddenly a woman's voice called out. "*Khâhar vâysâ!* Stop!" A door closed behind her. "I need your help, Sister."

Anna slowed. Who was calling her? Probably a nurse. Maybe even the night nurse who'd attended her. But Roya had said not to stop. Not to engage with anyone. Still, if she didn't, the nurse would suspect something, wouldn't she? Anna ignored her. She was only fifty feet from freedom. Just fifty feet.

The woman let out a stream of Farsi, fast and furious. Anna couldn't understand the words, but the tone was unmistakable. She was probably saying something like, "Don't you have ears? What is wrong with you?" But Anna was too close to freedom to stop. Best to pretend she hadn't heard. If the woman followed her out the door, perhaps Roya could say or do something. She kept going.

The woman's voice followed her, closer now. It felt like tiny birds were fluttering in her stomach. The woman was coming after her. Anna's hands were shaking. She hid them in the folds of her uniform. It couldn't end this way. Not after everything. She was only twenty-five feet from the door. She tried not to break into a run.

Suddenly a door opened behind her, and a man's voice called out in a stage whisper. A Guard? A patient? A doctor? He spoke to the nurse in Farsi. Anna couldn't understand. She didn't want to. Was he telling her to shut up? That it was late and people were trying to sleep? The woman argued back. Her voice was low, but insistent. Anna imagined her flailing her arms and pointing to Anna. She only had fifteen more feet. She kept walking. Ten.

The man's voice replied. His irritated tone sounded like he was criticizing the nurse. The nurse tried one more time. Anna reached the door. She opened it and sailed through. She was out. A well-worn dirt path led from the door around the corner of the building.

She glanced in both directions. A bush with red flowers stood on one side of the door, and a spotlight cast elongated shadows from it across the path. Anna wedged herself behind the bush. Roya crouched a few feet away. Anna hurriedly explained what had happened. Roya nodded, told Anna to stay where she was and stood up, brushing twigs and leaves off her uniform. She was pacing back and forth near the door when the woman who had pursued Anna came through.

"What do you think you're doing, Sister?" the woman asked. "I've been trying to get your attention."

"Just getting some air, Sister," Roya said.

Anna caught a glimpse of the women's faces in the light. The nurse—Anna could see that she was wearing a uniform—threw Roya a suspicious glance. "Who are you?"

"This is my first shift here. I transferred from Pars Hospital." Roya heaved a sigh. "This place…well, it is more depressing than I imagined."

The woman planted her hands on her hips. "The nurse I am looking for was not as tall as you."

Anna's heart stopped. She was petite. Roya was at least four inches taller. The woman had obviously noticed.

"She just came out. Did you see her?"

There was silence for a moment. Oh god, what would Roya do? Anna held her breath.

Finally, Roya said, "It was me, Sister. I just came outside. Surely, I am not that tall. My brother used to tease that I was too short." She giggled.

The woman's silence told Anna she was measuring Roya, trying to decide if she was telling the truth. Finally the woman muttered, "Well, it's too late now. I do not need you anymore." She turned around, and went back in.

Roya waited a beat, then exhaled into the silence. So did Anna. The silence deepened, but Anna was elated. It was the silence of freedom.

§

The air had never felt so sweet, the darkness so soft, the stars so bright. Anna floated down the path. She was free. She would never again take it for granted.

"How did you arrange this, Roya? I can't believe it. You—"

"Hurry." Roya picked up her pace. "We are not safe yet."

Anna followed as they made their way toward the street.

"No," Roya whispered. "Walk beside me. If anyone stops us, we are two nurses on break."

But it was the middle of the night and no one stopped them. They exited the hospital grounds and crossed the street. The only sounds were the thuds of their rubber-soled shoes on the pavement. The mullahs had decreed that women must only wear footwear with rubber soles, Anna recalled. The tapping of heels against the floor was considered too arousing.

Anna matched Roya's pace, but she was breathing fast and hard. An adrenaline rush had fueled her escape, but now that she was out, she realized how weak and out of condition she was.

"It is not much farther," Roya said encouragingly. She turned a corner onto a commercial street with small storefronts crowded together. There were no lights in the windows, and the street was deserted except for a car parked at other end. "There." Roya pointed.

Anna squinted. She could just make out the figure of a man in the driver's seat. They continued walking and, when they reached the car, Roya threw open the door. Hassan was behind the wheel. He was drumming his fingers on the steering column. He stopped when he caught sight of Anna.

Anna smiled. Hassan had been telling the truth when he came to see her in Evin. He had helped her escape.

"Climb in the back," he said quietly. "Quickly."

Anna obeyed. Roya sat in front. Within ten seconds, Hassan started the engine and they pulled out. The tires screeched as they melted into the streets of Tehran.

Forty-six

"How did you do it?" Anna asked.

Roya answered. "Hassan has...resources."

"But this...I would never have...I am so grateful."

Hassan cut her off. "Don't thank us yet. Your journey is just beginning."

"What journey?"

"Listen carefully, Anna," Hassan said. "You are going to be on a bus at daybreak. It will take you to Bazargan."

"Bazargan?"

"It is a small town—part of Maku—near the border with Turkey. You will be met by a Kurdish man. He will be wearing a cleric's garb. He has a car. He will have a valid Iranian passport for you and enough money to get you over the border."

"An Iranian passport? How did he get it?"

Hassan didn't answer. "The bus will drive to the customs terminal. You will meet him in front of the building. After you get through customs, he will drive you into Dogubeyazit, about twenty-five kilometers inside the border of Turkey. From there, you will change your rials into lira and dollars."

"Why dollars?"

"They take dollars in Turkey. They love them," Hassan said. "Once you are in Dogubeyazit you will buy a bus ticket to Ankara where you will go to the US Embassy. Once you arrive, the embassy will contact your father and get you an American passport. From there you will fly to America."

Anna clapped her hand over her mouth. She wanted to believe the nightmare was coming to an end, but reality told her to remain cautious. "Who arranged this?"

"All of us," Hassan said. "Baba-joon, your father—"

"Baba-joon?"

Hassan peered at her in the rearview mirror. "You have suffered enough. You don't belong here. We know you did not kill Nouri."

Anna eyed his reflection steadily. "Does that mean you know who did?"

Hassan hesitated. "I have suspicions, but no proof."

Anna wondered if his were the same suspicions as hers. She reviewed what Hassan said, and she could almost taste her freedom. It was so close, just a breath away. But she couldn't dwell on it. She had unfinished business. "I can supply the proof. But it's at the house. I need to go there to get it."

Hassan pulled to the side of the road. He twisted around, his eyes wide. "You know who killed Nouri?"

"I had nothing but time in Evin. To think and reflect. Yes, I know who killed him. And I need to set things right."

Hassan stared at Anna as if he wanted to say something, but Roya chimed in. "Are you crazy? There is no time to waste. You must leave Iran before they realize you are gone. You will come to my house—we will hide you until dawn. Then you will get on the bus. That is the plan."

"Roya, this is something I need to do before I leave."

Roya shook her head. "You cannot go back to the house in Shemiran. The Guards are monitoring it."

Anna crossed her arms. "Are they there all the time? Twenty-four hours?"

Roya glanced at Hassan.

"No," he conceded. "But they can show up at any moment."

Anna's chin jutted out. "You're a Guard. You can deflect them if need be. I must do this. It will only take a few minutes. Then we will go to the Samedis."

Roya was still shaking her head. "No. It's not possible."

"Look." Anna's voice was unyielding. "I...I know things between Nouri and I fell apart. But it wasn't always that way. In the beginning, when we met...when we first came to Iran..." Her voice cracked, and she fell silent. She bit her lip. When she spoke again, her voice was strong. "I need...I want to make things right. For Nouri. I owe it to his memory. To who he used to be. And the promise of what we might have become."

"Out of the question," Roya said. "It has been arranged. Baba-joon will come to my house with the bus ticket. He wants to say good-bye."

"Tell me," Hassan said. "Who killed Nouri? Once you are safely gone, I will see that justice is served."

Anna's chest went tight. In Evin, then in the hospital, she'd had all the time in the world to think things through. Now there wasn't a moment to spare. The truth was that her need to seek justice was not motivated simply by her memory of Nouri. The grief at losing her baby was motivating her, too. The baby hadn't been conceived in love, she knew, but she'd come to hunger for the child anyway. She'd planned to shower it with all the love and attention she herself never had. But whoever killed Nouri—and framed her for the murder—had robbed her of that chance.

She could leave it to Hassan. She did believe—now—that he wanted to see justice served. But what if he couldn't make good on his promise? Family was everything in Iran. In many cases, it was the only thing Iranians had left. How could she be sure Hassan would step up to the plate? Or that Baba-joon would let him? In times of crisis, a family often unites to face a common enemy. It was too risky. If anyone took action, it had to be Anna. Even if it meant staying in Iran for a few more hours.

"Roya, Hassan, I know you mean well. But it must be me. There is no time to argue."

"That much we agree on," Hassan said. "But doing this might mean you'll be caught. And this time they will make sure you never escape.

Are you prepared to take that chance?"

Anna jiggled her foot. "I thought it would be impossible to get out of Evin. But you made it possible. If Allah, or whatever god exists, wants me to leave Iran, it will happen."

Hassan and Roya murmured in Farsi. Anna thought Hassan wanted to let her go, but Roya kept shaking her head.

Anna cut in. "Hassan, if I find what I'm looking for at the house, there is one last thing I need you to do."

§

The house Anna had lived in with Nouri was shrouded in empty darkness. An official document was taped to the gate, which made Anna wonder if their belongings had been confiscated. If so, what she was searching for might be gone. She hesitated, then climbed out of the car and hurried to the gate. It was unlocked, which gave her more pause. Were there people inside? Maybe the Foundation had allowed squatters to move in. They could be sleeping in her bed.

Silently, she opened the gate, squeezed through, and stopped at the edge of the patio. The house looked abandoned. There were no shoes or objects on the patio, no lights inside, nothing to indicate anyone was occupying the house. But how to know for sure? She shook off her fear, opened the gate wider, and beckoned to Hassan and Roya.

The tiny pool in the yard was clogged with leaves from the chenar tree. They swirled in slow motion. Clearly, no one had been attending to it. A wave of sadness washed over her. Imagining the destruction was one thing; seeing it was another. Then she squared her shoulders. There would be time to grieve later. She went to the front door and tried to open it. It was locked. She turned around. Hassan and Roya were watching her. Roya flipped her palms up in a question.

Anna and Nouri had always left a key buried in a small box under the chenar tree. She backtracked to the tree, knelt down, and scrabbled in the dirt. She retrieved the box, removed the key, and hurried back to the door.

The faint stench of rotting garbage assaulted her as they entered the house. Perversely, Anna considered it a good sign. No one was there—if someone was, surely they would have emptied the trash. She looked around. Silent shadows loomed, heavy and thick. Anna tiptoed around them, reluctant to disturb their weight by turning on lights.

She let out a soft cry as she walked into the living room. Even in the dim light she could see the mess. Someone had tossed the place. Bookshelves were stripped; shards of china that had once formed beautiful bowls were flung into corners. Someone had stolen the framed photographs, knickknacks, and candlesticks. The cushions of the couch were gone, too.

Anna went into the kitchen. Most of the drawers were open and gaped at her from different angles. Her good silver was gone; so was her Wedgewood china. As she passed the knife rack, she noticed the steak knives had disappeared too. To be used as evidence against her, no doubt. Anna felt tears rimming her eyes. All this needless destruction. She turned around to Hassan and Roya. "I'm going upstairs. I'll just be a minute. You stay here and watch for the Guards."

In the bedroom she nearly flipped on the light, then caught herself. Her fingers still on the switch, she shivered at how close she'd come to making a mistake. Roya had a point. There was no guarantee that what she was attempting to do would work, and time was scarce.

She stripped off the nurse's uniform and threw on a pair of jeans and a t-shirt, then grabbed the chador hanging on a hook on the door. She opened the safe in the bedroom—thankfully, no one had changed the combination—and felt around in the dark. Nothing was inside. She wasn't surprised.

"Hurry, Anna," Roya murmured from downstairs.

Anna glanced out the window. The curtain of night was lightening to gray. Dawn was not far off. Anna closed the safe. Coming out of the bedroom, she hung the chador over the railing and climbed to the third floor. The closet. She grabbed the doorknob and twisted. It opened easily. She felt her brows knit together. Shouldn't it have been locked?

She peered inside. Five shelves were stacked with linens, blankets, and cold weather clothes. For some reason, the items here hadn't been ransacked. She wondered why, then pushed the thought away. She moved aside the blankets on the top shelf and inspected the back of the closet. She saw nothing except smooth wall. She did the same with the second shelf. Still nothing. It wasn't until the third shelf that she saw what she was looking for. The bare outline of a panel built flush into the wall, painted the same color. A secret compartment. Probably a second safe. One that Nouri had never told her about.

Anna couldn't resist a triumphant smile. She remembered how Laleh had retrieved a bottle of liquor from the Samedis' secret safe the day Baba-joon was taken. How Laleh suddenly realized she'd probably revealed something she hadn't intended to and clammed up. Anna also recalled how Laleh, fresh out of architecture school, bragged about contributing to the design of their Shemiran house. This had to have been Laleh's idea.

Anna's triumph was temporary. She ran her hands along the frame, looking for a latch or crack to release in order to open it. But everything around the panel was smooth. The safe was locked. And there was no combination assembly. She frowned.

Hassan called up. His voice was raw with tension. "Anna. We must go."

"Can you find a knife in the kitchen? Small, but with a sharp blade?"

"Anna, please."

"Just do it." Even she was surprised by the power in her voice.

Hassan hurried upstairs and fished a switchblade out of his pocket. "Use this." He handed it to Anna. "But be quick."

She flipped open the blade and slid it along the tiny crack at the top of the panel. It wouldn't go in. She turned to Hassan. "You try."

He leaned into the closet, studied the panel, ran his fingers along the top and bottom. Then he wedged the blade along the panel at the top. This time it went in. Hassan slid the blade from right to left, and as he did, they heard a click as if a latch had been tripped. The front of the panel protruded from the wall about half an inch. Anna pulled it open.

Inside was a treasure trove of gold coins, stacks of rials, necklaces, rings, and bracelets. There were also papers, which looked like bond or stock certificates. Small velvet bags with drawstrings. Brooches and earrings. Anna's jaw dropped. Hassan stared. Nouri *had* been skimming from the Martyrs' Foundation. He'd been storing the plunder here. She looked at Hassan. He was watching her, waiting for her reaction.

But Anna was still processing it. She tried to guess how long Nouri had worked for the Foundation—about four months, she thought. She dipped her hand into the safe and picked up a sapphire necklace. A vague memory came over her. Wasn't this necklace worn by one of the guests at their wedding? She thought she recalled Laleh—or was it Maman-joon—complimenting the woman who was wearing it. She'd bought it in Antwerp for a steal.

As she fingered the necklace, Anna's eyes grew hot. A petty thief. That was what Nouri had been reduced to. Someone who had to steal, then fence the possessions of people he knew—his parents' friends—to make ends meet. Sadly, it was the perfect job for someone in his circumstances. Perhaps the only job someone like him could have done. He knew who had what. He told the Foundation who to target, and the Foundation followed through. Anna tried to swallow, but her throat was thick. Despite her repugnance at what Nouri had done, she understood that he'd been providing for them the only way he knew.

"What is it?" Hassan asked.

Anna didn't answer. There was plenty of blame to go around. Anna hadn't known what Nouri was doing, but she should have. She'd been so miserable, so eager to leave Iran, that she never wondered where their money was coming from. She assumed Baba-joon was still supporting them—although, in retrospect, she saw that was impossible, given that his possessions had been confiscated, and he was in jail. Had she not been so wrapped up in her own despair, perhaps she would have known the Foundation wasn't paying Nouri enough.

She stared at the sapphire necklace. Weren't there earrings to match? Yes. She remembered the woman at the wedding touching her ear, blushing with false modesty as Maman-joon made a fuss over the jewelry. Laleh had praised it too. How the set was one of a kind.

So exquisite and stunning. Now, Anna searched for the earrings. They were not in the safe. But they were part of a set. Why would Nouri fence them separately? Unless he was desperate. Or someone else was.

Anna's eyes narrowed. She knew who had the earrings. She hoped it wasn't too late.

Roya's voice, full of barely controlled panic, cut through the silence. "Hassan, a car has pulled up. I think it's the Guards!"

Hassan straightened up. He and Anna exchanged glances. He waved his hand at the safe. "Close it up." He went down the steps, calling out to Roya. "I will take them to the alley in back. When we are out of sight, get Anna to the car." He called over his shoulder. "Anna, make sure you lie down in the back of the car. On the floor. So no one can see you."

Anna looked out at the rooftop. Strips of purple now streaked across the gray. They would lighten to pink, followed by a bright sunrise over the horizon. She turned back to the safe and scooped up a handful of the stash, including the sapphire necklace. She threw it into a bag, grabbed her chador, and hurried down the steps.

Forty-seven

Dawn broke as they raced through the streets of Tehran. Anna was squeezed on the floor between the front and back seats. Every time the car bounced, a jolt of pain streaked up her spine. Hassan and Roya kept their mouths shut. Anna steeled herself for what was coming. Hassan had spoken to the Guards as Anna asked—they were following in another car.

She knew the route from her house to the Samedis, and a series of sharp turns told her they'd arrived. Hassan killed the engine and got out, and Anna heard the Guards' car pull up behind them. The engine was cut. A moment later Hassan's voice murmured in Farsi.

"He's telling the Guards to get out of the car," Roya said quietly. "Now he's leading them around to the back of the house." Anna nodded to herself more than to Roya. It was proceeding as planned. The gate squeaked as it was opened. Hassan called out in a low voice.

"Be quick. Go."

Roya pushed the seat forward and Anna climbed out of the car. Hassan joined them, and they slipped through the gate.

"Did you happen to pick up a key at your house?" Roya asked.

Anna shook her head.

Hassan looked at his watch. It couldn't be much past six in the morning. He nodded to Roya, who knocked on the door. There was no response. Hassan shifted. "It's early."

Roya rose on tiptoe and peeked into the front hall through a glass inset in the door. She stepped back, startled. "Look!"

Hassan peered through the glass. His eyebrows arched.

"What is it?" Anna asked, her pulse suddenly throbbing like an engine.

"There are suitcases on the floor," Roya said. "With a black manteau draped over one of them."

Anna let out a relieved breath. It was not too late. "Knock again."

Roya did, louder this time.

A few moments passed, and thumps and rustles rose from inside. The door opened. Bijan was tucking his shirt into his pants. He had grown a beard, which had come in more gray than black. He looked worn out and wrinkled, like a used canvas bag. When he saw Hassan and Roya, he looked puzzled, but when he recognized Anna in her chador, his eyes widened.

"I do not understand." He gazed from Hassan to Roya. "The plan was to meet at your house."

"She insisted on coming here." Roya shrugged.

"She has something to do," Hassan added.

"Hello, Baba-joon," Anna said.

Bijan stared at Anna. Something bright and shiny appeared in his eyes. At first Anna thought it might be joy at seeing her after so long. But then she realized it was the beginning of a tear. He knew, Anna thought. He'd figured it out.

Still, his outward demeanor was calm, and he kissed her on both cheeks. "I am overjoyed to see you, my daughter. Your travails have been difficult."

"Where is Laleh?"

Bijan's eyes blazed with awareness. To his credit, he didn't prevaricate. "She is leaving Iran today. Just like you," he added.

At that moment, Maman-joon started down the steps. "Who is it so early, Bijan?"

She wore a bathrobe. Her hair was unkempt, her skin pasty. She looked like she'd just rolled out of bed but, when she saw Anna, she froze in the middle of the staircase. Her mouth formed a perfect "O."

"What is she doing here?" Maman-joon spit out. "Get her. Quick.

Call the Guards. And the komiteh. She must be stopped."

No one moved.

"What's wrong with you?" Maman-joon swept her arm in a gesture that included them all. "She killed our son!" She hurried down the steps and headed for the telephone.

Baba-joon blocked her path and grabbed her by her shoulders. The weight of sorrow embedded itself on his face. Anna suspected it would never fade. "Parvin," he said, "Anna did not kill Nouri."

"What are you talking about?" Parvin screeched, her voice rising. She stretched her arms out protectively, as if warding off evil spirits. "She is an evil jinn. She has cast a spell over you. How else could she have escaped from jail? We must purge her from our lives."

Anna ignored Maman-joon's rant and looked at Bijan. "Where is Laleh?" she repeated.

From the top of the stairs a clear voice rang out. "I am here." Everyone turned and looked up. Laleh stood at the top of the landing. She was dressed for traveling in a beige pants suit. And she held a pistol in front of her. It was aimed at Anna.

Maman-joon staggered backwards. "Laleh! What is this? What are you doing?"

Laleh didn't answer. She pointed with her chin toward Anna. "How did you get out?"

Anna motioned toward Hassan and Roya. "They helped."

Laleh snorted in contempt. "I should have known. Traitors!"

Roya stiffened.

"Where did you get that?" Bijan gestured toward the gun.

Laleh didn't reply.

Now that the moment had come, Anna felt strangely calm. Even the threat of a bullet couldn't stop her. "You killed Nouri. Your brother. My husband."

"You couldn't stand him. You were going to leave him."

"I never stole from him."

Laleh smiled coldly. "I'll wager now you wish you had."

"Look in the hem of her manteau. *I'll* wager you'll find a pair of earrings that match this." Anna pulled out the sapphire necklace. "Earrings that Laleh intends to fence when she gets to London."

"Very good, Anna." Laleh started down the steps, still pointing the pistol at Anna. "But you're wrong. The earrings are in my purse." She waved the gun at the others. "And if anyone tries to stop me, I will shoot."

Her tone was resolute. Anna took a step back.

Maman-joon clasped her hands together as if in prayer. "What are you doing, my child? Put the gun down before something terrible happens."

"Maman, you are a fool," Laleh hissed. "All you cared about was planning parties and weddings and making sure we were friends with the right people. I do not care about any of that. Shaheen and I will make our own way." She took the steps down. "And Hassan, you and Roya, with your phony piety...you disgust me."

Maman-joon's hands flew to her head, and she pulled at her hair. She rocked from side to side. "Laleh, azizam." She sobbed. "Stop this. We will make it right. You didn't do anything. It was *her.*" She thrust a finger toward Anna. "Hassan, you know the truth. Call the Guards. Have them take her away. Forever, this time."

No one moved. Parvin's sobs grew more frantic. "I'm begging you. Please!"

All eyes were still on Laleh. Anna wondered if she was enjoying her moment. They heard the sound of a car pulling up to the house. A horn blasted. "That must be my taxi. Everyone stand back."

Maman-joon, still weeping, tried to throw her arms around Laleh, but Laleh shoved her aside. Parvin crumpled and dropped to the floor.

Laleh headed toward the suitcases. "Nouri wouldn't listen. He refused to cut me in. I had no choice, you see."

Hassan stepped in front of Laleh, blocking her path. "You are not leaving."

"You don't want to do this, Hassan."

"Laleh, I am arresting you for your brother's murder."

"I do not think so." She fired the gun directly into Hassan.

There was a moment of silence. A look of astonishment came

across Hassan, and he clutched his gut. Maman-joon screamed. Hassan collapsed. Blood poured out from his body. Roya covered her face with her hands. Bijan looked horrified. Hassan struggled for breath.

A blur of action followed. Bijan lunged toward Laleh and seized the gun. At the same time, there was a commotion at the rear of the house. The Guards broke down the back door and rushed inside.

Anna knelt over Hassan. "Hold on, Hassan. Stay with me. We're going to get you help."

The Guards reached the foyer, aiming their machine guns at the group. Laleh recovered first and pointed to Anna, who was still bent over Hassan. "It was her!" she cried. "She shot him! My father wrestled the gun away from her. She is an American. Trying to escape Iran. See her suitcases? Arrest her. Take her away."

Maman-joon looked up and wiped her hand across her eyes. "What my daughter says is true," she chimed in. "I saw it with my own eyes." She motioned toward Anna. "She killed my son! And now she's shot his best friend. She is an American spy."

The Guards, clearly confused, looked first at Anna, then Hassan. One of them started toward Anna, but Bijan stepped forward.

"No. The women are lying. My daughter shot this man." He gestured toward Laleh. Anguish was etched on his face.

The Guards hesitated. They aimed their machine guns at Laleh but glanced cautiously at Hassan. Barely conscious, he nodded. "He is right," Hassan croaked. His eyes closed. The Guards grabbed Laleh and pushed her towards the door.

"Maman, Baba, please. Don't let them take me! You know the truth!" Laleh screamed.

"Bijan!" Maman-joon screeched. "Do something!"

Bijan hesitated. Then, "I did."

Forty-eight

The late summer sun was high in the sky when the bus pulled out of the terminal. Anna sat in the back, surrounded by women, old and young. Two of them cuddled babies on their laps, others sat with older children. The women flashed her shy, but curious, smiles. They had to be wondering about the woman with a few stray strands of blonde hair traveling alone.

She smiled back. She couldn't believe that twenty-four hours earlier she'd been a prisoner. Now she was on a bus to freedom. While she understood that she would be dealing with the consequences for years to come, for now she was content to let the exhilaration wash over her.

Exhaustion, too. The past few hours had been tumultuous. After the Guards took Laleh away, the fevered pitch of the morning ebbed, leaching out the emotion, leaving a colorless gloom in its place. Maman-joon wandered through the house murmuring nonsense. She looked so fragile Anna thought a tiny breeze would topple her. Still, Anna couldn't summon up any compassion. She was more concerned with Baba-joon. Seeing him watch his wife, knowing both their children had come to ruin, she doubted he would ever smile again.

Roya had jumped into the ambulance with Hassan and accompanied him to hospital. She promised to call as soon as she knew something. The paramedics said it was a good sign he was still breathing.

As soon as they were gone, Bijan sighed and went into his study. He emerged with an envelope. "This is for you."

Anna took the envelope and opened it. Inside was a wad of rials. Plus a letter. She unfolded the letter. It was written in Arabic, and some kind of official looking seal was stamped on the top.

"What does it say?" she asked.

"It is a letter signed by the chairman of our local komiteh giving you permission to travel alone. You must show this to anyone who tries to detain you. Or if there are roadblocks on the way."

"How did you get this? I didn't know you—"

He cut her off. "You do not need to know."

Anna searched his eyes, knowing it must have cost him dearly. He returned her gaze, his expression unreadable.

"This and the money should get you through to Bazargan. Remember, once you get off the bus, the Kurdish man should still be outside the customs terminal. He will be dressed as a cleric. He will have a passport for you. An Iranian passport."

"I understand."

"Listen to me, Anna. That passport will have a proper exit stamp, which—"

"You mean a visa?"

Bijan nodded. "Similar. It permits you to exit Iran. You will need it. Otherwise, the border guards in Bazargan and Turkey will question you. And because your Farsi isn't good, they might discover you are American. If that happens, they may accuse you of espionage—of being a threat to the regime. They could lock you up again. You are not to talk to any customs officials under any circumstances. Do you understand?"

Anna nodded.

"You must find the cleric. He will take you across the border by... another...route."

"If he is smuggling me across the border, why do I need the passport? Can't I just go to the American Embassy and tell them who I am?"

"Once you've crossed into Turkey, Turkish officials may demand to see an Iranian passport with the proper exit stamp. If you do not have one, they can detain you, just like the Iranians. For as long as they want. Only after you arrive in Ankara can you apply for an American passport."

Anna held up the letter. "What name is on this letter?"

"You are Roshni Omidi."

Fear suddenly slid around in her gut. She felt goose bumps on her skin. "Is that the name on the Iranian passport?"

"That I do not know. But the Kurd will. Remember, only when you get to Ankara can you resume your true identity. Do you understand?"

Anna nodded again. "A Kurdish man dressed as a cleric."

"You must connect with him."

"Who is this man? How did you find him?"

"I do not know. He called me."

Anna frowned.

"He was contacted by someone in America." The hint of a smile flitted across Bijan's face.

"My father."

Bijan nodded.

Her father hadn't abandoned her. He had been working to get her out all along. Her stomach twisted with an unfamiliar feeling. She thought it might be joy. "How does my father know this man?"

"How does anyone know the past?"

Bijan gave her final instructions on their way to the bus station. When they arrived he parked and went inside to buy a ticket. As he walked her to the bus, he handed it to her. "Do not talk to anyone if you can avoid it. They must not find out you are American."

Once again she nodded.

Bijan leaned over and kissed her on both cheeks. Anna threw her arms around him. His familiar scent—a mix of tobacco, soap, and saffron—wafted over her. She blinked rapidly. "You are a wonderful man. And father-in-law."

He shook his head, but his eyes filled.

Her own vision blurred with tears. Then she turned around and boarded the bus. As she took her seat, she saw him watching her. She waved through the window. Her last image of Tehran was of a sad, broken man at a bus station, raising his arm in farewell.

Forty-nine

The bus had no air conditioning, and even though it was late September, Anna was sweating under her chador in minutes. It would have helped to take it off—she was wearing jeans and a t-shirt underneath—but that was impossible. She opened the window, but the bus was passing through the desert north of Tehran, and a hot breeze scalded her skin. She felt dizzy. She hadn't totally recovered from the miscarriage. She leaned her head against the wall of the bus and tried to nap.

An hour later, the scent of saffron and lemon drifted over her. She opened her eyes. The women around her were breaking out food. Chattering brightly, they passed around pita sandwiches, vegetables, and fruit. Anna's stomach growled, and her mouth watered. She hadn't eaten since yesterday, and she had no food of her own. She turned her back on the women and faced the window, but the aromas of the food, the women's laughter, and her own hunger tormented her.

A tap on her shoulder made her turn around. One of the women seated in front held out a sandwich. "*Ghazâ?*" she asked.

Anna looked at the sandwich, then back at the woman, and nodded. The woman smiled.

"*Mamnoon.*" Anna took the sandwich and wolfed it down. "*Che khoob.* It's good." The woman smiled again. It was just a simple kindness, but Anna was so grateful that tears stung her eyes.

By mid-afternoon the bus slowed and came to a fitful stop. A roadblock loomed ahead. The revolutionary government was flexing its muscle by setting up checkpoints in cities and highways in order to examine papers—ostensibly checking for rebels and spies. The door to the bus opened, and three young men boarded, machine guns at the ready. Anna slumped in her seat and jiggled her foot. What would happen when they got to her? Would they figure out that she was a foreigner? Would her pale complexion give her away? She tucked her hair in and pushed the rusari on her chador low on her forehead.

Suddenly, the woman who'd offered her a sandwich poked her friend beside her and whispered in Farsi. The friend twisted around, stared at Anna, then whispered across the aisle to a young woman holding a baby. The infant was sleeping. The mother looked doubtful, but after a moment, got up and thrust the baby at Anna.

Anna's heart thudded. She knew what they were doing. She dipped her head at the young mother and cradled the infant. The child, swaddled in a light blanket, wiggled in its sleep. Anna held her breath that the baby wouldn't wake up and cry.

The officers, or whoever they were, stomped to the back of the bus. They appeared to be young, but youth, with its idealism and self-importance, could be dangerous. One demanded to see the papers of the woman whose baby Anna was now cradling. The mother handed them over. She refused to make eye contact.

Oh, god, Anna thought. What if the mother's papers indicated she was traveling with a baby? Would the soldiers figure it out? The soldier inspected the papers. He stared at them, frowned, then studied the mother, who still wouldn't make eye contact with him. He handed the papers back. Anna sighed in relief. She wondered if the soldier had actually read them. Perhaps he wasn't even literate. Maybe it was all bluster, like with so many of the revolutionaries. She focused on the baby but, out of the corner of her eye, she could tell the young man was watching her. His eyes flickered over her. The baby was squirming now, opening and closing its mouth. It was waking and wanted milk. Anna nuzzled the infant.

The soldier turned and backtracked to the front of the bus just as the baby opened its eyes. The infant had probably sensed that Anna wasn't its mother. Its features scrunched into a grimace and it let out a lusty scream. As its wail reverberated through the bus, the woman in the seat in front called out to the soldier.

"Now look what you've done. You woke the baby."

Anna rocked the crying infant.

The soldier shrugged as he disembarked from the bus. *"Bebakhshid.* I'm sorry."

Anna took a relieved breath and handed the crying baby back to its mother. Once again, she was reminded how kind Iranians could be.

As the late afternoon sun dipped in the western sky, the bus arrived in Bazargan, a suburb of Maku, which occupied a rocky mountain gorge in northwestern Iran. She had imagined an isolated dusty border town and was surprised when they drove through crowded streets lined with sturdy buildings, past a cathedral and even a mosque—although its minarets and dome looked more Russian than Persian. Then again, they were almost as far north as Armenia.

As they approached the customs checkpoint, traffic slowed. Bazargan was a major crossing into Turkey, and cars and trucks were lined up at least half a mile from the border. But the terrain had changed, and once more they were in the high desert with rocky cliffs and mountains. The women nattered on, sharing rumors about suspected border closings and red tape.

Finally, the bus pulled into the terminal, a one-story building with a flat roof. Everyone filed off and was immediately waved inside by uniformed officers. Anna searched for the cleric without success. She was supposed to wait for him outside, but the guards gave her no chance to step out of line. She was forced to follow the others inside. Her stomach pitched.

She walked into a large room with a counter at one end. The counter was divided into five booths, each with a glass window, but only one of the booths was open. If she stayed in line, she would eventually reach the only customs official on duty. Bijan had told her to avoid talking to anyone, but if she broke out of line to go outside, the guards would ask her why, which, for a woman traveling alone in the Islamic Republic, was dangerous. Despite the letter from the Tehran komiteh, her stomach tightened into a hard knot.

Thankfully, the line moved slowly. The man behind the booth screened each passenger, asking questions and scanning documents. He seemed overly thorough. One by one the women who had been so nice to her on the bus passed the official's scrutiny. The young mother with the baby gave Anna a farewell nod.

Almost an hour passed, but no cleric appeared. Anna was now at the front of the line. She rubbed the back of her neck under her chador. Her insides turned liquid with fear. She couldn't see a way to avoid talking to the official.

"Mitoonam komaketoon konam?"

Anna went blank. What was he saying? She turned around. A woman behind her gave her a gentle shove. Anna took a tentative step forward.

"Ajaleh kon!" the man gestured with an irritated wave.

She knew what that meant. "Hurry up." As she approached the counter, he let out a stream of Farsi, so fast she couldn't understand. She looked at him, still blank. He repeated himself. She pulled out the letter from the komiteh in Tehran and slid it across the counter. He scanned it, frowned, shook his head, and spewed out another stream of Farsi. This time Anna forced herself to concentrate and made out a word here and there. He was asking for her passport. Which, of course, she didn't have.

She wanted to melt into the floor. Everything was falling apart. She would be sent back to prison. She looked for the women who'd helped her on the bus, but they'd left the building. She turned back to the official who suddenly spoke to her in English.

"Where is your passport?"

Anna couldn't help register a jolt of recognition. She was about to reply when she realized her mistake. The customs official saw it too.

"Where are you from?" he asked in a curt voice.

She kept her mouth shut.

"Where do you live?"

"*Man dar Iran zendegi mikonam,*" Anna replied in Farsi.

The official took a long look at her, then snorted. He cried out. "Guards. Come! Hurry!"

Almost immediately, two men with machine guns flanked Anna. The customs official explained that she had no passport and that she seemed to understand English.

"America?" one guard asked.

The official nodded.

"*Bâ man biyâ,*" one of them said. "Come with me." The guards grabbed her and started walking her to the back of the building. Anna panicked. She hadn't come all this way just to be apprehended again.

Suddenly, a man dressed in a cleric's garb rushed into the building. He was breathing hard, and beads of sweat dotted his forehead. He gazed around, saw Anna, and arched his eyebrows. He hurried over and gave her a big hug, all the while talking in a rapid stream of Farsi. Anna managed to catch a few words. "*Khosh âmadid!* Welcome. Finally. Where have you been?"

"Who are you?" one of the guards barked.

The man relinquished Anna and stepped back. He straightened up, his expression turning serious. "*Salâm, barâdar!* Good evening. I am Amir. This is my niece. I will be taking her on pilgrimage. I'm so sorry. *Bebakhshid!* I was lost. *Man gom shodam.* Trying to find the terminal."

The guard glanced at his companion, then at the cleric. "Why does your niece not speak Farsi?" His eyes were suspicious.

"Yes, yes." The cleric bobbed his head, as if he hadn't quite understood the question. He spoke slowly in Farsi so Anna could understand. "She is French." He pointed to her. "She speaks French, English, and German. But she is converting to Islam and, Inshallah, soon will speak perfect Farsi." He smiled beatifically. "I am her uncle, you see. Her mother is French. She is married to my brother. Her mother, that is. They have just returned to Iran. But they visited the Ayatollah when he was in Paris, you know. He is acquainted with our family."

The official glared at Anna, but the cleric stepped in front of her, using his body as a shield between them. "Where have you been, my dear?" he asked in Farsi. "I expected you so much earlier. Yesterday, in fact. *Dirooz*."

"The bus. *L'autobus était en retard. Et très lent.*"

He nodded approvingly.

"*Mamnoon, mamnoon.* Thank you," he said, bobbing his head toward the guards, "...for taking care of my niece."

"She has no papers, Amir. Just this letter. Where is her passport?"

"*Baleh. Baleh.* Yes. Yes. Her mother has it." He squinted through a window at the setting sun. "But it will soon be time for prayers. Inshallah, we will return tomorrow when we are ready to travel." He motioned to Anna to follow him out.

But the guards kept a firm grip on her while they conferred, talking over her head.

The cleric intervened. "Brothers, we have snatched her away from the infidels. She will be one of us. A good Muslim woman. She has already started down the path. *Allâho Akbar.* Let me continue her education."

The guards looked at the official. He scanned the letter again, wrote down the name in the letter, then clipped it to a clipboard. Anna could hardly breathe. She needed the letter. But the cleric seemed unperturbed, and the guards relinquished their grip. The cleric took Anna by the arm, and hustled her out of the building.

Fifty

A few minutes later, Anna was in a small green car driving away from the border crossing.

"Thank you. *Mamnoon*," Anna said. "You saved my life."

"You were smart to pick up on the French," he said in well-spoken but accented English. Anna was surprised. He grinned and peered in the rear view mirror. "*Khoob*. Good. We are not being followed."

Anna started to relax, then sat up. "The letter. The one from the komiteh. We'll need that, won't we?"

The cleric smiled. "Not anymore."

Anna was not sure whether to believe him. She was not sure of anything.

As they neared Maku, the landscape slowly changed into an urban setting.

"Where are we going?"

"To my home. You need to eat. And rest. When it is dark, we will cross."

"Where?"

"That I cannot tell you. But you will soon be on your way to Dogubeyazit."

She studied the man. Apart from the clerical garb, Anna saw a lined face, a salt-and-pepper beard and dark curly hair graying at the temples. His blue eyes were almost as turquoise as the peacock that had been smashed to bits at the Samedis. His cheeks were ruddy, as though he spent time outdoors. "What is your name? What should I call you?"

He paused, then grinned and brushed his hand down his robe. "You may call me anything you want…but Amir will do."

They drove to a small stucco house in a residential section of Maku. As they got out and approached the door, Anna saw a tiny strip of wood at eye level on the side of the door. At first she thought it was just a decorative ornament, but when he pressed his fingers to his lips, then touched it, she asked, "What are you doing? What is that?"

"It is a *mezuzah*."

Anna felt her eyes widen.

Inside he stripped off the clerical robe, balled it up, and tossed it into a corner. "You may take off your chador." He went into the kitchen.

Anna took off the chador and sat on the couch. Unlike the nondescript exterior, the interior of the house was warm and comfortable. A Persian carpet covered the floor, and the walls were blue and pale yellow, with a crown molding of repeating flourishes. A mirror with a gilt frame hung on one wall, and what looked like a mobile dangled in front of the window. When she got up to inspect it, she discovered it was actually an elaborate votive candle holder, with stained glass, stars, and crescent decorations. A breakfront in one corner contained photos of Amir and a woman, along with a younger woman, and a young man. They were all in Western clothing.

She heard the rattle of dishes and the tinkle of metal coming from the kitchen. A few minutes later, Amir carried out a tray of food and two plates. Anna was ravenous and devoured the hummus, flatbread, chicken kababs, and a rice and vegetable dish. It was the best food she'd ever tasted. "Did you cook this?"

He pointed to the photographs on the breakfront. "My wife. But she is not here. We thought it would be better for her to visit the grandchildren today."

"Please tell her how delicious it is."

He smiled.

"How do you and my father know each other?"

He chewed thoughtfully as if considering how much to tell her. "I am a Kurd. Many of us in this part of Iran are."

Anna nodded.

"And I am a Jew. It is a rare combination. There used to be more of us, but...well...you did not come for a history lesson."

"But I'm interested."

His smile turned enigmatic. "You know the expression 'the enemy of my enemy is my friend'? Certain circumstances came together some years ago."

"What would those be?"

"It would be better for your father to tell you. Let me just say that I am in his debt. This is my way to repay it."

Anna wondered what sort of "friendship" had developed between a former Nazi scientist and a Kurdish Jew. The Kurds had been fighting for independence for centuries. The Nazis had allied themselves with the shah's father during World War II. She frowned.

Amir changed the subject and told her to rest in the living room while he filled the car with petrol. But Anna couldn't relax. Her nerves jangled with the anticipation of finally leaving Iran. At the same time she was still wary. So much had gone wrong. For so long.

He returned just as darkness was falling. "It is almost time," he said. "Put on your chador."

She picked it up. "What about my passport?"

"I will give it to you."

Once again they set out in Amir's car. The dark night was sliced with bars of moonlight; still, Anna had no idea where they were headed. Traffic had eased and soon they were climbing into the mountains. The higher they rose, the chillier it grew. Anna was glad for the chador. As he swung around a narrow road pitted with rocks, Anna gripped the edge of her seat. The farther they went, the more the road deteriorated, and eventually, it narrowed to nothing more than a wavy mountain path that looked like it was made for goats.

"Do not be alarmed."

But Anna was tense, and soon the path tapered to a trail so narrow

Amir was forced to stop the car. Amir gestured for Anna to get out. "Be careful."

As she climbed out of the car, she saw why. The mountain crowded in on one side, but what passed for the road was barely six feet across, and if she stepped too far, she would fall over the edge of a steep cliff. Even worse, the path was so narrow there didn't appear to be enough room for the car to get through. He fingered his beard. Fear twisted Anna's gut. Despite his protestations, was Amir lost? Would they be forced to backtrack? She didn't see how. The path was too narrow to turn the car around, and she couldn't imagine driving down an entire mountain in reverse. The old familiar desperation picked at her.

Meanwhile, he spread his arms, as if measuring the width of the path. Then he did the same to the car. He turned around.

"I must drive through alone. Once the path widens, I will come back for you."

"No!" she cried out. "You can't leave me! What if...I mean, what if..."

"Do not worry. I will return."

She tightened the chador around her. What if this was a trick? What if Amir was using this opportunity to abandon her? It was cold. And dark. She had no idea where she was. How was she going to survive? All she had was a little money and a chador. No passport, no identification. She no longer even had the letter—the customs official had kept it. She shivered, feeling the tension in her neck. "How do I know you'll come back?"

He laid his hands on her shoulders. "You have my word."

But Anna was not convinced. She had heard too many words. Empty words. Cruel words. Words with no pearls of truth between the shell of lies.

"What if you don't make it?"

"I will."

She watched Amir get back in the car and flick on the headlamps. He started the engine, and slowly inched forward. She heard the quiet crunch of wheels on rocks. The grumble of the engine. She was afraid for him, for her, for everyone. The car rolled forward. So far, so good. Then he started to round a curve. He couldn't be more than an inch from the edge of the cliff. She held her breath. Slowly the car disappeared from sight.

She didn't know what to do. Pace? Stand still? She hugged her arms. She was still standing in the middle of the path when she heard a whine far off in the distance. She craned her neck. The air was clear, but she couldn't see anything. The whine became a drone, and she realized it was coming from overhead. She looked up and staggered back just as several jets, their lights winking in the night sky, roared past in formation. For a brief moment, she panicked, thinking the planes were coming for her. Then she realized that she was being paranoid. But they *were* going somewhere.

She was so absorbed by the planes that she didn't hear Amir return, and when he tapped her on the shoulder, she jumped. The roar still reverberated in the air. She pointed to the jets, no more than tiny lights in the sky. "What are they? Where are they going?"

He looked up and squinted. "It is difficult to tell in the dark, but I would guess they are bombers. Warplanes."

"Bombers?"

"From Iraq. They look like they're headed toward Urmia. It is near the border. Maybe Tabriz."

"War?"

"Between Iran and Iraq. It has been coming for months."

Anna watched the jets streak across the sky and eventually disappear. Another war. What would become of Bijan and Parvin? Would they survive? What about Hassan and Roya? And Charlie? Would war free Charlie and the other hostages? She hoped so.

"But this is no business of ours," he said briskly. "Come. The car is safely through the pass."

Anna brought her focus back, and they walked around the bend. The car was waiting. They got in and slowly descended the other side of the mountain. After an hour of more hairpin turns and narrow passes, the ground gradually leveled. The clear moonlit night revealed the dusty desert terrain with which Anna was so familiar. She rolled down the window. She tasted grit in her throat.

Five minutes later, Amir said, "We are in Turkey."

Anna gazed through the windshield, then the side windows. Relief flooded through her, and her grin was so broad the muscles around her mouth felt stiff. "How long until we get to Dogubeyazit?"

"Not long."

The road flattened out. It was well-paved and straight, with white lane markers down the center. If Anna didn't know better, it might be any two-lane highway in America. She wanted to sing and dance and laugh. To celebrate.

He kept driving for another ten miles or so, then slowed just before a dirt road intersected the highway. He turned onto the dirt road and stopped the car.

"Why are we stopping?"

"You will see. It is a surprise."

Anna's high spirits abruptly flagged, and her dread returned. Amir never had any intention of letting her go. She got out of the car, her face set in a grimace. Should she run? How far could she get? Or should she just stay and make a stand? She might be able to scratch his face, maybe even seriously, before...before what?

She was still debating what to do when another car glided toward them from the opposite direction. Cool silver gleamed in the moonlight. She took a sharp breath, fearing the worst. The car made the turn onto the dirt road and came to a stop. A uniformed chauffeur got out and opened the rear door. An elderly man climbed out. He was wearing a dark suit, tie, and his shirt was so white the moonlight bounced off the collar. He was carrying a briefcase. Anna blinked. The man looked familiar. She blinked again.

"Papa?"

"Anna."

Her father was here. In Turkey. He had come halfway around the world to get her.

A muscle in his jaw twitched. He went to Amir and shook his

hand. Amir handed him something. Her father dug into the briefcase and gave him something in return.

Amir looked at Anna's father. "I have repaid my debt." He faced Anna. "Farewell, my dear niece."

Anna grabbed his arms, hugged him, and kissed him on both cheeks.

Amir slipped into his car. He started the engine, gave them a wave, and drove away. She turned to her father.

He cleared his throat. "I am to tell you that Hassan will recover. The girl, Roya—I believe that is her name—is tending to him."

Anna grinned. Roya was a real nurse now.

Her father's expression darkened. "The Samedis' daughter has been taken to Evin Prison. Your mother-in-law has collapsed. She has been taken to an institution."

"And Bijan?"

"He will stay in Iran."

Tears poured down Anna's cheeks. Tears she hadn't been able to shed for months. Tears for Bijan, for Parvin, for Laleh, and most of all, for Nouri. Her father stayed quiet, as if he understood. Anna wasn't sure how long she cried, but eventually, the tears stopped. Once she was able to talk, she said softly, "I think I know now why you wanted me to get married in Virginia. You wanted to protect me. You knew that—if everything fell apart—it would easier for me to get divorced in the States."

Her father gave her a curt nod, as if he was embarrassed that she felt compelled to raise the subject at all.

"But Nouri...you have to know..." Anna swallowed. "Nouri wasn't...evil...when we met. None of them were. It's as if an entire country—an entire culture—slipped off its axis. Black became white. White became black. Kind people were unkind. Good people were bad. Do you understand, Papa?"

Her father cleared his throat again. "I...I have an idea."

Of course he did. Anna suddenly had the sense that her father had endured much more than he'd ever revealed. And that it had cost him more than she knew. She tightened her lips. She wanted to know it all: his life in Germany, his relationship with her mother, and, especially his dealings with a Kurdish Jew from northwestern Iran. But they would have time to talk. Days and weeks and months and years. She slipped her arm around his waist.

"I'm ready to go home, Papa."

Author's Note

This is a work of fiction. Several years ago when I was casting around for a new novel to write, I was chatting with another author about the themes I wanted to explore—I am drawn to stories about women whose choices have been taken away from them. How do they react? Do they simply surrender? Become victims? Or can some survive, even triumph over their travails?

As we talked, I remember becoming captivated by a personal story told to me some years before. It contained elements of what I thought would be a great tale: young lovers who become ensnared by history, family complications, and the inherent conflict of a political and cultural revolution that turned some people into heroes, others into cowards. I imagined writing about the journey of a brave young woman confronted with almost insurmountable obstacles. The only problem was that there was no crime involved, and I write crime fiction. When I said that to my author friend, he looked at me as if I was a little strange, and said, "It's fiction. Find one."

I took his advice.

A caveat: Although *A Bitter Veil* is fiction, it is grounded in extensive research. For better or worse, the Iranian Revolution is one of the most well documented periods of world history, and I pored through many books, both fiction and nonfiction. I also read many articles and memoirs and viewed timelines, films and videos. Some of the texts are listed below. I also interviewed and talked to at least five Iranian-Americans who lived in Iran during the revolution. They shared their experiences, their journeys, and their fears. One of them vetted the manuscript, specifically searching for factual and cultural errors. Any mistakes that remain are mine alone, for which I apologize in advance.

Not surprisingly, perhaps, none of the Iranian-Americans I talked to wanted their names made public. They should know I will be forever in their debt. Because of their generosity, I was able to tell Anna's story.

There may be some who think I have unfairly created or perpetuated stereotypes in this book. It was never my intention to demonize the Iranian people or the revolutionaries who toppled the shah. However, history teaches us that the chaos and destruction of a political and cultural upheaval can cause human beings to act in extreme ways. It has happened before—the French, Russian, Chinese, and Cuban revolutions come to mind. It also happened in Iran. To that end, my object was to show the dissolution of a marriage, a family, and a culture, all of which could not stand up to the stress that revolution imposes. I hope the critics will take that into account.

Finally, I hope that I have faithfully illustrated the great love the Iranian-Americans I talked to have for their country and the culture. It is a love that will endure.

Reading List

Christiane Bird
Neither East Nor West: One Woman's Journey Through the Islamic Republic of Iran
(Pocket Books, 2001)

Ariel Sabar
My Father's Paradise: A Son's Search for his Jewish Past in Kurdish Iraq
(Algonquin Books of Chapel Hill, 2008)

Marina Nemat
Prisoner of Tehran
(Free Press, 2007)

Abbas Milani
The Persian Sphinx: Amir Abbas Hoveyda
(Mage, 2000)

Marjane Satrapi
Persepolis
(Pantheon, 2003)

Azar Nafisi
Reading Lolita in Tehran
(Random House, 2003)

Mahbod Seraji
Rooftops of Tehran
(New American Library, 2009)

Betty Mahmoody with William Hoffer
Not Without My Daughter
(St. Martin's, 1987)

Dalia Sofer
The Septembers of Shiraz
(Ecco/HarperCollins, 2007)

Ryszard Kapuscinski
Shah of Shahs
(Harcourt Brace, Jovanovich, 1985)

Debra Johanyak
Behind the Veil
(University of Akron Press, 2007)

Words of Paradise: Selected Poems of Rumi
(Viking Studio, 2000)

Stephen Kinzer
All the Shah's Men
(J. Wiley & Sons, 2003)

ALSO PUBLISHED BY ALLIUM PRESS OF CHICAGO

Visit our website for more information

www.alliumpress.com

⊗

Set the Night on Fire
Libby Fischer Hellmann

Someone is trying to kill Lila Hilliard. During the Christmas holidays she returns from running errands to find her family home in flames, her father and brother trapped inside. Later, she is attacked by a mysterious man on a motorcycle. . . and the threats don't end there. As Lila desperately tries to piece together who is after her and why, she uncovers information about her father's past in Chicago during the volatile days of the late 1960s . . . information he never shared with her, but now threatens to destroy her. Part thriller, part historical novel, and part love story, *Set the Night on Fire* paints an unforgettable portrait of Chicago during a turbulent time: the riots at the Democratic Convention . . . the struggle for power between the Black Panthers and SDS . . . and a group of young idealists who tried to change the world.

⊗

Beautiful Dreamer
Joan Naper

Chicago in 1900 is bursting with opportunity, and Kitty Coakley is determined to make the most of it. The youngest of seven children born to Irish immigrants, she has little interest in becoming simply a housewife. Inspired by her entrepreneurial Aunt Mabel, who runs a millinery boutique at Marshall Field's, Kitty aspires to become an independent, modern woman. After her music teacher dashes her hopes of becoming a professional singer, she refuses to give up her dreams of a career. But when she is courted by not one, but two young men, her resolve is tested. Irish-Catholic Brian is familiar and has the approval of her traditional, working-class family. But wealthy, Protestant Henry, who is a young architect in Daniel Burnham's office, provides an entrée for Kitty into another, more exciting world. Will she sacrifice her ambitions and choose a life with one of these men?

THE EMILY CABOT MYSTERIES
Frances McNamara

Death at the Fair

The 1893 World's Columbian Exposition provides a vibrant backdrop for the first book in the series. Emily Cabot, one of the first women graduate students at the University of Chicago, is eager to prove herself in the emerging field of sociology. While she is busy exploring the Exposition with her family and friends, her colleague, Dr. Stephen Chapman, is accused of murder. Emily sets out to search for the truth behind the crime, but is thwarted by the gamblers, thieves, and corrupt politicians who are ever-present in Chicago. A lynching that occurred in the dead man's past leads Emily to seek the assistance of the black activist Ida B. Wells.

Cʒ

Death at Hull House

After Emily Cabot is expelled from the University of Chicago, she finds work at Hull House, the famous settlement established by Jane Addams. There she quickly becomes involved in the political and social problems of the immigrant community. But when a man who works for a sweatshop owner is murdered in the Hull House parlor, Emily must determine whether one of her colleagues is responsible, or whether the real reason for the murder is revenge for a past tragedy in her own family. As a smallpox epidemic spreads through the impoverished west side of Chicago, the very existence of the settlement is threatened and Emily finds herself in jeopardy from both the deadly disease and a killer.

Cʒ

Death at Pullman

A model town at war with itself . . . George Pullman created an ideal community for his railroad car workers, complete with every amenity they could want or need. But when hard economic times hit in 1894, lay-offs follow and the workers can no longer pay their rent or buy food at the company store. Starving and desperate, they turn against their once benevolent employer. Emily Cabot and her friend Dr. Stephen Chapman bring much needed food and medical supplies to the town, hoping they can meet the immediate needs of the workers and keep them from resorting to violence. But when one young worker—suspected of being a spy—is murdered, and a bomb plot comes to light, Emily must race to discover the truth behind a tangled web of family and company alliances.

CPSIA information can be obtained at www.ICGtesting.com
Printed in the USA
LVOW060230240512

283084LV00001B/8/P